Red-Hot
COLLECTION

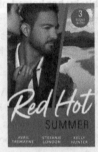

May 2018

June 2018

July 2018

August 2018

Red-Hot Honeymoon

JOSS WOOD

ANNE OLIVER

DEBBI RAWLINS

MILLS & BOON

Published in Great Britain 2018
by Mills & Boon, an imprint of HarperCollins*Publishers*
1 London Bridge Street, London, SE1 9GF

Red-Hot Honeymoon © 2018 Harlequin Books S.A.

The Honeymoon Arrangement © 2015 Joss Wood
Marriage in Name Only? © 2013 Anne Oliver
The Honeymoon that Wasn't © 2006 Debbie Quatrone

ISBN: 978-0-263-26698-6

09-0718

MIX
Paper from
responsible sources
FSC
www.fsc.org
FSC™ C007454

This book is produced from independently certified FSC™ paper to ensure responsible forest management.

For more information visit: www.harpercollins.co.uk/green

Printed and bound in Spain
by CPI, Barcelona

THE HONEYMOON
ARRANGEMENT

JOSS WOOD

To Sandi, so far away but still so close to my heart. Also for Sandi's Chris, who brings my little technie toys. Thanks bunches!

PROLOGUE

'MINIMALISM, MODERNISM OR IMPRESSIONISM?'

Finn Banning looked up from his seat in business class into the lovely face of a navy-eyed blonde with her hand resting on the seat in front of him. A ten-second scan told him that her body was long, lean and leggy, her waist tiny, her bright blonde hair falling way past her shoulders. Another five seconds of looking into those impish flirty eyes told him that she was Trouble. With a capital T. God, he hoped she wasn't sitting next to him on this long-haul flight back to Cape Town from JFK.

Over the past two months his life had been turned upside down and inside out and he didn't want to make small talk with a stranger—even if she was supermodel-gorgeous.

But he couldn't help the corners of his mouth kicking up in response to the mischief in those amazing eyes.

'Graffiti,' he replied when she cocked an arrogant sculpted eyebrow.

Her mouth twitched in what he suspected was a smile waiting to bloom.

'Whisky or bourbon?'

'Beer.'

She tipped her head and tapped her foot, encased in what looked to be, under the hem of dark jeans, low-heeled black boots. 'Rugby or cricket?'

He'd never played either as he'd spent every spare moment he had at the dojo. 'I was on the UCT crochet team.'

Her mouth twitched again with amusement as the other eyebrow lifted. 'You went to the University of Cape Town? Me too! What year? Degree?'

'Journalism. Is there a point to these questions?'

'Sure. I'm trying to decide whether you're worth flirting with or whether I should ignore you for the rest of the flight.'

She flashed him a megawatt smile that had his groin twitching and his heartbeat jumping. An elegant hand gestured to the empty seat next to him.

'My seat.'

'Ah…' he replied. Of course it was.

Finn watched as she tossed that bright head of relaxed curls and pushed some of them out of her eyes. Reaching for the strap over her shoulder, she dropped her leather rucksack to her feet and shrugged out of her thigh-length brown leather coat to reveal a taut, tight white T-shirt that covered small and perky breasts. *Nice.*

She folded the coat and stood on her toes to push it into the bin above their heads and that white T-shirt rode up to reveal a tanned, taut stomach and a beaded ring piercing the skin above her belly button. He watched, bemused, as she picked up the leather rucksack, pulled her tablet and earphones from the bag and tossed them on the seat. Holding her rucksack in her hand, she pulled a shawl from it, and as the bag tipped a thin, familiar silver foil packet fell out of a side pocket and landed on his thigh.

Finn picked up the condom and held it between his thumb and forefinger, waiting for her to look at him. When she did, instead of giving the blush he'd expected, she just flashed him another lightning bolt smile and nipped the condom out of his grip.

'Whoops! Maybe I should introduce myself before I throw prophylactics in your direction. I'm Callie Hollis.'

'Finn Banning.'

She wasn't shocked that he wasn't shocked, Finn thought as she tucked the condom into the back pocket of her jeans. Then again, after eight years as an investigative journalist before switching over to travel journalism nothing much shocked him any more. He'd seen the worst of what human beings could do to one another and, since it wasn't the first time he'd had a condom tossed in his lap by a beautiful woman, it didn't even make a blip on his radar.

Callie brushed past his knees and dropped into the seat next to him, wiggling her butt into the soft cushions and letting out a breathy sigh. She was all legs and arms and he would bet his last dollar that she hated economy class as much as he did—at six-two, for him it was like trying to sit in a sardine can—and that she figured the ridiculous price for a business class ticket was worth every cent.

Callie dropped her head back against the seat and then rolled it in his direction. 'So…married or single?'

'Why does it matter?' he asked.

Callie grinned. 'Well, I do this flight every month or so, and it's been a *looooong* time since I've had someone sitting next to me who I'd want to flirt with—normally my travelling companions are old, dull or ugly. And besides, when the guy is as hot as you flirting is fun—and I'm really good at it.'

He had no problem believing that and told her so. 'It must be because you're so shy and timid,' he added, his tone super-dry.

Callie laughed—a deep, belly laugh that made his stomach clench and his groin jump. 'That's what my best friend Rowan says all the time. Anyway, we were talking about flirting… If you're single you get the full treatment. If you're married I behave like a normal person.'

'I'm in between. I'm engaged.'

'Pooh.' Callie pouted. 'Well, your loss—because I flirt really, *really* well.'

He absolutely believed that.

Callie wiggled in her chair again, and tucked her legs up and under her. 'So when are you getting married?' she asked, and he could see that she'd dialled back the charm.

'In three or so months' time.'

She fiddled with the clasp of her seat belt and looked at him, puzzled. 'I don't get the whole marriage thing. What's your reason?'

Finn stared past the lovely face to the darkness beyond her window, frowning when a quick, instinctive answer didn't fall from his lips. Shouldn't that be a minimum requirement when he was contemplating spending the rest of his life with someone?

Her question raised all the issues that he'd been struggling with lately. Were he and Liz doing the right thing by getting married just because Liz was five or so weeks pregnant? It was the twenty-first century—they didn't need to get married to keep living together, to raise a child together. Were they complicating an already complicated situation? It wasn't as if their relationship had been fantastic lately, and he was mature enough to know that a baby was hard work and might put more strain on the frayed rope that was keeping them together.

On the other hand, being parents might bring them closer...

God—a baby. He was still taking it in. He wanted to be an integral part of his child's life and he was excited about becoming a dad. Maybe the birth of his own child would fill the hole that had appeared in his life when James died three months ago. A birth for a death, it seemed...*right*.

Fitting. Fated.

Finn rubbed his jaw. He was approaching his mid-thirties

and he wanted to be a brilliant father to someone. James had been one to his stepbrothers, to him. He wanted to create a family of his own—something he'd only truly experienced when he was fourteen and he and his mum had joined the Baker gang—a single dad and his three sons. He wanted to be part of something bigger than himself and he and Liz had been good together once. Maybe they could be again. Actually, they didn't have an option. They *had* to make it good again.

'So, why are you getting married?' Callie asked again.

He frowned at her, warning her off the subject. 'None of your business.'

Callie's low chuckle floated over him. Warning ignored, then.

'Of course it's not, but I'm always fascinated as to why someone would be interested in tying themselves down for ever and ever and ever...'

'Love?'

'*Pffft*. That's just an easy excuse—a myth perpetuated by movies and books.'

'You don't believe in love?' Finn asked, intrigued despite himself. Because, deep in his soul, he wasn't sure if he believed in the fairytale version either.

To him, love was taking responsibility, showing caring, companionship and loyalty, and he firmly believed in those. Besides, Liz hadn't got pregnant by herself, and if he was part of the problem then he would be part of the solution.

Right now it seemed that marriage *was* the solution.

He saw something that he thought was sadness flicker in Callie's eyes.

'I believe the only pure love people have is for their children, and some people don't even have that. No, love is a generic term we use to feel safe. Or comfortable? Possibly

co-dependent?' Callie suggested, twisting in her seat as
the aircraft started to move down the runway.

'Is that what you see love and marriage as? Co-depen-
dency?' He couldn't believe that he was having a conversation about his upcoming marriage with an absolute
stranger. Reticence was his usual style, along with reserve
and caginess. He *asked* the questions, dammit, he didn't
answer them.

Callie shrugged. 'I think that a lot of people use love
and marriage as an escape from whatever is dragging them
down. Just like some people escape to drugs in order to
feel happy, others escape to love.'

Whoa. He was occasionally cynical about love and relationships, but she made him look like an amateur. He
was cautious, thoughtful and rational about the concept.
He took his time to become fully invested in a relationship and he never made quick or rash decisions. Which was
probably why he was feeling so out of sorts about getting
married—he hadn't had nearly enough time to think the
whole situation through, to process the changes.

And he was still dealing with the death of the only father he'd ever known. Finn pushed his fingers to his right
eye to stop the burning. Would he ever get shot of this
ache in his heart?

Callie placed the tips of her fingers, the nails shiny and
edged in white, on the bare skin of his forearm. 'Sorry—
I'm being an absolute downer. I'm just naturally sceptical
about love, marriage and relationships. It's a crap shoot
and I'm not much of a gambler.' Callie bit her bottom lip.
'I admit that I'm a little too outspoken and opinionated—'

He couldn't help his sarcasm. 'A *little*?'

'Okay, a lot—but I do wish you happiness and success.'
She tucked her foot up and under her backside again, and
sighed theatrically. 'Both my brother and father—neither
of whom I thought would *ever* get hitched—are getting

married within the next couple of months, so I'm going to have to learn to keep my cynical mouth shut.'

Despite having only known her for twenty minutes, Finn knew that was impossible.

'Thank goodness that Rowan—my best friend, who is about to marry my brother—is an event planner and she's organising both their weddings. I just have to show up and look pretty.'

Pretty? She could don a black rubbish bag and still look stunning, Finn thought. Those eyes, those cheekbones, that pink tongue peeking out from between those plump lips... He wondered what she would taste like, how those breasts would fit into his hands, about the baby softness on the inside of those slim thighs...

Whoah!

What the hell...? Rein it in, bud, before you humiliate yourself. You're engaged, remember? An almost father, an about-to-be husband.

Knowing that she'd said something of importance that he hadn't picked up because in his head he'd been tasting her skin, he mentally rewound. 'Wait...you say your best friend is a wedding planner?'

'Mmm. Actually, she does all sorts of events, but she's great at weddings.'

'My partner—fiancée—is going nuts. Apparently there isn't a wedding planner in the city who'll take on organising a wedding at the last moment.'

'When are you getting married...tomorrow?'

'As I said, we'd like to get it done in three months or so.'

Liz wanted the wedding done and dusted before she started to show as she wasn't comfortable displaying her baby bump to her conservative relatives.

'And finding a wedding planner is something I have to do in the next couple of days.'

'Why isn't the bride-to-be looking?' Callie asked. 'Shouldn't that be her thing?'

'Liz is in Nigeria for the next six weeks, so finding a wedding planner has become my job.'

'What's she doing in Nigeria?'

God—more questions. He didn't think he'd met anyone more inquisitive and so unreservedly blatant about it. *So, Sherlock, why haven't you shut her down yet?*

'Liz is a consulting engineer working on an oil rig.' He saw her open her mouth and held up a hand to stop the next barrage of questions. 'This friend of yours…the wedding planner? Is she any good?'

Callie nodded. 'She really is. She started off by doing kids' birthday parties and then she did a Moroccan-themed wedding which was amazing. In eighteen months she's done more than a few weddings.'

'Can I get her number?'

'Sure.' Callie nodded. 'If you allow me one last word on marriage.'

'Can I stop you?' Finn raised a dark eyebrow. 'And just *one* word? How amazing.'

Callie ignored his quiet sarcasm. 'It's not from me but from Nietzsche…'

Good looks and good brains too? Callie was quite a deep little package.

'Nietzsche, huh? Do enlighten me.'

'He said something about love being many brief follies and that marriage puts an end to said follies with a single long stupidity.'

Huh. Some German philosophers and some navy-eyed blondes were far too smart for their own good.

'I need a drink.'

Callie grinned. 'People frequently say that when they're around me.'

Finn didn't find that hard to believe. *At all.*

CHAPTER ONE

Three months later...

CALLIE, ABOUT TO pull the door open to their favourite watering hole, the Laughing Queen, frowned as Rowan held the door closed and stopped her from walking inside.

'What?'

Rowan narrowed her eyes at her. 'Can you try and remember that this is a *business* meeting? That my client and his fiancée have called their wedding off two weeks before they were supposed to say I do. Do *not* flirt with him!'

Callie, purely to wind Rowan up, flashed her naughtiest smile. 'Why not? Maybe me flirting with him will cheer him up.'

'Don't you dare! I swear, Cal, just behave—okay?'

'I always behave!' Callie protested. Okay, that wasn't true, so she quickly crossed her fingers behind her back. For most of her adult life, whenever she'd found herself back in Cape Town, she had normally ended up in this bar, getting up to some mischief or other. Jim and Ali, the owners, loved her because she always got the party started and they ended up selling much more liquor than normal.

'Just no dancing on the bar or impromptu line-dancing, okay? Or, if you have to, pretend that you don't know me.'

'Hey! I'm not so bad!'

Rowan was thinking of Callie's early twenties self, or

maybe her mid-twenties self…maybe her six-months-ago
self. The truth was that it had been a while since she'd
caused havoc in a pub. Or anywhere else.

Normally, whenever she was feeling low or lonely, needing to feel outside of herself, she headed for the nearest
bar or club. It wasn't about the alcohol—she'd launched
many a party and walked out at dawn stone-cold sober—
it was the people and the vibe she fed off…the attention.

So why, after a decade, was she now boycotting that
scene? Had she totally lost every connection to the wild
child she had been? That funny, crazy, gap-toothed seven-
year-old who'd loved everyone and everything. That awesome girl she'd been before everything had changed and
her world had fallen apart.

Sadness made her throat constrict. She rather liked the
fact that at one point in her life she'd been totally without
fear. That was how she usually felt in the middle of a party
she'd created: strong, in control, fearless.

Maybe she should just start a party tonight to remind
herself that she could still have fun.

When she repeated the thought to Rowan, her mouth
pursed in horror.

'You are hell on wheels,' Rowan grumbled, letting go
of the door handle and gesturing her inside.

'And *you* were a lot more fun before you got engaged
to my brother,' Callie complained, stepping into the restaurant. She waved at Jim, who was standing behind the
long bar at the back of the large harbour-facing restaurant.
'What happened to my wild, backpacking, crazy BFF?'

'I'm *working*.' Rowan said through gritted teeth. 'This
is my *business*.'

Seeing that Rowan looked as if she was about to start
foaming at the mouth, Callie slung an arm around her
shoulder. 'Okay…chill. I'll behave.' She couldn't resist
another dig. 'Or at the very least I'll try.'

'I was nuts to bring you along tonight,' Rowan complained, leading them to an empty table in the corner and yanking out a chair.

Callie took the seat opposite her and flipped her hair over her shoulder. Seeing Rowan's irritated face, she realised that she might have gone a little too far, so she placed her hand on hers and squeezed. When Rowan's eyes met hers Callie met her dark eyes straight on. 'Relax—I'll behave, Ro.'

Rowan scrunched her face up and when she opened her eyes again let out a long sigh. 'Sorry. It's just that I feel for this guy. I mean, can you imagine calling it quits so close to the wedding?' Rowan picked up a silver knife from the table and clutched it in her hand. 'What could have gone so badly wrong so late in the day?'

Callie heard the unspoken question at the end of Rowan's sentence. *And what if it happens to us?*

'Easy, Ro. Seb adores you and nothing like that is going to happen.'

'Bet Finn didn't think that either,' Rowan muttered.

Finn? Callie stared at her. Finn Banning? The guy on that flight back from JFK? The one she'd never quite managed to forget? The one she'd recommended Rowan to as his wedding planner? Black hair cut short to keep curls under control, utterly mesmerising grape-green eyes and that wide-shouldered, long-legged, slim-hipped body. The man who had starred in quite a few of her night time fantasies lately.

'Finn? You've got to be sh—' Callie caught her swear-word just in time. With Rowan's help she was trying to clean up her potty mouth. And by 'Rowan's help' she meant that she had to pay Rowan ten bucks every time she swore. It was a very expensive exercise. 'You've got to be *kidding* me.'

Rowan placed their order for a bottle of white wine with

a waitress before answering her. 'Sadly not. Anyway, he's the strong, stoic, silent type—not the type of guy who you can commiserate with. So don't let on that you know.'

Of course she wouldn't. She was loud and frequently obnoxious, but she wasn't a complete moron.

She had a low-grade buzz in her womb at the thought of meeting Finn again—jilted or not. She still had a very clear picture of his super-fit body dressed in faded jeans, his muscles moving under a long-sleeved black T-shirt, sleeves pushed up to his elbows lounging in the seat next to her; his broad hand, veins raised, capable and strong, resting on his thigh. His quick smile, those wary, no-BS-tolerated eyes...

She had amused him, she remembered, and that was okay. He'd looked as if he needed to laugh more. And, more worryingly, those hours she'd spent with him were the last she'd spent in any concentrated, one-on-one time with a man.

Maybe she was losing her mojo.

'So, how long are you in the country for this time?'

Rowan changed the subject and Callie sighed with disappointment. She wanted to gossip a bit more about the luscious Finn.

As a fashion buyer for an upmarket chain of fashion stores Callie was rarely in the country, constantly ducking in and out of the fashion capitals of Europe and in New York and LA. Trips back home were rarely for more than a week or two—three if she was at the end of a three-month rotation. Wasn't she due for a three-week break soon? Hmm...she'd have to check.

'I'm flying out to Paris in a little while and will be away for a week.'

'Aren't you sick of it, Cal? The airports, the travelling, the craziness?' Rowan asked. 'I could never imagine going back to my old lifestyle, kicking it around the world.'

'But, honey, you stayed in grotty hostels and hotels. I travel the easy way—business class seats, expensive hotels, drivers, upmarket restaurants and clubs.'

Rowan had been a backpacker—a true traveller. Callie wasn't half as adventurous as her friend; unlike Rowan she'd never visited anywhere that wasn't strictly First World.

Upmarket First World. She was that type of girl.

Callie frowned. Rowan had a look in her eye that told her that she was about to say something she wouldn't like. She'd been on the receiving end of that dark-eyed look many times since her childhood and she leaned back in her chair, resigned. 'I know that look. What's wrong?'

Rowan pulled in a long breath. 'I don't know... I'm just concerned. Worried about you.'

Callie fought the urge to roll her eyes. 'Why?'

Rowan stared down at her hands. 'Because...um...'

'Jeez—just spit it out, Rowan,' Callie said, impatient.

Rowan's eyes flashed at her command. 'Well, okay, then. Seb and I are concerned because we think you might be becoming...what's the word?...brittle, maybe.'

What? 'Why?'

'You gobble up life, Cal, like nobody else. You love people and you talk to anyone. Within two seconds everyone adores you and wants to be your best friend. You are the only person I know who can walk into a party and within half an hour have everyone doing shots and then the conga. Men want you and girls want to *be* you.'

Well, that was an exaggeration—but it was nice that Rowan thought so. 'So where does the worry and the brittle part come into it?'

'Being bubbly and funny and outrageous has always been a part of you, but we sort of feel like you've been acting lately. It's almost as if you're trying a bit too hard...'

'I am not!'

Callie instantly denied the accusation. Except that Rowan's words stung hard enough for her to know it was the truth. And hadn't her recent actions shown her how hard she now had to work to dredge up the flirty, party-hearty girl when it had used to be constantly and consistently easy for her?

Maybe she was getting old. Or bored. Or maybe she just needed sex. Or all three.

Rowan traced the pattern of a bold flower on the table-cloth with her finger. 'I read an article the other day about people feeling out of sorts as they approach thirty,' Rowan explained. 'Maybe you're wondering if you're on the right path, whether your life makes sense.'

'Of course my life makes sense,' Callie retorted.

She earned spectacular money doing a job she could do with her eyes closed, she was constantly meeting new people, buzzing from cosmopolitan city to cosmopolitan city. Dinner in Paris…lunch in Rome. Looking at beautiful clothes and making the decisions on what to buy and for whom. She dated cosmopolitan, successful men.

She loved her job. She'd always loved her job. She *still* loved her job…okay, mostly loved her job. She'd been doing it for a long time—she was allowed to feel iffy about it occasionally.

Over the last six months the designers seemed to have become a lot more diva-ish, the cities a bit grimier, the hotel rooms even more soulless than normal. The men more man-scaped than she liked and a great deal more bland.

Maybe she needed a holiday. Or an affair…

'And how's your love-life, Cal? Who's the lucky guy of the moment?'

There Rowan went again—reading her mind. When you'd been friends with someone for more than a quarter of a century it happened. Often.

Callie sipped her wine before answering. 'I'm currently single...'

'You're *always* single,' Rowan corrected her.

'Okay, if you're going to be pedantic then I'll say that I'm currently not sleeping with anyone. Is that better?'

She dated lots of different men and slept with very few of them. Despite her party-girl, flirt-on-two-legs reputation she was very careful who she took into her bed. And she usually found out, during dinner or drinks, that they were married, bi, involved, arrogant or narcissistic. So she normally went to bed alone.

'Marginally. So why aren't you tearing up the sheets with some hunk?' Rowan asked.

Callie twisted her lips. 'Not sure, actually. Nobody has interested me for a while.'

Rowan shoved her tongue into her cheek. 'How long is a while? A week? A month?'

Callie looked at Rowan and tried to ignore the flash of hurt. She knew that Ro was teasing, but saying it like that made her sound like a slut—and she wasn't. She really wasn't. She didn't bed-hop or treat sex casually, but neither was she a nun.

'I haven't slept with anyone for about five, maybe six months,' she admitted quietly.

Rowan instantly looked apologetic. 'Sorry, honey, I didn't mean to sound judgemental. Teasing, maybe—judgy, no.' Rowan waited a beat before speaking again. 'Why not, Cal? You like men and men like you.'

Callie wished she could answer her but she couldn't—not really. Like her avoiding the party scene and her occasional dissatisfaction with her job there was no reason—nothing she could put her finger on. She just hadn't met anyone lately whom she wanted in her bed...in her body. Nobody she liked enough to make the effort.

She just couldn't put her finger on why, and she was

getting a bit tired of her self-imposed celibacy. She liked sex—she needed sex.

'I genuinely don't know, Ro. It just hasn't happened lately and I refuse to force it.' Callie shrugged before sitting up straight and putting a smile of her face. 'Anyway, it's not the end of the world. I'll find someone sooner or later who I'll want to tumble with. In the meantime I have a great, interesting life.'

Rowan bit her lip—a sure sign that she was about to say something that Callie might not like.

'Is it possible that your life is *too* great?'

'Huh? What?' Callie wrinkled her nose, puzzled.

'Your life is so busy, so crazy, and you are so virulently independent—do you have any room in it for a man? A lover? Someone who might be something more than a temporary arrangement? Can it be, darling Cal, that you're too self-sufficient and busy for your own good? Or is it a defence mechanism?'

Okay, had Rowan acquired a psychology degree along with her engagement ring? What was this all about?

'What is *wrong* with you? I came out for a drink—not to be analysed.'

Rowan pulled a face. 'We both had screwed-up childhoods, Cal. My parents and their inability to see me—your mum leaving when you were a little girl. Our push-the-envelope crazy antics got worse and worse the older we got and ended up with you writing off your car when you were eighteen. I landed in jail shortly afterwards.'

'Just for a weekend.'

'That was long enough. That was a hell of year, wasn't it?' Rowan shook her head at the memory.

It had been a hell of a year, indeed, Callie agreed silently.

'After both incidents we…settled down, I suppose.

We're so much better adults than we were kids,' Rowan continued.

'Speak for yourself,' Callie muttered. All she knew for sure was that she'd felt more alive when she was a kid and a wild teenager than she did now. Right now she just felt...*blah*. Not brittle—just *blah*. As if she was a cardboard cut-out of herself.

Rowan sent her a quick, worried look. 'While we're on the subject of your mother, I need to tell you that...'

They were on the subject of *her mother*? Since when? And, oh, hell *no*—they were not going to go there. Not tonight, not tomorrow, not ever. Her mother was long, long gone and not worth wasting time and energy discussing. They most certainly were not on this subject and would never be...

Good try, Ro.

Callie quickly shook her head. 'Don't.'

Rowan held her stare and Callie knew that she was debating whether to get pushy and pursue the topic. Luckily Rowan's mobile rang and she scooped it up off the table. Judging by the soft look on her face, she quickly deduced that it was her brother Seb on the other end, cooing into her ear. She genuinely loved the fact that Seb and Rowan were so unabashedly happy, but their sappiness frequently made her feel queasy.

She couldn't imagine acting like that—being so intertwined, so in tune with another person. It just wasn't her.

Callie looked up when a hand touched her shoulder and saw Jim, the owner of the bar, smiling down at her. He bent to kiss one cheek and then the other, and when he was done she allowed his big fingers to hold her chin.

'Where have you been, hun?'

'Here and there.'

'We've missed you,' Jim stated.

Callie grinned. 'You've missed me starting tequila

shooter competitions which invariably turn into massive parties which lead to your till feeling very full at the end of the evening.'

'That too.' Jim dropped his hand and tipped his head, his expression enquiring. 'Listen, I've got guys at the bar wanting to buy you a drink. You up for company or must I tell them you're not interested?'

Callie didn't bother looking at the bar. She just wanted to talk to Rowan and, if she was lucky, say hi to Finn Banning again. She shook her head. 'I'm not in the mood, Jim—and, besides, I told Rowan that I'd keep a low profile tonight and behave myself.'

'Why do I suspect that that is very difficult for you to do?'

Callie heard the deep, dark voice and whipped her head around to look up and into Finn's face. Tired, she thought, but still oh, so sexy. Purple shadows were painted beneath his eyes and his face looked drawn and thinner. His back and shoulders were taut with tension and his mouth was a slash in his face. She wanted to kiss him and cuddle him at the same time. And she thought that he needed the cuddling a lot more than he needed the kissing.

The last couple of days had clearly put him through the wringer. Experiencing that kind of pain, Callie thought, being that miserable, was why she never got emotionally involved. She'd experienced emotional devastation once before and it wasn't something she ever wanted to deal with again.

However, despite looking like a love refugee, he still looked good. Sage and white striped shirt over faded blue jeans and flat-soled boots. Curls that looked wild from, she guessed, fingers constantly being shoved into them, and a four-day beard. Tough, hard, stoic—and more than a smidgeon miserable.

Yeah, there was that tingle, that bounce in her heart's

step, the womb-clench and the slowly bubbling blood. *This* was what pure attraction—lust—felt like, she remembered. This crazy, want-to-lick-you-silly feeling she'd been missing.

Jim melted away and Finn looked at her with those sexy light eyes. She felt her face flush, her breath hitch.

Sexy, hot, *sad* man. What she wouldn't do to make him smile—she *needed* to make him smile.

'Now, why would you think that?' Callie asked him, projecting as much innocence as she could.

He slapped his hands on his hips and narrowed his eyes at her and she hoped he couldn't tell that her heart was thumping in excitement. He pulled his lips up into a smile which tried but didn't quite make it to his eyes.

'The passage to the bathroom facilities is covered in framed photographs of the parties that have happened here. Not so strangely, you are in most of them—front and centre. Oh, yeah, you're just trouble looking for a place to happen.'

Callie batted her eyelashes at him, her eyes inviting him to laugh with her…at her. 'My daddy told me that talent shouldn't ever be wasted.'

'Your daddy is probably on Prozac.' The smile lifted higher and brushed his eyes.

Progress, she thought.

He shook his head, bemused. 'Trouble. With a capital T. In flashing neon lights.'

Callie left Rowan and Finn discussing the dissolution of all his wedding plans—his eyes had gone back to being flat and miserable, dammit!—and went to sit on a small table on the outside deck, overlooking the harbour. On the mountain behind her lights from the expensive houses twinkled and a cool breeze skittered over the sea, raising goosebumps on her bare arms.

She tucked herself into her favourite corner, out of sight of the bar patrons, and put her feet up on the railing. The sea swished below her feet.

The noise from the bar had increased in volume and, as Finn had observed earlier, usually she'd be in the thick of the action—calling for shots, cranking up the music, and dancing…on the floor, on a bar stool or on the bar itself.

Nobody could ever call her a wallflower, and if they had to then she'd be an exotic one—climbing the wall with her brightly coloured petals and holding a loud hailer.

Where had she gone, that perfect party girl, loud and fearless? She'd cultivated the persona after the car accident—after she'd made a promise to her father and brother to pull herself away from the edge of destruction. It was the only way she'd been able to find the attention she'd craved and she'd got it—especially from men.

She got a lot of attention from men. Apparently it was because, as a previous lover had once told her, men felt good when they were with her: stronger, bolder, more alpha.

Whatever.

But Rowan was wrong. She didn't need a man in her life. Her life was fine—perfect, almost. She had absolutely nothing to complain about. She loved her life, loved her job, the world was her oyster and her pearl and the whole damn treasure chest. She liked her life, liked being alone, being independent, answerable only to herself. Her life was super-shiny. It didn't need additional enhancement.

Besides, as she had learned along the way, to a lot of the men she dated she was a prize to be conquered, a body to possess, a will to be bent. They loved the thrill of the chase and then, because, she didn't do anything but casual, they ended up getting competitive—thought they could be the one to get her to settle down, to commit. That they were 'the man'—had the goods, the bigger set of balls.

They tried to get her to play the role of lover or girl-friend and she always refused. And when their attention became a bit too pointed—when they showed the first signs of jealousy and possessiveness—she backed off. All the way off.

She'd never met a man she couldn't live without, couldn't leave behind. And if she ever had the slightest inkling that she might feel something deeper for someone she was dating she called it quits. She told him that her life was too hectic, too crazy for a relationship, and that wasn't a lie. It just wasn't the whole truth.

She always left before she could be left. It was that simple and that complicated.

Thanks, Mother.

Callie rubbed her forehead with her fingertips, noticing that a headache that was brewing. *Too much thinking, Callie. Maybe you do need a good party after all.*

A brief touch on her shoulder had her jumping and she whirled around. *Finn.* She put her hand on her heart and managed a smile.

'Sorry, I didn't mean to frighten you—you were miles away.' He held a beer bottle loosely in his hand; his other was in the pocket of his jeans. He had a couple of masculine leather and bead bracelets on one wrist and a high-tech watch on the other.

'Hi.' Callie waved him to an empty chair at her table and looked past him into the restaurant. 'Where's Rowan?'

'She met someone she knew at the bar.' Finn yanked the chair out and sat down, stretching his longs legs out in front of him. 'You okay?'

'Shouldn't I be asking that of you?' Callie replied. She leaned forward and asked softly, gently, 'What happened with your fiancée?'

Pain flickered in and out of his eyes. 'You are the nosi-

est woman I've ever met,' he complained, after taking a
long pull of his beer.

'I am—but that doesn't mean I'm not deeply sorry that
it happened. Besides, men usually love talking about themselves,' Callie replied.

'Not this one,' Finn replied.

Okay. Back off now, Hollis. Give him some space. 'Can
Rowan help you sort out the mess of cancelling the wedding?'

'Luckily, she can. I was just going through the final
non-arrangements with her; people are sympathetic but
they still need to be paid. Understandable, since pretty
much everything that needed to be ordered has already
been ordered.'

'I bet Rowan refused to be paid,' Callie said on a small
smile. 'She has a heart as big as the sun.'

Finn nodded. 'She did, but she will be—just like everyone else. It's not her fault that things went pear-shaped.'

Pear-shaped? Callie lifted her eyebrows in surprise.
Pretty tame word for being jilted. 'So, what happened?' she
probed again. Yeah, she was nosy—but this man needed
to talk…he needed a friend. Who wouldn't, in his situation? She might be nosy but she could also be a damn
good listener.

Finn shook his head. 'I know that you use your eyes
as weapons of interrogation, but I'm not going to go there
with you.'

Fair enough, Callie thought. He had a right to his secrets. She just hoped that he had someone to talk to—to
work this through with.

Finn rolled his head in an effort to release some of
the tension in his shoulders. He tapped his index finger
against his thigh. 'I *can* tell you that my biggest hassle is
that I landed a pretty sweet gig—writing articles about
the best honeymoon destinations in Southern Africa. Liz

and I were going to spend three weeks travelling…a few days at each destination. My publisher is not going to be happy that I'm doing it solo.'

Callie leaned forward and made a performance of batting her eyelashes. 'Take me—I'll be your substitute wife.'

Finn managed a small grin. 'I'm violently allergic to the word "wife"—even a pretend one.'

'Well, at least you'd be miserable in comfort.'

'If I end up keeping the assignment—which I very well might not.' Finn ran his hands over his short hair and blew out his breath. 'So, tell me why you're sitting here in the dark instead of causing chaos in the bar?'

Callie could clearly see that he'd closed the door on any further discussion about his non-wedding. She looked down into her drink and wrinkled her nose. 'I'm not in the mood to be…'

'Hit on all night?'

'That too. And someone walked in about fifteen minutes ago who I kind of said I might call. We made plans to have supper, then I had to fly to Milan on short notice—'

'Fashion-buying emergency?'

Callie lifted her nose at him in response to his gentle sarcasm. 'Something like that. And I lost his number, and I'm…'

'Not that interested any more?'

She bit her lip. 'Yeah. Not that interested.' She looked out across the ocean to the silver moon that hung low in the sky. She saw the craters, picked out the shape of the rabbit, and sighed.

When she dropped her head her eyes met Finn's and impulsively she reached out and tangled her fingers in his. She ignored the flash of heat, the rocketing attraction. It wasn't the time or the place.

'I'm sorry you're hurting. I'm so sorry for whatever happened that's put such sadness in your eyes.'

Finn licked his lips before staring at the ocean. 'Well, it's not rocket science. I was supposed to be getting married in less than two weeks.'

Callie shook her head, knowing that whatever it was that had mashed up his heart it was more than just losing his ex. 'I think that getting over her will be a lot easier than getting over whatever else has happened.'

Finn's eyes widened and she was surprised when he managed a low, harsh chuckle. He picked at the label on his bottle, not meeting her eyes. 'We changed our minds, decided that marriage wasn't what we wanted—that's all that happened.'

No, it wasn't. But Callie wasn't going to argue with him. 'Well, I am so, so sorry—because it's hurt you badly.'

And for some strange reason the thought of you being hurt makes me feel physically ill.

Finn stood up abruptly and Callie turned to see Rowan approaching them. Finn surprised her when he bent down and kissed her cheek, taking a moment to whisper in her ear.

'Callie, you are part witch and part angel and all sexy. I'm leaving before I say or do anything stupid around you.'

Callie inhaled his aftershave and couldn't help rubbing her cheek against his stubble. 'Like...?'

'Like suggesting that you come home with me.'

His comment wasn't unexpected, and she knew men well enough to know that he was looking for a distraction—a way to step out of the nightmare he was currently experiencing.

Ah, dammit! She wanted to say yes, but she wasn't going to be any man's panacea for pain—even one as sexy as this. If they slept together she wanted it to be because he wanted her beyond all reason and not just to dull the pain, to forget, to step outside his life.

She had to be sensible and she forced the words out. 'Sorry, Finn, that's really not a good idea.'

Finn raked his hand through his hair. 'I know…' He held her eyes and shrugged. 'I really do know. Rowan, hi—I was just leaving…'

CHAPTER TWO

A HALF HOUR LATER Finn tossed down the keys to his house and stared at the coffee-coloured tiles beneath his feet for a moment. Blowing air into his cheeks, he walked through the hall and down the passage to the kitchen, yanked open the double-door fridge and pulled out a beer.

Looking over to the open-plan couch area, he saw the pillow and sheet he'd left on the oatmeal-coloured couch. He'd spent the last few nights on that couch, not sleeping. He couldn't sleep in the bedroom—and not only because he no longer had a mattress on the bed.

Finn rubbed his forehead with the base of the cold bottle, hoping to dispel the permanent headache that had lodged in his brain since last week. Tuesday.

Along with the headache, the same horror film ran on the big screen in his mind…

God, there had been so much blood. As long as he lived he'd remember that bright red puddle on the sheets, Liz grunting beside him, as white as a sheet. He remembered calling for an ambulance and that it had seemed to take for ever to come, remembered Liz sobbing, more blood. The white walls of the hospital, the worried face of the obstetrician. Being told that they had to get Liz into surgery to make sure they didn't lose her too.

It had taken a while for that statement to make sense, and when it had pain had ricocheted through his body and stopped at his heart. Their baby was gone. He also remembered their final conversation as he'd perched on a chair next to her bed, knowing that she was awake but not wanting to talk to him.

'I lost the baby,' she'd said eventually.

'Yeah. I'm so sorry.'

Liz had shrugged, her eyes sunken in her face. 'I feel... empty.' She'd turned her head to look at the flowers he'd bought for her in the hospital gift shop. 'I want to go home, Finn.'

'The doctors say in a day or two. They want to keep an eye on you. You lost a lot of blood. Then I'll take you home.'

Liz shook her head. 'I want to go home—back to Durban, to my folks. We didn't tell anyone I was pregnant so I don't need to explain.'

She fiddled with the tape holding a drip into her vein. When she wouldn't look at him—at all—he knew what she was about to say.

'I don't want to get married any more. We've lost the reason we were both prepared to risk it. We loved the baby but we don't love each other—not enough to get married.'

He rubbed his hands over his face. 'God, Liz. Why don't we take some time to think about that?'

'We don't have time, Finn. And you know that I'm right. If I hadn't fallen pregnant we would've split. You know it and I know it.'

'I'm sorry.'

'Me too.' Liz looked at him then, finally, with pain and sadness and, yes, relief vying for control of her expression. 'Can you cancel the wedding? Sort out the house?'

'Sure.' It was the least he could do.

'And, Finn? I don't want anyone to know that I lost the baby. Just say that we called it quits, okay?'

Now, four days later, he was sad and confused and, to

add hydrochloric acid to an open wound, stuck with all the bills for a wedding that wouldn't happen.

Finn wrestled with the dodgy lock of the door that led out to the balcony and stepped out onto the huge outdoor area. He loved this house—mostly for the tremendous view. From most rooms he had endless views of False Bay, the wildness of the Peninsular, the rocking, rolling Atlantic Ocean. Out here on the balcony he felt he could breathe.

Liz loved the house too, and because she'd spent more time here than he had it seemed as if it was more hers than his. His name might be on the mortgage agreement, but she'd furnished and decorated the place—filled it with the things that made it a home. He supposed that he'd have to go through the place and pack up her stuff—which was pretty much everything. The house would be empty. But to him it felt mostly empty anyway.

They'd tried so hard to play the part of a happy family, but innate honesty had him admitting that, while he was devastated at the loss of their child, he wasn't heartbroken about the wedding being called off. Losing Liz didn't feel like something that had derailed his world, and shouldn't it? Shouldn't he be feeling—*more*? More pain? More confusion? More broken-hearted?

Instead of mourning the loss of his lover he was mourning not being able to hold his child, not being a dad. Although most of his and Liz's conversations lately had revolved around the wedding, they had obviously talked about the birth. They'd been excited—well, *he'd* been excited, Liz had been less so. They'd talked about what type of birth she wanted, had tossed a couple of names around, and he'd been in the process of moving his gym equipment from the third bedroom to the garage so that they could use the room as a nursery.

He felt lousy—as if his world had been tipped upside down. Was it crazy to feel so crap over losing a half-formed, half-baked person to whom he'd contributed DNA but whom he'd never met? Was this normal? Was his grief reasonable? God, he just didn't know.

And how much of his grief was over the baby and how much of it was the residue of the pain he felt about losing James? It felt as if his heart was wrapped in a dull, grey, icy, soggy blanket. The only time he'd felt as if it had lifted—even a little bit—was earlier this evening, when he'd been talking to Callie. For some reason that crazy flirt had managed to lift his spirits. It had been a brief respite and one he'd badly needed.

Finn drank again, leaned his forearms on the railing and stared hard at his feet. He knew that most people thought that because he was a travel journalist that he was a free spirit—that he was a laid-back type of individual—but nothing could be further from the truth. He was a Third Dan black belt in Taekwondo, held a black belt in Jiu-jitsu and, like the other two, his Krav Maga also demanded immense amounts of control and discipline.

But no amount of control, self-discipline or philosophising could rationalise this pain away. Because he'd tried. He really had.

He needed time, he decided—a lot of it—to sort out his head and his heart. Time to think through all he'd recently lost. His baby, his dreams of a family, even his stepdad. He needed time to get back on his feet, to make solid decisions, to work through the emotion of the last couple of weeks, months, years.

And even though he'd been so tempted to ask Callie to come home with him—sleeping with her would have been the perfect way to step out of his head—he knew that he needed to be alone for a while, to keep women at a distance, to work through what had gone wrong with Liz and how.

Ten days, he told himself, and he would be on a plane

to Kruger National Park for the first leg of his Southern Africa trip. Ten days and he could get some distance from this house, from the memory of the blood, Liz's ashen face, from the craziness of cancelling the wedding. Ten days and he would have an excuse to avoid all the calls from his friends and family. He wouldn't have to open the door to any of his three brothers who were taking turns to check up on him, making sure that he was okay.

Finn sighed. Ten more days. A part of him wished he was hiring a kitted-out Land Rover with rooftop tents and heading out into wild, crazy Africa. But visiting upmarket honeymoon destinations wouldn't be a kick in the pants either.

As Callie had said, there was something to be said for licking his wounds in luxury.

If he actually got to keep the job.

The travel magazine had forked out a shedload of cash, and some of the hotels had sponsored his stay in exchange for an honest review of their honeymoon experience. He would be writing the story but he was supposed to take his wife's opinions into consideration as he did so…except now he didn't have a wife to take.

He had to talk to Mike, his editor—and sooner rather than later.

Tomorrow Rowan would send out a blanket email to the wedding guests on his behalf and Mike, as a guest, would receive said email and soon put two and two together. Finn scrunched up his face, annoyed that he hadn't contacted Mike sooner. Cape Town was a small city and he might even have heard already.

Finn glanced at his watch. Ten-thirty. A bit late to call, but that couldn't be helped. He pulled his mobile from his pocket and looked up Mike's number, sighing as he pushed the green button.

'I wondered when you'd get around to calling me,' Mike answered without any preamble.

Finn rubbed his forehead. 'Yeah, it's been a bit mad. I presume you've heard that the wedding is off?'

'Yeah. Sorry.'

Finn heard Mike clearing his throat and jumped in before he could speak again.

'I'd still like to do the assignment.'

'It's a bit pointless without a wife,' Mike said.

'Can't I leave the honeymoon bit out and just write on the lodges themselves?'

'It's scheduled to be part of the honeymoon issue, Finn, with honeymoon and wedding advertising. The article has to concentrate on the honeymoon aspect.'

Finn swore.

Mike's voice in his ear sounded worried and frustrated. 'Tell me about it. I'm in a Catch-22 situation. The publisher agreed to foot the bill, as did many of the hotels, because *you* were writing the article. One of the world's best adventure and travel journalists writing on honeymoons. They loved the idea. And the promo people have already started working on the edition. You're part of that.'

Finn swore again.

Take me—I'll be your substitute wife.

He almost smiled, remembering Callie's words from earlier.

Wait, hold on... What had she said?

Take me—I'll be your substitute wife.

Could that possibly be a solution? Taking Callie or someone else with him?

'Can I take someone else?' he asked Mike.

Mike's long pause strained Finn's patience. 'I don't see why not,' he said eventually. 'It's not like anyone is going to ask for your wedding certificate or proof that you're married. The two of you would just need to be seen to be having fun. Enjoying the experience. Got anyone in mind?'

He did, actually. Someone who was vivacious, charming, loud, flirtatious, possibly crazy. 'Yeah, I do.'

'Is she someone I know?' Mike asked slyly.

'Judging by the way she talks to everyone and anyone, you probably do.'

'Who is she?'

'Let me talk to her first and see if her coming with me is an option,' Finn said, cautious.

Instinctively he knew that taking Callie—inviting Callie—would be a very good move for him. He'd get to keep this plum assignment and he'd have the company of someone who was a bundle of fun. On that flight back from New York they hadn't stopped talking, and Finn could see why men dropped their tongues to the floor around her. She had a surfer's body—broad shoulders, toned arms, flat stomach and that long, curly blonde hair. But when you looked past the body and face to the brain beyond it you got the shock of your life—because the woman was bright, knowledgeable, and as sharp as a spear-tip.

At her core, she had a lust for life that was contagious. And best of all—unless something had radically changed recently—she had absolutely no interest in relationships and commitment and would be an entertaining companion. She'd be distracting enough to keep him from feeling too sorry for himself.

'Well, talk to her and come back to me. And if you don't take her you'll have to take someone else to complete the assignment,' Mike told him before disconnecting.

Finn slapped his mobile in his hand, considering all his options. He tried to be honest with himself. He had to admit that he was attracted to Callie. If they were spending time in close proximity to each other—he didn't think that honeymoon suites came with twin beds—he'd want to sleep with her. Hell, he wanted to sleep with her now. So sue him. His heart might be battered and bruised, but his junk was in perfectly good working order.

So *sleep with her. It's not like you haven't had flings before. She could be your rebound girl—your way to get over and through this bleak time.*

She wouldn't say yes…

How do you know unless you try?

Finn, thinking he might be going off his head, scrolled through his contacts on his mobile. Rowan would have her number and after sweet talking her out, he had Callie's mobile number. Taking a deep breath, he pushed the green phone icon.

'Hey, how do you feel about being my fake wife?'

The next morning Callie rushed around her apartment, trying to get ready. It was crazy that when she was travelling for work she was super-organised but when she was back home all her wheels fell off. This morning wasn't the first time she'd forgotten to set her alarm, and now she was late for work. So she'd be late? She worked long enough and hard enough that nobody would make a fuss.

Callie pulled a pale yellow dress over her head and scrambled in her cupboards for the pair of nude sandals she wanted to wear with it. Finding them eventually—she really needed to clean out her overflowing cupboards—she smiled as she remembered the very odd conversation she'd had with Finn last night about being his fake wife.

She'd always thought that the 'wife for hire' premise in romance novels was odd, because she couldn't conceive of a situation in the twenty-first century when a fake wife would ever be needed.

But gorgeous Finn needed a wife. She was sorry that she couldn't help him out, but thanks to the eye-watering mortgage she paid each month on this flat, her job—even when she wasn't crazy about it—always came first. Which was a shame, because she could totally see herself swanning around five-star resorts, drinking cocktails and snuggling up to her husband's hot bod—fake…real…who cared?

With her hair and make-up done, Callie headed to the kitchen. She pulled open her fridge door with more hope than expectation and twisted her lips at the bare shelves. There was absolutely nothing to eat and she was starving.

But she knew of a house where there would be blueberry muffins and a hot pot of coffee. The downside was that she'd be even later for work than normal, but maybe she'd take the morning off, or even the day. The house was only a couple of minutes away, and a large part of the reason why she'd bought this expensive flat in this gated community.

Awelfor, red-bricked and old, was her childhood home. In it were her favourite people; Seb, her brother, her best friend and almost sister-in-law Rowan, and Yasmeen, their housekeeper.

But she was so much more than a housekeeper, Callie thought ten minutes later, when she stood in the big, bright sunny kitchen at Awelfor, bending over to hug Yasmeen. This tiny, fiery Malay woman was her north star, her homing beacon. Awelfor would not be home without her.

Yasmeen pulled away and lifted her hand to Callie's face. Her black eyes narrowed. 'You're too skinny and you look tired. When are you going to spend more time on land than you do in the air? And when are you going to find a man and have some babies?'

Situation normal, Callie thought. It was fine for Yasmeen to be a spinster, but not her. *Do as I say and not as I do* was Yas's position on this subject.

Callie rolled her eyes and snagged a muffin—choc chip, not blueberry, yum!—from the plate in the middle of the wooden table that dominated the kitchen.

'Don't nag me—nag them,' Callie retorted, gesturing to Seb and Rowan who had walked into the kitchen, both of them wearing that just-had-spectacular-wake-up-sex look.

Lucky rats. Callie wrinkled her nose when Finn's gorgeous face flashed onto her eyeballs. She'd love to wake up to morning sex with *him*.

Seb crossed the kitchen to where she perched on the corner of the table, munching her muffin. As usual, he kissed her temple and gave her a quick hug. Her brilliant, nice brother. She was so happy that he'd found Ro—that they'd found each other.

It almost, but not quite, made her believe in true love. If it existed then Seb and Ro had the best chance of experiencing it.

Callie was startled out of her musings by Yasmeen's hand slapping her thigh. She yelped and looked at her accusingly. 'What?' she demanded.

'Have you *ever* been allowed to sit on the table instead of at it?' Yasmeen demanded, hands on her hips. 'That's what chairs are for.'

Callie pulled a face at Rowan, who was laughing at her, but jumped off the table and pulled a chair out to sit down. 'Yas…?' she wheedled, using her best little-girl voice.

'Yes, I know—you want a stuffed omelette,' Yasmeen replied, heading to the fridge.

'You know me so well,' Callie purred.

'I should. You've had me wrapped around your little finger since you were a baby,' Yas retorted, pulling items out of the fridge. 'Make yourself useful and grate some cheese.'

Seb poured them all some coffee and placed a cup on the table in front of Callie. 'Aren't you late for work?' he asked, glancing at his watch.

Callie shrugged. 'I let them know. Besides, I have so

much holiday time due to me that I can take a morning here and there.'

She unwrapped the cheese and placed it on the cutting board Yasmeen had placed in front of her. Yasmeen passed her a grater and Callie got to work.

'Hey, Ro?'

'Mmm?' Rowan looked up from her job of cutting red bell peppers. In Yas's kitchen everyone helped. Including Seb, who was dicing mushrooms.

'I had a call from the sexy Finn last night.'

'What sexy Finn?' Seb demanded. 'Is this another European man you're dating?'

Callie laughed. 'No, this is Ro's client Finn. The one we went to meet last night.'

Callie pinched some cheese and popped it into her mouth. After chewing, she told them about Finn's crazy be-my-fake-wife offer.

Rowan looked at her, bemused. 'Are you mad? Take him up on it!'

'I'm flying to Paris, Ro, I have a job.'

'You've just said that you have so much holiday time owed to you,' Ro argued.

'Stop encouraging her to act crazy, darling,' Seb told Rowan. 'And running off with a man she doesn't know would be crazy. Talking about crazy—Cal, we need to talk.'

The mood in the room instantly turned serious as Seb cleared his throat. Rowan frowned and bit her bottom lip. Yasmeen stopped beating the eggs and Seb stared down at his pile of fungi.

Something was up, and whatever it was she knew from their response that she wouldn't like it. 'What's going on?' she asked.

Seb sent Rowan a pleading look, but Rowan just shook her head. Seb looked at her, fear and worry and, strangely, a touch of excitement in his deep blue eyes. 'Cal, I have to tell you something.'

Callie shook her head, knowing instinctively that she didn't want to hear whatever he was going to say. She held up her hand. 'I don't want to know.'

'Laura is coming home.'

Crap. Dammit. Hell.

Laura. Her mother. *Their* mother. The woman, as Seb had told her a few months back, he had reconnected with. Oh, she'd always suspected that he'd kept track of her; he was a brilliant ethical hacker and there wasn't any information he couldn't find.

'I want to see her again and she's returning to Cape Town for a visit.'

Seb had a stubborn look on his face and she knew that his mind was made up.

'Are you paying for her to come home?' Callie demanded.

Seb's lack of an answer was confirmation that he was.

'If you bring her back to Awelfor I'll never forgive you,' Callie whispered, her stomach now in a knot, twisted with tension and long-ago suppressed hurt.

Her mother had walked out when she was seven. As far as Callie was concerned she'd had twenty years to come back home. It was way too late now.

'I wasn't planning to—not yet,' Seb said in a quiet voice. 'She's coming home for a three-week visit and we've agreed to meet. She wants to see you too.'

Callie shook her head wildly. 'Hell, no! No to the max. *No!*'

Seb held up his hands. 'I know that this is a shock, but…'

Callie pulled in a deep breath and pushed back the hurt, the feeling of abandonment, the constant ache for her mother. Her eyes turned cold and her face tightened.

'When is she due to land?' she asked quietly, thinking that this was what Rowan had started to tell her the other night. She had been trying to warn her about Laura's arrival—trying to get her head wrapped around the idea of Laura returning.

Sorry, Ro, not even marginally interested.

Seb checked his watch. 'Today is the eleventh; she's flying in on the nineteenth. Will you be back in town by then?'

Callie grabbed her mobile from her bag and quickly pulled up her diary app. She cursed when she saw that after Paris she didn't have any trips scheduled for a couple of weeks. Three, to be exact. It was the end of a three-month rotation—but why, oh, why did it have to be now?

She'd be home at exactly the same time as her mother would be in the city. That wouldn't do. That wouldn't do at all. She wouldn't risk running into her, having her arrive on her doorstep, popping into Awelfor and seeing her here. She wouldn't take the chance.

She'd endured twenty years of silence and Laura didn't just get to rock up now and make demands. She'd made her choice when she left—she had to live with it now.

'Will you try to be here?' Seb asked quietly, rephrasing his question.

Callie shook her head before yanking her bag off the chair and heading for the door. 'Hell, no. I don't have a mother—I haven't had one for twenty years. So Laura can just go back to wherever she came from and I don't want to talk about her again. *Ever!*'

'Cal—' Seb pleaded.

'Don't mention her name again, Seb,' Callie muttered, before stepping out of the door, blinking back tears. It had to be the bright sunlight making her cry because her mother—*Laura!*—wasn't worth a single one of her tears.

Looking down at her mobile in her hand, she thought

that she couldn't be in the country, breathing the same air as Laura. She'd rather do anything else, *be* anywhere else. Even—

'Finn? It's Callie. You called me last night? If you haven't married, proposed to or found anybody else to be your wife since we spoke last night I might be your girl.'

CHAPTER THREE

CALLIE LEFT AWELFOR and headed directly to Simon's Town, the pretty town to the east of the city of Cape Town. Her father had set up a branch of his sea kayaking tours there after handing over the family property business to Seb. Patch loved his life as a kayak guide and tour operator. Like her, he was vivacious and open; if she had any charm at all she'd inherited it all from him.

Callie sat on the low wall that separated the promenade from the beach and watched Patch converse with his customers while his assistants unloaded the kayaks from the trailer that he'd driven onto the beach. He was still tall and broad and handsome—quite a silver fox, Callie thought. Thank God he'd finally given up dating vapid and beautiful women—mostly younger than her—and was about to marry a woman his own age.

He and Annie seemed to be blissfully happy, and after what Laura and the crazy gold-diggers had put him through she was happy for him. He deserved to be loved and loved well. And, judging by the perpetual grin he was sporting lately, Annie loved him very well indeed.

Callie let out a whistle that Patch had taught her as a kid and Patch instantly turned, his fantastic smile lighting up his face. She might have had a screwed-up childhood, and maybe Patch hadn't been the perfect father, but it had been a very long time since she'd doubted that he loved her. He was one of her best friends and the strongest rope keeping the balloon that was her life tethered to the ground.

Patch bounded across the sand and immediately pulled her into his arms, warm and strong. She buried her head in his neck, sucked in the smell of him and felt her tilting world settle down. Patch ran a hand over her hair before kissing her temple and stepping away from her to sit on the wall next to her.

'Seb told you, huh?'

'Yeah.' She suddenly remembered that her mother had been his wife and wondered how *he* was handling the news. 'How do you feel about her returning?'

Patch shrugged. 'Doesn't mean much to me except for how it affects you and Seb.'

Callie sank her bare feet into the warm sand and wiggled her toes. She bit the side of her lip and stared out to sea. 'I'm running away...'

Patch cocked his head. 'You are? Where to?'

'Well, it's not quite settled, but there's this guy and he needs a—a friend to go on a trip with him.'

'Uh-huh?'

'He seems nice, and he's just gone through a rough time, and we seem to like each other...' Callie waved her hands in the air. 'Not as...you know...but I think we could be friends... He needs a friend.'

'Most of us do,' Patch agreed. 'And you want to avoid seeing Laura.'

Callie waited a beat before turning anxious eyes to his face. 'Am I wrong? Should I be meeting her?'

Patch ran his hand over his jaw. 'Honey, for the last ten years, ever since you totalled your car at a thousand miles an hour, I have trusted you to do the right thing—not for me but for yourself. I still trust you to do that.' He reached for her hand and held it. 'That thing we call intuition? That little voice? It's your soul talking. You can trust it.'

'My intuition is telling me to go on this trip with Finn.'

'Then do it,' Patch said, before frowning. 'Wait—is this Rowan's client? The travel writer?'

'Mmm.'

Patch smiled broadly. 'Tell him to come kayaking with me—maybe he'll do an article on the tours.'

Callie had to smile. Her dad was her rock, but he was never shy about putting himself forward. Ah, well, she thought as she sat with him in the morning sun, you don't get apples from orange trees.

Callie buzzed Finn through the gates of her complex in Camps Bay and walked onto the wide veranda that encompassed most of her second-storey luxury flat. She leaned her arms on the railing, watching as he steered his expensive SUV into her visitor's parking space. He left his vehicle and Callie watched as he stretched, his T-shirt riding up his abdomen to reveal a ridged stomach that had to be an eight or ten-pack and the hint of make-women-stupid obliques.

She did appreciate a fine-looking man, Callie thought, and they didn't come much finer than Finn Banning. Sexy, and also very successful She'd researched him and read that he had been an award-winning investigative journalist before switching to travel journalism, where he was raking in the praise.

What had really gone wrong with his engagement? Why had they called it off? Why would any woman walk away from that?

Maybe there was something about Finn Banning that she didn't know yet—and that worried her. Especially if she was considering spending three weeks in his company.

After she'd called him from Awelfor she'd spent ten minutes convincing him that she wasn't joking about being his 'wife' and avoiding his probing questions around why she'd changed her mind. She'd ended the conversation with the suggestion that if he still thought that taking her along was a good idea he should pop by for a drink at sunset.

And here he was—still hot, still sexy, still sad and still, apparently, wifeless.

He was her get-out-of-the-country card. Okay, the truth was that she didn't need him to go anywhere—she had enough cash at her disposal to go anywhere she wanted. But since she was taking a month's holiday at very short notice wherever she went she would be going alone. Normally she wouldn't mind being alone, but at the moment she needed a distraction from her thoughts—from thinking about Laura.

She'd thought she'd buried those feelings of betrayal and abandonment but apparently it only took the knowledge that Laura was heading home to pull them all back up to the surface.

If she went anywhere alone she'd think and wallow and feel sad and miserable. But if she went with Finn she'd have a sexy man to distract her; she'd have to be happy and flirty and…well, *herself*.

She could shove all thoughts of Laura back into the box they'd escaped from.

Finn pulled off his sporty sunglasses and held them in his hand as he looked around the complex, eventually seeing her number on the front wall. He rubbed the back of his neck as he stopped a couple of feet from her door—a gesture that told Callie he wasn't totally comfortable with this idea and was thinking of backing out.

'Finn…hi.' She leaned over the balcony to look down at him, not aware that she was giving him a super-excellent view of her hot pink lace-covered breasts. 'The door is open. Come on up the stairs and hang a left. It's too gorgeous an evening to be inside.'

Finn nodded and walked through the front door. She

heard the thud of the door closing behind him, and his rapid footsteps told her that he was jogging up the stairs. Through the wooden patio doors she saw him entering her lounge, looking around at the eclectic furniture and her wild, colourful abstract art. He dropped his glasses, mobile and keys on her coffee table and looked at her across the room.

His eyes caught hers and a small smile played on his lips. 'Hello, possible fake wife.'

Callie laughed, immediately at ease. What was it about him that instantly had her relaxing? She felt she'd known him a lot longer than she had.

She watched as Finn stopped, as everyone always did, at the wall of photo frames. She watched his eyes skim over the photographs, quickly taking in her history—her journey from being a daredevil kid to a daredevil teenager to who she was today, whoever *that* was.

Finn spent more time than people usually did staring at the photos, eventually turning to look at her, his eyebrows raised. 'You're up a tree.'

'I frequently was.'

He pointed to a frame. 'You look like you're about forty feet up.'

She grinned. 'Forty-two feet—my dad measured it after his heart restarted.' She shrugged and waved her wine glass around. 'They told me not to climb it, so I did.'

'How old were you?'

'Five? Six? Somewhere around there.'

'You must have been a handful.'

'You have no idea. I thought I was indestructible. I had zero sense of self-preservation and was willing to try anything once—or four times. And if my brother was giving something a whirl—well, I would too. Surfing, diving, climbing, skateboarding, cycling…'

'And I thought *I* was a hellraiser. Your mum must have pulled her hair out,' Finn said, walking towards her.

Callie swallowed and looked away. Her mum had let her run wild—not particularly worried that Callie might crack her head open or break a limb. She would just shake her head before disappearing into her bedroom and locking the door behind her.

Then one day, a couple of weeks after her seventh birthday, she'd disappeared for ever.

Finn stepped out onto the veranda, gratefully taking the beer she held out to him. She dropped into the corner of her fat couch and tucked her bare feet up and under her bottom, gesturing to Finn to take a seat. When he'd sat down in the chair next to her he looked out at the sea view and the dropping sun and sighed.

'Nice place. How long have you lived here?'

'I bought it about five years ago. I love it, but I'm seldom home,' Callie explained, picking up her wine glass and taking a sip. She turned and looked at his profile, strong in the fading light of the day.

'So what's happened that you're suddenly available to come travelling?' Finn asked. 'And why are your eyes redrimmed and puffy?'

Damn, that cosmetics rep had *so* lied. The eye cream that had cost the equivalent of a small house did *not* suck away the bags of fluid left there by a massive crying jag.

Callie couldn't meet his eyes. Mostly because she felt her own prickling with tears again and she never cried in company—especially not around sexy, fit men. 'It's not important.'

Finn shook his head. 'I suspect it's very damn important to you.' Then he lifted one broad shoulder. 'But, since I hate people prying, I'll leave you with your secrets.'

Thank you, she thought sarcastically, a little put out that he hadn't pushed. Did that mean that she actually *wanted* to tell him her sad tale of maternal neglect? *Blergh*—she didn't do sob stories. Especially her own.

Callie pulled herself out of her funk and tilted her head. 'So, it turns out that I can be free for the next four weeks or so. Do you want to explain your crazy proposal to me again?'

Finn stretched out his long legs, which ended in a pair of battered trainers. 'As I explained, I landed an assignment to write an article on upmarket lodges, focusing on the honeymoon aspect of said lodges. The magazine is Europe-based, a leader in its field, it has a huge readership and it's a plum assignment.'

'Of course it is.'

Finn was hot property—he wouldn't be writing for just any old magazine.

'With the wedding imploding I either have to give up the assignment or find someone to go with me.'

'As your wife?'

'As my editor said, nobody is going to ask for proof of my marriage. If I take someone who looks reasonably happy to be there with me I think I can get by without having to explain that the wedding was called off two weeks before the big day,' Finn said, his voice even but his expression pensive. 'I really don't want to give up the opportunity to get my foot in the door with *Go Travel*; they have a bunch of staff writers and rarely issue assignments to freelancers.'

But they did to you.

As she'd thought: hot property, indeed. And not just as a writer. The man had a body that you could strike tinder off.

Callie resisted the urge to fan her face with her hand as a bead of sweat trickled down her spine. Yes, it was summer in Cape Town, but her hot flush had nothing to do with the evening heat and everything to do with imagining him naked above her, his fabulous eyes locked on hers as he pushed himself home. She'd be tight and he'd be big, and he'd reach that special spot deep inside and rock her to screaming...

'Callie?'

Finn's voice pulled her out of her side trip into fantasy land and she waved a hand in front of her face, knowing that her cheeks were fire-red. 'Wow, it's so hot out here.'

'Actually, a cool breeze has picked up and the temperature has dropped a couple of degrees,' Finn countered, sending her a knowing smile. At least she thought it was knowing—for all she knew he could be thinking that she was loopy.

She fumbled for her wine and downed half a glass before resting it on her cheek.

'You okay?'

Just peachy, trying to deal with the fact that you are the first man I can imagine sleeping with for far too long.

'Fine.'

Liar, liar, womb on fire....

'Anyway, back to your trip. When are you supposed to arrive at your first destination? Where *is* the first destination?'

'The Baobab and Buffalo Lodge, which is on a private concession next to the Kruger National Park. We're booked in for a few nights.'

Holy fishcakes—when they said 'upmarket' they meant *upmarket*. Callie knew that the Baobab and Buffalo Lodge was booked solidly for years at a time. It was a six-star safari experience all the way.

Callie leaned forward, her eyes uncharacteristically serious. 'Cards on the table, Finn. What exactly does it entail? What do you expect from me?'

A ghost of a smile flitted over Finn's face. 'All it entails is you hanging out at expensive lodges and hotels, taking part in some of the activities, eating yourself into a coma and drinking yourself under the table. All on my expense account.'

'And the cons?'

'You have to do all of that with me.' Finn placed his ankle on his knee and picked at the label of his beer bottle. 'I'd like someone I can talk to—someone I could have fun with…someone who I know is not going to go all hearts and flowers on me, thinking that this will be the start of something special. I am in no way, shape or form looking to extend this beyond the holiday, nor looking for anything more than a friendship.'

Okay, she could understand that. Everybody needed time to regroup after a break-up, and of course he didn't want to get involved. And she was perfect for that as she didn't go hearts and flowers on any man, ever. And she was fun.

Well, she hadn't been fun for a while, but that was going to change. She'd pull herself out of her funk and go back to being the old, crazy, happy, party-like Callie.

She needed to be that Callie again.

Callie cocked her head. Time to pull out the big guns. 'And this *fun*. Where does it stop? In other words, are you expecting sex out of this deal?'

Finn's light eyes bumped into hers. 'It would be a nice side benefit but not a deal-breaker.'

Callie heard the honesty in his words and tone but thought she should just make sure. 'So I could still go with you and not be pressurised into having sex with you?'

Honesty had her silently admitting that she probably would—old Callie wouldn't have hesitated!—but she'd prefer to have it out in the open.

'Making me repeat it in another way isn't going to make my words more true. But if it makes you happy…' Finn lifted that broad shoulder again. 'Sex—if it happens—

will be a bonus, not an expectation. And totally without strings.'

Callie nibbled the inside of her lip, desperately trying to be sensible. She couldn't believe that she was seriously considering his offer, but on the other hand how often did the opportunity to visit such wonderful places in luxury—for free!—fall into one's lap?

How often did a person get the chance to do something so different on someone else's dime? That would be *never*. She'd be a fool to pass this up.

But she wasn't an idiot. She had to be marginally sensible about this. She was thinking about going on holiday with a stranger—a man she'd met twice. If he turned out to be a psycho she would be at his mercy, neck-deep in a situation that might become very sticky, very fast.

But he didn't give off any creepy vibes, and she had pretty good intuition. *It's your soul talking...you can trust it.* She suspected he was exactly what he appeared to be: a guy who'd had the emotional carpet yanked from underneath his feet; battered, who was bruised and trying to find his feet, to regroup.

But was she prepared to risk her life on her intuition?

'I'll need character references.' she blurted out, hoping that he would understand that she needed to protect herself. 'Just to make sure that you aren't a weird psycho. I can give you references too, if you want.'

At that, Finn did smile—possibly the fullest and most genuine smile she'd yet to see from him. 'Nah, I'm good. I already know that you're slightly psycho,' he teased.

'Funny...' Callie muttered, although in truth he was. It was a relief to realise that behind that gruff, stoic exterior was an offbeat sense of humour. When you travelled with someone a GSOH was the minimum requirement.

Callie put down her glass of wine and linked her fingers around her bare knee. 'Are you sure about this, Finn?

You don't know me. After two days with me, you might want to shoot me.'

Finn lifted the beer bottle to his lips, took a long sip and swallowed. 'If we were at a resort and I had to say to you that I wanted some time alone, some quiet, what would you do?'

Callie thought for moment. 'I'd find something to do— go hang out by the pool, read my book, flirt with the barman. I'd give you your space.'

'And if I said let's go bungee jumping or white-water rafting?'

'I'd say go on your own,' Callie replied quickly. She held up her hand and looked at him askance. 'Is me being a thrill-seeker part of the requirement? Because if it is then I might have to bail now. You might be Indiana Jones, but I'm not a run-through-the-jungle-barefoot type of girl.'

She had been at one time. Right up until her late teens— until her car accident—she'd tried anything wild or woolly once...probably twice.

Finn's mouth twitched with amusement as he glanced towards the photos on the wall before looking back at her. 'Fair enough. You might change your mind.'

No, she wouldn't. He could take that to the bank.

'You have a better chance of falling pregnant,' Callie quipped before turning serious again. 'Look, Finn, I'm honoured and flattered that you've asked me to go with you, but this will only work if you feel you can be honest with me, that you can treat me like you were taking a mate with you.' Her brows pulled together. 'Why *aren't* you taking a friend with you? Surely you have someone you could ask?'

'You keep forgetting the honeymoon angle.' Finn pushed his hand through his short curls. 'The magazine is paying through the nose for me to do this, and there is no way they will allow me to go on my own or with a mate.

They were expecting me to go with my wife, at the very least my girlfriend, at the very, *very* least with a woman.' Finn placed his beer on the wooden coffee table between them. 'So what do you think? Yes? No? Hell, no?' Finn raised a solid black eyebrow.

Callie nodded. 'I think so.' She slowly answered him. 'Let me have a bit more of a think.'

Why was she hesitating, being coy about this? She wanted, *needed*, to get out of Cape Town, and Finn was offering her a brilliant way to do that. She found him easy to talk to, he seemed to like her, and she was attracted to him.

What was holding her back?

Exactly that, she realised. The fact that she was so immensely attracted to him. Nobody had ever created such an intense longing in her and that made her wary…a little scared. If she were less drawn to him she wouldn't have any doubts and she'd be packing her bags already.

You are so weird, Hollis, Callie told herself. *Fruitcake nuts.*

'I'd love to know what is going through that very sharp brain of yours, Callie.'

There was no chance of her telling him what she was thinking. *I know that you were about to be married, and that you're probably hurting and missing your fiancée, but I'd really like to have you leaning over me, sliding on home…*

She didn't think so.

On the other hand she really didn't want to be someone's backstop. If Finn was making love to her then she wanted him to be *with* her, thinking of her and not of the lover he'd lost. She wasn't prepared to be his escape, his emotional aspirin, a distraction from the pain. She'd be his friend, but if he made love to her then it would be because he wanted her.

While she was prepared to be a fake wife, she refused

to be a second choice or a substitute lover. Maybe if she knew why he was so suddenly single she would have a better idea of how emotionally battered he really was. And the only way to get that information was to ask.

'Why *did* your engagement blow up?'

Finn glared at her. 'You are like a dog with a freakin' bone. Do you ever give up?'

Innate honesty compelled her to speak. 'No.'

Callie stared at him with big eyes as he stood up, walked around the table and gripped the arms of her chair, caging her in. Callie sucked in air and along with it the masculine, indefinable essence of Finn. A kick of spice, a hint of citrus, a tiny bit of natural musk. The hair on her arms and on the back of her neck stood up and she felt her skin prickle as his eyes locked on hers.

'Are you always this stubborn?'

Callie shook her head. 'Sorry to tell you that I haven't even hit stubborn yet.'

'Crap. Well, let's see if a little distraction will work,' Finn replied, his voice silky. 'And if my kisses don't distract you at least they'll get you to shut the hell up...'

Callie sucked in her breath as his mouth brushed her lips. Harder, thinner, masculine lips that knew exactly what they were doing as he nipped and teased her mouth. His hand came up to clasp the side of her head and he tipped her face sideways. Then his kiss deepened and his mouth became more insistent, asking—no, *demanding*—more.

'Kiss me, Callie. Open up and let me taste you,' he muttered against her lips.

Callie couldn't do anything but obey—didn't have the thought processes to do anything but follow where he led.

Instead of plunging inside, forcing its way in, his smart tongue explored her bottom lip, teased the corners of her mouth, deliberately avoided tangling with hers.

Frustrated with his teasing, Callie pushed against his

chest and, keeping her mouth locked on his, found her way to her feet, looping her arms around his back and pushing into his hard frame. Breast against chest, stomach against his steel erection, mouth under his. Needing more, she pushed her tongue into his mouth, sliding it against his and taking the kiss from hot to steamy to erotic, from wild to crazy.

His hands raced down her back, palmed her butt and lifted her up and into him. Her legs automatically wound around him and she tipped her hips so that his erection could rub her clit as his kisses—God, was it possible?—got deeper and steamier.

She wanted more…she needed more… This was just sex, lust! Six months was far too damn long, Callie realised from a place way, way outside of herself. She needed him—Finn—now.

Her hands were sliding down the back of his shorts, trying to feel that magnificent ass she'd been fantasising about, when Finn pulled his mouth off hers. He lifted his hand from the inside of her bra and one arm kept her anchored in place. He brushed her hair off her cheek and tucked it behind her ears. He looked rueful.

Callie felt her feet touch the floor and she held on to his arm to make sure that she wouldn't topple over.

'Ah…um…what was that?'

'God knows. But, after that I guess sex is closer to being on the table than before.'

Finn stepped away from her, seemingly unconcerned that he still had a steel pipe in his pants.

His words dumped a figurative bucket of cold water over her head. What *was* it about him? He just had to touch her and she was under his spell, ready to go where he led. She never lost control in a sexual situation—her head was always in the game.

'That's why I'm wary,' Callie admitted eventually, unable to stop licking her bottom lip, hoping the taste of him lingered there.

Finn's black brows pulled together. 'Sorry—lost you. What?'

'We have a hectic attraction. It could blow up in our faces,' Callie explained. 'It could burn hot and die fast, and if that happens while we're on holiday then we'd be up the creek without a paddle.'

Finn jammed his hands in the pockets of his shorts. 'We'll be together for three weeks. Do you normally lose interest that quickly?'

Sometimes, Callie wanted to admit. But with him she was more worried about feeling something deeper than basic lust than finding herself bored. Bored, she could fake her way through, but he intrigued her; he was a puzzle she longed to solve and that rarely…okay, *never* happened to her. And if she was this attracted to him—physically and mentally—so soon, then spending twenty-four-seven with him might make her feel so much more.

Dangerous.

Callie stepped away and held up her palms. *Okay, get a grip and shut this down before it goes any further. Get you head in the game, Hollis. Someone has to be sensible here and it looks like you've drawn the short straw.*

'Finn, I get that you're hurting, that you need a distraction from your crappy life. You've just broken up with your fiancée and that's got to be seriously painful.'

And I'm using you to escape dealing with my mother.

Finn just folded his arms and kept his face blank.

'You should know that I never treat sex casually, that I am very selective about who I bring into my bed.'

'Okay. Good to know.'

Callie blew out her breath. 'And you should also know that I'm not going to be your means of escaping that pain.'

And, conversely, I'm not going to use you to escape my memories.

Finn frowned. 'Lost you. Explain.'

She waved her hand in the space between them. 'We obviously generate some heat between us, and I have no doubt that sleeping with you would be fun, but we can't ignore the fact that until recently you were in a highly committed relationship. That relationship came to a skidding halt and pretty much went over a cliff. Fair to say that?'

Finn shrugged. 'I suppose.'

'So, to carry on with that analogy, I'm not going to sleep with you until I am fully convinced that you have come out of that coma and are mostly recovered. I'm *not* a way to dull the pain.'

Finn stared at her for a long time, his green eyes speculative. Eventually, ever so slightly, his mouth lifted at the corners. 'This isn't all about me and my relationship, is it? You're also running from something—or *someone.*'

Maybe. Possibly. Okay, dammit, yes.

'And that's why you've been crying.' Finn rubbed his jaw with the palm of his hand. After a long silence he lifted his muscled shoulders in a weary shrug. 'Look, Callie, I'm probably not ever going to tell you about the mess that was my almost-marriage, but would you think I was spinning a line to get into your pants if I said that I'm not that heartbroken? That I'm sad but also relieved?'

She heard something that sounded like the ring of truth in his voice but she didn't know him well enough to trust him. 'Maybe you're just telling yourself that to make it easier to cope with. People love to lie to themselves.' She saw Finn's mouth open to start his protest but she shook her head to stop him. 'Look, Finn, let's just take it slow, okay? One day at a time, as friends and companions. Let's not force it, okay?'

He looked as if he wanted to argue, but then she saw him swallowing his words, saw his nod.

'Yeah, okay, I suppose that's sensible.'

Finn lifted his hand to brush her cheek with the backs of his fingers. Callie could only look at him, her blood roaring through her veins and pooling between her legs. If he didn't go soon she was going to forget any doubts she had and drag him to the floor.

'That being said, I'm going to go.'

Callie licked her lips as her brain tried to restart. 'Um… okay.' Him going would be a very good idea.

'You'll let me know your decision? As soon as possible? Like tomorrow?'

Callie handed him a blank look. 'Uh…what decision?'

Finn grinned. 'About being my fake wife?'

Callie blushed. God, her brains were fried. 'Sure, as soon as possible.'

She opened her mouth to add a blanket yes to whatever he wanted, wherever he wanted, as long as he would kiss her like that again. At the last minute her rationality kicked in and mentally slapped her to bring her to her senses.

'I'll see you out.'

'Don't bother.'

Finn stepped towards her, dropped a quick kiss on her temple before heading inside and picking up his wallet, keys and mobile. He turned and looked at her, and the corner of his mouth kicked up.

'Yeah, I think you and I could have some fun. And, Cal?'

'Mmm?'

'No more crying, okay?'

CHAPTER FOUR

FINN HEARD HIS doorbell ring and cursed as he lifted another box onto the tower of boxes he was creating in his hallway. God, Liz had a lot of stuff, he thought as he turned sideways to navigate through the thin aisle between boxes to get to the door.

It would be a brother again, holding a six-pack and a takeaway, coming to keep him company in his darkest hour. He appreciated the beer and the food, but instead of their sympathy he wished that they'd give him something useful, like help with shifting and packing boxes.

He rolled his eyes as the doorbell pealed again and reached out to yank the door open. 'You can only come in if you're prepared to work, you lazy—'

He blinked at the vision on his doorstep. Instead of one of his big, brawny, young stepbrothers Callie, dressed in a short sleeveless sundress, stood in front of him, her blonde hair pulled up into a tail and most of her face covered by huge dark sunglasses.

'Oh, sorry. Wasn't expecting you.'

Callie pushed her glasses up into her hair and smiled. 'I can see that, since you're shirtless and shoeless. Who *were* you expecting?'

'Ah, one or more of my brothers—stepbrothers. They pop in most evenings, usually around this time.'

'Coming to check up on you?'

'Yeah.'

Callie placed a hand on her heart. 'That's so sweet.'

Finn grimaced. 'I appreciate the sentiment but I wish they would just stop. Because I'm not talking they think that Liz is to blame and that I need comforting.'

'*Is* she to blame?'

'Mutual decision,' he replied quickly, seeing the trap and dodging it. 'Anyway, because not all men are Neanderthals, they've been worried about me because Liz and I were together for a long time. I have so many offers for beer or lunch or dinner I could scream.'

Callie didn't say anything and he, like a rookie, just kept on talking.

'So I drink the beers and eat the food and try to convince everyone that I'm okay.'

'Are you?'

Callie took his right hand and held it between hers. She looked up at him from beneath those ridiculously long lashes, her expression earnest and concerned. She wasn't just asking for form's sake, he suddenly realised, she genuinely seemed to care. And her empathy—not pity or sympathy—melted one of the many icicles attached to his heart.

Finn thought about her question for a minute and left his hand where it was, his fingers entangled with hers. 'Mostly. I will be a feeling a lot more relieved when you say yay or nay.'

'Yay,' Callie said as she dropped his hand.

Finn looked down at her, not sure that he'd heard her correctly. 'What?'

'Yes, I will be your fake wife.' Callie said, her eyes dancing. 'Thanks for asking me.'

Finn felt relief course through him and was surprised at the wave of—hell—*happiness* that followed. He was going to be able to complete this amazing assignment, get out of this house and step out of his life, thanks to this phenomenal woman.

'That's the best news I've heard all day. Thanks, Callie.'

'I should be thanking you; it's an amazing opportunity to see some places that I haven't seen before.'

'And to get out of Dodge as well.' Finn folded his arms and raised a brow. 'Want to tell me why?'

Callie didn't miss a beat. 'Want to tell me what really happened to stop the wedding?'

'Touché.'

He wasn't going to open up and neither was she. Better that way, Finn decided, even though he was damn curious.

'So, do you want to come inside?'

Finn thought that she was about to say no but then she straightened her spine and pushed her shoulders back, lifting those small breasts. 'Yeah, okay. There's a couple of things we need to chat about.'

'That sounds ominous.' Finn gestured her inside and noticed that she had no problem negotiating the boxes. 'Liz's stuff. I'm packing it up and shipping it home to her parents.'

'Ah.'

Callie moved away from the boxes and looked at the now stark living room. All the things that had made it a home were gone—the scatter cushions, the art, the ornaments, the photo frames.

'The furniture—hers or yours?'

Finn shrugged. 'The couches and the furniture are mine. I'm pretty much handing over the rest of the house. She bought most of it and there's nothing much I want to keep.'

'Nothing?'

Finn shook his head. 'I'm not sentimental when it comes to stuff.'

He'd used to be but wasn't any more. Only with a gun

to his head would he admit that he'd kept all the sonar scan pictures of his baby—the baby that hadn't made it past four and a half months. Finn swallowed and steeled himself against the wave of pain. Okay, maybe he was a little sentimental about some things.

He pulled in a deep, restorative breath and along with it Callie's sweet perfume. She smelled so sweet and fresh, and he realised that *he* had to smell as if he'd been working his tail off all day—which he had—so he backed away from her.

'There's some wine or beer in the fridge—glasses in the cupboard next to the fridge. Help yourself. I'm just going to take a quick shower, if that's okay.'

'Sure, take your time.' Callie grinned at him. 'It'll give me time to snoop.'

'Snoop away—you won't find anything interesting,' Finn told her, before belting up the stairs to the en-suite bathroom off the guest bedroom.

As per normal, he glanced at the closed door of the room on the left and sighed. He really should try to move back into the master bedroom again. But he still hadn't replaced the mattress on their—*his*—bed, so what was the point? Maybe after he came back from his 'honeymoon' he'd try again.

Maybe. Or maybe he'd just get a whole new bed.

She liked Finn's house, Callie decided, liked the openness and the space. And the view was one of the best she'd seen. But the lack of anything personal surprised her; Finn was a world traveller—surely he would have picked up a memento here and there? Art? Pottery? Photographs?

Nothing in the house suggested that he'd lived here on an ongoing and permanent basis with his fiancée. Which was weird—weren't houses supposed to be shared? Granted, she wasn't an expert on co-habiting, but shouldn't the house be a place of compromise? Shouldn't there be a photograph of his family…his brothers? A trophy? A flat screen TV? Books…? Something that suggested that this was his house as much as hers?

For Finn's sake she hoped that his ex hadn't been an 'everything that's mine is mine and what's yours is mine too' type of woman. Maybe his priorities were a big screen TV and an internet connection—she'd dated more than a few men like that. Or maybe he simply wasn't a sentimental, collect-mementos-along-the-way type of guy.

Callie turned when she heard his footsteps behind her and saw that Finn had showered and dressed in a pair of black athletic shorts and a plain red T-shirt.

He ran his hands over his wet curls and sent her a small smile. 'Did you get some wine?'

'I didn't get that far.' Callie followed him into the kitchen and stood on the other side of a granite counter as he opened a cupboard door to pull out a glass. 'You look very fit—do you go to the gym?'

Finn pulled a face. 'No. Martial arts.' He opened the fridge and she saw that it held nothing but a bottle of unopened wine, a mouldy block of cheese and some eggs. Someone hadn't been cooking or had been living on takeout.

Not healthy.

'What type of martial arts?' she asked, resisting the urge to mention his lack of food. Even if she was going to be his 'wife', she wasn't in a position to nag him about eating properly and taking care of himself. But, damn, she wanted to.

'Pretty much everything, actually. But I concentrate on Taekwondo and jiu-jitsu, occasionally taking a side trip into Krav Maga—'

'Notoriously difficult—out of the Israeli army.' She saw

the surprise flicker in his eyes at her even knowing about Krav Maga—but, hey, she read. A lot. 'Are you ranked?'

'You are the nosiest woman I've ever met,' Finn complained—not for the first and, she knew, not for the last time.

'And—I'll say it again—you're one of the few men who don't like talking about themselves.'

'So why do you keep asking?'

"Cos you're *fascinating*,' Callie replied, shoving her tongue into her cheek.

'Flirt.'

Callie dropped into a quick curtsy. 'Thank you, sir. So, what's your rank?'

Same question, phrased another way. His quick smile and the elaborate roll of his eyes told her that he was enjoying their banter. It would do him good to laugh, to smile.

'I'm ranked highly.'

She sighed dramatically at his answer. 'Trying to get information out of you is like trying to get blood out of a stone.' Callie took her glass of wine and sipped. 'Why don't you buy mementos of the places you've been?'

He blinked at the change of subject as he twisted the top off a bottle of beer. 'What? Like tourist tat?'

Callie sent him a patient look. 'Come on, Finn. Like you, I travel a lot and I know what is tat and what is art. And *everybody* sees something along the way that calls to them. I picked up a stunning vase in Murano that I treasure, a piece of street art in Rome. What do *you* buy?' She gestured to the soulless house. 'This is your house—why isn't there anything of you in it?'

Finn took a long sip of beer. 'You're going to nag me until I tell you, aren't you?'

'Actually, if it's a touchy or personal subject I won't. I know that I'm relentless, and curious, but I do respect your right not to talk. Just say *pass* and we'll move on.'

Callie shook her head and caught his look of surprise. 'This agreement we have doesn't include sharing our secrets. Well, you're welcome to share yours but I'm not sharing mine.'

Finn raised the bottle to his lips again and shook his head looking bewildered. That was okay, Callie thought. Bewildered she could live with. Annoyed or bored would make her think that she'd overstepped the mark.

'So why is there nothing personal in your house?' Callie grinned at his exasperation. 'What? You didn't say pass!'

'You are going to drive me crazy—I can just tell.' Finn closed his eyes and scratched the spot between his eyebrows. 'When I bought the house Liz moved in. She travelled as well, but she spent six weeks away and then a month at home. Her schedule was set but I could be away for two months, home for a week and gone again. She asked me time and time again to help her decorate the house—but, hell, I'm a guy. I'd rather watch sport or…watch paint dry. So one day she dumped all my stuff and all her stuff in the middle of the lounge—right over there—in front of the TV. There was a rugby match I wanted to watch so we had to sort through it. The whole process made me realise…'

'Pray tell?' Callie's lips quirked when he paused for dramatic effect.

'…that I buy crap and shouldn't be allowed anywhere near art galleries or home décor shops. If it's cheap and nasty, tasteless and fake, I *will* buy it.'

Callie's laughed bounced off the walls, and she was still chuckling when Finn led the way to the veranda, where Callie took a seat on an antique bench that had been converted into a swing.

'It's really better for everyone if I just hand over my credit card. Nobody gets hurt that way.'

Finn took a seat on a cane chair and propped his feet

up on the coffee table. After a minute of comfortable silence he spoke again.

'So, you said that there were things we needed to discuss?'

'I did.' Callie kicked off her sandals and felt comfortable enough to tuck her feet under her bottom on the denim fabric of the swing. 'I put in for a month's holiday today, and I also managed to organise it so that I don't have to fly to Paris this week. So I am, in the most virginal sense, all yours until we go.'

'That makes it easier, because there are a couple of things we need to sort out before we go.'

'Like?'

'Like the lawyers for the magazine would like you to sign an indemnity form, and they'd also like you to go for a full medical—just to cover their legal asses.'

Callie wrinkled her nose. 'What a pain.'

'I use the same travel clinic all the time. I'll make an appointment for you.' Finn rested his beer bottle on his flat stomach. 'You'll need clothes that are suitable for five and six-star resorts—'

Callie looked down at her designer sundress and lifted her eyebrows. 'Finn, I am a fashion buyer—I think I have the clothes covered.'

'Glad *you* do,' Finn grumbled, looking frustrated and miserable. 'Because I sure don't. I keep thinking that I have to get my act together and I keep putting it off. I hate clothes-shopping.'

'You always looked okay to me.' Better than okay—mighty fine, in fact. And his clothes were nice, too. 'So, does your ineptitude with home decoration extend to your wardrobe?'

Finn tipped his bottle up to lips. 'Yep. In spring and autumn Liz would drag my ass to the shops. She'd choose and I'd pay.'

Callie's lips quirked. Shopping was something she *could* help him with. After taking a big sip of wine, she stood up and jerked her head, indicating that he should get up too. 'Let's go.'

'Where?'

'Up to your bedroom.'

When she saw his eyes widen and a gleam appear, she rolled her eyes and thought that she should explain—quickly.

'Since you're giving me an all-expenses-paid holiday, the least I can do is to help you out with your wardrobe. I'll go through your clothes, pick out what's suitable, and then we'll go shopping for what you need.'

Finn looked suddenly and momentarily panicked, but she put it down to the fact that no man—especially one as masculine as Finn—wanted to spend any part of his evening discussing clothes.

'Trust me…it'll be painless.'

'I don't think that having you in my bedroom is a very good idea,' Finn stated as he followed her through the house and up the stairs.

'We're taking it slow, one day at a time, and today is not *that* day, Banning,' Callie told him as they hit the top floor. 'Where's your bedroom?'

Finn gestured wordlessly to the closed door on their right. Callie opened it and walked into a white-on-cream, endlessly pale bedroom. Placing her hands on her hips, she lifted her eyebrows as she took in the cream and white striped walls, the deep beige curtains and the neutrally shaded pillows piled high on the floor.

She felt as if she'd stepped into a dairy.

'Wow…' she murmured.

'I hate this room,' Finn muttered, standing at the door, glaring.

'It's not that bad…it just needs some colour,' Callie

said, forcing herself to sound cheerful. She gestured to the bed—a white wood canopied monstrosity that dominated the room. 'You must also have hated the mattress.'

'What?' Finn barked.

'The mattress—it's gone.'

Finn shoved both hands into his hair and dropped his head, for a brief instant looking like a little boy who'd been slapped. Then his face changed and turned hard and determined.

'You know what? Let's not worry about checking what I have that I can take. I'll just buy a whole new wardrobe.'

Callie started to argue, but stopped when she saw the misery underneath the fury. 'That's an expensive exercise,' she said carefully, knowing that there was something fundamental that she was missing.

'I can afford it,' Finn said and gestured for her to leave the room.

Callie knew that it wasn't the right time to argue with him, to try and push his buttons. He wanted her out for some deeply private reason, so she left the bedroom and headed for the stairs. She waited until they were halfway down before speaking again.

'Still want me to help you shop for clothes?'

Finn's tension seemed to fade as he closed the door behind him. His white teeth flashed. 'Hell, yes. I might come back with one of those khaki vests with a hundred pockets and pants that unzip at the knees to become shorts.'

Callie shuddered at the thought, not entirely convinced he was joking. 'You *definitely* need help.'

Finn's broad hand, warm and exciting, encircled her neck as they walked down the stairs. 'In more ways than one. So, what are we ordering for supper?'

She loved spending other people's money, Callie thought, holding up two shirts for Finn that she really liked. And it was so much fun shopping for a guy. Finn didn't think so, but she did. They'd only been at it for a couple of hours and he was starting to wilt—the lightweight.

There was a pile of bags in Finn's SUV already, and with the clothes now on a low couch in this store she thought he would have everything he might need for the next couple of weeks—possibly years. She'd made him buy belts and shorts, designer tees and shirts, shoes and ties, and she'd had a blast.

'Anything else, Callie?'

You knew you were a professional shopper when the sales clerks knew you by name, Callie thought. 'No, I think that's it, Annie. If you'd like to start ringing that pile up, I'll take these to Finn so that he can try them on. We'll meet you at the counter in a few.'

'Sounds like a plan,' Annie agreed, and Callie left her to gather up the clothes while she walked into the three-cubicle dressing room, the shirts over her arm.

The first two were empty, and she skidded to a halt as she saw Finn's reflection in the third changing room mirror through a gap in the curtains.

She couldn't pull her gaze away from the perfection that was his body. He was wearing nothing more than a brief pair of pants, and his body rippled with muscle as he shoved a shirt back onto a hanger. His legs were long and muscled, his tanned shoulders broad, his butt round and tight. His broad chest and rippled stomach made all the saliva in her mouth disappear.

How was she supposed to go on holiday with him, knowing how much she wanted him? This gnawing need to know what he felt like, how he made love, how he would feel as he filled her, completed her, was unusual for her, and it scared her as nothing else ever had. Yes, she needed to explore his body—but she also wanted to dig below his cool, calm and controlled surface to see what was underneath.

That wasn't good. She always kept her distance from men who made her feel too much, who intrigued her. They were dangerous. They made her want more than sex, more than a brief affair, and nobody had made her want more like Finn did.

It didn't matter how much she wanted him, she reminded herself. She could want and wish and pray, but the people she needed to stick around never did. *Remember?*

That cold dose of reality didn't make her desire for Finn disappear. Her mind might realise that he was dangerous but her body still craved him.

She could never allow herself to risk getting to know him too well. She couldn't get emotionally attached to him. But she wanted to know his touch, his taste, how it felt to have that powerful body giving and receiving pleasure.

Finn's eyes met hers in the mirror and he just stared at her, half naked, his desire for her blazing from his face. She watched, fascinated, as his penis grew into an erection from nothing more than looking at her. Finn didn't try to hide his reaction. Instead he just kept his eyes locked on hers, his hands on his hips.

'Keeping my hands off you is going to be a problem,' he said, his voice low and slow. He turned to face her and yanked the curtains open.

Callie licked her lips and shook her head, trying to be sensible.

'I'm not thinking of my failed engagement or my ex. I promise that I am not thinking of anyone but you,' Finn growled.

She heard the frustration and the truth in his voice. He wanted her—possibly as much as she did him.

How was he able to look inside her head and see what she was thinking? He seemed to be able to intuit immediately and correctly what she was thinking without her saying a word.

Nobody had ever managed to do that before.

'Too soon,' Callie stated, sighing as she felt her panties dampen. 'It really is, Finn.'

An F-bomb shattered the loaded silence between them and then Finn's hand shot out and grabbed her wrist. Yanking her into the cubicle, he jerked the curtains shut and the shirts she held fell to the floor.

Finn took her chin in his hand and tipped her head up. 'Have you ever stood in front of a fire and wanted to be in the heart of it? Inside the colours…the heat? Yeah, you have—because that's how you were looking at me just now. Like I was the fire and you wanted to feel my heat. You want me…'

She wanted to deny it but she couldn't. Of course she wanted him—she'd been fantasising about him for months. But it was just lust and attraction and the fact that she hadn't had an orgasm in far too long.

Didn't she deserve to feast on him just a little?

'It's just lust. I haven't felt it for a while,' she told him.

'It's a crazy chemical reaction. But we can handle a little chemistry, can't we?'

Yes—no. Maybe… What did she know? Her brain had long since shut down.

'So let's test the theory. Kiss me, lose yourself in my mouth. Right here, right now. Let me taste all of your heat, your passion.'

How could she say no? A hot, no-holds-barred kiss? She wanted it as much as he did. Just to test the theory, of course. People had sex-based relationships all the time— hell, *she'd* had sex-based relationships all her adult life. What was so different about Finn? *Nothing,* she resolutely lied to herself. Yes, he was hot—yes, he set her nerve-endings on fire—yes, he made her lady bits squirm. But she'd had good-looking men before. She'd handled them and she'd handle Finn Banning.

She would—even if it killed her. And this was her chance to prove it.

Then Finn's mouth covered hers and she realised that she was right to be hesitant, right to be a little scared. Because she'd never been held like this, touched liked this—*God*, tasted like this.

His arms were strong, his hands tender, one on her hip, the other holding the back of her head, keeping her mouth to his. She could feel the heat of his bare chest as her breasts smashed against it, could feel his erection brushing her stomach, hard and wonderful. But his mouth...

She would never get enough of his taste, of the way he sipped and then suckled and then, to mix it up, swirled his tongue around hers. He gently bit her bottom lip, then soothed the sting away with a swipe of his tongue. And while his mouth was busy decimating hers his hand started to explore her body.

She felt his fingers moving over the bumps of her spine, drifting across her bottom, sneaking under her skirt to feel the backs of her thighs, tracing her thong where it disappeared between her butt cheeks. He skimmed her happy place, and when she wiggled against his hand slid his finger under the cotton to her entrance, slipping through the heat and wet to that tiny bundle of nerves.

Callie felt her knees buckle and Finn instantly tightened his arm around her back, plastering her to him as her legs widened, allowing him deeper access. One finger, then two, and his thumb was brushing her clitoris.

'You feel so amazing...' Finn muttered against her mouth, green eyes blazing.

'We should stop.'

'Hell, no,' Finn muttered. 'Just this once...don't think... just lose yourself.'

'We can't have sex in a changing room cubicle, Finn,' Callie protested, trying to being sensible.

'We're not going to make love. You're just going to come, and I'm going to watch you fall apart in my arms.'

'I can't—'

'Yeah, you can—and you will,' Finn told her, hooking a small stool with his foot and dragging it over to them.

Turning Callie around, he placed her hands on the mirror before lifting her right foot up onto the stool. Bunching her skirt in one hand, he lifted it slowly to reveal her lacy thong. He pulled it to one side and stared at her waxed strip, tracing it with one finger before sliding that finger into her folds. Callie watched, turned on, as he started to pleasure her, sliding his finger over her clitoris and into her vagina in a slow, steady, orgasm-building rhythm.

His other hand came up to undo the buttons of her shirt, leaving it to fall open and show a hint of her ivory bra. His tanned hand was dark against her lighter skin—and then it disappeared beneath the cup of her bra to cover her breast. Instantly her nipple swelled into his palm, demanding attention.

His fingers worked in tandem to devastate her control—fingers in her panties and fingers rubbing her nipple—and soon she couldn't help her harsh breathing as she climbed up and up, reaching for that ultimate release, that burst of concentrated pleasure that she hadn't experienced in far too long...

'Look at you...so hot, so close,' Finn growled in her ear. 'See how beautiful you are.'

Callie almost didn't recognise the woman in the mirror—the one standing in Finn's arms. Her hair was messy, her face flushed, and her eyes were a deep, dark mesmerising blue. She looked wild and out of control.

'You're so frickin' hot I could come just looking at you.'

Finn pushed another finger into her channel and flicked her clit with his thumb. Callie shuddered in his arms.

'Come for me. Right now.'

At his command Callie fell apart in his arms, instinctively bucking against his fingers as she milked every last sensation from the experience. From a place far away, where fireworks were exploding inside her brain, she felt Finn stiffen against her, his erection against her back. She heard his low moan and then felt the hand that was on her breast leave her to grab himself, covering his penis as he turned away and came into the palm of his hand.

In a shop's dressing room. In the middle of the day. *Dear God.*

His muttered curse bounced off the walls of the dressing room and pulled her back from that happy place.

'I haven't done that since I was a horny teenager.' He sent her a hot, frustrated, embarrassed look. 'Apparently I have absolutely no control around you.'

Ditto, Callie thought. She rested her head against the mirror as he backed away from her, aftershocks still skittering through her body. The fact that they—two people who'd been around the block, the world—had no 'off' button when they touched was a huge warning that they should keep their distance.

She couldn't handle him—this. This nuclear reaction couldn't be controlled so it should be contained, and the only way to contain it was not to light the fuse.

She needed control. Control made her feel safe and secure. Control meant that her mind and emotions could stand apart and let her body have its fun. If all three got in on the action, as they had minutes before, then she was toast.

Finn quickly shucked his underwear, giving her a quick peek at a black thatch of hair and his still mostly erect penis. He swore as he used his underwear to clean up. 'That was *not* supposed to happen.'

'I don't think any of it was,' Callie said, closing her eyes.

She heard him stepping into his jeans, the rasp of the zip, a long sigh.

'Are you okay?'

Callie opened her eyes and stepped away from the mirror. She smoothed down her skirt as Finn pulled on his T-shirt.

Finn sent her a long, concerned look as he repeated his question. 'Callie, talk to me. Are you okay?'

Callie looked up at the ceiling. 'Yeah. Wow. Yes. But I think that we should get going. They're going to come looking for us soon.'

On cue, Annie's hesitant voice drifted from the entrance of the fitting rooms. 'Callie? Everything all right?'

Callie's lips twitched as she replied. 'We're coming!'

Finn started to grin. and Callie slapped his shoulder in warning. 'If you say *Been there, done that* I swear I will slap you!'

CHAPTER FIVE

FINN STEERED HIS SUV into the empty parking space in front of Callie's front door and frowned when he saw the tall blond guy sitting on her front step.

'I thought you said you were single,' he said to her bent head. He didn't like the fact that white-hot jealousy speared through him. The thought of any other man having her, being with her, while the delicious scent of her was still on his fingers, the memory of her falling apart in his arms was still so fresh, made him feel ill.

Callie picked up her head and frowned. 'I am. Why?'

He glared at the man—who just looked at them, waiting for them to leave the car. 'Pissed off male sitting on your steps.'

Callie looked out through the front windshield and pursed her lips. 'Older brother.'

Ah. Relief—which was bizarre, because he had no claim to this woman. 'Can he wait five minutes? We need to talk.'

Callie sat back and nodded. Finn ignored her brother's thundercloud face and turned in his seat to face her, making sure that the windows were up so no part of this conversation could leak from the car.

He thought about how to start, what exactly he wanted to say. They hadn't spoken since leaving the shopping mall and he thought that they needed to clear the air before this went any further.

'So, a little chemistry, huh?'

Callie broke the tense silence, verbalising his thoughts. How did she manage to do that?

'If you can call that explosion "a little chemistry",' Finn muttered, wanting to bang his forehead against the steering wheel. 'That was crazy. I've never...' Finn swallowed his embarrassment. 'Never lost it like that before. We had hot sex in a changing room, Callie!'

'Well, it wasn't really...' Callie blew air into her cheeks. 'Yeah.'

Callie's tongue touched the centre of her top lip and he held back his groan and cursed the stirring in his pants.

'This was supposed to be a simple arrangement!' he muttered, more to himself than to her.

'It's still simple,' Callie argued. 'We're going on holiday together, I'm going to pretend to be your wife, and we're going to end up in bed sooner or later. And, judging by that craziness, probably sooner.'

'I'm old enough to know that explosive sex has a way of making stuff extraordinarily complicated.'

'We're also old enough to work our way around that,' she said.

Finn frowned at her as he stared at her profile. '*Whoah*... Let me get this straight. Are you saying that you are *happy* to have sex? You said you wanted to take it day by day.'

Callie blushed and threw her hands up in the air. 'I don't know what to think! I'm still in orgasm land! And I'm still wrapping my head around the fact that we did *that*, in a semi-public place, at noon, in a busy shop where I know the sales ladies.'

She buried her face in her hands.

'I'm never going to be able to go back in there. They *knew*, Finn!' Callie pushed her fingers into her hair as she lifted her head. 'We didn't give where we were and what we were doing a moment's thought, Finn. Hell, we didn't think *at all*!'

We didn't think at all... Her words made him push back into the seat, his breath hitching. That was it—exactly it. The biggest problem he had around this woman was that he didn't think. He just had to put his hands on that warm skin, had to kiss that luscious mouth, and his freaking brain switched off.

And he needed to think—needed time not only to work through the runaway fire that was currently his life but also why she had the ability to short circuit his thought processes. He needed to think about how he was going to handle this craziness between them so that neither of them ended up scalded.

Callie stared out of the window. 'Would you prefer that I didn't come with you?

'No! Where the hell did *that* come from?' Finn shot back, panicked at the thought of her backing out. And not only because he needed a 'wife' so he could do his job.

Finn let out a long stream of air. Dammit, it was his turn to be sensible, to take a step back from the situation and use his brain. His big brain.

He needed some distance from her; his body needed to get closer but *he* needed space to think.

'Maybe we should just get through the next couple of days, get on the road and, as you said, see what happens—okay?'

Since Callie looked relieved at this reprieve, he knew that it was the right decision, that he was on the right track.

'Okay.'

Callie nodded, but her next words surprised the hell out of him. Whatever else he'd expected her to say it wasn't this:

'And still no hearts and flowers at the end?'

Finn nodded his agreement. 'Definitely not.' He gestured to her brother, whose look had now passed pissed off and was on its way to furious. 'You'd better go—he's been waiting long enough.'

Callie wrinkled her nose. 'Yeah.' She opened the door and swung her legs out of the car. 'Hey, Seb.'

'Callie. Is that who you're running away with? Want to introduce us?'

Finn heard the whipped out words before Callie slammed the door behind her. Hitting the button to take down his electric window, he made a production of putting his seat belt on before starting the car.

'No, I am *not* going to introduce you. Why are you here?'

'We need to talk about Laura and why you're running off with some stranger to avoid seeing her,' the brother stated as Callie brushed past him to her front door.

Finn, not able to delay his departure any longer without being caught out, reversed and sent a last look at her.

Who was Laura and why was Callie running from her? And why was he so curious to find out all he could about her? And why did he hate the stricken look he'd seen on her face when her brother had mentioned Laura's name?

It was the journalist in him, he told himself as he accelerated away. It was his job to be curious—about people as well as places.

And apparently, he thought as he turned the corner, his job now also included deception and lying to himself as well.

Crazy.

In her lounge, Callie tossed her bag onto the couch and faced her brother, hands on her hips. 'I don't appreciate you rocking up on my doorstep unannounced and looking for a fight.'

Seb, tall and strong and looking as frustrated as she

felt, pushed his fists into the pockets of his jeans. 'When my sister storms out of her house—'

'*Your* house.'

Seb glared at her interruption. '*Her* house and refuses to take my calls for three days I am allowed to rock up here and have it out with you. We're all worried about you.'

'So I hear,' Callie retorted. 'Apparently my life is now too good and I am too independent. I remember a time when you thought the exact opposite. There's just no pleasing you, is there, big bro?'

'That happened a long time ago and it has no bearing on this situation. Look, Ro and I—'

Ro and I. It had used to be *Callie and Ro.* They'd used to be a team—best friends. Had Seb driven a wedge between her and her best friend? Had he surpassed her in importance? It was natural if he had, but Rowan had always been her rock, her sounding board, her port in a storm. Now she was Seb's.

Callie had never felt so alone in her life. Oh, wait, maybe she had. For the first couple of months after Laura had left. First couple of months, years, most of her life…

You're being silly and sentimental and emotional, Callie thought as she walked over to the doors to the veranda and yanked them open, looking for some air. It had been a crazy couple of days—culminating with a very hot, very sexy, very confusing encounter in that dressing room— and she was exhausted and played out. Ro was still Ro, and she still loved her, but it just didn't feel as if anyone was standing in *her* corner right now.

But that was okay. It was time to pull on her big girl panties and kick some ass. And her brother was a great target.

Callie leaned against the frame of the now open door and turned back to him. 'Look, Seb, I absolutely understand and respect your right to talk to your mother, and I'd appreciate it if you'd respect my right not to.'

'She's your mother too. Don't you at least want to know why she left?' Seb demanded.

So like Seb, Callie thought. Analytical and clear-thinking. If he understood the cause he could make sense of the problem. For her it was a lot more simple —cut and dried.

'She left you and me—bottom line. I don't care what her reason was. She left. When you have kids you put *them* first, not yourself.'

'In one of her letters she said that her life was overwhelming—that was why she retreated to her room, why she eventually left.'

Callie threw her hands up in the air in exasperation at his explanation. 'Overwhelming? God, Seb, she was a stay-at-home mother with a housekeeper and a rich husband who spoilt her rotten. That's a stupid excuse. There are millions of women all over the world who have a lot less, who live in terrible circumstances, and who don't walk out on their kids.'

Seb shrugged. 'I don't disagree with you, but I still think that I need to meet with her—that *you* need to meet with her. To hear her side and to find closure, if nothing else.'

'I don't need closure. I'm perfectly fine,' Callie said stubbornly.

'All your issues are rooted in Laura leaving,' Seb stated, still pushing.

Callie ground her teeth together, trying to keep a hold on her bubbling temper. 'I do *not* have issues!'

Seb snorted. 'Honey, you delude yourself. You're crazy independent because you refuse to rely on anyone in case they let you down. You're consistently single because you don't trust anyone to be there long-term.'

From the couch Callie heard the strident ring tone of

her mobile and she walked over to answer the call, grateful for the interruption and the opportunity to get hold of her temper before she slapped her brother.

She saw Rowan's name on the display and barked a tense greeting.

'My fiancé there?' Rowan asked, after saying hello.

Callie answered in the affirmative and Rowan ordered her to put her on speaker phone. Callie shrugged, did what she said and held up the mobile in her hand.

'Seb!' Rowan's voice sounded frustrated. 'What did I say to you?'

Seb grimaced. 'I know, but—'

'Leave your sister alone. If she doesn't want to meet Laura, then it's her decision—not yours.'

'But—'

Rowan didn't give him a chance to explain. 'We spoke about this. We agreed that you would leave her alone! *God!*'

'But—'

'Respect her right to make her own decisions, Hollis.'

After that bombshell Rowan told Callie to take her off speaker phone, and Callie lifted her phone to her ear, watching as her brother threw his hands up in the air.

'As per usual, you two have ganged up on me. I'm out of here,' Seb stated, before turning and heading for the front door.

'He's left and he's not happy,' Callie told Rowan, not feeling quite so alone as before.

Callie could imagine Rowan's shrug. 'So? I might love him to distraction, but he's still messing with my best friend and nobody—not even him—does that. I'm the only one with that privilege.'

Callie felt tears prick her eyes. 'I love you, you know.'

'I love you too, kiddo.' Rowan sighed. 'I just need to ask you one question.'

'Okay.'

'Do you know what you're doing, Cal?'

Callie sank into the corner of the couch and tipped her head back. 'I don't have the foggiest idea. Can you come over? I need you.'

'On my way.'

Maybe, Callie thought as she placed her mobile on the couch next to her, she wasn't quite as alone as she'd thought.

Callie, her bags in a pile next to the door, pulled open the front door and sucked in her breath as she caught sight of her fake husband. Finn was dressed for travelling in a pair of lightweight grey linen shorts and a black and white checked shirt over a snow-white T-shirt that skimmed his broad chest. His arms were muscled and tanned, and the only jewellery he wore was a high-tech watch that could probably launch spaceships.

His eyes widened when he saw her. 'You look fantastic, fake wife.'

Callie grinned at him. 'Thank you.'

Callie knew that she looked good in the pink-orchid-coloured swing dress with its copper leather belt and drawstring neck. She'd kept her accessories and make-up minimal, and she wore flat, gold sequinned sandals. She knew she looked the part of a stylish woman about to embark on her honeymoon.

Did she have everything for her bogus honeymoon? Clothes—check. Passport—check. Accessories and toiletries—check. Jewellery, simple, classy, to go with all her outfits—check.

Except for one glaringly obvious exception… Hell, she wasn't wearing a wedding ring!

Finn caught her expression and frowned. 'What's wrong?'

'Your fake wife needs a fake ring,' she said, lifting her arm and wiggling the fingers of her left hand.

Finn twisted his lips as he stepped into her hallway and wound his way around her bags. 'I didn't even think of that.' He looked at his watch and sighed his annoyance. 'Liz still has the engagement ring I bought her.'

Callie's mouth dropped open. 'I am *not* wearing your ex's ring!'

A shallow dimple appeared in Finn's cheek. 'You're pretty picky for a wife who isn't actually my wife!'

Callie lifted her nose. 'I still have standards—fake or not.'

Finn sighed. 'I suppose we could pick up something at the airport.'

Callie lifted her eyebrows. The only jewellery stores at the airport were high-end and very expensive, and she couldn't justify him splurging for a ring that she'd only wear for three weeks. She quickly did a mental stroll through her jewellery collection in the hope that she had something remotely engagement-ring-like. Then she remembered the large velvet jewellery box Seb had left with her just after he'd got engaged to Rowan.

'It's mostly Grandma's jewellery, with a couple of pieces our mother left behind,' he'd said. 'You should have them.'

Callie hadn't wanted to keep the box and she'd never bothered to look inside. It was still at the back of her lingerie drawer, where she'd shoved it a year or so ago.

She still didn't want to open it, but this was an emergency.

'How much time have we got before we have to leave?' she asked Finn as she turned towards the stairs.

'A half hour or so,' Finn replied. 'Why? Do you have some diamond rings stashed upstairs?'

'Maybe,' Callie replied, hearing Finn's footsteps behind

her. She turned, faced him, and for once they were eye to eye. 'It might be better if you stay down here.'

'Why?'

'My room. It's a bit messy.' *Catastrophic* was a better word, Callie thought.

'I've seen messy before,' Finn told her.

'Not like this, you haven't,' Callie assured him. Seeing the stubborn look on his face, she sighed and shrugged. 'Don't say I didn't warn you.'

Dear God! Finn looked around the master bedroom, his mouth open wide enough to catch flies. Who had so many clothes and why were they scattered everywhere?

When he managed to find his voice, he croaked the words out. 'Newsflash, Callie: clothes can be put back into cupboards as well as taken out.'

Callie stepped over a pile of shoes as she headed to her dresser. 'No point,' she said over her shoulder. 'While I was trying to decide what to pack I realised that I have far too many clothes—'

'Seriously? I would never have guessed that!' Finn said from the doorway, thinking that if he went in he might not find his way out. *Ever.*

Callie ignored his interruption. 'And I decided that I need to clean out my wardrobe. That pile is for Rowan, that pile is for the secondhand shop, and that pile is to be donated.' She waved her hands around the room.

Finn leaned a shoulder into the doorframe and crossed his arms. 'Damn...' he muttered again.

Callie yanked open a drawer in her dresser and Finn's mouth went dry as she tossed a pile of rainbow-coloured thongs and bras onto a chair. They were skimpy and frothy and ultra-feminine.

'I get samples from the designers I do business with,' Callie said, seemingly oblivious to the fact that he was mentally stripping her in an attempt to see what she wearing under that sexy, stylish dress.

It would probably be the same sexy deep pink, he decided. Callie was nothing if not colour co-ordinated.

'I can't remember when last I actually went to a store and bought clothes. That's why I had so much fun shopping for you.'

With difficulty Finn raised his eyes to her face and tried to look as if he had heard her. But he was a guy—distract him with sexy lingerie and his brain headed south. With his blood. And his hearing.

'Ah—got it.'

Finn watched as Callie pulled out a large jewellery box and, cradling it in both hands, walked back towards him. She skirted the bed and sat on the side closest to him, on top of a pile of jackets, putting the box down next to her. A wistful, sad, wary look passed across her face and he straightened, all thoughts of sex and lingerie gone. This box meant something to her, and he wasn't sure if it was a good or bad something. Probably a mixture of both.

Then, very surprisingly, she stood up, picked up the box and thrust it towards him. Finn caught it as it hit his chest and she dropped it from her grasp.

'Look in there and see if you can find something that I can wear. If there isn't anything then I'm afraid you're out of luck. I'll be downstairs.'

Finn frowned as she slipped past him and ran down the stairs. Putting the box on the bedside table, he switched on the light and flipped the lid. His breath caught at the blink of gold inside. It was a pirate's treasure box, he thought, bubbling with thick gold chains and bracelets and the occasional flash of a precious stone in a pendant.

Lifting up a handful of chains, silver and gold, some with pendants and some without, he saw that there were smaller boxes below and dumped the chains on the bed.

The first box held earrings—mostly old-fashioned, but there was a nice pair of diamond studs he could see Callie wearing. The next box held rings, and he pulled in his breath as he ran his fingers over the jewels.

Of the eight or so in the box there were at least four that would pass as engagement rings, and three had matching wedding bands. One ring fascinated him: it looked older than the others—a big diamond, with spikes of platinum radiating in another circle embedded with tiny diamonds. A thin band sat under the diamond and he presumed that was a wedding band.

Finn held it under the light and on the inside could just make out the date: June the sixth, 1909.

That'll do, he thought, tucking it into the pocket of his pants.

He quickly replaced the boxes he'd taken out and dumped the tangle of chains back inside the larger box. Snapping the lid shut, he walked across to the near empty cupboard, found a shoebox and tossed the shoes inside on to the floor. Sliding the jewellery box into the shoebox, he used his height to stretch up and hide the box behind another pile of shoeboxes.

He wondered why he was bothering. If any thieves broke in and found themselves in Callie's bedroom while she was away they'd think she'd been ransacked already and leave.

Finn tried to close the cupboard doors and wondered why Callie wouldn't deal with the box herself. Why would a woman who obviously loved clothes—and, he presumed, accessories—ignore a box full of such amazing jewellery? Why couldn't she even open it to look inside for a ring she needed?

Strange. But interesting. Curiosity, he reminded himself, and he didn't need to indulge it. Not where Callie was concerned.

Finn rubbed the back of his neck, thinking that she couldn't do the jewellery box and he couldn't do his bedroom. Maybe they deserved each other.

Finn left the room and jogged down the stairs. He found Callie sitting on a chair in her hallway, legs crossed and her foot jiggling.

She looked up at him with those amazing reticent eyes. 'Did you find something?'

'Lots of things,' Finn said, keeping his voice easy. 'That's quite a little treasure trove you've got there. That box should be in a safe, by the way.'

Callie lifted a bare shoulder. 'I wouldn't know. I've never looked inside.'

'Why not?' Finn asked the question although he knew that she wouldn't answer.

'It's complicated and I have my reasons.' Callie stood up and held out her hand. 'Let's see it.'

Finn pulled the two rings from his pocket and dropped them into her hand. He watched as she stared at them. She looked as though she was trying to place them, but after she'd given the tiniest shake to her head she picked the wedding ring up to take a closer look.

'It's really pretty.'

'It has a date in 1909 inscribed on the band,' Finn told her.

'It must be my great-grandmother's—Seb told me that some of the family pieces were in the box,' Callie replied, sliding both rings over the ring finger on her left hand. 'They fit. Yay.'

'Good.' Finn smiled lazily. 'That was easily sorted. Just promise me you'll get the box into a safe deposit box or just a safe. There were quite a few bigger and better diamonds and precious stones than that one.'

Callie shifted on her feet. 'Maybe.' She nudged a suitcase with her foot. 'Shall we go?'

'Yep.' Finn looked at the pile of suitcases on the floor and sighed. Okay, they were going for a while, but two large cases and a carry-on seemed a bit excessive. But judging by what had been left behind she probably thought that this was—what had she called it the other day?—a capsule wardrobe. He thought it looked like backache waiting for a place to happen.

'Okay, grab your stuff and I'll wait for you in the car,' he said, teasing her.

Callie looked surprised, then confused, and then her eyes cleared as he realised he was joking. 'Carry on like that and I'm going to cut you off from fake sex.'

Finn slung the tote bag over his shoulder and pulled the bigger of the two suitcases up onto its wheels. 'Fake married for two seconds,' he grumbled as she opened the front door for him, 'and I'm already on rations for sex I might not even get. This is a tough gig.'

'You were the one who wanted to get married,' Callie reminded him. 'Didn't I tell you that it was a bad idea? I'm sure I said something about it being a long stupidity...'

Six hours later Callie stood in the tasteful lobby of the Baobab and Buffalo, sipping a welcome glass of champagne while Finn took care of the details surrounding their stay at this first six-star resort.

According to their itinerary they would be staying in the honeymoon suite for one night before being moved to another room for the rest of their three-night stay. Since bookings at the Baobab and Buffalo were harder to come by than hen's teeth, and since this entire 'honeymoon' was sponsored—and fake—Callie knew that they were in no position to complain.

And, really, what was there to complain about? The resort was utterly fantastic. The main building was built in grey stone and lavishly but tastefully decorated. Judging by the discreet signs, there was a business room, a library, various lounges and dining rooms. Callie walked across the lobby, intrigued by the double-volume doors and the view beyond the glass.

Stepping onto the long veranda, she gasped at the endless view of bush beyond her. Wild and wondrous. There was a watering hole for wildlife at the bottom of the cliff below, and verdant green terraces led to an infinity pool that seemed to cling to the edge of the cliff.

Well, wow.

Callie turned at a touch on her shoulder. 'Mrs Banning?'

Callie turned and looked into the eyes of a gorgeous redhead. 'No. I'm Callie—' Then she remembered that she was supposed to be married and flushed with embarrassment. Her brain kicked up a gear as she tried to explain her gaffe. 'Sorry—I'm still operating on my own name.'

The redhead grinned. 'I absolutely understand; I'm recently married myself. I'm Clem—welcome to the Two B.'

Callie had read her fair share of celebrity magazines and instantly recognised this ex-model, who'd once been engaged to one of the world's most notorious musicians. From socialite to living on an upmarket game reserve. Now *that* was a life-change.

'Thank you. It's beautiful.'

Clem sighed. 'It really is. I'm still in awe of what Nick's managed to build here.'

Clem jammed her hands in her khaki shorts and gestured to a dark-haired man who stood at the other end of the veranda, talking to a man dressed in the same uniform of khaki shorts and navy polo shirt.

'That's Nick and his right-hand man, Jabu. They are the heart and soul of the Two B. Sorry, that's what we call this place. The Baobab and Buffalo is such a mouthful.'

Callie watched as Nick and his wife exchanged a look across the veranda that blazed with passion and lust. Callie felt as if she needed a fan or a long drink of water when they finally looked away from each other, but Clem turned back to Callie, acting as if she *hadn't* just eye-bonked her husband.

'What are you hoping to do here? Or are you just planning to hibernate in your room and…well, do what honeymooners do?'

How the hell was she supposed to answer that question? She didn't even know the answer to any of the questions *she* had with regard to her and Finn's relationship—the fake one or the real one!

Were they going to sleep with each other? *Duh.* That was a no-brainer—as soon as they had to share a bed they'd be all over each other…there was no way they'd be able to resist. And that would be the start of their three-week fling. It would be hot and sexy and rollercoaster-crazy and she had to remember to keep her emotional distance. *No spilling the secrets of your soul, Hollis!*

Callie frowned at the rogue thought. What was wrong with her? She had always been able to separate sex and emotion—why was she worried that she wouldn't be able to do it with Finn? *Because you like him,* Callie admitted reluctantly. *Because you'd like to be his friend, have him be yours.* And that meant taking a step away from being 'safe' and unattached; it would take her into uncharted territory…

'Callie?'

Callie blinked at her hostess. 'Sorry, I zoned out. Tired…'

Clem laughed and patted her arm again. 'No problem—I understand. I was so exhausted after my wedding day I could barely string a sentence together.'

Yeah, that wasn't it. Looking into Clem's beautiful, open, happy face, Callie felt the urge to spill her secrets.

Actually, I'm not really married. I'm running away from reconnecting with my long-absent mother.

And I want to sleep with Finn; he's exciting and intriguing and the first man in for ever who I can imagine myself falling for. But I'm scared that he's the one man that I will like more after I've slept with him—not less. I already like him more than I should. Hell, I knew that I liked him more than was wise on the plane home from JFK—and this is all very scary for me. And he's on the rebound and I never, repeat never, sleep with men I can fall for.

So I'm confused. And more than little terrified.

And I really don't like being either.

Callie suspected that Clem would understand.

Callie sighed her relief as she saw Finn walking towards them, a Two B butler two steps behind. She gathered her wits and made the introductions. 'Finn Banning—meet Clem. She and her husband own and run the Baobab and Buffalo.'

Clem's eyes narrowed slightly and her smile was a little cool. 'You're the journalist doing an article on us?'

Hmm, it seemed that the fiery redhead wasn't fond of journalists—then again, with her history with the profession Callie couldn't blame her.

'I am,' Finn said easily, his hand resting low on Callie's back, his fingers just above her butt cheek. It was a very possessive, familiar gesture—one perfectly suited to a newly married man.

'We don't normally allow reporters to write about the Two B; we're booked for years in advance and don't need the publicity. We're doing this as a favour to the owner of *Go Travel* who's a regular visitor.'

Clem kept the smile on her face but there was a note of protectiveness in her voice that was unmistakable. Finn's fingers flexed on Callie's back and Callie knew that he'd heard Clem's warning too.

Finn sent her an easy smile. 'I'm morally bound to write on my personal experiences and I already know that my experience here will be utterly fantastic. We're so lucky to start off our honeymoon here.'

Clem relaxed and Callie released her pent-up breath. Finn casually sipped from the glass of champagne he'd been handed on walking through the front door.

Clem nodded at the papers in his hand. 'I've tweaked your itinerary to showcase the best of what we can offer honeymooners—which is an utterly unique and memorable experience.' Clem pulled a face, humour back in her eyes. 'I'm sorry, it doesn't leave much time for long, lazy mornings spent in bed, but it will be exciting and amazing.'

Wow. If all the lodges were going to pull out the stops the way Clem was doing then Callie was in for one hell of a holiday.

'We're grateful for your personal touch,' said Mr Charmer at her side.

'Then Sarah, your personal butler, will take it from here. Enjoy your stay,' Clem said, before turning away to walk towards her husband.

Nick immediately opened his arms and Clem snuggled up into his side. Callie briefly wondered what it would feel like to love a man like that—to be loved like that. To feel so absolutely, utterly secure in yourself and in his love that you could slide into a conversation and into his arms without either of you missing a beat, as if it was the most natural action in the world.

Love, it seemed, could work for some. But Callie knew that she wasn't one of the lucky few. No, she was better off on her own, walking her own path.

That way she could be in control and could stop her heart from walking off the side of a cliff and splattering on the rocks below.

CHAPTER SIX

Instead of walking them to their room, as he'd expected, Sarah led Finn and Callie to an open game-viewing vehicle and invited them to climb inside. As he hoisted himself up into the vehicle he noticed that their luggage was neatly stowed in the back of the vehicle, just behind the second row of bench seats.

Finn settled himself next to Callie, conscious that the sun was starting to set and the temperature was falling; the day's heat was giving way to the chill of the first, unexpectedly early cold front, suggesting that autumn was just around the corner. Callie pulled out a shawl from her bag and wound it around her shoulders as Sarah accelerated away.

When they drove back through the impressive entrance Finn realised that they were leaving the security of the electric fenced estate and were heading into the reserve itself—wild and beautiful.

This is more like it, he thought, his eyes scanning the bush for signs of wildlife.

Within five hundred yards of the gate they saw a herd of springbok and a female warthog with her piglets. Then they saw a fish eagle in a tree, and Sarah pointed out a reclusive eland bull in a thicket of acacias.

This is Africa, he thought, breathing deeply. *The sounds and sights of the bush.*

A part of him wished that Sarah would dump them in a clearing and pull out a tent. He needed the solitude and peace of nature. After this crazy couple of weeks he wanted to wind down, and he couldn't think of a better way to do it than being alone in the bush. But because this was the Buffalo and Baobab he suspected that their idea of getting up close and personal with nature would be much better.

He'd barely finished that thought when Sarah veered off the dirt road onto a grassy track. Within a hundred metres she'd stopped in a clearing and Finn looked around.

They were on the edge of a cliff, and he could hear the muted sound of a river smacking on rocks below them. In one of the huge wild fig trees overlooking the river he could see a tree house, nestled into its strong branches. Except that it was less house and more platforms—three of them in all, staggered up the tree. The bottom platform looked to be a bathroom, complete with shower, the second held couches and a table, and the highest one, he presumed, would hold a bed. A bed that was open to the African sky and the elements.

Finn hopped out and slapped his hands on his hips, grinning wildly. 'Oh, this is so cool! But what happens if it rains?' he asked Sarah, taking a moment to be practical.

'Retractable roofs and screens. We monitor the weather pretty closely, and if there's a chance of rain we come down and secure the platforms. Tonight is clear, though,' Sarah said. 'Cool, but no rain.'

'Excellent,' Finn replied. He turned to look at Callie, who was looking at the tree house in horror. 'Callie...?'

'My room is up *there*?' she whispered, staring at the huge tree.

Oh, so this wasn't what she was expecting. Finn hoped that she wouldn't make a scene—not on their first night. Besides, thousands of people all over the world would give their right arm and a considerable portion of their bank account to sleep under the stars in a luxury tree house on an African game reserve.

'Problem, honey?'

Out of the corner of his eye he could see Sarah stiffening, her welcoming face turning wary. *Please don't turn out to be a city girl diva, Callie,* he silently begged her.

'Look, I think the idea of sleeping in a tree house is seriously wonderful, but—well, this is a game reserve, right? And game reserves have wild animals. And some of those animals—like leopards—like to climb trees! I do *not* want to be a leopard's breakfast!' Callie stated, with a touch of hysteria in her voice.

Sarah bit the inside of her lip to keep from smiling. 'The tree house is completely animal-proof, Mrs Banning.'

Whoah—*Mrs Banning.* That sounded weird.

But Callie didn't seem particularly fazed about what she was being called. She was still fixating on ending up on the local leopard's menu. 'You're sure?'

'Very. We would never put our guests at risk,' Sarah assured her. 'Obviously we ask you to confine your movements to the platforms. If you do so, you'll be absolutely safe. And I'll leave you with a radio and a mobile phone to call me if there is any problem at all.'

A hyena barked in the distance and Callie jumped.

Sarah looked around. 'That being said, I'd prefer that we get you into the tree house. It's not safe to hang around in the bush.'

Callie practically scampered off the seat to stand between Sarah and Finn. Finn took her cold hand in his and linked their fingers together. Sarah walked around to the back of the Land Rover and looked at their pile of luggage. Well, Callie's pile of luggage. He just had one suitcase.

'Let me see you inside and then I'll come back for the luggage.'

Finn shook his head. 'Nah, I'll help. Cal, do you need all these suitcases or can you get away with just one?'

Callie pointed to the smaller case and her tote bag. 'I just need those two.'

Sarah looked relieved as she reached for Callie's bag.

Finn leaned past her and snagged his suitcase and Callie's tote bag. 'I've got it,' he told Sarah, who had started to protest.

'I'll store your other bags at the lodge, Mrs Banning.'

Mrs Banning. Still weird.

'We've set out a picnic dinner for you, including some wine and beer. There is also a selection of spirits and mixers. If you are unhappy with our selection please just call Reception and we'll have someone deliver anything you require,' Sarah said as she led them to the tree house.

As they walked up the stairs Sarah secured a gate behind them, and Finn could see the unobtrusive but strong netting under the first platform that would prevent leopards or any other creatures from making a nocturnal visit. He pointed out the animal-proofing to Callie and watched her shoulders drop a half-inch. He allowed himself a small grin as Sarah showed them the facilities, which included a shower, his and hers basins, and a slipper bath on the edge of the platform that overlooked the river and the valley below.

The second floor held comfortable couches and chairs, a hammock strung between two branches, and a small dining table covered with cloche dishes and champagne bottles in ice buckets. There was a small chest freezer containing soft drinks and beer, and a steel wine rack holding five bottles of exceptional red wine.

How much did they expect them to drink in one night? Finn wondered.

'I'll leave you to explore the bedroom on your own,' Sarah told him, gesturing to the mobile and the radio on a side table. 'You'll hear lions and hyenas, typical bush noises, but do not hesitate to radio or call me if you are uncomfortable or encounter a problem. Nick will collect you at six a.m. for a guided tour—which is a pretty big deal because he rarely does them any more.'

'Why not?' Callie asked.

'Pretty wife in his bed...' Finn explained, and was enchanted by her blush.

'Also the fact that he has two kids under the age of three who are up and roaring around at that time,' Sarah added, before bidding them goodnight and leaving them to their night under the African stars.

Within minutes they heard the Land Rover pulling away and Finn turned to Callie and gestured to the view. 'So, what do you think?'

'Pretty shoddy digs...' Callie teased. 'They've gone to absolutely no trouble at all.'

Finn watched as she walked to the edge of the platform and placed her hands on the safety railing. 'Want some champagne?'

Callie looked at him over her shoulder and wrinkled her nose. 'No, thanks. Actually, I'd love a beer.'

Finn poured beer into a glass for her and brought it and his own bottle over to where she stood. In silence they scanned the river, saw a pod of hippos on the far bank, and watched as the sun tossed ribbons of gold over the treetops.

Finn saw her shiver as the temperature dropped further and allowed the backs of his fingers to drift over the bare skin of her shoulders. 'You're cold... This wind has a bite to it. Why don't you change into something warm and I'll start a fire in the pit?'

Callie looked around. 'Where are our bags?'

'Sarah took them to the bedroom area,' Finn replied.

'Ah, the bedroom area. Bet you it's a massive bed covered in white linen and a mosquito net, surrounded by candles.'

'That's a sucker bet,' Finn replied.

Callie took a nervous sip of her beer before lifting her eyes to Finn's. 'So, are we still paying it by ear?'

He'd never met a woman as direct as Callie before. He liked that—respected it. He didn't need to play games with her.

But she wasn't ready to share herself with him yet, Finn realised. He could see reluctance in the hitch of her shoulders, the slight shake of her fingers—although that might be from the cold—and in the worry in her eyes. She would share his bed one of these days—just not yet. And that was okay. He could wait until the time was right.

And, in the spirit of honesty, he knew the more time he had between his break-up and sleeping with her, the better handle he'd have on this entire situation. *Damn*, it would all be so much easier if he didn't like her quite so much— and if she didn't make his junk want to do a happy dance whenever she breathed.

So. Much. Easier.

Finn's expression turned serious. 'I have the sense that your flirty nature doesn't often translate into bedtime fun.'

Callie tipped her head. 'How do you figure?'

'Well, if it meant less to you then we'd have already ripped each other's clothes off.'

Callie looked out at the stygian darkness. 'It wasn't always like that. I was a lot more impetuous when I was younger.' She held up her hand to explain. 'I wasn't a slut— I just didn't take sex as seriously as I do now. It used to just be a romp…some slap and tickle…fun…'

'It still can be,' Finn said, his eyes locked on her face.

'I know, but these days I prefer to have a little bit of friendship with my sex. Just a smidgeon—I don't expect more than that—but liking is a prerequisite, respect is a bonus.'

'I like you.'

'I like you too, but...'

Finn quirked an eyebrow. 'But?'

'But...' Callie sighed. 'I'm just not—'

Callie stopped speaking and Finn waited for her to finish her thought. She just wasn't *what*?

Callie sighed. 'Ready. I'm just not ready.'

Yeah, and that was a lie. There was another reason why she was hesitating, why she was treading carefully. She wanted him—he knew that...had no doubts about that. So something else was causing her to hesitate. What was it and why was he so desperate to know?

Callie was waiting for his reply, buy there was nothing that he could say except, 'We won't be doing anything together until you are a hundred per cent comfortable with me, Cal. So try and relax, stop worrying, go and get warm. We can share a bed without me jumping you, I promise. Actually, tonight I'd love to sleep in this hammock. It looks super-comfortable and I've slept in far worse.' Finn took a long sip of his beer. 'Go and put something warm on, honey.'

Callie nodded, put her untouched beer on the table and walked to the stairs leading to the sleeping platform. Finn watched her gorgeous ass moving up the spiral staircase and felt the action in his pants.

All he had to do was follow her, start kissing her, and she'd be his. He knew that. God, it was tempting. But he didn't want to have to coerce her, tempt her, persuade her. When they made love it would be because it was a mutual decision.

It had something to do with the respect that Callie had been talking about earlier.

'Finn! This bedroom is *amazing*!' Callie called down

to him. 'Come up here and look at this place. It would be like having sex in the clouds—I mean, sleeping with you in the clouds—I mean... *Aaarrrgggh! Dammit!*'

Finn grinned, happy that he wasn't the only one who had his mind in the bedroom.

'Ignore me.' Callie's low voice drifted down to him.

Yeah, not easy to do, Finn silently assured her as he swallowed his chuckle.

Callie pushed her plate away and groaned as she leaned back in her chair. She'd expected a cold supper. She hadn't expected delicious prawns, spicy fish fillets and perfectly cooked steak. There'd also been a couscous salad and a watermelon, olive and feta salad, along with crusty bread and a variety of dips.

After the flight from Cape Town and two glasses of red wine she was feeling lazy and hazy and very sleepy. At nearly eight it was fully dark, and the soundtrack of the African bush had started to play. The crickets chirping was a familiar sound, and there was the power saw noise of the African cicada beetle. Occasionally a fish eagle would let rip with a *heee-ah, heeah-heeah*, and from somewhere that sounded far too close they heard the yelping, woofing and whining of what Finn said was a family of black-backed jackals.

It was noisy, Callie realised. *Very* noisy.

Finn, his strong features looking even more handsome in the low light of the paraffin lamps, looked at her across the table. 'There's chocolate mousse in the cool box.'

'I wish I could. I'm stuffed.'

Like her, Finn had pulled on jeans and a hooded sweatshirt against the cool night air. The blazing fire in the pit kept the worst of the chill off, but this was a place that invited you to have a warm shower and then to snuggle under the down duvet on the bed upstairs, warm in each other's arms.

It was an attractive proposition, Callie thought. But Finn had reiterated his wish to sleep in the double hammock. He'd found another down duvet in a storage cupboard on the bathroom platform and announced that he'd be super-warm wrapped up in it in the hammock.

'You look tired,' Finn commentated, lifting his glass of red to his lips.

'I am.' Callie leaned her arms on the table. 'It's been an interesting week.'

'You should've been in Paris by now.'

Tearing around the city, rushing from designer to designer, not having a moment to enjoy the city in the spring... Callie thought that she would much rather be here.

'You never told me what happened that you could suddenly take me up on my offer to be a fake wife.'

Could she tell him? Would he understand? Callie ran her finger around the rim of her full glass. He was treating her to three weeks in luxury—maybe he deserved an explanation. And, geez, they were going to be in each other's company for three weeks—they were going to *have* to talk! They were going to be friends whether they liked it or not. It was up to her to keep things casual.

'I'm running away—trying to avoid someone,' she said, looking into the fire pit. So much for keeping it casual!

'Yeah, I sort of realised that.' Finn stretched out his legs and rested his wine glass on his folded arm. 'So, who is Laura and why are you avoiding her?'

Callie jerked her head up. 'Where did you hear that name?'

'The other day, when you were arguing with your brother. Who is she?' Finn asked again.

Well, she'd started this conversation, she couldn't shut it down now.

'My mother,' Callie said, slouching down in her chair, crossing her feet at the ankles. 'She left us. We haven't heard from her since I was seven. Seb, my brother, has been tracking her movements around the world for years—he's a hacker and can do that—and they started exchanging emails. The result of which is that Laura is coming home for a three-week visit, landing—' Callie checked her watch '—in about an hour. She and Seb are going to reconnect, and everybody wants me to meet her too. Well, "everybody" being Seb.'

'And you made damn sure that there was no possibility of that happening by leaving the city with me? That's why you changed your mind about coming?' Finn said, his voice deep in the darkness.

'Yeah. I needed to leave and you gave me a damn good excuse.' Would he think she was a coward? That she was being immature? Why did it matter so much that he didn't judge her?

Finn pulled his legs in and sat up. 'So why don't you want to meet her? Why don't you want to hear why she left?'

That question again, Callie thought.

'Because it doesn't matter! Because nothing she can say—and, trust me, I've thought of every excuse she could come up with—would make me feel better, would make me understand. I was *seven*, Finn. Seven! I needed a mother. Especially since my dad dealt with my mother leaving by hooking up with younger and younger women. They were mostly after his money, and weren't interested in his little daughter hanging around. Seb was twelve, and he dealt with her leaving by withdrawing into his sports and computers.'

Callie heard her voice rise and made a conscious effort to remain calm.

'If it wasn't for Rowan, who lived next door, and Yasmeen—'

'Who is she?'

'Our housekeeper—and I suppose my real mother in every way that counted,' Callie explained. She pushed her hair off her forehead and shoulders. 'Look, I know I sound harsh, but I can't meet Laura. I don't want to...'

'Don't want to meet her, like her, risk being hurt by her again?'

'Yeah.'

He got it—he understood. *Damn*. There were those fuzzies in her tummy again. She could get used to those. *Not* a good idea.

Finn rested his forearms on his thighs and looked up at her, sparks from the fire reflected in his eyes. Callie, feeling as if he'd taken a peek into part of her soul, thought that he'd heard enough from her, so she turned the spotlight onto him.

'So, you mentioned your stepbrothers? How many do you have?'

Finn half smiled. 'Three. All younger. They're driving me nuts lately.'

'Why?'

'They were, to put it mildly, upset that the wedding was called off. As I said, because they know me, and know that I never go back on my word, they assumed that the break-up was Liz's idea. I haven't bought food for two weeks because someone always pitches up at my house with beer and take-out.'

'Nobody rocked up that night I had dinner at your house,' Callie pointed out.

'I sent them a group message while I was upstairs and told them I would kick their ass if they didn't give me a night on my own.' Finn pulled a face. 'The next night I had all three of them coming to check up on me and had to spend half the evening reassuring them that I was okay.'

'And are you?' Callie asked. 'Okay?'

'Mostly. I'm glad to still be on this assignment, working. Glad of the distraction that is you.'

Callie smiled at that. Whatever they had cooking it was, she had to admit, a hell of a distraction. 'It's surprising that your younger brothers are so protective of you.'

'We're protective of each other. They're my brothers. My mum married James when I was fourteen and he already had the boys. Mum died when I was seventeen, and James acted as my legal guardian for a while.'

'Where's your real dad?'

'Who the hell knows? Jail? Dead? In a gutter somewhere?' Finn said harshly.

He rubbed a hand over his face, and when he finally met her eyes she made sure that her face was impassive.

'Pretend I didn't say that, please? I never talk about him and I have no idea where that came from.'

Maybe their bottle of wine had contained some magic truth potion, because she'd had no intention of telling him about Laura. Or maybe it was the fact that they were absolutely, utterly alone under an African night sky…

Or maybe it was because they liked talking to each other.

And she thought that *she* had had a messed-up childhood. God, they were a pair, Callie thought.

Finn cleared his throat before speaking again. 'I've always protected my brothers—yanked them out of scrapes, had their back. I've been their rock, their calm in the storm. This break-up has been the first crisis I've had that they've witnessed and they want to be there for me.'

'And your stepdad? How does he feel about your break-up?'

Finn shrugged and kept his shoulders up around his ears. 'Dunno. He died about six months ago.'

'I'm so sorry, Finn. You two were close?'

'Yeah. He was the best man I ever knew…' Finn cleared his throat. 'I adored him.'

God. He had a waste-of-space father, a dead mother, and his stepdad, whom he'd loved, had recently passed away. He'd broken up with his fiancée two weeks before his wedding. Was there anything else that life could throw at the poor guy?

Enough now, she told the universe, annoyed on his behalf. *Seriously. Just enough, already.*

Callie leaned forward and touched his knee in silent support. He hadn't stopped grieving, she realised. Probably wouldn't for a while. Losing his fiancée had undoubtedly pulled all those old feelings of grief over losing his stepfather to the surface again.

Oh, yeah, there was far too much emotion swirling around for them to sleep together. Because there was no chance that sex would be about just sex after a conversation like this. For her it would all be tangled up with the urge to soothe, to comfort. And to him she would be just a distraction…

Thinking that it would be prudent, and smart, to close this conversation down, Callie pushed her chair back and stood up. 'I'd really like a shower. I feel grubby.'

Finn stared up at her for the longest time before lifting one broad shoulder. 'Sure.'

Callie looked at the stairs that led to the dark bathroom area below them and bit her lip. 'Is there a torch anywhere?'

Finn stood up. 'I'll go down and light some lamps for you. There's a big tub on the deck if you'd prefer a bath.'

A hyena whooped in the distance and Callie shivered. 'Not that brave. I'm not entirely sure if my standards of animal-proof are the same as the lodge's, so I'd rather not take the chance.'

'The bath is at least twenty foot off the ground, Hollis,' Finn told her, smiling.

'There might a genius leopard out there who has the situation sussed,' Callie suggested, only half joking.

'You're a nut,' Finn said with on a shake of his head and a grin. 'Go get your PJs while I sort out some light for you.'

'Thanks.' Callie bit her bottom lip. 'I don't suppose you'll stand guard, will you?'

Finn touched her bottom lip with the pad of his thumb. 'The only way that will happen is if I'm in the shower with you.' Finn dropped his thumb when she shook her head. 'No, I didn't think so.'

Snuggled down in the enormous bed on the top platform, Callie couldn't keep her eyes off the magnificent night sky. It looked as if God had taken a handful of diamonds and tossed them against a sticky backdrop, allowing them to hang there in a perpetual grip. She'd never seen stars like this before—she almost felt she could reach out and touch them.

She was beyond tired, Callie thought, and wished that sleep would come. But every time she closed her eyes she was jolted by another strange sound. The rustle of something in the tree—probably just the breeze, or a bird—had her constantly on edge. It was *not* the genius leopard, she kept telling herself. And just when she felt her eyelids starting to close those pesky jackals would start their yelping again, and then something would grunt and the hyena would laugh.

Callie was over her night under the African stars and was not finding anything remotely amusing. She was exhausted, slightly chilled, and—though she hated to admit it—a lot scared. She realised she *liked* having walls and windows between her and the night, locks and safety chains. She didn't like feeling as if she was a snack on the buffet of the African savannah, and it didn't matter how much Mr Cool downstairs reassured her: this was *not* natural! Or maybe it was *too* natural.

Again—walls, doors, windows! That was what God had created them for!

The sounds of the night dropped away and Callie felt her eyelids drooping. She was on that wonderful edge of sleep when she felt a rumbling in her chest, felt electricity charge the air. Instantly the night sounds ceased as a deep-throated grunt echoed across the bush. Oh, crap!

Callie scrambled up in bed and pulled the duvet over her head.

The grunt increased in intensity and she felt the sound invade her chest, skitter down to her nerve-endings. *Lion!* Callie sucked in her breath and wished that she could belt out of bed and run all the way back to Cape Town. The deep grunts tailed off and she bit her lip, waiting for the next sound. Just when she thought that the lion had stopped he let out a massive, deep-throated roar that raised every hair on her arms.

God—oh, God—oh, God. Finn had to call the lodge. There was a lion below them. Who could sleep with a lion below them?

'Finn!' she whispered.

Finn didn't reply.

Throwing back the covers, Callie grabbed all her courage and belted for the stairs. She cursed when she stubbed her big toe against a table. The roars were still reverberating through the night. In bare feet she scampered down the steps and by sheer chance located the radio and mobile on the table, where Sarah had left them. Her shaky hands fumbled with the unfamiliar device.

'Whatcha doing?' Finn's drowsy voice came from the direction of the hammock.

'Finn! There's a lion below us!' Callie hissed. 'We've got to call the lodge!'

'Um, okay. Why?'

'Because there's a *lion*!' Callie shouted. 'Below us!'

'Lions don't climb trees, Hollis, especially animal-proofed trees,' Finn drawled.

If she hadn't been so freaked out Callie would have heard the amusement in his voice.

Another roar rolled through the stygian darkness and Callie jumped, dropping the mobile which skittered away. She swore and peered down at the pitch-black floor. She couldn't see the phone so she swore again.

She was going to owe Rowan a lot of money after to-night.

'Cal, calm down, honey.' Finn's voice was low and steady, a beacon in the darkness. 'Leave the phone and head over here.'

Thinking that sounded like a very good plan, Callie inched her way over the deck to the bulky outline that was Finn lying in the hammock. When she stood next to him he lifted his hands and in one smooth movement lifted her, so that she lay on top of him. Rolling her off, he pulled the duvet out from under her and pulled her up so that her head rested on his shoulder.

'Uh...what are you doing?'

'Trying to get you to settle down so that we both can get some sleep,' he muttered.

His hand rested on her lower back and she snuggled up to his warmth.

'Now, listen to me, city girl. A lion's roar can be heard up to five miles away, and I promise you that lion is no-where near us. Yeah, he sounds amazing, but he's not about to eat us—so calm down, okay?'

'I still think we should call the lodge,' Callie protested on a huge yawn.

'What would we tell them? A lion is roaring? *Yeah, that's what they do in the wild, Mr Banning.* They'll think that I have the tiniest pair of balls in creation,' Finn scoffed.

'I'll call them and tell them that *you* aren't scared but I am terrified.'

Finn's sigh brushed the top of her head. 'There's nothing to be frightened of. Listen. He's stopped.'

Callie lifted her head and, true enough, the grunts and roars had stopped. She was just starting to relax when another rumbling loud roar split the night. Callie yelped and buried her face in Finn's neck, plastered herself tightly against him, hoping to climb inside.

Finn sighed. 'Or maybe not.'

Finn's hand stroked her neck, her hair, her back. His voice was low and warm and calming. 'You're safe, Cal, I promise.'

Callie shivered in his arms.

'Breathe, angel,' he told her.

Callie pulled in long deep breaths, felt his warmth and his strength and breathed again. Then her eyelids started to close and she pulled in another deep breath.

In Finn's arms, fast asleep, feeling warm and safe, she didn't even hear the next roar that shattered the night.

CHAPTER SEVEN

THEY DINED OUTSIDE the following evening, at a beautifully
laid table on the lawn of the lodge, under another magnificent star-heavy sky. In the distance they could see a storm,
the lightning lighting up huge thunderclouds. They could
taste the rain in the air but were assured that dinner would
be long over before the storm hit, so they sat back to enjoy
the exceptional food placed in front of them.

Finn noticed that the lead singer of a popular band sat
with a pouty waif at the next table, and beyond them he
recognised an English politician with a woman who was
definitely not his wife. If he were a tabloid journalist he
would be having a field-day right now; he might be feeling a bit sleazy but he'd be making a fortune, he thought.

He looked across at Callie, who was leaning back in her
chair, holding her wine glass, her eyes fixed on the storm
on the horizon. God, she was beautiful, he thought. He'd
always thought that she was attractive, but now, after seeing her without make-up and dozy with sleep, or animated
and thrilled while she bottle-fed two orphaned cheetah
cubs, or pensive while watching a pride of lions take down
a zebra, he was slowly realising that she was more than
pretty and deeper than he'd thought.

He'd thought that he would be taking a bubbly flirt on
holiday with him, but the woman he was with—even if
he'd only spent two full days in her company—was less

bubble, more substance. And sexier than he'd believed possible.

Finn dropped his hand and surreptitiously rearranged himself under the table, feeling as if his pants were suddenly a size too small. Since he'd woken up with her clinging to him like an octopus he'd been super-aware of her all day. The length of her legs, the freckles on her chest, her white-tipped fingernails. God, if he was noticing a woman's nails then he was in deep, *deep* crap.

He'd thought he was going on holiday with Flirty Callie but instead he found himself with Intriguing Callie, and he wasn't sure he could handle her. Flirty Callie he could brush off—ignore if he had to. This other Callie had him wanting to dig a little, to see what was below the surface.

Finn took a sip of his Cabernet and pushed his dessert plate away. Then he manoeuvred his chair so that he was sitting next to her, facing the storm. He could smell her perfume and feel the heat of her bare shoulder when he touched it with his.

He slid his hand under hers and linked her fingers with his. He saw the quick, searching look she sent him and ignored it. If she asked he'd say that this was what married people did—touched each other—but the truth was that he couldn't sit there and *not* touch her.

'Tell me about your jewellery box.'

There was so much else he wanted to know about her— he had a list of burning questions—but this topic seemed the safest, the most innocuous.

He heard her quick intake of breath, felt her eyes on his face.

He slowly turned his head and lifted his eyebrows. 'Why would a woman who loves clothes and shoes and accessories not wear some of that fabulous jewellery?'

Callie crossed one leg over the other and her swinging foot told him she was considering her response, choosing her words. He didn't want the bog standard answer she obviously wanted to hand him—he wanted the truth. He'd rather not know than have her spin him a line.

'Don't wrap the truth up in a pretty bow—give it to me straight.'

The foot stopped swinging and the sigh was louder this time. She took so long to say anything that Finn began to doubt that she would speak at all. When she did, her voice was low and tight with tension.

'That was the first time I'd seen the box for…oh, fifteen years. It lived on my mum's dressing table and as a little girl I'd spend hours playing with her bangles and necklaces. Her rings.'

Finn tried not to wince at the thought of little Callie playing with the two and three carat diamonds he'd seen.

'Some of the jewellery was my grandmother's—my father's mother's—passed down through the family. A lot of it is my mother's. My father constantly bought her jewellery in an attempt to make her happy.'

Ah, well… 'I take it that the buying of jewellery didn't work?'

'Not so much. Neither did the pretty clothes and the gym membership and the credit cards.' Callie shrugged. 'She didn't want to be a wife…a mother. To be chained to my dad, the house, us. She gave birth to the expected son and was horrified, I once heard, to find herself pregnant with me. She'd never really wanted children, and apparently finding herself pregnant with me was a disaster of magnificent proportions.'

'Who told you that?'

Callie crossed her legs and shuffled in her chair. 'People say that kids don't remember stuff, but I do. She screamed that during one of their fights.'

'I'm sorry.' It was all he could say—all he could think of to say. Finn removed his hand from hers and put his arm around her shoulder, leaning sideways to kiss her temple. 'But people do say stuff they don't mean in the heat of the moment.'

'Except that her leaving me—us—made that statement true.' Callie took a large, serious sip from her glass. 'Anyway, the jewellery—she left it behind. It meant nothing to her. So why should it mean anything to me?'

God. Imagine knowing that your mother was out there somewhere but not interested in knowing whether you were dead or alive, happy or sad. People should have to take a test before they were allowed to become parents, Finn thought. His father should head up the queue.

Callie turned her head and blinded him with a big smile, perfect teeth flashing. 'Now, don't you go all sympathetic on me, Banning. I had a father who adored me and spoilt me rotten, an older brother who adored me and spoilt me rotten, and a housekeeper-cum-nanny who—'

'Let me guess,' Finn interrupted, making sure that his tone was bone-dry. 'Who adored you and spoilt you rotten?'

Callie laughed. 'I have a fabulous life, and I'm on holiday with a nice man.'

'I prefer sexy.'

This time her smile was more genuine. 'So I have nothing to complain about!'

Being abandoned by your mum is a pretty big deal, Callie, Finn told her silently. *Even if you choose to think it isn't. The one person who is supposed to put you first, love you best, stand in your corner left you. That's got to cause some deep scars on your psyche.*

Feeling the need to banish the sadness from her eyes, Finn nudged her with his shoulder. 'Want to take a walk down to the lookout over the waterhole and see if any wildlife has come down for a drink?'

Callie immediately nodded and a sparkle returned to

her eyes. 'Yeah, let's do that.' She stood up and folded her arms. 'How come I find myself telling you stuff?'

Finn wanted to make a joke but he couldn't. 'I don't know, but rest assured you're not alone. I keep doing the same thing.'

Callie bit her lip. 'Maybe we should stop?'

Finn held out his hand. 'Yeah, maybe we should. The thing is, I don't know if we can.'

There was nobody in the lookout and nothing at the waterhole except for a lone bull elephant. They watched him and the storm for a while, but Callie's thoughts were miles away. On Finn and their bizarre situation, and on the fact that every time they drew a line in the sand they managed either to smudge it or step right over it.

Maybe it was time to draw a line that couldn't be removed, stepped over or just plain ignored. But how to do that?

Callie yawned and felt his arm come around her shoulders. Without thought she circled her arms around his trim waist and laid her cheek on his chest.

Smudging that line again, Hollis?

Callie felt Finn's kiss on her hair. 'Tired?'

'Mmm…'

Callie moved her hands to his abs and Finn sucked in his breath. In response she scraped her nails across his cotton-covered skin. A quick glance down and she realised, by the tenting of his pants, that he had a hair trigger response to her touch.

This wasn't smudging the line—this was obliterating it. Was she prepared to go there? She had about five seconds either to take this to the next level or to back away.

Callie knew herself well enough to know that she wasn't going to step away. She was facing a fire and for the first time in, God, so long she was going to jump right in. But this time she was going to be a little wiser and don a fire suit.

'Finn?'

'Yeah?' His voice was husky with desire and so sexy.

'That thing that happened in the dressing room…I keep thinking about it.'

She knew exactly when he stopped breathing, when he finally sucked in much needed air. 'Okay. Where are you going with this?'

'Our room only has one bed, and if I climb into it with you I'm going to be all over you.'

Callie forced herself to walk out of his grip, to pick up the bottle of beer he'd brought with him and take the last sip. To keep herself from jumping him, she held the bottle in a loose grip.

Finn groaned. 'Good to know. Want to get going, then?'

She smiled at the hopeful note in his voice before quietly murmuring, 'Holiday romances seldom work out.'

'That's what I've heard.'

'People tend to put on rose-coloured glasses and, because they know their time together is short, the experience can be intense, powerful.'

'I guess.'

Callie rolled the bottle between her palms. 'I'm at a bit of a crossroads in my life and I'm questioning so much. I'm not thinking as straight as I usually do, so don't let me get forget that this is a couple of weeks of pure fun, okay? Don't let me get seduced by the luxury and the romance and the fact that I like you.'

That was the line in the sand, she decided. They could chat and talk, share confidences and make incredible love, but she had to remember that this was going to end. It was too easy to forget who they were and why they were here. It was not real life. They were on a fake honeymoon—emphasis on the *fake*—surrounded by romance and luxury.

She could easily get swept away and inadvertently slip on a pair of those rose-coloured glasses.

They were two strangers who hardly knew each other—not a couple on their honeymoon. They could have fun, even sex, but they had to keep it real. She wasn't in a place to consider a relationship beyond the three weeks. Sure, it would be easy to fall for Finn, but it wouldn't last because it wasn't based on anything real.

She—*they*—had to keep their eyes open, their heads in the game. If she had sex with him she would finally know how he felt, tasted, moved. and then she could stop thinking about him—and sex—all the damn time.

Callie turned her head and sent him a direct look. 'We're on the same page?'

He rubbed his hand over his jaw before nodding briskly. 'Yeah. Just to be clear, are you saying that you'll sleep with me?'

The tip of her tongue touched her top lip and her skin flushed with anticipated pleasure. *Yeah, that was the plan.* Callie held his eyes.

'Well, sleep isn't what we'll be doing, exactly.' He made a move towards her but her lifted hand stopped him in his tracks. 'I don't want to be seduced, Finn.'

She saw a moment of confusion and then his face cleared. 'No hearts and flowers, no expectations.'

How did he seem to know without her having to explain? It was unsettling, but reassuring at the same time.

Finn touched her bottom lip with the pad of his thumb. 'Only in my bed, honey. I promise. Sex is on the table—everything else is off it.'

They could do this, Callie thought as they made their way out of the hide and across the lawns to their new room behind the main lodge. If they were smart and sensible, and if they kept their heads, they could have three weeks of fun and walk away unscathed.

They *had* to do this, Callie amended as Finn took her hand in his. They didn't have another option.

In their private chalet within the protected grounds of the lodge Finn took her hand and led her out onto a dark, private veranda, where moonlight glistened off the bubbles created by the hot tub that sat in one corner. Callie watched his face as he reached behind her and slid down the zip of her simple A-line dress, pulling the collar away from her neck and allowing the silky sage-green fabric to fall to the wooden deck. She stood in her violet strapless bra and matching panties, open to his appreciative gaze, watching his eyes as one index finger traced her collarbone, her shoulder, the top of her right breast.

He looked entranced, engrossed, fully involved in touching her, learning her shape, making her a memory. *Don't get fanciful,* she warned herself, closing her eyes as his finger touched her nipple and it tightened and peaked immediately.

'This is about sex, about pleasure, about a three-week affair,' Callie gabbled, closing her eyes at the intense pleasure his touch aroused in her.

'Shut up, Callie,' Finn murmured gently.

You've had these before, remember? she told herself. *You sleep with him until it stops being fun and then you stop. It's not rocket science.*

Except that Finn touching her didn't feel like just another sex act, just another pursuit of physical pleasure. It felt like something more. Deeper, more important.

Finn's mouth brushed her ear. 'Stop thinking,' he muttered. 'Just feel me touching you, enjoying your smooth skin, tasting you, smelling you. You do the same to me.'

His breath tickled her cheek and the touch of his finger on her skin had heat pooling between her thighs, causing a rush of moisture to her panties. He had barely even started and she was already ready for him to take her—*right now*. Oh, this was going to be amazing, incredible…

'I think you should kiss me,' Callie said against his cheekbone.

'I think I'll go up like a cracker,' was Finn's wry reply.

Callie dropped her gaze to his pants and sucked in her breath. Unable to stop herself, she ran her finger down the long, rock-hard length of him.

Finn grabbed her wrist and pulled her hand away. 'Yeah, also not a good idea.'

'I need you to—'

'Honey, I know exactly what you need.' Finn lifted his hand and tipped her chin up. Their eyes slammed together and held. 'Trust me to take care of you.'

'I do…'

'You sure?'

'If you can make me forget who I am in a semi-public dressing room, I have no doubt that you can do it now.'

Finn waited a beat before he shot his arm out, encircled her hips and slammed her into him. As her mound made contact with his erection his tongue swept into her mouth. He tasted and tormented her, swirling her away on a whirlpool of pleasure. His hand slid into the back of her panties and he palmed her butt with his broad hands, dipping lower, stretching the silk over his wrists so that he could touch her inner thighs and explore her feminine folds.

Callie shuddered as she fumbled for the buttons on his shirt, ripping off the last one in her haste to feel his broad chest and his hard, ribbed stomach.

'Want you…want you…want you…' she chanted, standing on her tiptoes to nibble his jaw, to swirl her tongue down his neck.

Finn pulled his hands out from her panties and with one deft flick her bra fell between them. Callie couldn't have cared less; her nipples were rubbing through the hair on his chest and if he didn't touch her soon, in all those important burning places, she was going to scream.

Loudly.

Unable to wait, she took one of Finn's hands and placed it on her breast, tried to direct his other hand to her crotch. But instead of taking her direction Finn stepped away from her and shook his head.

'No—you're saying *no*?' Callie cried, her fists on her hips. She couldn't believe that he was stepping away, that he was backing off.

Finn had the audacity to laugh at her before his eyes turned serious. 'I have a feeling that you normally call the shots in the bedroom, but this time—this first time—I'm running the show, angel.'

His thumb rubbed her cheekbone and she forgot her thought.

'You said that you trusted me. Take your panties off.'

Callie looked at him, her mouth drying at his command. She was always in the driving seat when it came to sex—she set the pace—and it felt strange and wildly intoxicating to relinquish control. Her heart was pumping at a mile a minute.

She licked her lips before hooking her thumbs in the band of her panties and shimmying them over her hips. Finn looked at her lightning-shaped strip of pubic hair and his lips twitched. When he lifted his eyes again the humour had been replaced by flat-out desire.

'That's new.'

'Shut up…' Callie growled. They could discuss her beautician's creative streak later.

'Go and sit on the edge of the hot tub—feet in the water, legs open.'

Callie turned her back to him, walked up the steps to the tub and stepped over the ledge, dropping her feet into the hot, gorgeous water. She sighed her pleasure and couldn't help wondering what was coming next.

'Yeah, keep your eyes closed,' Finn told her. 'This is about you—only you.'

God, could she stand it? Callie thought as she obeyed his instruction. Immediately her other senses were heightened: she could taste the approaching storm on her lips, could smell the citronella in the candles that she heard Finn lighting, could feel bubbles popping against her feet and her calves.

The crickets were in full chorus again, and she thought she heard the bark of a zebra.

Callie had no idea where Finn was. She had heard the rustle of his clothing as he undressed, but after that nothing more. He'd gone Ninja on her, but she couldn't open her eyes—not until he told her to.

'Open your legs, Cal.'

Callie shivered as his voice caressed her skin, causing goosebumps up and down her arms. 'Wider, honey. Yeah. So pretty. No, don't open your eyes. Let me look at you.'

Callie sat on the edge of the tub, her eyes closed, feeling wild and free and as much a part of this savage place as the predators and the prey. Time slowed and the seconds ticked over sluggishly. She was content just to sit there and let her about-to-be lover look at her.

An owl screeched, a candle spluttered, and Callie yelped as hard hands pulled her knees further apart and a dark head appeared between her thighs. Then his mouth, hot, wild and experienced, dropped onto her sex and she bucked against him, her cries blending into the sounds of the night.

Callie gripped the sides of the tub as Finn pleasured her with his lips, his tongue, slid first one finger into her, then two. She arched her back as her orgasm built, desperate for Finn to push her over the edge. But just as she crested he pulled back, and she keened her disappointment. He allowed her to fall, just a little, before building her up again.

He repeated the torture until he lifted his head, looked her straight in the eye and, with his fingers still inside her, issued another order. 'Come for me. *Now.*'

And Callie responded, just as he knew she would, instantly gushing over his hand, her inner muscles gripping his fingers and seeking all the pleasure he could give her. Finn kept his eyes locked on hers, thoroughly captivated by her uninhibited response.

When she finally stopped shaking he pulled his hand away and lifted his arm to grab her waist and pull her into the middle of the tub. She wound her legs around his hips and felt the divine friction as her clit rubbed against his penis, revving her up again. She rode him and felt vindicated, powerful, when his eyes crossed.

Taking him in her fist, she positioned him so that his tip was at her entrance. His bicep bulged with the effort of keeping from ramming himself inside her.

'No condom,' he muttered, his arms shaking.

'I'm on the pill,' she told him. 'And I'm clean. I haven't had sex for over six months and I had a medical three months ago. You?'

'Same. Clean. Trust me?'

Callie didn't bother to reply. She just slid onto him and smiled at his expression, which combined relief with pure, unadulterated pleasure.

'God, you feel so good.'

Finn lifted a wet hand and pushed her hair back from her face. 'You ready to go again?''

'*So* ready.'

He lunged up and into her, his arms a vice around her waist. 'Then hang on, baby.'

Callie managed to push herself away just enough to

look into his eyes. She touched his mouth with the tips of her fingers. 'Finn?'

'Yeah?'

'Come for me. *Now.*'

And, with a roar that was as wild as the bush around them, Finn did exactly as she commanded.

'In the nineteenth century the local tribe in the area knew it as Mosi-oa-Tunya. Translated, that means the smoke that thunders.'

Callie stood gripped the railing in front of her and watched, utterly fascinated, as millions and millions of gallons of water thundered over the edge of the falls into a gorge over one hundred metres below them.

'The Victoria Falls is known as the greatest curtain of falling water in the world,' Finn told her, his face wet from the droplets of spray. 'The spray can be seen from miles away at the height of the rainy season. Apparently more than five hundred million cubic metres of water per minute plummet over the edge, over a width of nearly two kilometres.'

'Thank you, guidebook Finn,' Callie said dryly.

Finn pushed his wet hair off his forehead. 'It *is* an incredible sight, though, isn't it?

'It so is,' Callie agreed.

Finn placed his forearms on the railing and lifted his head to squint up at her. 'I wish we were here in winter,' he said, with a pensive look on his face.

'Why? Apart from the fact that it would be about a hundred degrees cooler than at the height of summer?'

Callie felt as if she was walking around in hot soup and she was melting from the inside out. Africa in late summer, early autumn, was still furnace-hot, she thought. And the towns of Livingstone and Victoria Falls, situated next to the massive river, had killer humidity as well. They were, she'd decided, minutes after landing in Livingstone, Zambia, three hours ago, after a chartered flight from the Baobab and Buffalo, standing above the devil's boiler house.

'Well, in winter, when the water levels are low, you can walk along the lip of the falls. There are rock pools there, and one is called the Devil's Pool.'

That made sense, Callie thought. After stoking the fires of hell, Satan would want to cool down.

Then Finn's words sank in and her eyes widened. 'You can walk across....' she waved at the massive falls behind her '...*that*?'

'Well, there'd be a lot less water.'

'That's insane! People *do* this?' Callie cried, her stomach clenching at the thought.

'Sure. You walk across the rocks, swim through some pools, and then there's this other pool, right at the lip of the falls. The rock lip stops you from going over.'

'And you'd do that?' Callie asked in a squeaky voice.

Finn shrugged. 'Sure. It would be a kick.'

Callie closed her eyes. 'That's insane. It's official: I'm sleeping with a mad man.'

Finn straightened and pushed a long wet strand of hair out of her eyes, tucked it behind her ear. 'Talking of sleeping... This morning was so rushed we haven't had a moment alone for me to ask—are you okay?'

Callie frowned. 'Sure. Why wouldn't I be?'

'You said that it had been a while, and we did it a couple of times last night. You're not sore or tired or—?'

Callie grinned, touched by his concern. She was a little stiff, a little uncomfortable, but she wasn't about to admit that. 'Finn, I'm twenty-eight—not a hundred and eight.'

'Just checkin'.' Finn rubbed his thumb over her cheekbone. 'I had fun.'

Hoo-boy. So had she. 'Me too.'

'Want to do it again?'

Callie made sure that her tone was flippant, carefree. 'Sure—since you're *marginally* good at it.'

She put her tongue in her cheek to make sure that he knew that she was teasing.

In a flash Finn scooped her up into his arms and swung her towards the railing. 'Can you swim?' he asked, grinning down at her.

Callie wound her arms around his neck in a chokehold as she squealed hysterically. 'Put me down, you jerk!'

Finn swung her towards the railing again. 'Tell me I'm the greatest you've ever had.'

'The best ever!' Callie shouted in his ear, tightening her arms. 'I promise!'

Finn finally allowed her legs to drop to the ground, but Callie kept her arms around his neck, peeking out from over his arm. His hands were running up and down her spine.

'You were pretty spectacular yourself, Cal.'

Callie dropped her head back to look into his face. His eyes looked warm and tender, and his mouth—that wonderful mouth—was heading towards hers. She allowed him one brush, two, then a quick taste of her tongue before pulling back and stepping away. Sleeping with him was one thing, but the banter, the teasing, the outright affection had to be curtailed—or at the very least controlled. Or else they'd forget that their fake relationship was...well, fake, and they'd end up in all sorts of emotional trouble.

'I don't want a relationship,' she stated baldly.

He met her eyes. 'Me neither.'

She wanted to tell him that she *really* didn't. She couldn't allow her feelings to be engaged, couldn't hand her heart over and trust its well-being to the hands of another person. As a little girl she'd done that. Her mum had been her entire world and she'd left. Just left.

I can't and won't allow myself to break the habit of a

lifetime and fall for you in any way, shape or form, she told him silently.

She made herself smile at him. 'Just so that you know: I am going to use you and abuse you, then callously toss you aside at the end of three weeks.' *I'm going to treat you like just another short-term prospect...some bed-based fun,* she added silently. *And that means no digging into the past, sharing secrets or stories. It means being sensible and unemotional and playing it super-cool.*

Finn nodded. 'Use, abuse and toss away. Got it.' The corners of his eyes crinkled with laughter. 'You are the most honest woman I've ever met, angel.'

He'd called her that before, and it sounded so natural that she wondered if he even knew he was doing it. Short-term lovers shouldn't have nicknames, but she didn't have the guts to ask him to stop. She rather liked it.

Callie looked down the gorge to the river, to what looked like a tiny speck on the water. Her attention captivated, she leaned forward and immediately felt Finn's hand on her elbow, placed there for protection. She would have to be an idiot to lean far enough over to lose her balance and go headfirst down into the gorge, but Finn's protective instinct warmed her from the inside out.

Don't go there, Hollis. Use, abuse, toss.

'Is that a boat?' Callie asked, pointing to the river so very far below them.

'Yep. That's one of the white-water rafting boats.' Finn nodded. 'I want to do that tomorrow. Want to come with me?'

Callie twisted her lips. 'That would be a no.'

But there was a tug of excitement in her belly—a wish that she could say yes, that she could experience the thrill of riding those rapids. She hadn't done anything to make her adrenalin pound since she was a teenager who'd loved pushing the envelope.

And she wouldn't. She'd promised Seb and her dad. But, *damn*, she'd loved it.

'Aw, come on!' Finn placed a hand on her back to steer her down the path, away from their lookout point.

'You have more chance of being impregnated by a member of the zombie apocalypse.' She leaned her shoulder into his. 'You'd better not die. I'll be narked if my holiday and my recently revived sex life is interrupted by having to ship you home in a body bag.'

Finn grinned at her. 'No worries. It's safe.'

'It's madness!' Callie hissed.

But it wasn't—it really wasn't. It looked fun and exciting and thrilling, and she hoped Finn loved every second of it.

She knew that *she* would. Damn, she could just do it and they wouldn't even know. But she'd promised. And promises couldn't be broken, she reminded herself.

CHAPTER EIGHT

CALLIE, IN A teeny bikini, sat on the deep step of the tepid hotel pool, a virgin mojito by her elbow and her face shielded from the early-afternoon sun by an enormous straw hat. Finn, dressed in a pair of board shorts and holding a beer in his hand, sat next to her, reading a travel magazine.

'I should be working,' he muttered as he flipped a page.

'This *is* working,' Callie assured him. 'You're researching the hotel's facilities.'

Finn didn't lift his eyes from the page. 'I'll go with that. Jeez, what a crock!'

Callie leaned into his shoulder. Judging by the mighty mountains in the photograph, she realised that he was reading an article about the Himalayas.

'What's the problem?'

Finn flicked the magazine with his thumb. 'This journalist is writing about Durbar Square in Kathmandu and being factually incorrect—which annoys the hell out of me. If you're going to write about a foreign place be respectful and get your damn facts straight!'

Callie's lips twitched in amusement. 'I'll keep that in mind if I decide to make a career change.'

'Smart-ass,' Finn muttered, but she saw his quick smile before he refocused on the offending article.

Callie heard her mobile ring She reluctantly stood up

and went to her lounger to answer it. It would be Rowan, or Seb, or her dad calling to check up on her. She could, she thought with a smile, only tell Rowan that she was having fabulous sex…

'I'm fine…I'm happy…I haven't done anything stupid yet,' she said, her voice full of laughter.

'Hello, Calista.'

Callie stiffened and her heart started to pound. She recognised that voice—it was the voice she heard in her dreams. Callie checked the unfamiliar number on her display. 'Who *is* this?' she demanded, although she had no doubt.

'It's your mother.'

Callie shook her head. 'Funny, that—I don't *have* a mother. She left while I was in hospital, getting X-rays for my broken arm and cracked ribs.'

'You always were a challenging child.'

Like you'd know. 'Says the woman who sneaked out through the door and didn't come back.'

'I'm back now.'

'Twenty-plus years too late and I don't care. Who gave you my number? Seb?'

Silence answered that question. 'Tell him he sucks. Don't call me again, Laura, we have nothing to say to each other.'

'Calista—'

Callie pushed the button to disconnect the call and bit down on her lip, concentrating on that pain in an attempt to ignore the throbbing clenching of her heart. Laura sounded exactly the same: her voice low and melodious. She had a beautiful voice, Callie remembered. She'd loved to hear her sing.

God, she couldn't think about her—couldn't start to remember. She didn't want to remember—didn't want to open that Pandora's box. She'd always sung when she was happy...which hadn't been that often.

One phone call and a host of memories flooded back—her laughter, her scent. Callie banded her arms across her stomach, trying to keep the pain at bay. She didn't want to remember, to start thinking about her, about everything she'd lost...

She needed something to distract her—something to make her forget. Callie threw her mobile back into her tote bag and looked to Finn. *He* would make her forget. One touch of his hands on her skin and she would be taken away to a place where no thought was necessary. A place of pleasure and delight...

Callie dived into the pool and surfaced by the step. She tugged on Finn's big toe and when he looked at her lowered her eyelids in a gesture that she hoped was sexy and alluring. 'Want to go back to the cabana and play?' she asked.

Finn pulled his glasses off his face and folded them carefully. He looked at her for a full minute before asking, 'Who called you, Cal?'

Callie pulled in her top lip and shrugged. 'No one important.' Her hand slid up his leg and gripped his knee. 'Let's go and fool around.'

'Nope.'

Callie's mouth fell open in astonishment. The man hadn't been able to keep his hands off her last night and some of this morning and now he was saying *no*? When she most needed him?

'Excuse me?'

Finn held her eyes, his expression inscrutable. 'As tempting as that offer is...no, we're not going back to the room to fool around.'

'Why not?' Callie demanded, finding her feet in the pool.

'Tell me who was on the phone, Cal.'

She didn't want to discuss her mother—that was the point! She didn't want to go there. Didn't want to revisit her bad childhood and her mother issues.

Suddenly she craved the rush of adrenalin, the freedom of doing something extreme, something to get her out of herself. She wanted to be Wild Callie, Free Callie. So if she couldn't have sex in the middle of the day with her fake husband then she'd do something else to get her adrenalin pumping, to distract her.

A part of her knew that she was lapsing back into old childhood habits—as a child and teenager she'd tried every daredevil stunt she could, either to attract attention or to distract herself from her mother-free life. But, God knew, after hearing her mother's voice for the first time in over twenty years, she more than needed a distraction.

Patch and Seb would understand why she had to break her promise.

'Fine.' Callie tossed her head and glared at Finn. 'Then I'm going back to the room, getting dressed, and then I am going to go and bungee jump.'

'Yeah? No. You're not.'

Now he was presuming to tell her what to do? She didn't think so!

'Since I am an adult, and since I am not asking you to pay for it, how do you think you're going to stop me?'

Finn drained the rest of his beer and placed the empty bottle on the side of the pool. He folded his arms and she wished she could crawl into them, rest her head on his chest and allow the tears that she was holding back to slide down her face. But that was impossible. Because Callie Hollis was a tough party-girl. She didn't cry.

'Obviously I can't stop you, if that's what you're determined to do, but yesterday you said that you didn't want to bungee, to do white-water rafting or the microlight over the Falls experience. You said that extreme sports isn't something you do any more.'

'Changed my mind,' Callie retorted.

Please don't sound so concerned and worried. If you do, I might break down totally.

'I can see that. Want to tell me why?'

Callie shook her head. 'I changed my mind. I'm allowed to do that, Finn!'

'Stop treating me like an idiot, Callie! Ten minutes ago you were happy and relaxed and then you got a call. Now you're more wound up than a spinning top! Whoever called you has put you over the edge and now you're acting like a...' Finn's words trailed off.

'A lunatic? A crazy person? A bitch?' Callie asked. God knew she felt like all three. But she didn't owe him an explanation for changing her mind—why couldn't he respect that? She didn't owe anyone anything! Besides, in the past couple of days she'd spoken more about her past than she had in twenty years!

'Now you're putting words in my mouth.'

How was she supposed to fight with him, argue, when he was so calm, so controlled, so unfazed? It was like arguing with a pile of soil—incredibly frustrating.

'Did your mum call you? It was her, wasn't it?'

Oh, God, don't go there, Finn, please. 'I'm not discussing this.'

Finn rested his forearms on his knees and Callie could see the disappointment in his eyes, on his face.

'Okay, Callie, I give up. Go bungee-jumping—do whatever the hell you want.'

'All I wanted to do was make love with you!' Callie cried.

If he'd just said yes, like any normal man, they wouldn't be fighting, wouldn't be having this torturous conversation.

'No, you wanted to use me as a distraction from her call,

from whatever she said, what she made you feel,' Finn replied, his tone low. 'And while I'm happy to have you any time and anywhere, angel, might I remind you that you weren't prepared to be a means for *me* to escape the pain of my break-up? Well, ditto back at you, babe.'

Callie squeezed the rope of wet hair that hung over her shoulder. 'You couldn't even hear what I was saying, so you're jumping to some very big conclusions, Banning!'

Finn tapped his sunglasses against his leg. 'Am I wrong?'

Callie tried to lie—she did—but while her tongue formed the words she couldn't push them past her lips. Unable to hold Finn's stare, she looked up at the deep blue sky before whirling around and plunging back into the pool, allowing her tears to mix with the chlorinated water.

Damn him. All she'd wanted was some crazy sex to help her forget. Was that such a big ask?

Okay, so today had been weird, Finn thought, as he left their room at The Thunder, a small, luxurious boutique hotel situated on the banks of the mighty Zambezi River. He was heading for a huge deck suspended above the river, which offered—according to the pile of literature the manager had left for him to peruse—superb views of wildlife coming down to the river to drink and magnificent sunrises and sunsets.

Right now all he hoped was that it held a certain navy-eyed blonde who was currently avoiding him.

Finn ran his hand through his wet hair before jamming his hands into the pockets of his stone-coloured linen shorts. After their argument she'd swum lengths in the pool, only stopping forty-five minutes later, when her breath was laboured and her limbs were shaking. Her eyes had still been tight with tension, red-rimmed either from the chlorine or her tears, and her lips had been a thin line in her face.

Thinking that he'd pushed her enough, and that she needed some time to cool down, he'd avoided her for the afternoon, taking his laptop and notes and finding a secluded spot in the hotel's library to start work on his honeymoon article.

When he'd surfaced hours later it had been early evening, and when he'd returned to their room Callie's scattered clothes and her light fragrance in the air had told him that she'd already dressed and left for dinner.

She wasn't on the deck, he realised, looking over the tables. Twisting his lips, he walked to the bar area—and there she sat, at the end of the bar, a margarita in her hand, holding court. Two guys his age and older man were hanging off her every word, tongues practically resting on the bar.

On the other side of the bar Finn leaned his shoulder into the wall and watched her, unnoticed by anyone but the barman. *Look at her,* he thought, *so bold, so attractive, such a fake.* This Callie, this consummate, charming flirt, wasn't who she really was. *All* of who she was.

The real Callie was softer, more vulnerable, a great deal deeper than the person currently charming the pants off her admirers. This woman was harder, phonier, a great deal more Hollywood.

But sexy—always so damn sexy.

The man in him—her lover—got a kick knowing that she would share his bed tonight, be with him tonight. He shrugged. That was his ego talking. It was normal to like the idea of men envying him his woman.

His woman. Wow. Yet for at least the next two weeks she was. Fake wife or not, they were sleeping together, and that allowed him a certain measure of possessiveness. It didn't mean anything serious.

Did it?

Irritated with himself, Finn peeled himself off the wall and walked up to the bar, deliberately placing a hand low on Callie's spine. He felt her stiffen and caught the wary look she tossed his way.

'Evening,' he said, making eye contact with each of her admirers. Being men, and obviously not stupid, they received his non-verbal *back-the-hell-away-from-her* message loud and clear. Within minutes they all had somewhere they needed to be, and he was soon alone with Callie.

He ordered a beer from the barman and looked into her lovely face, immediately clocking her sad eyes, her wariness.

'We still fighting?' he asked gently.

'I was fighting more with you than myself,' she admitted, twisting the wedding ring on her left hand.

'Okay,' Finn replied. He didn't understand, but as long as he was not knee-deep in the brown stuff he was good. 'Do you want to talk about it?'

'Not really.'

He should be happy at that answer, since talking always led them into uncharted, emotional territory, but he couldn't help feeling a little disappointed. He wanted to help her, to work through that brief conversation with her mother that had rocked her world this afternoon.

He was whipped, he decided on an internal sigh. He was feeling protective of her and possessive of her, acting affectionate around her and calling her *angel*. But he felt as if he'd known her for a lot longer than the few weeks he had, and in a sense he seemed to read her better than he ever had Liz. He knew her instinctively.

He was stepping into quicksand and he should back up before he found himself nose-deep in mud and struggling to breathe.

'Okay. The sun is about to go down and I think the sunset is going to be absolutely amazing. Let's go watch it.'

Callie jerked her head in a quick nod and slid off her stool, her long, sleeveless halterneck dress skimming her slim body. The indigo colour lightened her eyes and set off the tan she'd managed to acquire in a few short days. Her naturally curly hair was pulled into a messy plait.

She looked sensational and smelt even better.

Finn picked up her glass and his beer and watched her buttocks sway as she walked towards the open doors and onto the deck. He was pleased when she made her way to a vacant table perched on the end, right over the river and private.

He placed her drink on the table in front of her, pulled out a chair and waited until she was sitting down before settling himself into his own chair. He took a long swig of his beer. He was not going to ask what had gone wrong today.

Finn just sat there, happy to swat mosquitoes away as the sun finger-painted the evening sky with bold oranges and pinks.

A waiter replenished their drinks, brought them a snack of homemade chunky bread and flavoured olive oil to dunk the bread into, and Callie just looked out onto the dark river, her profile exquisite in the low light provided by lamps and citronella candles.

She slapped her bare arm and grimaced at the mess left by a bloodsucking mosquito. 'I'm being eaten alive,' she complained, and he was glad to break the silence—even if it meant discussing the mozzies, which were big enough to pick them up and carry them away.

Which reminded him... 'Did you take your anti-malaria pill?'

Callie winced. 'Dammit, I forgot.'

Finn shook his head. 'Jeez, Cal, you *can't* forget. Malaria is not fun. Take it when you get back to the room, okay?'

'Okay.' Callie agreed, leaning forward to rest her arms on the table between them. 'So, today was—'

Finn lifted an eyebrow.

'—difficult.'

Finn scratched the back of his neck. 'Difficult? No. Confusing? Hell, yeah.'

Callie broke off a piece of bread, dunked it in the oil and popped it into her mouth. Finn urged himself to be patient. She'd explain in her own time. Oh, wait—he wasn't supposed to be waiting for her explanation. *Remember the point about backing the hell up?*

'Oh, Finn, look! There's a massive bull elephant coming down to the river. Oh, he's a big boy.'

Okay, so she still wasn't ready to talk. Why did he want her to? Why did he want her to trust him with her mind, her feelings, as well as her body?

Callie leaned forward, her elbows on the table and her chin cupped in her hands. Finn couldn't resist picking up his mobile and aiming it in her direction, trying to capture the look of admiration on her face.

The flash went off, Callie blinked rapidly, and he looked down at the captured image.

Callie's eyes were scrunched closed and the image was blurry and out of focus. He deleted the image and shook his head. Well, what did he expect? It had been that type of day.

Then again, surely things could only get better from now on, he thought.

Finn leaned back in his chair and his attention was caught by a couple a short distance from them. She had a huge smile on her face and was gesticulating wildly. He just looked shocked. Fantastically happy but utterly shocked. Finn felt dread settle in his stomach. He knew what she was telling him.

The man's loud whoop and his bouncing out of his chair to lay his cheek on his partner's stomach was a pretty good clue. She was pregnant and he was excited. Finn swallowed when the guy kissed that still flat feminine stomach and then reached up to cover her mouth with his.

He understood that wave of love. He'd never loved Liz as much as he had when she'd told him he was going to be a father. He'd thought that she'd hung the moon and stars.

Unable to watch them any more, Finn turned his head and stared out onto the river, fighting the urge to tell them not to get too excited, that bad things could and did happen. Happiness could be fleeting.

Caught up in the business of the last week—the elephant rides and the game drives, the amazing sex—he'd managed to shove his grief aside. To forget, just for a little while, why he was here…with Callie. He'd managed to have a break from mourning the loss of his baby, the loss of his dream of having a family, his stepdad—all of it.

Grief, hard and sour, rolled over him and memories flashed on the big screen in his head. He saw his bedroom, the blood, Liz's white face.

He couldn't resist looking across the room again at the excited couple. He didn't know if he could ever be that excited again, ever trust in happiness like that again. Nothing compared to the joy he had felt about becoming a father, and to have it ripped away was an experience he never wanted to repeat.

Maybe in a couple of years, after a great deal of thought, he might be ready to think about another relationship, about trying to create a family with someone again, but not yet—not when he was so raw and his emotions were all over the place.

The waiter put the menu down in front of them and Finn

felt his stomach roil at the thought of food. He couldn't
eat—not now. Right now he needed to be alone, to lose
himself in his writing, maybe do a couple of chapters of
the anecdotal travel guide he was busy compiling.

It was either that or lose himself in Callie's body. And
he couldn't do that—not since he'd taken the moral high
ground earlier in the day. Besides, maybe they needed a
break from each other…from sex. God, did he *really* think
that? Shoot him now! But he needed to step away from the
quicksand and he couldn't use her as a crutch. She wouldn't
be around in a couple of weeks and what would he do then?
No, he had to backtrack, put some distance between them.

He was going to act like an adult now, not scuttle from
the room because a random couple were expecting a baby.
That was just stupidly ridiculous. He was going to sit here,
enjoy the evening, the balmy night. He was with a gorgeous, entrancing woman who fascinated and frustrated
him in equal measure. He was not going to fall into the
vortex of grief—not tonight.

'Are you okay?' Callie asked, her eyes flashing concern.

'Sure.'

'You're not still mad at me because I acted like a loo-
ney tune today?'

'I was never mad at you.' Finn saw that she didn't buy
that statement and he smiled. 'Okay, I was a little frustrated.'

'You had a right to be,' Callie admitted. She blew out a
long sigh. 'I can be a very frustrating woman.'

He smiled at her self-deprecation. 'You're also a smart-
ass and a flirt and as sexy as hell.'

The light dimmed in Callie's eyes. 'Yet you turned me
down today?'

Finn covered her hand with his, linking their fingers.
'That wasn't because I didn't want you.'

Callie pushed her hair back with her hand. 'I know; I

was using sex as a distraction and that wasn't fair—to you or to me. I'm so sorry, Finn, it was wrong of me.'

He wanted to tell her that not five minutes ago he'd wanted to do the same thing to her, so he wasn't exactly a saint. He slid a glance to the expecting couple and sighed. God, he and Callie were a pair. Outwardly successful, talented, in the prime of their lives.

The truth was that they were both pretty screwed up in different ways.

Callie sent him a small smile. 'You keep shifting in that chair—it looks like you're uncomfortable. Why don't you move to this chair?'

Finn looked at the chair to her right and realised that it would put his back to the couple—just what he needed.

Shifting over, he settled his long length in the new chair and immediately felt more relaxed, a lot more comfortable.

Callie pushed her hand under his and slid her fingers between his. 'We're really bad talkers, aren't we? I'd rather literally spill my guts than do it emotionally, and I suspect you are the same.'

'Yeah.'

'That being said—and I know that I have absolutely no right to say this—I want you to know that if you want to talk I'll listen.'

Finn squeezed her hand, shocked at the thought that he was tempted to do just that. But they'd made a decision not to be sucked into anything deep, anything important—not to be seduced by the romance and the company and luxury.

No, he needed to put distance between them, and talking wouldn't help with that. It would just make him ache for more.

Finn squeezed her hand again. 'Back at you, angel.'

There he went again with the endearments. God, could he get *nothing* right tonight?

CHAPTER NINE

CALLIE, DRESSED IN a short terry robe, her hair wet from the shower, was curled up in the corner of a cane couch on their private veranda, a bowl of fruit salad in her hand. Finn was half perched on the railing, the riverbank vegetation below him and the mighty Zambezi river behind him, the early-morning sun beating down on his bare chest.

After their meal last night they'd both retreated to their respective corners by silent agreement. He'd gone out onto the balcony and hunched over his computer and she hadn't disturbed him. Instead she'd showered and gone to bed, taking a little time to catch up with her e-reader. She'd fallen asleep somewhere around midnight and hadn't heard Finn coming to bed, but she'd woken up curled up half on him. It had been an easy slide completely on to him and she'd sighed when he'd entered her, filling her.

It had been easy and languorous and sexy.

'Croc on the sandbank,' Finn told her, pointing so that she knew where to look.

Now or never, Hollis, Callie thought. *Are you going to back away and pretend that you didn't notice what you noticed last night? Leave the status quo? Or are you going to make this situation more complicated than it needs to be? And if you get him to open up, then he has a right to do the same to you. You ready for that? Getting to know him better will make it so much harder to walk away...*

Callie spooned up a strawberry and slowly chewed. She understood that she was taking a risk, but she knew that Finn needed someone to talk to about the horror of the last few weeks. Because it was eating him up.

When he thought she wasn't paying attention his eyes would reveal his sadness, his grief. His lower lip would tremble before he flattened it out and then he'd pull in a deep breath. Yeah, the man was in pain and he needed to talk. It was more important that he do that than it was for her to protect her heart.

Her wounds were old and mostly healed, but his were raw.

'Did you love your fiancée?'

Finn's laugh had absolutely no humour in it. 'You go straight for the jugular, don't you? I loved her, but probably not as much as I should have.'

Thought so. So, now are you going to ask the really hard question?

Yeah, she was.

'So, how far along was Liz when she miscarried?'

Finn wobbled and grabbed the railing to steady himself as the colour ran from his face. He stared at his bare feet for so long that Callie didn't think he'd ever answer her.

'Four and a half months,' Finn said finally, his voice rough. 'How did you know?'

Callie placed her bowl on the coffee table and wrapped her arms around her bent knees. 'I've always thought that there was something more to your break-up than—well, just a break-up. Then I saw your reaction to that couple last night. It was written all over your face.'

Finn grimaced. 'And I thought I hid my reaction so well.'

Callie pushed her unbrushed curls out of her eyes. 'Not so much. I take it that you really wanted the baby?'

Finn slowly nodded. 'I really did... I've always wanted to have a family—a wife, a couple of kids.'

'Because of your own dad?'

Finn took a long time to answer her. 'My dad was useless. That's the kindest word I can find to describe him. He'd come back, make these elaborate promises to us, siphon money off my mum and disappear again. It was always just Mum and I, and life was tough sometimes. I wanted a dad I could rely on.'

'James was that person for you?'

Finn nodded. 'He really was. He taught me about family.'

'And when Liz told you she was pregnant it was your chance to have the family you'd always craved?' Callie gently pushed. 'Tell me about losing your baby, Finn.'

Finn rubbed his jaw in agitation. 'She just started to bleed that night. We were at home. I've seen war—reported on war—seen some pretty horrendous stuff, but there was always a distance been me and the event. This was up close and personal. Blood...so much of it.'

That's why he got rid of the mattress, Callie realised. *Oh, Finn, honey.*

Callie knew that if she spoke, if she uttered a word of sympathy, she'd lose him.

'They took her to Theatre, did a D&C, what is that, anyway?'

'Basically, they just go in and...' Callie bit her lip '...clean everything out.'

Finn briefly closed his eyes. 'Anyway, when she came out of Theatre we had a discussion and she suggested that we break it off. She said that we were only together for the baby. That if she hadn't fallen pregnant then she doubted we would've been together any more.'

Callie's respect for Liz rose and she placed her hand on her heart. 'That was enormously brave.'

Finn frowned at her. 'What?'

Callie lifted her shoulder. 'She was brave, Finn. It would've been so much easier to go through with the wedding, to go home and pretend that you still loved each other, that you could love each other again like you should. Instead she chose the hard route—the one that took courage. Cancelling the wedding, exposing herself to gossip, to questions. In her most painful moment she looked for the truth—you've got to respect that.'

Finn stared at her. 'I never thought about it like that.'

'She deserves some credit for making a tough choice when she could've lied to herself *and* to you.' Callie smiled softly. 'You have great taste in women, Banning,' she teased.

The corner of his mouth lifted. 'Apparently so.'

'Could they tell whether your baby was a boy or a girl?'

Finn's broad shoulders rose and fell. 'I have no idea. To me it just felt right that he was a boy.'

Callie rested her chin on her kneecap. 'I bet you named him after your stepdad.'

Finn's mouth lifted at the corners in another reluctant smile. 'Witch. Yeah, I did. In my head I called him James—Jamie—same as my stepdad.'

You're still in mourning, honey, for both your stepdad and your lost little boy.

'Does anyone know, apart from me, about the baby? About what you lost?'

Finn shook his head. 'We hadn't told anyone that she was pregnant and Liz asked me to keep it like that. She's pretty private and her folks are conservative.'

'I think coping with all the questions about why you broke up so close to the wedding would be hard enough; having to explain about the miscarriage too would probably have sent her running into the night,' Callie said, empathising.

'You seem to understand her a lot better than I ever did,' Finn said, his voice sad.

'I'm a woman—and you feel bad because you wish you could've loved her more.'

Finn stared at the wild African bush that edged the opposite bank of the river and Callie sensed that it was time to be quiet, to leave him to his thoughts.

After a couple of minutes he spoke again. 'I feel stupid for mourning like this. God, I can't even call him a baby—he didn't get that far. He was an entity that I never met! That's what I've been battling with—the idea that I can be so devastated when I hadn't even met him yet.'

'Don't feel stupid. You *are* allowed to mourn losing him, Finn. It doesn't matter that his time with you was brief, or that he wasn't even fully formed yet. He was a soul and you loved him. If you lose love you are always entitled to mourn.'

'When my stepdad died—God, it was six months ago, but it still feels like it was yesterday—I lost my mentor, my rock, my best bud. Losing the baby made me feel like I'd lost him all over again.'

He might be slow to talk but, *dang*, he definitely needed to, Callie thought. This was heavy baggage to carry on your own.

Finn turned his back to her and gripped the railing with his hands, his head dropping to his chest. Callie knew that he was fighting tears and that he'd hate for her to see them.

Staying where she was, she asked another soft question. 'Did you bury your stepdad? Does he have a grave? A headstone?'

'No. He wanted his ashes scattered out at sea. Why?' Finn, now back in control, turned to face her but kept his white-knuckled grip on the railing behind him.

Callie shrugged. 'It's nice to have a place to go to remember, to cry if you need to. A place where you can think about your stepfather and your son.'

'It's a nice idea, but I don't.' Finn released the railing and walked over to the coffee table. He drained the half-glass of orange juice he'd left there earlier. 'Can we change the subject? I'm feeling a bit like a specimen under a microscope.'

Callie looked up at him and saw his shuttered eyes, his now implacable face. Yeah, he was done talking. And that was okay, she thought. She'd got a lot more out of him than she'd expected to.

And she'd given him something in return. She wasn't sure what. Maybe a little comfort, a little support. And that was more than okay—she had it and he needed it.

She was beginning to think that there wasn't much that she *wouldn't* give Finn.

Including, if she wasn't very, very careful, her heart.

After Livingstone they were sent back to South Africa and booked into a sprawling, Vegas-type casino on the outskirts of the country's capital. Callie had been looking forward to this portion of their trip the most, but instead of loving it, as she'd expected to do, she wanted to go back to easy summer days and hot summer nights—in bed as well as out.

She didn't want fancy rooms or air-conditioning. She wanted to hear the call of the fish eagles, to smell the electricity of a wild storm. She didn't want to hear the *ker-ching* of slot machines or the whoops of overdressed, over-perfumed people.

Callie leaned back in her chair in the restaurant section of a popular bar and hoped Finn wouldn't take his time fetching her wrap from their hotel room. Then again, their room was about a mile from the entertainment area, so she might only see him again in an hour or two.

Callie gave a man approaching her table a look that said *don't even think about trying to chat me up* and he halted in his tracks and turned away. Fishing her mobile out of her purse, she pushed a speed dial number and blocked her other ear so that she could hear when Rowan answered.

'Uh…Cal. I didn't expect you to call tonight.'

'Why?' Callie demanded, laughter in her voice. 'Are you out having fun with my wicked witch of a mother?'

The long silence that followed her comment was all the confirmation she needed. Callie felt her stomach cramp and she stared at the table, fighting the burning sensation in her eyes.

'Where are you?' she croaked out.

'Awelfor,' Rowan finally answered.

'He allowed her to come *home*?'

'Callie—'

Callie heard a familiar guffaw in the background and her clenching stomach launched up her throat. 'Is my dad there?'

'Yeah, Seb invited him and Annie round for dinner.'

'With *Laura*?' Callie clasped her neck with her hand. 'Am I the only one who still has a problem with the fact that she left for over twenty years and we haven't heard from her since? That she abandoned me—us? How can you all just sit there and laugh and drink and pretend what she did was okay?'

'Honey—'

'Don't *honey* me. God, you all suck…' Callie whispered into the phone, before jamming her finger against the red button.

Hauling in air, she looked around for a waiter but there wasn't one to be seen. She needed a drink and she needed it now. More than that, she needed to forget that her family—the people who were supposed to love her most—were laughing and drinking and eating with Laura as if she'd done no wrong. How could they just forget? Just forgive?

And her dad? How *could* he? He was supposed to be on her side.

She didn't want to think about her mother and she couldn't consider forgetting or forgiving. No, what she needed was a distraction. Something to take her mind off her mother, her family and the aching void in her heart.

Callie looked around and through the window to a pub, where she saw a group of well-dressed adults. They looked sophisticated and successful and badly in need of a party.

Well, *she* was their girl.

He'd lost his fake wife, Finn thought, bemused, holding her wrap in his hand and back in the restaurant where he'd left her. Finding Callie was going to be a nightmare. Was it asking too much for her to have stayed where he'd left her?

Hearing a loud chorus of male laughter from the adjacent pub, Finn had a sinking feeling that he'd find her wherever the action was—and it sounded as if the action was next door.

Heading that way, he walked through the frosted doors and there she was, standing behind the bar, a bottle of tequila in her hand, happily pouring shots into the grubby glasses lined up in front of her. The bartender next to her had two bottles in his hand and was filling up the glasses too.

A mound of lemon segments sat on the plate in front of the fifteen-strong crowd and Finn shook his head when he saw that there were women in the group as well. It seemed that Callie could charm members of her own sex into drinking competitions as well.

He'd only been gone an hour. How the hell had she get managed to get front and centre and drinking in sixty minutes? God, bartenders must love her. Finn shook his head as Callie licked salt off her hand, tossed back her drink and sucked on her lemon, pulling the inevitable 'tequila face'.

She was a handful, and a man would have to have steel balls to take her on.

You are not that man, he reminded himself. *You are not in a place where you can even think about getting emotionally involved with another woman; Callie is your rebound fling. It doesn't matter that she totally gets you about the miscarriage, that she understands how it feels to lose something you've never had, that she's fun and smart and so sexy.*

It was the wrong time and place. He'd thought long and hard about getting involved with Liz, longer and harder about Liz moving into his house, and here he was, after a few short weeks, thinking about taking on a girl with a wild streak.

It would be crazy. And yet a reckless part of him wanted to. He wondered what it would be like to love her, to be loved by her. To have her there when he came home, to think about her when he was away. And he knew that he *would* think about her when he was gone—he knew that he wouldn't be able to compartmentalise her as easily as he had Liz.

Callie would demand so much more from him than Liz—or any other woman he'd ever met.

He didn't have it in him—not now and not any time soon—to give her a quarter of what she wanted or expected. Or deserved. Callie deserved the world and he didn't have it in him to give it to her.

'Hey, hubby!' Callie waved the tequila bottle at him, her eyes slightly squinty.

Finn pushed through the crowd to stand directly opposite her. 'You're on the wrong side of the bar, wife. How did you get there?'

Callie smiled broadly and pointed to a sophisticated-looking couple. 'Kelvin and Neil are celebrating their anniversary and these are all their friends!'

'Uh-huh?'

'And I offered to buy them a drink—to toast them—and they said yes, and then we got talking about our favourite shooters, and I showed Grant here—' she laid a hand on the barmen's shoulder '—how to make a champagne shooter, and we had some of those. Now we're doing it old school.'

'Ah…' Finn winced at the thought of what she'd spent, throwing liquor down strangers' throats. Correction: what *he* was about to spend—because Callie, dressed in a slinky black cocktail dress, certainly didn't have a credit card tucked between her magnificent breasts or under the thin cord of her tiny, tiny thong. He knew this because—well, because he'd happily watched her climb into, and out of, and back into that dress hours earlier.

And he couldn't put the booze on his hotel bill—even *he* wouldn't get away with forty-plus shooters on his expense account.

One half of the anniversary couple stood up and held his hand out for Finn to shake. He looked more sober than the rest of his crew. 'Your wife is an absolute delight and such a hoot.'

'Thank you,' Finn replied, looking at his wife, who was leaning across the bar, squishing her boobs with her elbows and giving herself a hell of a cleavage. Even the gay boys seemed fascinated by the view. Her breasts might be spectacular, but he was distracted by the fact that her eyes were more violet than blue—a colour he'd come to associate with Callie being upset or sad.

'Something happen while I was gone, angel?' he asked quietly.

Her smile was bright and bold and perfectly suited to this fake place. 'Yeah, I started a party! I haven't done that for a while. I have my mojo back!'

Oh, yeah, something had happened. Another call from her mother? Maybe…

'Honey, you never lost it.' He jerked his head as he put his hand in his back pocket to pull out his wallet. 'Time to go, angel.' He flipped open his wallet and pulled out a credit card, which he handed to the amused barman.

'Awww, I don't wanna…' Callie whined.

'I have a surprise for you waiting in our room,' Finn lied.

He just had to get her to the room; he knew that as soon as Callie fell onto the bed she'd be dead to the world, and he doubted that she'd remember that he promised her a surprise. After all, tequila was well known for its coma-inducing and amnesiac qualities.

As he'd suspected Callie's eyes lit up, and she skipped around Grant to come over to his side of the bar. 'What is it?'

'You'll have to wait and see.' Finn took the credit card slip and his eyes widened at the total. Damn! How many shooters and how many bottles of champagne had they gone through?

The barman sent him a sympathetic look. 'Sorry, sir.'

'She's going to bankrupt me,' Finn muttered, taking back his card. 'Let's go before you do any more damage.'

'Got to say goodbye first,' Callie told him, and Finn waited while she kissed cheeks and exchanged hugs as if she was saying goodbye to her best friends. Good grief, she'd only met these people an hour or so ago.

'Be happy, people!' Callie yelled at them as he steered her towards the door.

Most of them—Callie included—were certainly not going to be happy in the morning.

Callie rolled over in the massive bed and feeling as if she had a bowling ball bouncing off the inside of her skull.

There was a time, she thought on an internal whimper, when she could party herself stupid and wake up the next morning raring to go.

That time had passed, she decided mournfully. Squinting, she sat up on her elbows and forced her eyes open to look at the gold and white garish suite. *Ack.* If her husband—real, that was—had brought her here for her honeymoon she'd have stabbed him between the eyes with a fork.

Talking about husbands—where was hers?

He'd slept with her—she had a recollection of him waking her up to swallow some aspirin some time close to dawn—but she didn't recall him leaving their bed. She needed him right now. Mostly to order coffee and to hand her some more aspirin.

Note to self: *I can no longer drink like a twenty-year-old.*

Second note to self: *tequila is nasty and no longer your friend.*

But her brother and her best friend and her father and soon-to-be stepmother had spent last night laughing and drinking and socialising with Laura.

She'd wanted a distraction, to forget, and it had worked for a while. But this morning she still felt hurt and betrayed and she had a hangover. Talk about adding fuel to the fire. Callie tucked her hand under her cheek, ignoring the trickle of tears leaking from her eyes.

Hurting, she wondered if she was being harsh in not wanting to engage with Laura. *Was* she just being stubborn? Unfair? Why was reconnecting with her so much easier for Seb than it was for her?

She closed her eyes and remembered those long nights sobbing in her room, her ten, fifteen, eighteen-year-old self wondering what had been so wrong with Laura's life—with *her*—that she'd had to leave. What had she and her dad and Seb done that was so wrong that she'd had to leave and never call or write? Was she sick…poor—dead?

She'd spent most of her nights worrying about Laura and her days pretending that she was fine, so that her father and Seb wouldn't worry about her.

It had taken all the emotional energy she had.

And now she was supposed to just wipe her past away because Laura had decided that it was time to reconnect? *No.*

Callie felt the bed dip behind her and Finn's warm, broad hand stroking her bare back. Within seconds she felt comforted, calmer, as if she could cope with whatever life threw at her. What was it about this man that made her feel both brave and safe at the same time?

Finn was on her side, totally in her corner, all hers. Just as she'd known he would be.

'Angel, why the tears?'

She couldn't not tell him. It was her turn to let him in.

Callie rolled over and rested her forearm over her eyes. 'Something happened last night.'

'I know. What did your mother do?'

He just *got it*, she thought on an internal sigh. He got *her*. 'Had dinner with my father and brother and my best friend in my childhood home.'

'And you're mad at her? And them?' Finn pulled her arm from her eyes before rubbing a thumb over her cheekbone. 'I brought you aspirin and coffee; take them and we'll talk.'

Callie groaned as she pulled herself up so that she was leaning back against the padded headboard, the sheet tucked up under her arms. She picked the tablets out of Finn's hand and chased them down with a glass of water. He passed her a large mug of coffee, which she gratefully took.

Finn sat next to her, calm and strong, and his strength

seemed to flow into her. She could start to rely on having him around, she thought, having his calm presence in her life.

'So, start from the beginning and tell me about Laura.'

'It's a long story.'

'Nowhere else I need to be. No one else more important than you right now.'

She could see that truth in his eyes. Right now, right here, she was the most important person in his life and she loved it. Oh, dear God, if she wasn't careful she could love him.

Callie looked at his hand, big and tanned on her thigh. She took another sip of coffee before placing it on the bedside table. *Park any thoughts about love and for ever and talk to him,* Callie told herself. *You need to talk to someone.*

Pushing her curls behind her ears, she started trying to explain. 'I told you that I was a hell-on-wheels child. I tried anything once. And I mean anything, I had absolutely no sense of self-preservation. The highest tree, the tallest rock, the fastest bike, the biggest wave. Unfortunately I always bit off more than I could chew. The nurses and doctors at our nearest casualty department knew me by name.'

Callie drew invisible patterns on the sheet with her index finger.

'It was after another visit to Casualty, when my dad brought me home—with a broken arm and two cracked ribs—that we found out that that Laura had left us. For good.'

Finn held her thigh and his eyes encouraged her to go on. She'd never told anyone this before, but she felt safe with Finn.

'In my childish head I equated my being a wild child with her leaving. And, because I'm me, I thought, *What the hell? Let's make damn sure she had a good excuse for going.* I let it rip. I was wild, Finn. Crazy. I did stupid things, took incredible risks, put myself in danger. I went walking the streets at night, looking for trouble. I caught trains and buses into bad areas. I hitchhiked all over the place. I surfed huge waves, was a maniac on my skateboard and on my bike. Thank God that He protects the stupid.'

'Why did you do all of that?'

'Partly to justify her leaving—*Look how bad I am. I don't blame you for leaving*—and also because the adrenalin high was so damn good. I think I was also challenging my father's and brother's love. If they didn't walk away from me when I was so bad then they *did* love me. Crazy, huh?'

Finn stretched out beside her and rested his hand on her stomach. 'Not so much.'

'Anyway, the craziness got me out of my head, stopped me from feeling worthless and abandoned, and I craved it.' Callie stared at her hands. 'In my late teens that adrenalin high started to be more difficult to achieve and I started flirting with alcohol.'

She saw sympathy on his face, in his eyes, but not pity. She couldn't have handled pity.

'I got drunk and wrecked my car. I was damn lucky not to die.'

Finn swore. 'Angel...'

'Yeah. Well, that prompted my father and brother to tear me a new one and I was finally brought under control. I made a big deal of their authority and bossiness but secretly I loved it. I started to believe that they loved me and always would, and I promised them that I wouldn't do anything stupid again. So I cut out all the extreme stuff except the partying and grew up, I suppose.'

Finn looked puzzled. 'Yet that day in Livingstone you were prepared to break your promise to go bungee jumping? Oh, wait. It was a coping mechanism.'

'I needed to escape from myself. When she phoned I

didn't want to deal with all the old feelings that bubbled to the surface and I reverted to what worked. Sex with you or...' she pulled a face '...something else to make the adrenalin pump.'

Finn smiled. 'That's a hell of a backhanded compliment, Cal, but I'll take it.'

Callie couldn't smile—not just yet. 'God, it all sounds so stupid.' She pulled a face. 'It makes sense in my head.'

Finn's thumb stroked her knee. 'I'm not judging you, angel.'

Callie went on to explain how hurt she'd felt by her family having dinner with her mother and her need for distraction—which had prompted the party in the bar.

Finn took a sip of her coffee before asking, 'And you really don't want to see your mum? Meet her? Get an explanation?'

Callie shrugged. 'Do you think I should?' she asked.

His opinion was important to her; she respected and trusted it. And him. She trusted *him*. Dear God, she really did.

'I can't decide that for you, Cal. I can give you another perspective on it, but I would never presume to tell you what to do. First tell me why you're so against meeting her.'

Callie placed her hand on his and stared down at their linked hands. 'I haven't seen or heard from her in over twenty years. What's there to say? She missed out on every important day of my life and now she wants to make contact. Where was she when I needed a mother? Hotfooting it around the world! She chose to leave. I'm choosing not to acknowledge her return.' Callie lifted worried eyes to his. 'Am I wrong, Finn? Should I be able to just forgive her?'

'Again, no judging.' Finn lifted her hand and placed a kiss on her knuckles. 'Cal, my father is a shocking father and I have no freaking clue where he is. I worry about him, and sometimes I wish I could just talk to him, know that he's okay and find out why he made the choices he did. I'm not saying that I'd accept or forgive those choices— I'd just like to understand why he made them. And my two real parents are dead. I'd do anything to spend some more time with *them*.'

Finn spoke quietly but his voice was full of conviction and Callie listened carefully, soaking in his words.

'The other thing to consider is what if Laura chooses to stay in Cape Town? If she becomes part of your brother's life again? What then?'

Callie looked horrified. 'Oh, God, I never considered that possibility. I'm so close to Seb and Rowan... I would have to see her at family functions...' Callie closed her eyes. 'It would be horrible if we couldn't speak to one another. Oh, God, maybe I should just meet her.'

'Take a breath, honey. It's just something to consider. Cross one bridge at a time,' Finn told her, squeezing her hand to reassure her. 'You don't need to make any rash decisions—you just need to think it all through. You need to try and separate your emotions from your decision.'

'I don't know if I can.'

Finn kissed her bare shoulder. 'I believe in you. I believe that you can move mountains if you want to. You are one of the strongest women I have ever met.' He smiled into her skin. 'Crazy as a loon, but strong as hell.'

At his words Callie fell a little deeper, a little harder. This man might be exactly what she needed.

'How is your head?'

'Better.' Callie lifted her hand to her head and nodded. 'Yeah, definitely better.' She also felt lighter, because Finn had just listened without judgement. Acceptance, Callie thought. It was such a rare and beautiful thing.

'You hungry?'

'Starving!' Callie replied.

'Room Service? Or do you want to brave the hordes downstairs?' Finn asked.

Callie winced. 'Room Service, please.'

Finn nodded, his dimple flashing. He leaned back, his hands spread out on the covers, and cocked his head at her. 'So…how hungry are you really? Can breakfast wait?'

Callie tipped her head at his playful expression. 'Why?'

'I just thought that maybe you needed a rush of adrenalin? Please say yes.'

Callie's smile made her eyes crinkle and she placed a hand over them. 'Oh, God, I'm *so* going to regret telling you that.'

Finn placed his hands on her shoulders and pushed her onto her back. 'That wasn't a no. I didn't hear a no, so I'm going to take that as a yes.'

Callie sighed theatrically as she linked her hands around his neck and pulled his mouth down to hers. 'If you must…'

CHAPTER TEN

BUSH AND BEACH, Callie thought, digging her toes into the white sands of the Mozambique coastline. This was, hands-down, the best holiday of her life. And five days at the exceptionally luxurious, remote Manta Ray Lodge, on the Bazaruto Archipelago, was the best way to end their trip.

Callie sat up on her elbows and watched Finn walk out of the gentle surf, heading towards her after snorkelling above the reef just behind the breakers. He loved the sea, she realised. From scuba-diving to deep-sea fishing, to snorkelling, to kite-surfing—he wanted to do it all. She could easily see why he was so good at his job as a travel writer. He threw himself into every experience he was offered, wringing every drop of pleasure he could from the situation.

He was so gorgeous, she thought, watching as he walked up the beach to where she was lying on a towel in the sand. Tall, ripped, in peak physical condition. Hair pushed off his face and red board shorts clinging to those strong thighs. So drool-worthy.

She knew that body intimately—knew every toned muscle, every scar, the fact that one of his little toes was crooked. She knew that scraping her nails across his abs made him shiver and that he hated her blowing in his ear. She knew that he didn't have a favourite sexual position, that he liked to mix it up, and that he loved oral sex. That he could kiss her for hours without taking it further, that he always slept on his stomach, and that he needed to run or do a workout and have at least two cups of coffee in the morning before he could string a sentence together.

She knew he was loyal and responsible and that he loved his stepbrothers, and that he was mentally and physically tough. She also knew that she was on the very slippery slope to falling in love—if she wasn't there already. He was what she hadn't known she was looking for.

And he didn't want her—not like that. It wasn't part of the arrangement…the deal. *No hearts and flowers,* she'd said. How often had she said that? Along with *Don't let me be seduced, This is short-term, This is going to end.*

Use, abuse and toss.

She'd broken every rule they'd laid out from the beginning. She'd been so arrogant, thinking that she could control herself, control the situation, control her response to him. Life was rolling on the floor, laughing its ass off at her.

Even though she knew they couldn't be anything more she wanted to dream about a future with him. But there wasn't one—couldn't be one. Their jobs kept them both buzzing around the world, and she didn't need a man complicating her life—especially now. She had a mother who, after being absent for most of her life, was doing a very good job of that all by herself.

Was she just being seduced by the holiday? The romance of their surroundings? This wasn't real life. Real life had bills and work and family and jobs to complicate the situation. There was a reason holiday romances never worked out.

There wasn't any future for them. *Was there?*

Callie lifted her head as Finn approached her and sighed when his lips brushed hers in a gesture that felt so natural, so right. *Holiday romance,* she reminded herself, *not going to last.*

'I saw a scorpion fish and a small manta ray.'

'Cool...' Callie murmured as he dropped onto the hot sand next to her.

Finn looked around, catching the eye of a hovering waiter who walked over to them. Finn ordered a beer and Callie ordered a bottle of water.

'This is the life,' Finn stated, reaching for his sunglasses, which he'd left on top of her beach bag. He slipped them on and leaned back on his elbows, stretching like a cat in the sun.

Those sleek muscles rippled under tanned skin and Callie couldn't believe that her libido was buzzing again. She swallowed the urge to suggest they head back to their private, practically-in-the-sea chalet, just fifty metres away from them, so that she could worship that body. Instead she half turned, stretched out, and rested the back of her head on Finn's thigh.

'Talk to me.'

Above his wraparound shades a dark eyebrow lifted. 'Okay. About what?'

Callie sat up, put her back to the sea and faced him. 'Do you ever think of Liz? Do you miss her?' she asked, eyes down, wiggling in the sand.

'We were together for five years, Cal...so, yeah. I do.' Finn replied, his voice low. 'I was supposed to be sharing all this with her.'

Damn, that was a knife to her heart. 'I know. I'm sorry.'

'I'm not.'

Callie's head shot up and she met his rueful eyes. 'I don't understand.'

'She was right to call it quits. We'd stopped loving each other. Our marriage would never have lasted.' Finn pushed his hand through his hair, his eyes still on the sea. 'Getting married seemed like a good idea at the time. We'd talked about it and we'd been together for a long time. When she fell pregnant it seemed like the next step to take—a natural progression,' Finn explained. 'Then she lost the baby, and our last reason to be together was removed.'

'Do you see yourself in a relationship again?'

Finn took a long time to answer. 'I think I need to be on my own for a while.'

No surprised there, Callie thought.

'I never jump into situations with my eyes closed, Callie. I think everything through. I don't do quick and impulsive and crazy. Relationships that are meant to last take time and are hard work.'

His words rumbled over her and she could hear the conviction in his tone.

'I'm pretty sure that I don't want a long-distance relationship again, but that's all I can have until I give up my job and find something else to do. And that's not going to happen any time soon.'

You, me, us—we're not going to happen either. Callie heard his unspoken words. *That wasn't the deal.*

Callie stretched out her legs and dug her toes into the sand, her eyes burning behind her dark glasses. 'I'm really glad that I was able to be your rebound girl, Finn.'

Finn linked her hand in his. 'Maybe you should try being in a relationship some time, Cal.'

She forced herself to sound jovial, carefree. 'How come you get to be footloose and fancy-free but I should settle down?' she asked, making sure that she had a small smile on her face.

'Because you've only *ever* been footloose and fancy-free. I think that you would be a brilliant partner: you're fun, intelligent, and crazy good in the sack.'

Finn pushed his sunglasses into his hair and she caught her breath at the passion and...*affection?*...she saw in his eyes.

'And you'd be a stunning mum one day.'

Callie instinctively shook her head. 'Yeah, *that's* not going to happen.'

'Why not?' Finn asked gently.

Callie folded her arms against her chest and shook her head. 'I'm never putting any child through what my mother did to me!'

Finn grabbed her chin and tipped her head up, making her meet his eyes. 'Honey, you would never do to your kid what your mum did to you. No way, no how.'

Callie swallowed the lump in her throat. 'How do you know? I'm selfish, I bounce around the world, I'm totally self-involved.'

'No, you're not. That's who you pretend to be.' Finn cupped the side of her face in his broad palm. 'When you decide that you're strong enough to be brave, when you find someone you love enough to risk your heart, you'll hand it over because you're so damn generous. And when you bring a kid into the world you'll be incredible at that— because you know how not having a mum affected *you*.'

'I don't know if I can do either—hand my heart over *or* have a kid,' Callie admitted.

'One day…' Finn said, lying back in the sand and placing a forearm over his eyes. 'I can almost guarantee it.'

Except that right now, holiday romance or not, Callie thought bitterly, *I can't imagine doing that with anyone else but you.*

Stupid girl, she thought, standing up and walking to the super-clear water. She waded in, waiting for it to become deep enough so that she could dive. *That's why you shouldn't have deep conversations with Finn...why you should keep it light and frothy.*

Because deep conversations raised possibilities that she wasn't ready to think about or deal with. Deep conversations gave birth to dreams that would never come true, possibilities that would never be realised.

Wishes that would never be fulfilled.

After a light lunch of freshly caught prawns and garden salad, accompanied by a glass of dry white wine, Finn and Callie headed back to their room to escape the intensity of the midday sun. The private villa, tucked away into the palm trees just off the beach, was incredibly private—perfect for a honeymoon couple.

Except they weren't on honeymoon, Finn reminded himself again. She was his fake wife and they were having a very temporary affair. But for a moment just now on the beach he'd been tempted to suggest that he and Callie try and extend it into real life.

Then he'd pulled himself back to reality. Callie was a stunning travelling companion: easy to look at, fun to talk to, great in bed.

The end.

Despite sharing their secrets, the mental and physical connection they had, she'd never once hinted at wanting anything more from him, wanting to change the rules. *She* knew that this was a holiday romance, so why was he suddenly doubting it? What the hell was he thinking?

Finn closed his eyes and shook his head. Goddammit, he was losing his mind. This trip was not real life—this was an aberration, a step out of time. It wouldn't be like this every trip. It was usually hectic: a combination of stunning sights and experiences interrupted by long periods of boredom spent in hotel rooms and airport lounges.

It wasn't a life to build a relationship on. As for another long-distance one? Well, that hadn't worked out so well the last time he'd tried it, and Callie wasn't the type of girl he'd be able to stay away from for long.

Finn walked over to the small fridge in the corner of the

lounge area and took out a bottle of water. Cracking the lid, he took a long drink and watched Callie as she pulled her T-shirt up and over her head, revealing the top half of the pink and orange bikini she was wearing. A vision of her, round and bursting with life with his child, flashed across his retina and he groaned. No, he wasn't going to think of her in terms of for ever, in terms of creating a family with her.

Or being the man she fell in love with.

He wanted to be single, to get his bearings, and she was even more wary of commitment than he was. Why did he want to put his fist through that glass door at the thought of her loving and living with someone else? Handing over that very fragile heart to another man?

He was just projecting, influenced by the incredibleness of these past two weeks. This wasn't reality.

Get a grip, Banning. She's fun, good company and brilliant in the sack. That's it. You have less than a week left of this—of her—so get your head out of your ass, stop obsessing, and catch a clue. Instead of standing here, staring at her like a moonstruck whipped boy, do something!

So he would do what he…they…did best. Lose themselves in each other…

He gestured with his water bottle. 'Carry on,' he told her.

Callie lifted her eyebrows at him. 'Sorry?'

Her voice was prissy, but her sexy smile told him that she knew where he wanted to go and was happy to tag along.

'Shorts off.'

Callie's eyes deepened with passion as she slowly pulled down the zip to her brief denim shorts and shimmied them over her hips. When they dropped to the floor he looked at her standing there in the shadows, the shades drawn to keep the heat out.

'Top off,' he said in a croaky voice, and took another sip of water to moisten his mouth.

Callie reached behind her back and pulled one of the ties holding her top together before reaching for the other one around her neck. The two triangles joined her shorts on the floor and she placed her fists on her hips and stared at him.

He was rock-hard and ready to spring out of his pants—and he hadn't even touched her yet. Surely after so much sex he should be able to temper his reaction to her by now? But it took just one look into those amazing eyes for him to be ready to roll. Surely he should have more control?

Then Callie stepped out of her bikini panties and he knew that, with her, he had absolutely no control at all.

As he reached for her he wondered how he was supposed to walk away from her. From the amazing sex but also, even harder, from her sharp mind, her dirty sense of humour and the vulnerable, soft soul beneath that vivacious personality?

How?

It was past eleven at night when their plane finally landed in Cape Town, and nearly midnight when Finn swung his SUV into the driveway in front of her closed-up house. This was unlike any homecoming she'd ever experienced, Callie thought, staring at her tightly laced hands in her lap. She didn't want to be here, back in the city. She didn't want to go back to real life, to work, to a life without Finn to wake up to, to make love with, to snuggle up to at night.

She wanted to be back in Kruger, in the sweltering heat of Livingstone, on that white sand beach. Anywhere with Finn…everywhere with Finn.

Finn's white-knuckled hands gripped the steering wheel. 'So, this is it.'

Callie sucked in her top lip. 'Yep.'

'How long are you in the country for?' Finn asked, his voice low.

'I think I have a quick trip scheduled to Milan for next week. You?'

'Not sure. I have to get this article in and accepted, then I can choose between a dude ranch in Montana or the northern lights in Alaska.'

Callie made herself pat his shoulder. 'Poor guy. I'm sure both will be terrible,' she teased, and felt proud of herself. She wouldn't make this goodbye difficult by weeping and wailing. She would hold her head up high and go out on a huge smile.

Finn turned his head to look at her. 'They won't be as much fun without you.'

Callie felt the tears well. 'You can't say that. I'm trying to be brave, here,' she protested.

'Me too.' Finn blew out a long sigh before dropping his head back onto the headrest. He rolled his head to look at her. His eyes, deep with regret, caught and held hers. 'I still want you.'

Callie swallowed and her hand instinctively reached out to grip his thigh. 'I know. I want you too.'

'Last time for the road?'

'It's a really bad idea, Finn.'

'I know, but let's do it anyway. I need to burn you into my memory one last time.'

The next morning, for the first time in weeks, Callie didn't wake up to Finn laying hot, wet kisses down her back, or a hard, heavy arm across her waist, or warm male breath tickling her ear.

She was alone and she really didn't like it.

Rolling over, she looked at the dent his head had left on the pillow and, inexplicably, felt tears burn her eyes. How was she supposed to live without him? Be without him?

Exist without him? How was she supposed to love him if he wasn't even around?

Love? Was she in love? Could she be?

This was insane. Nobody fell in love after a month—especially her, a girl who didn't believe in love and happily-ever-after. But she couldn't deny it any more. She loved Finn—absolutely, utterly, probably catastrophically.

Callie sat up in bed and rested her head on her bent knees. This was *so* not a clever thing to have done. Finn was on the rebound—he didn't want a relationship, wasn't interested. She knew all this, but *she* was.

Should she tell him? A part of her wanted to, needed to. Callie had loved too few people in her life, had been loved by too few, to bury or ignore this amazing sensation when it came her way. It was what it was and it demanded to be expressed—to be validated, to be acknowledged. But she'd also told him that there would be no hearts and flowers, no demands for anything more, no complications. Was telling him that she loved him more important than keeping her promise? Especially since she knew that he didn't feel the same way about her?

What should she do?

Callie lifted her head when she heard footsteps outside her door and made herself look at him as he stepped into her bedroom. She had to look at him because she didn't know when she would again.

If she would again…

Love was love, but that didn't automatically translate into happily-ever-after. She knew that now. Her mother had said she loved her but she hadn't stayed; she loved Finn, and even if by some miracle he felt the same they had so many obstacles in their way. They both travelled extensively. How could they mesh their schedules so that they could build a relationship? Maintain it?

But she was getting way ahead of herself. She still had to decide whether to tell him or not.

'Hey, you're awake,' Finn said, handing her a cup of coffee.

'I am. Thanks.' Callie took the coffee and took a grateful sip, thankful for a reason not to talk.

'I brought your bags in,' Finn said, moving to look out of her window to the view of the sea.

Callie cocked her head at his quiet voice and knew that he was trying to ease his way out of her bedroom and her life. His fists were bunched in his pockets and his lips were pulled tight.

'I checked my email while you were sleeping. I'm heading for Alaska.'

Callie felt as if the coffee was threatening to come up her throat again. 'When?' she asked, her throat hoarse.

'Within a day or two.'

'That soon, huh?'

Callie carefully placed her coffee cup on the side table and swung her legs out of bed. Reaching for a robe that hung over the back of her chair, she pulled it on. Her hands were shaky as she tied it at the waist.

'So this is definitely goodbye?'

Finn turned and sat on the open windowsill. 'It should have been goodbye last night. We just make it harder the longer we draw this out.' His voice was low, but resolute.

He had no idea how hard it could be, Callie thought. He wasn't in love with her but she was with him.

'Do you think you'll ever fall in love again?' she asked, as a way to test these very turbulent waters. Just to make sure...

Finn's head snapped up in surprise at the question. 'I'm not sure I was in the first place.' He raked a hand through his hair. 'I don't know... I don't think so. If I was so inclined then it would've been with you, during this last month.'

Callie struggled to keep him from seeing how those words pierced her soul. She used every acting skill she had to make her voice sound light and flirty.

'So you're not in love with me, then?' she asked him, deliberately batting her eyelashes.

'Nope. Why? Are you in love with me?' Finn teased back, and she was faced with the do or die question.

Did she admit it and have their relationship end on an awkward, weird note—or did she let him leave her life thinking she was unaffected?

Never had a choice been so hard.

She tipped her head and dredged up a big, bold smile. 'What would you say if I told you I was?'

Finn took his time answering. 'I'd tell you what I've been telling myself: that we're blinded by the passion between us, that we stepped out of the reality of daily life and the romantic settings and the warm weather and the luxury changed the way we behaved. That we can't trust out judgement.'

Callie nodded. She'd thought about all of that, but none of it had changed her mind or her knowledge of what *was*. She loved him. Simply. Crazily. For ever.

He didn't love her. Oh, she knew that he loved her body, loved sex with her, but it wasn't the same thing. Callie rubbed her forehead with her fingers as her mind operated at warp speed, trying to decide what to do.

Then Finn took the decision out of her hands by walking over to her and kissing her gently on the lips before folding her into his strong arms.

'We agreed to walk away, Cal.'

Callie looked up at him, feeling so safe in the circle of his arms. Arms that would soon be gone. 'Guess it's time to rip off those rose-coloured glasses and get back to real life, huh?'

'In a couple of days…weeks…we'll settle down into that real life and this will feel like a dream.'

Callie buried her face in his neck. 'So I'll always be your dream girl?'

'You bet.' Finn stroked her hair. His long sigh blew into her curls. 'This wasn't supposed to get this tangled, this complicated.'

Still no *I love you*.

Callie tried to swallow the golf ball that was lodged in her throat. 'I'll miss you. Thanks for a brilliant time.'

'I'll miss you too. Thanks for being a brilliant fake wife.' Finn kissed the top of her head—the brush-off kiss for any man—and stepped away from her. 'Take care, Callie. And think about what I said about your mother.'

'Yeah.'

In her eagerness to avoid the first person who'd broken her heart she'd run away with a second person who'd just rebroken it. She had the intelligence of a pot plant, Callie thought, watching him walk across her lounge to the front door.

'Bye, angel.'

It took every iota of willpower she had, and then some, not to throw her arms around his knees and beg him not to go.

'Bye.'

Then the door snicked closed behind him and she felt her heart cleave in two. Overwhelmed, she sank to the floor and wrapped her arms around her head, trying to shield herself from the burning miasma of pain that engulfed her.

It didn't help, she realised. Nothing would—not for a while. She knew this. She'd been here before.

CHAPTER ELEVEN

CALLIE MADE HERSELF get up the next morning, forced herself to put on a pretty dress, curl her hair and do her makeup. Her world might be falling apart but there was no reason for people to know that she was too. Besides, if she pretended hard enough and long enough that everything was fine then maybe it would be. Eventually.

She was making herself a smoothie, in an effort to start losing the pounds she'd picked up drinking cocktails on the beach with he-whose-name-could-not-be-mentioned, when her doorbell rang. She considered ignoring it and had just decided to do that when it pealed again.

Dammit! Thinking that she wasn't in the mood to see anyone, to explain anything, she stomped through to the front door and looked through the peephole at the distorted image of a tall blonde woman. It took her a minute to recognise the blue, blue eyes of Laura, the tall frame, the long face.

She looked older, Callie thought, her heart accelerating. An older, harder, tougher *me*. Even through the peephole she could see that she looked as if she'd lived a hard life—too much sun, booze, too many cigarettes. Callie wanted to tell her to go away, that she didn't want to see her, but she couldn't push any words past her thick tongue.

'Cal-belle? Honey?'

Callie could hear her voice clearly through the wooden door.

'I know that you're there. I heard your footsteps.'

Cal-Belle. God, she hadn't heard that in over twenty years. Her mum's pet name for her—Laura's pet name for her.

'Callie, I know that you don't want to see me, and I understand why. I do—I really do. But I just couldn't leave, fly back to Sao Paulo, without trying at least once.'

Callie kept silent but let Laura speak. She wanted to be strong enough to walk away but she couldn't—not yet.

'There's so much I want to say to you, so much I want to explain.'

Callie, feeling drained and very, very vulnerable, didn't even realise that hot, thick tears were rolling down her face. All she could think was that she wanted Finn... needed Finn. She needed his strong arms to hold her up, his voice in her ear telling her that she was okay, that she would always be okay, that she could do this.

But he wasn't here. Like her mother, when she needed him most he was AWOL. The people she loved most had the ability to let her down the hardest.

Hardening her heart, she finally managed to speak. 'I'm not ready to talk to you, Laura. I don't know if I'll ever be ready.'

She didn't think she could even open the door.

'I've made a lot of mistakes, Callie, but the biggest one was walking out on you and your brother.'

You think?

'I want to tell you that I'm sorry, and if this is the only way I get to do it—through a closed door—then this is how I'll do it.'

Callie slipped off her shoes and quickly moved to the right, to the thin sliver of tinted glass that allowed her to see out but kept visitors from looking in. Laura was looking at her fingernails and her foot was tapping on the terracotta tiles. She looked bone-deep scared.

Callie remembered what she'd said to Finn about Liz, about how courageous her decision to end their relationship had been. Wasn't it equally courageous of Laura to face her, to ask for forgiveness after so long? She had to know that it wouldn't be easy, that she might not get it, but she was still willing to try.

Her mother was standing there offering an explanation—something that Finn desperately wanted from his own father. And she was alive. Finn's parents weren't. If she turned Laura away now, would she regret it for the rest of her life?

'Callie?'

'Can you hang on a sec? I just need a moment.'

Callie paced the small area of her hallway—the place where Finn had made love to her the night before. *Finn*... He'd made her better, she realised. Stronger. He'd left behind a little of his strength and a lot of his wisdom.

She could almost hear his deep voice in her ear. 'You don't have to accept or forgive her choices—just understand why she made them.'

Not now, she thought. *I'm still reeling because you're not here*.

'You can move mountains. You don't need her to be happy. And I'm still with you.'

He was, Callie realised. Oh, she missed him desperately, but he'd left a part of himself with her. His belief in her. She *could* move mountains, she *could* be happy—one day, maybe. She was stronger than she thought.

She could choose either to hang on to her bitterness towards her mother or she could set herself, and her mother free. She could listen to what she had to say and then decide whether she wanted Laura back in her life—*wanted*, not needed!

She might not be able to make a certain travel reporter

love her, but, by God, she could do this, she could face her mother.

Callie turned back to the door and wrenched it open. 'Come in and talk, but I'm making no promises beyond this meeting.'

Laura bit her lip as she stepped into the hall. 'I understand.' She glanced down, transfixed by the rings on Callie's hand. 'Oh, my goodness. You're wearing them! And on your wedding finger!'

'I'm not married,' Callie hastened to explain, lifting her hand. 'You *know* these rings?' she asked, confused.

'Sure. Your father bought them for me from an antique store to celebrate your birth.' Laura placed the tip of her finger on the raised stone. 'They were the only rings I ever wore.'

Callie looked up at the ceiling and let out a deep breath. Of course they were. Because this was her life and nothing could be simple.

It wasn't a surprise that Alaska in the dead of winter was cold, Finn thought, looking out from his hotel window into the weird light that was supposed to signal dusk—at two in the afternoon! In an hour or so it would be pitch-dark and the sun had only appeared four hours earlier. Crazy place, crazy life.

Fairbanks, Alaska, in the dead of winter and he was alone. Oh, the Northern Lights were amazing, awe-inspiring, incredible—all the adjectives so many writers before him had used and the ones he intended to avoid when he finally got around to writing his article. But his was a strange life, and one he wasn't sure he wanted any more.

He still hadn't turned in his honeymoon article and he wasn't sure when he would. Writing—always so easy—had become a task of herculean proportions. *Why?* His life, apart from no longer having a fiancée he seldom saw in it, was pretty much back to normal. He was back on the road, he had an editor squawking at him, and he was alone. So what was the problem?

He *liked* being alone, he reminded himself. Apart from his three weeks with Callie he'd always travelled alone and he was used to it. He didn't have to think of anyone, could jump into his work without distractions, didn't have to worry that he was neglecting anyone.

So, Einstein, if you like it so much then why are you feeling so damn miserable? Okay, he got that it was okay to miss Callie. They'd spent practically every minute together for most of the past month, so that was to be expected, wasn't it? He was allowed to miss her laugh, her piggy snores, waking up and realising that she was wrapped around him like a vine. And naturally he missed the sex. That was normal, right?

What *wasn't* normal was the crater-sized hole he felt in his heart at not seeing her again, not hearing that laugh, that piggy snore, not waking up to the feeling that he was being smothered.

This was the way he should have felt when he and Liz broke up, he thought. Wretched—as if the world had no colour, as if he was just going through the motions. Everything he should have experienced after losing his fiancée he was now experiencing in this cold, cold place on the other side of the world.

Was it just delayed reaction? Was he transferring his feelings for Liz on to Callie? He wished he was—it would help this crazy situation make a whole lot more sense. Unfortunately it had nothing to do with Liz and everything to do with that commitment-phobic wild-child woman he'd left behind in Cape Town.

He missed her…he wanted her. In his bed and in his life. Now and for ever.

That complicated and that simple.

He'd thought he could just walk away with a casual goodbye, with heartfelt thanks for helping him out of a jam and giving him the best short-term fling of his life. God, he was such a moron.

'What would you say if I said I was in love with you?'

Her memory drifted across his mind and he frowned, looking out into the nearly dark afternoon. Had she been trying to tell him something? Something crucial? At the time he'd just dismissed her cocky question as Callie being Callie, trying to push his buttons, teasing him as she often did. Then he remembered her serious eyes, the trepidation on her face that he'd ignored. Had he, in his quest to leave, to get back to normal, missed that she was trying to tell him that she loved him? That she wanted more?

In the dark, Finn moved to his laptop and moved his finger across the mouse pad, pulling up the folder named 'Angel'. Her face appeared on the screen and he stared at the images of her that changed every few seconds. Every photo he'd taken of her was filled with sunlight, with happiness, with joy. Everything his life didn't have now.

Finn shook his head. She was anti-commitment—she readily admitted to it. She thought that commitment and long-term were the emotional equivalent of the rabies virus. But she was also the woman who had resisted falling into bed with him, had tried to keep her distance because she'd said that she had the potential to fall for him. *Had* she? Fallen for him as he had for her?

Finn thought back on their relationship—to the glossy, sophisticated woman he'd first met and how her walls had slowly started to crumble. She'd begun to open herself up to him, to let him see glimpses of the lost little girl behind the charming, flirty façade. Finn knew that she wouldn't have done that for just any man, for just anyone. He'd got to her and she'd trusted him, let him look inside.

Trust was a very big deal for Callie...

Trust was a short degree of separation from love. For her and for him.

When Callie loved and trusted and decided to commit she'd do it with everything she had. He knew that without any hesitation. She'd toss her hat and every other of item of clothing she wore into the ring and go all out to make it work. She wouldn't cheat, she wouldn't run away, she wouldn't play games. She'd been hurt by love and she wouldn't want to hurt anyone *she* loved.

He remembered her question again. *What would you say if I said I was in love with you?*

I'd say I'm in love with you too, Cal, and call myself a million types of an idiot for not realising what you were trying to say earlier. I'd say my life without you isn't a life—it's just a random set of happenings that mean little.

I'd say I'm in love with you too...

Callie cursed Finn's lack of gardening skills as her shovel bounced off the hard soil in the corner of what had used to be a flowerbed. Didn't the man know that a garden required water? Pushing her hair off her sweaty forehead with the back of her hand, she looked at the shallow dent she'd made and sighed despondently.

This wasn't going to work. Oh, the bench looked stunning—a wooden three-seater, with a brass inscription screwed onto the back strut. Expensive, but worth the price—as was the case of beer she'd paid Finn's youngest stepbrother Michael so he'd let her onto the property and help her lug the bench into its position in the corner of Finn's yard overlooking the ocean.

To his credit, Michael had taken the crazy request from a strange woman in his stride and had refrained from asking too many questions. The ones he had asked she'd managed to fudge her way through.

Callie stood up and glared at the ground. She'd planned

to plant two rosebushes on either side of the bench, but now she thought she might take them away with her. There was no way they'd survive Finn's black thumb. Or lack of skill with a hose or a watering can.

Maybe she'd take them home and plant them in pots on her veranda—a reminder of the only man she'd ever loved.

She dropped the shovel to the hard soil and sat on the bench, resting her elbows on her thighs, thinking of Finn.

She could stay here for a while…hang out in his garden. After all, as she'd confirmed with Michael, he was still in Alaska and wasn't due home for a week or so. Then he was off to Patagonia—or was it Pakistan? She couldn't remember. But it didn't matter. He was away and she had time to deliver the bench, to plant the rose bushes—or *not* plant them as seemed to be the case.

God, she missed him. Missed everything about him.

They'd been apart two weeks and she still felt as if she was operating on only one cylinder, as if she was walking a tight wire. She'd tried to get back into the swing of things at work, taken a four-day trip to Milan, and had hated every second of it. Callie dropped her head and stared at the hard ground beneath her flip-flops. If her work didn't distract her from missing Finn then what was she going to do?

Go slowly mad? It was a very distinct possibility.

Man, life was just rolling on the floor laughing at her. Callie Hollis, party-girl and commitment-phobe, sitting on a bench, trespassing on her fake husband's—now *ex*-fake-husband's—property and trying to keep from falling apart because she was ass-over-kettle in love with a man she'd promised not to fall in love with.

Yeah, life was such a joke.

Callie felt a tear drop off her chin and land on the hard-as-concrete soil below. Well, that was a hell of a way to get the ground wet. Finn had turned her into a crier—she'd never cried before he came along.

'Bastard...' she muttered, feeling as if that was the final insult.

'Sorry?'

At the deep, familiar voice Callie jerked her head up and whirled around. And there he was, standing a couple of feet behind her, dressed in board shorts and an old T-shirt, a four-day-old beard on his jaw. God, he looked good. *So* good.

'What are you doing here?' she demanded in a thready voice.

Finn's mouth kicked up, just a little, at the corners. 'I live here. What's your excuse? And why do I have a bench at the end of my garden?'

Suddenly Callie didn't know how to explain. Would he think she was sentimental? Sappy? That it was a stupid idea?

As he walked towards her she leaned back so that her shoulder was covering the plaque on the back of the bench. Would he think that she'd overstepped the mark? That she was being too presumptuous?

'Why the bench, Cal?'

'A view like this needs a bench,' Callie muttered, unable to meet his eye. He was now standing close enough for her to smell his aftershave, to feel the heat from his amazing body. She closed her eyes and told herself that she couldn't stand up and fold herself into his arms any more, that she didn't have the right to do that.

'There are chairs on the veranda with the same view,' Finn said, and Callie opened her eyes to see his strong hand—the same hand that had loved her with such skill—stroke the arm of the bench.

She wished he was stroking her. She'd reached a new low. She was jealous of an inanimate object.

'It's beautifully made. Hand-crafted?'

'Yeah.' Callie wished he'd take off his sunglasses. She needed to see his eyes because he had that implacable expression on his face. 'You needed a bench…'

'So you bought me one? OK.'

Finn walked around the bench and squatted in front of her. He shoved his glasses up into his hair and Callie sighed when her eyes met his. They were liquid and full of heat. God, she could look into those eyes for ever.

Finn lifted his hand and his thumb stroked her chin. 'You're filthy. Were you trying to plant these rosebushes?'

'You should water your garden more often,' Callie complained.

'I should.' Finn placed his hands on her knees and stared into her face, his eyes no longer playful. Instead they looked serious and intense. 'What are you doing here, Cal? Really?'

Callie hauled in air and scooted down the bench so that he could see the brass inscription. 'I wanted to do this for you. I thought you needed a place…somewhere to think about them.'

Finn looked at the inscription and Callie saw his Adam's apple bob.

'"In memory of James, big and small".' Finn read aloud.

He rubbed his hands over his face before staring at the plaque again. She couldn't tell what he was thinking and she needed to.

'If I've been too presumptuous or if you don't like it no harm, no foul. I'll take it away again,' Callie gabbled. 'I just wanted to give you some place where you could… I don't know…'

'Think about them? Remember them?'

'Yes…' Callie whispered.

'Thank you, angel.' Finn's voice was barely above a

whisper itself. 'It's spectacular. A little overwhelming, but spectacular.'

Finn reached out to rest his fingers on the inscription, his chest heaving under that ratty T-shirt.

After a little while, he looked at her again. 'How did you get in here? How did you get on to the property?'

Callie lifted a shoulder. 'Rowan had the email addresses for all your stepbrothers. Michael agreed to help me. He left about a half hour ago. He asked me to explain the "James, big and small" but I told him to ask you. That it was your story to tell. He said he would.'

'And he will. My brothers are insatiably curious.'

Callie winced. 'I'm sorry. I shouldn't have. I was out of line. I shouldn't have done this.'

Finn rested his hand on her knee and squeezed. 'No—thank you. It's an awesome gift. I'm at a loss for words, actually.'

Callie, thinking that this was a great time to go, abruptly stood up. The rosebushes would have to stay, she thought. Maybe Finn would plant them, maybe he wouldn't. She'd done all she could. It was past time for her to leave—before she broke down and begged him to let her stay.

Finn allowed her to stand up and watched her walk away, each step pulling her heart closer to breaking again. Why did he have to be here? Why couldn't she have done this without seeing him? It was taking every bit of willpower she had to put one foot in front of the other.

She was on the other side of the pool when he spoke again. 'Where are you going, Hollis?'

Callie turned back to look at him, standing tall and strong in the midday sunshine. She gestured to the house and shrugged. 'Home, I guess.'

'You guess wrong,' Finn told her, arms crossed. 'You're not going anywhere.'

She couldn't help the bloom of hope in her heart or the lifting of her chin at his arrogant words. 'Excuse me?'

'The only place you're going is into a shower. With me.'

Callie reached out and grabbed the back of a pool lounger to keep her balance, hope draining away. No, she couldn't do this. She wasn't going back to an affair, to crazy sex in the shower and then going home alone. She wanted more—she needed more. As much as she wanted Finn, settling for a no-strings, only-when-they-were-in-town-together fling would kill her.

Because she loved him so damn much.

'We can't go back, Finn.' She managed to croak the words out. 'I can't do it again.'

'Do what?'

'Have an affair with you!' Callie cried. 'I just can't—not again. Not feeling like this.'

Finn took two strides to reach her, and when he did he held her face in her hands. 'What are you feeling, angel? Tell me.'

'Why? What does it matter?' Callie flung the words into his face.

'It matters, darling Cal, because *you* matter.'

Finn brushed his lips against hers gently, briefly, before picking his head up and looking back into her shocked face. 'Okay, then, I'll tell you what *I'm* feeling. I saw you and my world settled down. I feel complete. Seeing you here makes me feel like I'm home. Normal.'

'Wha—at?' Callie frowned, confused.

'I came home from the gym, kicked off my trainers and walked onto my veranda—and I saw and heard you, cursing me for not watering my garden. And my world, for the first time in weeks, was the right way up. Me coming home, seeing you, made sense.'

'Um…what are you saying, Finn?'

Finn's smile warmed her from her toes up.

'I'm saying that I'm in love with you. Fathoms deep in love with you.'

'Oh.'

Finn's mouth twitched. 'That's all you've got?'

Callie held up her hand, trying to process what he'd just told her. 'You're in love with me?' she asked, just to clarify, not sure she'd heard him properly.

'Seems that way.'

Callie rested her forehead on his chest. 'Okay...wow.'

Finn's hand drifted down her spine. 'Still not the response I was waiting to hear. Any chance of *I love you, too, Finn*?'

Callie lifted her head and frowned at him. 'Of course I love you. How could you think for one moment that I don't?'

'Oh, let me think... Maybe it's the fact that you told me that you were going to use, abuse and toss me. That you aren't interested in commitment, that you don't believe in love, that I was allowed to seduce your body but not your mind.'

Finn rested his hands on Callie's hips and his forehead on hers.

'Might I remind you that you left me with that "Thanks for being a brilliant fake wife" comment?' Callie replied tartly.

Finn brushed his mouth across hers, sighed, and did it again. 'Okay, I admit it—we are equally bad at falling in love. Admitting we are in love. But I *do* love you. So much.'

Callie linked her arms around his neck and reached up to rest her mouth against his. 'I love you too.' She tipped her head back and her eyes laughed. 'So...what do we do now?'

Finn shrugged, his hand resting on her bottom. 'Haven't

the foggiest idea except that we go back to my original plan.'

'Which was…?'

His grin was pure mischief. 'You and me in the shower. Naked.'

Callie, her heart about to explode from happiness, thought that sounded like a marvellous idea and led him into the house.

The next morning Callie, dressed only in one of Finn's T-shirts, followed him through the garden to the bench, a cup of coffee in her wobbly hand.

Was this real? Any of it? Had they really made love all night long? Soft and sure, tender and wild, they'd lost themselves in each other's bodies, safe and secure in their love and their need for each other.

But what now? Where did they go from here?

Take a breath, Callie, she told herself. *Take it minute by minute, hour by hour. You don't need to have it all worked out right now. Right now you need to sit next to your man, on this bench, and watch the sea dance beneath the mid-morning sun.*

Callie leaned back against the arm of the bench and draped her legs across Finn's lap. He drew patterns on her bare thighs with his fingertips, his relaxed face lifted up to the sun. He was beautiful and he was hers.

'I spoke to my…to Laura,' she told him after watching him for a while.

Finn turned his head to smile at her. 'Yeah? And…?'

Callie shrugged. 'Old story. Married at eighteen, feeling like life had passed her by. Needed to leave to "find herself".' Callie lifted her cup to her lips. 'I don't know if we're ever going to have a mother-daughter relationship but I can be civil to her. *You* got me through that conversation, by the way.'

'I did? All the way from Alaska?'

'I heard you telling me you believed in me, that I could move mountains. You gave me your courage.'

Finn pulled a face. 'If I had any courage I wouldn't have left you and put us both through hell.'

'Maybe. But at least we realised that real life sucked without each other.' Callie put her cup on the arm of her chair. 'Talking about real life… How are we going to make this work? How are we going to be together? I know you don't want a long-distance relationship and neither do I.'

'Are you willing to give up your job?'

God, that was a big ask, but she would if she had to, as she told him. 'I love my job—I do. I wasn't sure I did six weeks ago, but having you in my life just makes everything seem exciting again.'

Finn's hand tightened on her knee. 'I would give up mine too, if it meant spending more time with you. So how about neither of us giving up anything?'

Callie's brows lifted. 'And how do we do that?'

'We travel together. If you're in London or Europe, I'll write about something in London or Europe. If you're in the States, the same thing. We spend most nights together. If there's an assignment I feel like I really need to take then it had better not take longer than a week—because that's my limit. That will always be my limit to the amount of time I can be away from you.'

Callie looked at him, astounded. 'Are you sure?'

'Hell, yes. What do you say?'

Callie bit her lip. 'What happens if one of us gets sick of travelling? What if I want to stay at home and—?'

Finn's eyes sharpened. 'And…?'

'Work in the garden? Redecorate the house?' Callie's voice dropped. 'Have a baby?'

Finn cupped her face with his hand. 'Then we both quit

and do something else. There'll always be something else, angel, but there's only one you and me.'

Callie took his hand and kissed the centre of his palm. 'There's only you for me.'

'Good to know.'

Finn glanced at her left hand and after Callie had explained why her dad had given the rings to her mother played with the rings with his fingers.

'You haven't taken them off.'

Callie felt her heart speed up. 'Should I?'

'Since I intend to change your status from fake wife to real wife as soon as possible, don't bother on my account,' Finn told her, his eyes blazing with love and passion. 'Proper proposal and new engagement ring to follow in due course.'

Callie gurgled with laughter. 'Just as long as you remember that I am trouble with a capital T. In neon letters.'

Finn sent her an amused look. 'I wouldn't have it any other way. Talent, as you once told me, shouldn't be wasted.'

* * * * *

MARRIAGE IN
NAME ONLY?

ANNE OLIVER

CHAPTER ONE

AT LEAST SHE was going to die in spectacular fashion.

Chloe Montgomery clenched her fingers around the tacky tar-smelling rope and tried to imagine that she wasn't suspended *who knew how high?* above the pitch-black auditorium in one of Melbourne's finest entertainment venues.

A rough knot below her feet scratched her bare soles. The way-too-small-barely-there costume dug into her ribs, making breathing almost impossible—especially when every shallow gasp could be her last.

'You'll be fine, Chloe,' the guy behind her whispered as he made a final adjustment to the slim safety harness at the back of her waist. 'Trust me, you'll be the highlight of the evening's entertainment.'

'Trust you…' Her voice came out reed-thin, a touch hysterical and barely audible above the rushing sound in her ears. How was she going to get one note of Happy Birthday out when her throat was closing over? She was no singer at the best of times.

'Ready?' the guy murmured.

'Mmm-hmm,' she managed between tightly pressed lips. What insane reasoning had convinced Chloe that she was up for this—in any way?

Because she wanted—*needed*—to prove to her new boss

that she was an asset to her event-planning business. No task too hard, no unforeseen circumstance she couldn't handle.

So when the artist booked for the event was involved in a car accident on the way here, Chloe had stepped up to the plate—or, in this case, the rope. And if everything went as planned, she'd be lowered onto the birthday boy's lap, kiss him on the cheek, someone would be there to unfasten her harness and she could escape to the venue's kitchens, challenge met and dignity intact. Dana would be only too grateful and impressed and desperately keen to take on such a valuable, *flexible* employee full-time.

A single spotlight exploded into life, blinding her with its brilliance and holding her captive in its hot white light. The audience's hushed murmur of anticipation rose into the stratosphere and she could feel every pair of eyes focused on her. Chloe, who'd spent her life trying and mostly failing to be someone people noticed, was finally the centre of attention.

A pity she was going to be remembered for all the wrong reasons.

Thought fled as the rope shuddered and began its descent. *You're supposed to sing,* she reminded herself. *Find the target, focus on him.* She squinted through the glare to the table directly beneath her. The cake, flickering with candles amongst champagne flutes, red foil stars and silver-ware, marked her destination.

A man was staring up at her with a faint smile—or was it a smirk?—on his lips. Hard to tell in the spotlight's dazzle but there was enough candle-glow to make out that they were, indeed, very nice lips. Forget the lips—*imagine him naked*—wasn't that what people afraid of public speaking were supposed to do? It couldn't hurt here either.

Except that his wife had organised this surprise. Which reminded her she had a job to do…

Clearing the constriction from her throat, she launched

into a wobbly, out-of tune rendition of Happy Birthday, keeping her eyes pinned to his as she descended. *Not* imagining him naked. Much.

Brilliant timing; she sang the last note as she reached table height and safety. She had to manoeuvre herself and the rope a little to ensure she landed on his lap. Her body prickled hot and cold all over when her barely covered bottom came into contact with a pair of rock-hard thighs, and she had to shift slightly to keep from falling off. Which would be easy to do because her whole body was trembling.

Warm palms slid firmly to her waist to steady her and she stifled a gasp at the electrifying contact. How embarrassing. How *wrong*. She lifted her chin and met his gaze. Up close his eyes were blue. A piercing, blinding blue that, to her shame, melted her insides to mush. 'Happy Birthday…' she finished in her best Marilyn Monroe voice, then came to a breathless pause. What the heck was his name again? Oh, my, he was…

Not available, Chloe.

She leaned in to brush the expected kiss over his cheek, caught the whiff of his enticing masculine skin before his head turned and his lips were somehow on hers. Warm, firm. Friendly. *Too friendly.* Appalled, she peeled her lips away to stare at him. He stared back, those fascinating blue orbs sending all the wrong signals for a married man.

'I'm not the birthday boy,' he told her, before she could blink. He leaned closer so that his breath tickled her ear and murmured, 'But then you already knew that, didn't you?'

Huh?

He jerked a thumb at the man on his left and leaned back, his hands dropping away from her waist. 'Sadiq's the one you should be kissing.' The tone of bored cynicism belied the heat in his eyes.

She felt the safety harness being unclipped and realised

she was *still sitting on his lap*. And…she went completely still…was she turning him on?

Not waiting to find out, she slid off immediately, her legs barely supporting her. 'Hey, *you* kissed *me*,' she whispered into his ear, keeping her smile in place, but furious with his dismissive attitude and furious with herself for making the mistake in the first place.

She turned her attention to the handsome black-haired, dark-eyed man who'd have looked right at home in one of those desert romance books. Way less unsettling. He was watching the two of them with an amused look, apparently unconcerned she'd stuffed up so sensationally.

'*Sadiq,*' she said with forced brightness and leaned down to kiss him to a roomful of enthusiastic applause. She wished him an enjoyable evening or some such but her mind was stuck on the previous thirty seconds.

You already knew. The weird—and incorrect—accusation burned like a hot wire in her blood. How dared he—whoever the hell he was—insinuate she'd contrived this act to some-how seduce him?

Sexual harassment. The taste of bile rose up her throat. An employee's word over some fancy schmuck with the wealthy connections? Like that was ever going to happen. One word of complaint from him and Dana was *so* going to fire her.

Jordan Blackstone watched the blonde's pretty cheeks flush, her well-endowed cleavage on full view as she made a fuss of his friend, privately enjoying her discomfort…and more than a little disconcerted at his own. Thankfully, she'd stood up before things had got too awkward. Another moment of her cute rhinestone-encrusted butt squirming on his lap, he'd have been in real trouble.

Women were always contriving new ways to meet him and he had to admit this one was unique. As was his body's response to hers. He hadn't expected to find his dormant libido awakening so fast and so hard.

He watched her drop a quick kiss on Sadiq's cheek. His own lips tingled at the memory of how they'd felt beneath his. *Soft and sweet.* What the hell had possessed him? Sheer momentary madness obviously, because in that pulse-pounding moment he sure as hell hadn't been himself.

She didn't hang around. He'd barely blinked and she was gone in a flash of sparkles and skin. The sort of shimmering flash that lingered on your retina long after the moment had passed.

He shook his head to clear the image. Soft and sweet was just a facade. No matter that she'd played the innocent mistake game, she was the type of out-there, attention-grabbing, rich-man-hungry woman he avoided. And that costume—what there was of it—was obviously intended to over-enhance her curves. Even if said curves were every man's fantasy, it was hardly appropriate for this occasion.

And she couldn't sing to save herself.

He picked up his glass, drained the bubbly mineral water to moisten his throat, which he realised had gone dust-dry, and watched Sadiq blow out his candles. A hovering waitress whisked the cake away to cut and distribute to the roomful of elite guests.

The band struck up a party number and dancers hit the polished floor amongst the bobbing helium balloons. Jordan gazed at the ceiling as the rope snaked upwards and disappeared over a balcony. 'Well. That was...interesting.'

Sadiq chuckled. 'Not as interesting as the look on your face when the lady landed on your lap, my friend. And that kiss... Want to tell me what you were thinking?'

Jordan scowled. 'I *wasn't* thinking.' And that was the problem. He had to be grateful for Sadiq's request to ban the media from inside the venue or he'd be front and centre in tomorrow's gossip rags.

His friend leaned closer and spoke over the noise. 'A discreet word here or there and you could get lucky tonight.'

'I make my own luck.' A sultry image involving him peeling that costume from her lithe and voluptuous body danced on his eyelids. He blinked it away. 'And she's hardly my type.'

Another chuckle. 'You have a type?'

Jordan didn't bother to reply, just reached for the water carafe and filled his glass. *Not his type?* Hell, certain parts of his anatomy obviously begged to differ. She was hot, no question. And wasn't that all he was looking for in a woman these days? Hot and single and temporary?

The sounds of merriment swirled around him as the music quickened, its throb beating low and heavy in his sensitised groin. He drained his glass, then tugged at his collar. Ever since she'd plonked that sexy butt on his lap and he'd felt her womanly assets graze his chest, his clothing had felt two sizes too tight. He could still smell her fragrance—warm and spicy and sensuous, making him think wicked thoughts; like lying naked with her in front of a roaring fire, her skin flushed with heat from their love-making.

Then there were the eyes. The colour of aged Scotch. He hadn't missed that initial flare of attraction, that quick clash of heat on heat, gone before he could think *hot night in paradise*. No, he hadn't misinterpreted that, but recognition…? He frowned. Had he got it wrong?

Because after the kiss and the accusation, those eyes had burned with a very different kind of heat—indignation. If there hadn't been an audience, he had a suspicion he'd have felt the hot sting of that anger in one way or another.

And now that he thought about it, quite possibly he'd have deserved it. Maybe she was already in a relationship? But she hadn't worn rings—and why he'd noticed was beyond him.

He relegated the confounding incident to the back of his mind, glanced at his watch and pushed up. Unfortunate timing, but his mate's thirtieth birthday bash clashed with important business. He clasped Sadiq's shoulder on his way. 'Gotta go. Teleconference with Dubai in an hour.'

His friend nodded. 'Good luck. You're still on for lunch tomorrow?'

'I'll be there.' He dropped a light kiss on Sadiq's wife's cheek. ''Night, Zahira. Great party. By the way, I loved your surprise.'

Zahira's dark exotic eyes smiled. 'Wasn't she delightful? And so brave to step in at literally a moment's notice.'

Jordan, who'd already turned to leave, swung back. 'Is that so?'

'The original artist had an accident earlier tonight,' she explained. 'A member of Dana's staff volunteered to take her place.'

Jordan felt a prick of guilt. Not a professional entertainer then, but a girl with maybe no experience who'd stepped in to save the day. That accounted for the debacle of a performance. It excused her actions; it didn't excuse his. 'Good for her,' he mumbled. Then because he admired people prepared to give it a go and he'd treated her less well than he might have, he said, 'She deserves a bonus at the end of the evening.'

Zahira flicked him one of those unreadable female looks. 'I'll tell her you said so when I hand it to her, shall I, Mr Blackstone?'

An odd sensation prickled the back of his neck. 'That's not necessary—I'll tell Dana tomorrow at lunch.' He pulled his car key from his pocket. 'Enjoy the rest of the evening.'

Except for her boss, Chloe was the last to leave the building when she exited through the staff entrance at two a.m. She pulled on the worn leather jacket she'd bought at a charity shop and swung her backpack onto her shoulders, glancing at the sky's heavy underbelly and hoping she could make it home before it rained. The birthday boy's wife, Zahira, had stopped by with praise aplenty and a nice fat wad of notes. *And* Dana had asked her if she wanted to take on regular work. Chloe did a little happy dance right there on the footpath.

What an evening! One minute she'd been swirling raspberry liqueur sauce over the desserts and wondering how she was going to make ends meet, and the next she'd been dangling over a balcony in a borrowed costume and singing in public.

Of course, it hadn't *all* gone according to plan. She'd got the wrong guy, after all. And Mr Wrong had *smirked* at her—she was sure of it. She'd be the first to admit she couldn't sing, *and* she was dead scared of heights, but she'd tried, hadn't she? Jerk.

Then he'd kissed her. Tingles shivered through her body at the memory. The drugging taste of those lips, the way he'd held her safe on his lap so she wouldn't fall, his musky masculine smell. Until he'd all but pushed her off with some ridiculous accusation that she knew him.

Double jerk.

Chloe dismissed him with a snarl, then jammed on her helmet and headed for her scooter parked a few metres away and looking all the more ancient in front of a shiny new maroon SUV. *Forget him.* The important thing was she'd come out on top. So it hadn't been the world's best performance; she'd made twice as much money in one night than she had since she'd stepped back on Australian soil a fortnight ago, and a regular job with reasonable pay would give her a realistic chance to resave the money she'd lost.

She slowed her steps, rubbed her arms against the chilly winter air. And then it just might be time to consider reconnecting with her family. A friend she'd made while overseas had lost her chance to reconcile with hers when an accident had taken both parents. Chloe didn't want to have the same regrets.

A sharp *meep* spiked the air and she glanced at the parked car as its lights blinked, then behind her at the sound of brisk footsteps. A man was approaching, a black overcoat over one shoulder. He was tall and broad with a lanky stride.

As he drew nearer the amber street light turned his shirt a white-gold and washed over his face so she could make out his features. Dark brows, firm jaw. Generous full lips even at this distance.

She stifled a gasp inside her helmet. She knew those lips. She knew how they felt, how they tasted. Her pulse took off on its own wild journey as she watched him cross the footpath, open the door. He glanced at her over the roof as he climbed into his car but didn't recognise her with her helmet on.

Was she just going to stand there and let him go without giving him a piece of her mind? No, she was *not*. She was beside his big bad wheels in seconds, stepping off the kerb in front of him, rounding the bonnet as the lights beamed on. 'Hey!' She rapped on the driver's window. 'Hey.'

The window lowered halfway. Now she could see the blue intensity of his eyes, the thick brows above them raised in concern. 'Are you okay?' he asked her. 'Do you need assistance?'

She lifted her visor and stared at him. Watched the blue in his eyes grow deep and focused as recognition sharpened his features. 'I'm fine,' she said, without giving him time to draw breath. 'No, actually I'm annoyed. You're arrogant and rude and I don't know why you'd think I'd know you or why on earth you'd think I'd want to come on to you. Who are you anyway? No—' She slashed a hand through the air. 'Don't tell me—I don't want to know.' And flipped her visor down.

She hadn't given him so much as a microsecond to open his mouth. Jordan leaned back in his seat and watched her walk— rather, *stalk*—to the decrepit-looking scooter in front of him. She was even smaller than he'd thought and dressed entirely in black leather now with a lumpy backpack on her shoulders. So… He'd got under her skin, had he? Was she itching all over with the memory of that kiss?

He damn well hoped so.

Because he hadn't been able to rid himself of the feel of her compact body against his. Because she'd distracted him during an important conference call. Because she'd made him forget his coat, which was why he was back here at two o'clock in the morning.

And she was going to give him an exceedingly restless night.

Her scooter sputtered into life and took off down the street in a cloud of fumes. He gave her—and himself—a minute, then pulled away from the kerb and headed for home.

A short time later, he caught sight of her again when he drew up behind her at a red traffic light. The lights changed and she zoomed off ahead, her hair streaming behind her from beneath the helmet. Dammit—he wanted a chance to apologise, preferably while running his hands through that silky gold.

And that was the thing; he didn't go for blondes— especially small mouthy blondes. He preferred his women tall and dark, poised and sophisticated. But he'd felt the tiny quivers running through her limbs, the surprising fit of her small body against his. The fury in her eyes, all the more eloquent for its silence.

An almost-grin tugged at his lips. Any other night he might

have enjoyed the challenge—a night to slake his lust with a nameless woman. A woman who didn't know him. A feisty woman who'd give as good as she got. He had a feeling the little surprise package riding ahead of him ticked all three boxes.

But his conference call to Dubai hadn't gone as well as he'd hoped and his fist tightened on the steering wheel. Yes, he could have done with a bloody good distraction.

Suddenly, without warning, she veered to the side of the street. By the time Jordan had pulled over and climbed out with the honourable intention of asking if she was okay, she was standing on the footpath, helmet in hand, windswept hair tangled around her face, expression stony. Her free hand was curled into a fist and tapping against her thigh. Music floated from an all-night jazz bar nearby. A light rain misted the air.

'So I can add stalker to my list.' She shuffled her feet on the concrete, drawing his attention to clumpy knee-high boots.

He raised his hands to shoulder height. 'I'm on my way home. Forgot my coat earlier.'

She rolled her eyes. 'R-i-ght.'

'Look, I—'

'No, *you* look, whoev—'

'Stop!' He jabbed the air with a finger. 'Give me a chance to open my mouth, will you?'

A beat of silence filled the air between them. 'Fine.' She huffed out a breath, her spine stiff, mouth tight. 'Say what you have to say and leave.'

'This is my usual route home. I am not following you. And I *will not* follow you.' He paused, hopeful. 'Unless you ask me to.'

She didn't reply but he imagined he saw the tiniest glimmer of that earlier heat in her eyes, instantly doused.

'Though I do have to ask,' he continued carefully, 'are

you sure it's safe for a woman to be riding that thing alone late at night?'

'I don't need a bodyguard.' She glanced skywards. 'And I'd like to make it home before I drown.'

'Think that's possible?' He glanced at the scooter. 'That's not the most reliable-looking transport I ever saw.'

'The Rolls is in for a service.' She flicked at her dampening hair as the rain thickened but there was a touch of humour around her mouth and her voice had lost some of its sting.

'My name's Jordan. Jordan Blackstone.'

She studied his face a moment. 'Should I have heard of you?'

'Dana knows me,' he said, then, 'I've had one hell of a night, and I know you have.' He gestured to the nearby bar. 'I'll buy you a nightcap. I think we could both use one.'

'I don't drink and drive on an empty stomach, 'specially when I'm tired.'

'Coffee, then.'

'Thanks, but no, thanks.' She turned towards her bike.

Something inside him snapped—he didn't want to be alone tonight. He didn't want to go home and think about his messy situation. And he wasn't used to women turning him down cold.

'Wait.' He reached out, his hand encircling her wrist, keeping his touch light, giving her a choice. Her eyes widened at the contact but she didn't pull away. The tip of her head barely reached his shoulders, arousing his protective instincts. 'Is anyone expecting you?'

She hesitated. 'No. But my housemates will know if I'm… late.'

'What's your name?'

'Chloe.'

'Chloe.' He smoothed his thumb over the delicate skin at

her wrist, felt her rapid pulse thrumming in time with his own. 'I want a chance to explain about earlier.'

She shook her head but left her hand in his, confusing him further. 'Why?' Dark eyes skewered into his. 'It wasn't as if it was memorable or anything.'

That brought a smile to his lips. 'You enjoyed it as much as I did.' He couldn't resist; he shifted closer, smelled leather and spice and warm woman.

She didn't back away and he heard the tiny hitch in her breath, saw the flare of heat in her eyes even as she said, 'You really are an arrogant piece of w—'

'Ring Dana. If anything happens…'

'Nothing's going to happen.' She withdrew her hand and pointed up the street. 'See that neon sign? I'm going to sit down in there in the nice bright *public* light where there are people and eat a burger.' Then she pulled on her helmet.

He watched her shapely black-clad legs, the curve of her backside as she climbed onto her scooter, and his groin hardened at the mental image of her astride *him*, thighs clenched around his hips, her head thrown back in passion as she tangled her fingers in her own hair and shouted his name. His blood simmered and smoked in his veins. *I could give you the ride of your life.*

She didn't so much as glance his way before she zoomed off. Which was probably a good thing.

But it was a clear invitation and he jumped into his car and followed. The evening might not end so badly after all.

CHAPTER TWO

JORDAN GAVE HER a few moments to order and waited until she'd taken up residence at a table before following her inside. She was munching on a burger by the time he sat down opposite her with his own and a side order of fries.

He slid a foam cup in front of her. 'I didn't know what you like. Most people like cappuccino.'

'Not at ridiculous o'clock in the morning if you want a decent night's sleep,' she said around a mouthful of bun. 'But thank you.'

'You're welcome.'

'So are you a movie star or something? On one of those Aussie soaps? I've been out of the country for eight years. I'm not up on the latest celebrities.'

Obviously fame didn't impress her, which made for a refreshing change. 'I'm in the mining industry.'

She studied him curiously. 'Why did you think I'd know you, then?'

He shrugged, wishing he'd never made the accusation in the first place. Except he wouldn't have been sitting here sharing burgers with her if he hadn't. 'The company's had some publicity over the past couple of years.' Which he didn't want to go into. 'What I said… What I did…' He was unwrapping his snack but paused. 'I apologise. I was out of line. And you're right, it was rude and arrogant.'

'Something we can agree on.' She arched a slim brow. 'Do you make a habit of kissing random women?'

'Only beautiful ones who fall into my lap at birthday parties. About that—I'm hoping we can do it again sometime.'

She blinked, her burger halfway to her mouth. 'My sixty seconds of fame. I'm not likely to be repeating that any time soon.'

But he knew *she* knew exactly what he meant. As he watched her cheeks turned pink, her eyes darkened and met his for a few unguarded seconds before she reached for her coffee. She took a sip, leaving a tempting fleck of foam on her upper lip.

'I didn't know you filled in at the last minute until Zahira told me,' he went on. 'That was a pretty game stunt you pulled. I'm ashamed to say, I'd have had second thoughts about the safety of that rope myself.'

'Yes, well, that's me. Always up for a challenge.' She licked the foam off with the tip of her tongue and said, 'Apology accepted, by the way. But that doesn't mean I'm going to let you follow me home.'

'You don't need to worry.' No matter how he'd have preferred to end the evening.

She nodded. 'Thanks.'

'Eight years is a long time to be away.' She only looked around twenty. 'How old were you when you left?'

'Nineteen. I'm an adventureholic, couldn't wait to leave.' She snaffled one of his fries. 'The freedom and independence. No one telling you what to do. No one to tell you you're doing it wrong.' Her voice turned sombre and the light faded from her eyes.

A man? he wondered. And things hadn't ended well. 'So what brought you back?' *Or chased you away.*

She chewed a moment, studying the table. When she looked up again, she was smiling, but she didn't fool him for a second. 'Family,' she said brightly, mask in place. 'You know how it is.' A haunted desperation flickered in her eyes before she looked away again, fingers tense around her bun.

Yes, he thought, those same emotions running through him, he knew how it was to owe family, but his bet was still on the man. He waited until she met his gaze once more then murmured, 'What did he do to you?'

Colour drained from her cheeks. 'Who?'

'The guy who put those clouds in your eyes.'

'I don't know what you're talking about—there's no *guy*, I was talking about my *family*.'

He nodded slowly. 'They're glad to have you back, then? Your family?'

'They live in Sydney.' Biting her bottom lip, she rewrapped the remains of her meal in record time, screwed it up and stood. 'I have to go.'

'Hang on.' He stood too. 'Can I see you again?'

'I don't think so.' She swung her backpack onto her shoulders, swiped up her helmet. Cool, guarded eyes met his. 'Thanks for the coffee.' Her tone was reasonable enough but the message was clear and final. A one-eighty-degree turn-around from the vibes he'd felt earlier in the evening when she'd swung down towards him.

Fine. He didn't need the complication in his life right now, anyway. 'You're welcome, and ride safely.'

He resumed his seat, studying her through the windows as she walked into the damp night, her blonde hair washed moon-pale beneath the car park's lighting. What was her story? She'd said she'd come back for family but hadn't caught up with them? She'd tripped over her tongue with that one and hadn't been able to get away from him fast enough.

Nope. She could deny it all she wanted—only a love gone wrong would elicit that lost-soul response he'd seen in her Scotch-coloured eyes.

And he ought to know.

His gaze lingered on her a moment more, then he turned away. She worked for Dana; she'd be easy to find. Tonight he had more important things on his mind than casual sex and other people's problems.

Such as how he was going to sweet-talk Sheikh Qasim bin Omar Al-Zeid into buying his gold.

Jordan's mother had inherited the majority shares in Rivergold when his father had died, and she'd nearly bankrupted the company—his father's love and life's work. Jordan had finally bought her out with the trust fund he'd inherited on his thirtieth birthday, but it had taken him two years of solid work and little sleep to bring it up to anything approaching its former glory.

His fingers automatically felt for the leather thong beneath his shirt. And he was back in time to eight years ago and he could see his dad lying on his office floor, barely breathing when Jordan had found him. He'd not been there in time because he'd been too busy heating up the sheets with a fellow student when his elderly father had demanded he come home to Perth to discuss his latest poor academic performance at one of Melbourne's finest unis.

He was the reason his father had died that day....

'Jordan...you came...' His old man's voice was barely audible.

He dropped to his knees beside his father, knowing it was already too late. 'I'm here, Dad, the ambulance is on its way. Just hang in there a few more moments and they'll be here and we can have that talk.'

'I don't have...that long...'

He barely raised a trembling hand, and Jordan grasped it, felt the thin, papery skin, saw the grey pallor of his lined face, the glazed eyes sunken into his skull. When had his dad grown so old? But seventy-nine *was* old. He should have known the bull of a man wouldn't last forever. *Jordan should have been here.* He *should* have made his father proud. 'Hang on, Dad, just hang on. Please.' *One more chance to show you I'm worthy.*

'Jordan, promise me...' Even through the pain he was fighting, the way he'd fought all his life.

Jordan leaned closer, heard the wheezing sound in his father's chest. 'What, Dad? Anything.'

'You'll inherit Rivergold one day. My dream, the gold... for you and your mother. Study hard, make Rivergold proud. Make me proud...'

He closed his eyes, the effort of talking taking its toll, and Jordan watched him fading away through misted eyes even as the wail of approaching sirens split the air. 'I promise. Dad, you'll—'

'My nugget. Wear it for me.'

Jordan looked at the irregular thimble-sized chunk of gold on its leather thong resting on his father's chest—the first gold he'd discovered while prospecting in the remote Western Australian outback.

'It's yours now, son. Rivergold needs you.' He spoke faster now, wanting to get it all out before the end. 'I want my... gold in a necklace...give your mother. Those negotiations in the UAE...so important to me...'

'I'll make it happen, Dad,' Jordan said, and meant it down to the last cell in his body.

'Tell Ina I love...'

Then he was gone, his empty shell a shadow of his former self.

The paramedics hadn't been able to revive him. If Jordan had been there earlier, as requested, he might have been able to get him help in time. The man might not have had a heart attack at all. If he'd been there.

* * *

Jordan gulped down the remains of his coffee, bitter-tasting now, and reflected on the evening's tele-conference. Qasim hadn't mentioned it, but Jordan had heard via a source close to Sadiq that the prestigious Dubai jewellery manufacturer billionaire was also considering X23 Mining. X23's owner, Don Hartson, was Jordan's most bitter rival. *And married to Jordan's mother.*

How was that for irony? Not that she'd been any kind of mother to Jordan. The woman had married Hartson five minutes after Dad's death. Which had left Jordan to draw the obvious conclusion—Ina Blackstone had been having an affair behind her elderly husband's back.

Too distracted by her glamorous new lifestyle with a younger man, she'd let the company slide over the next few years, and, with Jordan powerless to prevent it, those negotiations his father had set up had fallen through.

But the day he'd turned thirty he'd bought out her shares, taken control of the company and reaffirmed the promise he'd made to a dying man.

He'd spent the last two years modernising Rivergold, refusing to lay off staff, some of whom had given his father years of loyalty. It had been tough—still was—but he was now consolidating. Increasing his exports. With Sadiq's contacts in the UAE, Jordan had been able to turn his negotiations to the reputed City of Gold once again.

And now that long-ago promise he'd made to his father was so close he could almost reach out and kiss it.

But apparently the elderly gold manufacturer had a reputation for extreme conservatism. Blowing out a slow breath that seemed to take a part of him with it, Jordan stepped out of the restaurant and into the chill evening. He'd never been one to toe the line, but for this long overdue deal he'd do whatever it took.

CHAPTER THREE

CHLOE'S HEART SKIPPED a beat when she checked her phone for messages while dressing for Sunday brunch and saw an email from her sister. It wasn't tragic news, thank God, but it was disturbing news just the same.

Donna's message was brief and clear and to the point and included a bank account number. Their parents were facing tough times. Losing the family home was more than likely. And since neither her brother nor Donna could help out financially *at this time*—her sister outlined their perfectly valid reasons why they *couldn't* in bullet point format—they'd really appreciate Chloe's financial support since she had a high-paying job and lived in a virtual palace with a member of the aristocracy.

Stewart. Chloe beat back the pain with a sharp stick and thwacked that stick at the man she'd fallen in love with. The gorgeous hunk of widower who'd employed her to care for his son then used her for sex, except she'd been too naive and blinded by love to see it that way until it was too late.

Of course she'd told her family; she'd relished telling them about her successes, her career as a nanny, the palatial home in rural England. The man in her life.

And four years ago when it had all turned to crap, telling them she'd made a mistake and that she didn't fit into the world of the rich and famous and never would hadn't been on her list of priorities.

She flicked the email off, tossed her phone in her bag. She'd have to come clean and tell Donna the bad news, and she wasn't looking forward to it.

An hour later, she swiped sweaty palms down her best jeans then adjusted the belt over her thigh-length tunic and hoped she'd dressed appropriately. She'd caught public transport to avoid the dreaded windswept, helmet-hair look. Hitching her bag higher on her shoulder, she stared at the massive two-storey mansion as she walked up the long, curved drive. Dana's early-morning phone call had come out of the blue. Sadiq and his wife had extended an invitation to Chloe to attend an informal meal as a thank-you for helping to make last night's entertainment a success.

She'd been stoked. Dana's Events was one of the city's premier event-planning businesses, catering to the elite, and this was a brilliant opportunity for Chloe to get to know the clients.

The only downside was the probability that Jordan Blackstone would be there. And after the relentless dreams she'd had of the two of them last night… The residual heat was still stroking her abdomen, and her skin felt tight and tingly. Worse, she was mortally afraid he'd see it in her eyes. He was the type of man who could read women's minds. He'd read hers last night, hadn't he? She should never have stopped for that burger. A momentary weakness she would *not* be repeating no matter how attracted she was to him.

Rich and influential, like Stewart. Not the type of man she needed in her life—a lesson she'd learned the hard way. And there were limits to how much risk one should take, both personally and financially. She'd learned that lesson the hard way too.

A smartly uniformed staff member welcomed her at the

front door. Chloe followed her across a huge tiled foyer where a heavy chandelier threw rainbows over brass and honeyed wood, along a wide passage hung with a mix of Eastern and European art.

The aroma of barbecued meat and Asian cooking wafting from the garden met her nose as she walked through an airy glass atrium filled with tropical potted plants.

Zahira turned from the intimate group of guests as Chloe stepped outside. 'I'm so glad you could make it, Chloe,' she said in her lightly accented voice, her dark eyes smiling. 'Welcome. Here's our brave little entertainer from last night,' she announced, and had every head turning their way. 'Chloe Montgomery, a member of Dana's capable team.'

'Hi.' She smiled at the group in general but there was only one pair of eyes she saw. Jordan Blackstone's. Blue and even more intense in the winter sunshine. Startling against his tanned complexion and spiky dark hair, which riffled around his temples in the breeze.

No avoiding him, she thought, as he said something to the knot of people he was standing with and began walking towards her. Her pulse thrummed fast and her breathing quickened while she watched him approach.

Unlike the rest of the guests who wore casual, he was dressed for business. A suit and tie for a Sunday brunch? Still, she couldn't help but be impressed by the clean-cut corporate image. Hopefully he was on his way to forge some million-dollar deal with some other mining magnate and she could relax and *not* think about sharing Sunday brunch with him in an entirely more intimate way.

'Morning, Chloe.' His smile was polite, his tone precise, almost professional. Only his eyes betrayed the hint that he hadn't forgotten last night's kiss either.

'Jordan. Hello.' She felt her face warm and prayed her

expression didn't give away her inner turmoil. Her dreams, her restless night.

Not to mention the fact that she'd almost blurted out her most private personal problems at the diner.

Then Zahira smiled enigmatically and made some vague comment about leaving her in Jordan's capable hands—which had her body tingling anew—and walked away, leaving the two of them standing alone together in the middle of the lawn.

'Would you like a drink?' he asked, motioning a waiter who was at her side in three seconds flat.

'Soda water, please. I skipped breakfast. Running late,' she added, though why she felt she had to explain...

'You didn't sleep well?'

Was that humour in his voice? 'Slept like a baby, thanks for asking.'

'The coffee didn't keep you tossing and turning all night?'

Not the coffee. But she *knew* he already knew that and was relieved when the waiter returned with her glass of bubbles. 'I was tired—that usually does it.' She took a cooling sip of her water and deflected his attention from her hot cheeks with, 'Do you always dress so formally for a barbecue?'

'I have a meeting in the city later.'

'Hello.'

Chloe looked down at the sound of the young voice to see a small girl with dusky skin and long black hair looking up at her. 'Hello, there.'

'What's your name?' she asked, fiddling with a gold brooch pinned to her dress. 'My name's Tamara. It means date tree. Mummy's is Zahira and it means blossoming flower and Daddy's is Sadiq and it means trooful. Daddy says I should always tell the troof.'

Chloe glanced at Jordan and they exchanged a smile before she leaned down. 'Your daddy's right. And my name's Chloe.'

'What does Chloe mean?'

'I don't know. I'll have to find out, won't I?'

Tamara's inquisitive gaze flicked between them. 'Is Jordan your boyfriend?'

'No,' Chloe said, startled. 'We…don't know each other very well.'

'Not yet,' Jordan murmured, sending ripples of awareness down Chloe's spine. He didn't look at Chloe as he ruffled the small girl's hair. 'How's it going, Tams?'

'I'm five now,' she announced proudly, holding up her fingers. 'And I go to school so I'm allowed to help light the candles on my daddy's birthday cake later.'

Chloe nodded. 'I'll be sure to be watching.'

'I think your daddy has something for you,' Jordan said, jutting his chin in the direction of the barbecue.

Tamara followed his gaze. 'Yum, sausages. Bye.' She waved a hand, setting a dozen gold bangles jangling along her arm, her frilly party dress shimmering in the sun as she skipped across the lawn to her father.

'She's a cutie,' Chloe said, meeting Jordan's eyes, still unsettled by the boyfriend question but determined not to let him see. 'And obviously likes to be the centre of attention.'

'Reminds me of someone else last night.' His eyes twinkled at her.

Oh, no. Too awkward. She loved attention but singing to an audience in a costume two sizes too small? And worse, kissing the wrong man? She coughed out a laugh. 'Please, I'd rather forget.'

'Well, I, for one, am not likely to forget any time soon.' He watched her without speaking a moment. Not that she was looking at him now—she was smiling and giving a finger wave to Tamara, who was holding up her sausage like a trophy—but she could feel the heat of his gaze, bathing her like sunshine and not letting her forget either. 'You like kids,' he said.

'You kinda need to if you want to work as a nanny.'

'Guess so. That job kept you busy a good while, then?'

Eighteen wonderful months of being a nanny to Brad while falling hopelessly in love with his father... *Don't go there.* She forced herself to meet Jordan's eyes. 'Only until I had enough money to get me to the next port of call.'

A tiny line furrowed between his brows, as if he was weighing up the truth of what she'd said. 'So...what else did you do while you were overseas? The usual waitressing to fund the campervan to Europe?'

'I wanted more than that,' she went on quickly, relieved the nanny topic was over. 'I picked grapes in France, trekked Nepal, worked on a trail restoration project in the Grand Canyon. Won a wet T-shirt contest in Rome and lost my money in—' Appalled, she bit her lips together. *Please tell me I didn't just say that.* To a man she barely knew. A rich and successful man who'd never have been so careless where money was concerned. She couldn't even blame her runaway tongue on too much wine.

This was the *however many* time in less than twelve hours that she'd said too much to Jordan Blackstone. It was *none* of his business. She should blame him. It was his fault she wasn't thinking straight.

'You ran out of funds,' he finished for her.

'Ye— *No.*' She chewed on her lip then plastered a smile on her face. He probably thought she had a gambling problem or something. 'Family—I told you already. Last night.'

'So you did,' he said slowly, watching her through eyes that were far too perceptive. 'I wasn't sure.'

Now he probably thought she'd come back to sponge off her parents. If he only knew it was the other way round. She eyeballed him back. 'Money's not important to me. Never has been, never will be.'

He didn't believe her, she could tell. And okay, money

hadn't been important until now. She looked away from his unsettling assessment and watched the wait staff setting platters of salads and aromatic Eastern dishes on a long glass table.

When she saw the tray of steaming barbecued delights arrive at the table, Chloe moved fast. 'Looks like the food's ready,' she said over her shoulder as she walked away. 'I'm starved.'

Chloe used the buffet meal to mingle with the other guests under the covered pergola. She didn't speak with Jordan again, but as she chatted she knew where he was at any given time by the way the hairs on the back of her neck tingled as if they were mini antennae seeking a signal.

So when Tamara asked her to come and look at her new cubby house, Chloe was only too happy to escape.

The little hideaway stood a metre or so off the ground. It was a perfect replica of a gingerbread house, crammed with child-sized furniture, books and toys. Tamara had just settled on a cushion when she jumped up and scrambled to the door. 'I forgot my princess crown in my bedroom. Wait, okay?'

'Okay.'

Chloe watched the child skip off across the manicured lawns in her designer dress and shiny shoes with what had to be a fortune in Dubai gold glittering on her arm and blew out a sigh.

Obviously this child was loved, indulged, no struggle to be accepted by her doting parents. Was just wanting to be loved and accepted for who she was too much for Chloe to ask? She stared around at the cubby, luxurious enough to live in.

Okay, money had never been a priority, but right now she could do with a fraction of that wealth. Who knew where her parents might end up without the home they'd lived in for forty years?

And why should she care? Why should Chloe Montgomery, an accidental offspring who'd never fitted in, never lived up to their expectations and had escaped overseas the moment she was old enough, feel any sort of familial obligation?

She rubbed a dull ache that had taken up residence in her heart since Donna's email last night. Because they were family, bonded through blood—however fragile that connection was.

As fragile as life itself, Chloe thought, remembering how devastatingly final Ellen's loss had been. Ellen had argued with her family and left without a goodbye and life had been sweet and exciting. But a couple of months ago her parents' car had been swept away crossing a flooded river in rural Victoria. Chloe would never forget the despair in Ellen's eyes as they'd said goodbye to each other at Vancouver airport.

A couple of months later, Chloe had decided maybe it was time to come home, too, and re-establish some sort of connection, but she'd needed just a little more cash…

Tamara scrambled up the little steps and burst through the doorway with a sparkling crown on her head and a skateboard under one arm. 'Can you read me a story?'

Chloe loved telling stories—making up her own adventures where the heroine always won in the end. She'd been doing it since she was Tamara's age. 'I can do better than that,' she told her. 'I'll tell you one.'

'How did last night's conference call go?' Sadiq asked Jordan as they wandered away from the group.

'I was right—I need to be there in person.' He tightened his jaw, stared out over the garden. 'If I can talk to Qasim face to face, I know I can convince him. I've made an appointment to meet with him next week.' He turned to his friend. 'You understand the way things are done there. What's it going to take?'

'Stability. Focus. Commitment.'

'You know me—I'm all three.'

'Where business is concerned, I agree one hundred per cent, but in other aspects of your life…?' Sadiq shook his head. 'It doesn't help when you're frequently in the media spotlight with a different woman superglued to your arm every night of the week.'

'Women have never interfered with my business priorities. They—'

'And Qasim's not going to like the possible repercussions for his own business,' Sadiq continued over the top of Jordan. 'He's old school, set in his ways, and has always been of the opinion that married men are more likely to put in the effort. He builds his business deals around that.'

'And you agree with that reasoning?'

Sadiq shrugged, as if it were nothing. 'I was brought up that way. Marriages have been arranged around business for centuries. My own marriage was arranged when we were ten years old.' His gaze searched out his wife amongst the women. She looked their way at that moment and they exchanged an intimate smile.

And Jordan felt something that might have been envy. If he were the type to play happy families. He'd learned he wasn't the hard way. He shoved his hands in his trouser pockets. 'I'm living proof that he's wrong. What's more, I'm going to prove it to him.'

'If anyone can, it's you.' Sadiq nodded encouragement. 'Still, it wouldn't hurt to have an advantage.'

'Like what?'

'Why don't you speak to Dana, check out Chloe's references?' A speculative gleam flicked briefly in his mate's eyes. 'Couldn't hurt.'

Frowning, Jordan studied him more closely. 'What do—?'

'What are you two looking so serious about?' Zahira appeared as if summoned by the couple's earlier exchange of glances and laid a hand on Sadiq's arm. 'This is no time for business talk—we've got a home-made party cake coming up. Tamara helped bake it and she's been looking forward to lighting the candles for weeks.' She looked about. 'I haven't seen her in a while. Do you know where she is?'

'I saw her heading in the direction of the cubby house with Chloe in tow,' Jordan said. He'd been watching Chloe all afternoon; he'd known exactly where she was at any given moment. He immediately turned in that direction. 'You two go ahead. I'll tell her she's been summoned.'

The little door was open and Tamara was still for once, utterly focused. They were cross-legged on the floor, facing each other, and Chloe was telling Tamara a story.

Jordan stilled too, equally intrigued, watching the way Chloe's small, slender hands moved as she talked. Listening to the vitality in her voice. Her flyaway hair was too messy for his taste, her eyes incongruously big in her small pixie face. But she could spin an adventure story out of thin air and make it sound believable. She could charm any age group. She could conquer high balconies and risky ropes at a moment's notice...

An impossible idea was coalescing at the back of his mind. Now the flicker of expression in Sadiq's eyes made some sort of sense. Didn't it?

Attraction aside, she wasn't the usual acquiescent kind of woman he dated, just as he very much doubted he was her type of guy—if she had a type. According to her, she didn't stay long in any one place so she'd probably never formed any close attachments. And that had to be an advantage because they could walk away at the end, no complications...

He smiled to himself. Not such an impossible idea. Chloe Montgomery might just be the up-for-anything kind of girl he needed.

CHAPTER FOUR

'...AND THE PRINCESS—'

'Princess *Chloe*,' Tamara corrected.

'Not Princess Tamara?'

'It has to be Chloe 'cos it's your story,' Tamara said, then took her crown off, reached across and set it on Chloe's head. 'And you have to wear this.'

'Oh. Thank you.'

Jordan relaxed against the cubby's frame even as his mind raced ahead with possibilities and potential problems.

'Okay, Princess *Chloe* wanted to learn to skateboard—'

'A pink skateboard. With sparkles.'

'Exactly.' She nodded. 'But her father the king wouldn't let her.'

'Why not?'

'Because he didn't understand his daughter. He thought she should be learning to do princessy things like practising her curtsey and learning how to wave. And he wanted her to be safe.

'So Princess Chloe left a note—so the king and queen wouldn't worry—and ran away from the palace. She sold her crown so she could buy food and journeyed to the far side of the kingdom with her sparkly skateboard to find someone who could teach her. She wanted people to like her because she was clever, not just because she was a princess.

'She was away for a long, long time,' Chloe continued. 'She knew that the king and queen would worry so she sent messages with the birds about what she was doing. She told them about the man she met who could spin straw into gold—'

'Like in Rumpelstiltskin?'

'Yes. And that she lived in a shining crystal tower. But when she fell out of the tower and had to live in the forest again she didn't tell them.'

'She didn't tell the troof?'

'No, Tamara, she didn't. And that was a very bad thing because one day a wicked witch came and took all the gold and the palace away from the king and queen and made them sleep in the stables with the horses. Princess Chloe found out and wanted to help.'

He wasn't hiding—still, Jordan felt as if he was eavesdropping on someone's private confession, but he couldn't tear himself away. Nor could he bring himself to interrupt Chloe's story to tell Tamara she was required for candle-lighting duties. Because the longer he listened, the more intrigued he became. Some gut instinct was telling him this was no ordinary fairy tale.

He watched her lean close to the child, blonde to brunette. 'She went home because they were her parents and she loved them and one day they'd get old and d— She'd miss them. On the way she met a handsome prince.'

Tamara nodded, approval sparkling in her eyes. 'Ooh, a *prince*.'

'He promised to help her find some real gold if she'd give him her skateboard. And she was so happy because now she could go home and take the palace back from the wicked witch and they could all live happily ever after.'

'With the prince too?'

'Ah, but he *wasn't* a prince, Tamara. He was an evil sorcerer in disguise. He turned her skateboard into a yucky slimy log.'

'Uh-oh...' Tamara clapped her hands to her cheeks in true drama mode. 'He didn't give her the gold?'

'No, he didn't. He put on his special invisible cloak and Princess Chloe didn't know where he'd gone...'

Chloe trailed off, suddenly aware that the light from the doorway had dimmed, and that they were no longer alone. Uncomfortable heat flooded her cheeks. She turned to see Jordan, one shoulder leaning on the doorjamb, hands in his tailor-made trouser pockets, his expensive-looking silk tie flapping in the breeze.

With his height and the cubby's elevation, his face was in her direct line of vision and he was making no secret of watching her. Or listening in. And judging by his preoccupied expression, he'd been there for some time. Thinking.

Thinking what? It had been too easy to put too much of herself into the story—a familiar habit, but not one she shared with others. Sweat sprang to her palms and she swiped them down the front of her jeans.

'What happened then?' Tamara demanded.

Jordan pushed away from the door. 'Tams, Mummy's looking for you. It's nearly time to light the candles.'

'Now?' She pursed her lips. 'But Chloe hasn't finished her story.'

'Tell you what,' Chloe said, while her mind whirled. 'Why don't *you* be the storyteller? Think about how it ends and tell me later.'

Tamara nodded. 'Okay. I've got to light the candles now.' She shot up off her cushion and ran to the door, launching herself at the man. 'Lift me down, Jordan.'

He swung her down with a chuckle. 'There you go.'

Which left Chloe alone in a cubby with no place to hide.

Not for long though because somehow Jordan squeezed through the doorway and took Tamara's place on the cushion.

He looked so incongruous against the mini furnishings, dominating the tiny space with his size, his masculine scent, his charisma. Under different circumstances, Chloe might have laughed. Or leaned in and got reacquainted with those lips. Instead, she sucked in air that suddenly seemed in short supply. 'What are you doing? The cake...'

'We've got a moment. They won't miss us.' He stared at her hair. 'It looks good on you, *Princess Chloe*.'

'What?' Oh. She pulled off Tamara's crown, set it aside, her laugh coming out hoarse and strained and fake. 'I love kids' stories, don't you? Kids' games are so much fun,' she rattled ahead as she pushed up onto her knees. 'I promised Tamara I'd watch—'

'She's got herself in a bit of a tight spot—the princess.'

The way he said it... *How much did he know?* Her heart skipped a beat. 'Yeah, but she's independent and clever, she'll find a way out. She'll win.' The game, the gold, the guy, it didn't matter. Right now, Chloe would settle for the gold.

'She should find herself a real prince and marry him,' Jordan said. 'Isn't that how the story should end?'

'Ah, but does she want to marry this real prince? He's not like her and she hardly knows him. Maybe he'll turn out to be the evil sorcerer's apprentice...'

'Or maybe he can help. Chloe.' He reached out, encircled her wrist with a warm hand. 'Stories aside, maybe *I* can help.'

'What do you mean? I don't need help—yours or anyone's.' She tried to pull her hand away but his grip firmed.

'I think you do.'

'Who are you to think what I need?' She lifted her chin and glared at him. 'Anyway, I don't know what you're talking about.'

'Come on, Chloe. You've spun enough fantasy for me to draw some very real conclusions. You're short on cash.'

He released her and she sank back down, clasping her hands around her knees and feeling like a deflated balloon. 'You should have made your presence known.'

'I wasn't hiding. You were too involved in your story to notice. Can we talk about this?'

'What's to talk about? I already told you, I don't need anything. Or anyone.'

'Give me a minute here, Chloe. I'm considering making you an offer I'd like you to think about.'

She regarded him warily. 'What kind of offer?'

'A partnership. A business partnership. With no risk on your part.'

'Well, *that* sounds risky for a start.' He continued watching her without speaking for a moment until her curiosity got the better of her. 'Why would you want to help me? You barely know me.'

'I reckon we can help each other,' he said slowly. 'You need money, right?' When she didn't answer, he continued. 'You're adventurous, you say you're up for a challenge, you enjoy travel. That makes you the right kind of girl to make what I have in mind work.' His gaze slid to her mouth. 'The fact that I'm attracted to you has nothing to do with it.'

She refused to melt into a mindless puddle of lust at the way his last huskily spoken words slid through her insides like sun-warmed treacle. 'You kissed me last night to make me feel bad.'

He lifted his darkening gaze to her eyes and the puddle grew to a lake. 'The next time I kiss you, I can promise you, you won't feel bad.'

She pressed her lips together to stop the sudden rush of blood there at the thought of an encore. She didn't doubt he was up to the task. If she let him. Which, she told herself, she didn't have a mind to, no matter how prettily he promised. He *had* made her feel bad with his arrogant assumption that she knew him. 'You didn't mention anything about kissing. You said business.'

His mouth twitched and what looked like humour danced in his eyes. 'So I did.'

She shut off all thoughts of carnal pleasure. 'Business is hardly my forte.'

He leaned closer so that all she could see was him. All she could smell was his musky scent. 'It doesn't need to be—it's mine. But I want to think on it before I decide, so I'd like you to have dinner with me tomorrow night. We could get better acquainted.'

His voice made her think of a still river with hidden depths. And something in his expression, something she recognised because she knew that feeling of desperation too, drew her interest. He pressed his advantage. 'How does seven p.m. suit you?'

She studied him a moment. The way his eyes changed from cobalt to denim to azure depending on the mood and the moment. The clean-shaven jaw that smelled pleasantly of some exotic aftershave, the modern spiky cut to his dark hair, the precise fit of his perfectly tailored clothes.

An evening out with a gorgeous guy—why not? And that was all it would be. 'Dinner, then.'

The following day Chloe worked a busy corporate luncheon, which didn't leave her time to think about the evening ahead or to quiz Dana about Jordan in a busy kitchen—except to learn that he was a long-standing friend and an absolute 'darling'. *Uh-huh*. No men Chloe knew had ever deserved that rep so she'd reserve judgement on that.

She made it back to the semi-detached house she shared

with a couple of flight attendants fifteen minutes before Jordan was due to pick her up.

And yes, he'd made it clear before he'd left for his meeting in the city yesterday afternoon that he intended picking her up, and in the end she'd given him her address and they'd swapped phone numbers. It was a given he'd have her references checked out with Dana before he offered whatever business partnership he had in mind.

Fine. She had glowing reports from her overseas employers. Nothing to hide. Unless... She shook her head determinedly. Almost impossible to trace—unless he was looking for a nanny. She'd been innocent, used. Betrayed.

Chloe threw on her seasons-old black dress of soft wool and pulled on matching leather boots while she searched for her clutch bag. She refreshed her make-up and ran a brush through her hair, deciding his gentlemanly insistence was appreciated in this instance.

Her quick search last night had revealed that Jordan Blackstone owned a gold mine in Western Australia. He was involved in some charity called Rapper One and, according to a recent magazine poll, was one of the country's most eligible bachelors. His love interests were plenty and varied and colourful, not to mention stunning and sophisticated, but it seemed there was nothing remotely dodgy about the man's business reputation.

And nothing remote about her body's response when she answered the knock on her door either. Yet another dark suit, expertly fitted and accentuating his broad shoulders, but tonight he wore a black shirt and tie, giving him a temptingly devilish air. Even his eyes looked black in the hallway's dim light.

'Hi,' she murmured in a breathy voice she hardly recognised. She felt herself sway towards his enticing scent and gripped the door handle tight to stop from grabbing his lapels and launching herself at him.

'Evening, Chloe.'

His smile... A sigh rose up her throat and her knees went weak. Had she forgotten the effect those lips had on her? 'Hang on...' *Water.* She dashed back to the kitchen and filled a glass, gulped it down.

She smoothed her dress, took a deep breath, then marched down the hall, her boots echoing briskly on the worn wood in time with the words in her head. *I am not going to fall for good looks and charm ever again.*

He was leaning against the doorjamb but straightened as she approached. His smile had worn off and he looked concerned, as if she might have changed her mind. 'Are you ready?'

'As I'll ever be.' She pulled the door shut behind them.

He gestured to his shiny car parked at the kerb. 'After you.'

She spent the short journey to the city on a razor's edge beside him, so flustered she couldn't remember what they talked about besides her busy day, yesterday's brunch. Melbourne's traffic.

The up-scale French restaurant was glamorous but intimate with cosy candle-lit alcoves. *'Bon soir, monsieur, mademoiselle.'* A polished waiter showed them to their private corner table, fussed over their napkins and poured water into glittering glasses. Jordan asked Chloe's wine preference, then ordered expensive champagne, which arrived almost before she'd finished speaking. The wine was poured, the bubbles fizzed. Lights danced over crystal and silver.

In the corner, a lone musician in a felt beret squeezed early-twentieth-century French tears out of a piano accordion, the soft sound reminding Chloe of a favourite brasserie in the heart of Paris.

Jordan raised his glass. 'To a successful evening.'

'*Bon appétit.*' She clinked her glass with his. The cold liquid tickled her throat on the way down.

'What do you fancy?' he asked, putting his glass down and reaching for his menu.

Was that a trick question?

But he showed no sign of meaning anything other than food, and, pushing erotic images from her mind, she cast her eyes quickly to the menu in front of her. *Concentrate on your* stomach, *Chloe.*

When they'd decided on their choices, Jordan signalled the waiter. '*Nous voudrions l'assiette des fruits et fondue de Brie pour les deux, s'il vous plaît. Pour le plat principal, mademoiselle voudrait le filet de saumon au beurre rouge et je voudrais l'entrecôte è la bordelaise.*' He placed the menu on the table. '*Merci.*'

The waiter inclined his head. '*Merci, Monsieur.*'

Chloe spoke French well enough but listening to Jordan speak it was like having the back of her neck stroked with rich velvet. She indulged in the sensation a moment before forcing her thoughts back to the reason she was eating expensive French cuisine without prices in the first place.

'So what's the deal here?'

He rotated the base of his wineglass on the cloth and met her eyes. 'I spoke with Dana today. With your references and what I've learned about you so far, I'm satisfied you're the best woman for the job.'

'Oh? And what if I don't want this *job*?'

'You will,' he said smoothly.

She took a sip of wine and studied him over the crystal rim. 'So confident?'

'I'm always confident.' He leaned forward slightly. 'For the record, though, how badly do you need cash, and just as important, why?'

She hesitated, then decided what the hell? She had nothing

to lose and maybe something to gain. 'My sister emailed me that my parents could lose the family home. They always put us kids first, sent us to the best schools and paid our tuition fees because they hadn't had the opportunity themselves and wanted it for us. I was the only one who disappointed them and now they're elderly. Donna expects me...'

They'd not been in touch for years except for birthdays and Christmas and Chloe had never got around to telling them about her humiliating breakup. 'I want to help.'

He nodded. 'Sounds reasonable. And I need someone to help me win a lucrative contract overseas. Which makes it perfect.'

'Huh?' She stared at him, incredulous. 'How can a woman with no business expertise possibly help you win an overseas contract?'

His voice was polished business professional. 'You'd accompany me to Dubai as my wife.'

Her mouth dropped open. 'Excuse me?'

'In return for a very large sum of money.'

In the ensuing silence she clamped her hands to her head to keep it from spinning away. 'How large?' she said, finally. Faintly.

She thought she saw a smile of satisfaction flicker at the corner of his mouth, then he named a figure that had her head spinning in the other direction. And it wasn't just the money; everything about this proposal had *dangerous* plastered all over it.

'You like to play games, Chloe, so let's play Mr and Mrs Jordan Blackstone for a couple of weeks.'

She almost choked on an invisible lump in her throat and all she could think was, 'Why?'

'Say yes and I'll explain.'

She shook her head. 'It's ridiculous. Impossible.'

'You're already married?'

'No. I just…can't up and go away with you.' *But that kind of money*, a tiny, desperate voice whispered. 'Dubai…?'

'Have you been there?'

'No.'

'But that adventurous girl would like to, right?' He nodded. 'Think about it, Chloe.'

Oh, she was. She surely was. Like how easy it would be to fall into another man's honeyed money trap.

'If you're worried about publicity, no one need know,' he assured her in a soothing tone.

'Oh, yeah? The media obviously loves you. What if they see us together and get snap happy?'

'I'll make sure they don't. I'm an expert at not being seen when I don't want to be seen.'

Ideas were tumbling inside her head. She was already calculating what she could do with that kind of money. First and foremost she could ensure her parents kept their home, with plenty left over. For once in her life she'd be the golden girl. This man could be the fabulous guy she'd told her parents about. *Win-win*.

She shook her head. Forget fabulous guy. *What* was she thinking? This man wasn't Stewart, nor was he ever going to meet her family. 'I only just met you. I may be a risk-taker but I'm not stupid.'

'No, you're not stupid—you're being cautious. We can discuss it, then—'

'Discuss it…'

His lucrative business contract.

A fortune in cash.

A fake marriage.

'Why would a wealthy, good-looking guy such as yourself consider such a drastic course of action with short, plain-speaking, plain-dressing Chloe Montgomery, I'd like to know? Surely you have plenty of willing candidates?'

'Don't put yourself down, Chloe, and others won't.' His blue eyes mesmerised her. 'I'm sure willing candidates abound, yes, but I pride myself on reading people. I need a woman with particular qualities and you tick all the boxes.'

She felt a strange warmth flow through her veins, as if he was paying her a compliment even though he hadn't resorted to the usual complimentary—and often empty—words. However, she said, 'I'm not going into this without all the facts I need to make an informed decision.'

He nodded. 'I have questions too.' He leaned forward, his eyes intense. 'Let's be absolutely clear here. This is a business arrangement. We'll both sign an agreement to that effect. If you decide not to go ahead, I ask that you keep what I'm about to say confidential. Are we agreed?'

'Okay.'

He talked to her about Rivergold Mining and honouring his father's last wishes. By the time he'd finished, their starters had arrived. The fact that he seemed to be upfront with no hidden agenda was reassuring.

Still… 'How long would this "marriage" thing have to last?'

'Just until the business deal's agreed on and we come home.'

She chewed on her lips a moment. 'I want the money up front.'

He regarded her steadily a moment, then withdrew a legal-looking document. 'Read this fully, sign both copies and I'll deposit half the agreed sum in your bank account. The rest will be deposited as soon as the deal's done.'

'You *were* confident,' she murmured, almost afraid to think about how carefully he'd planned this.

'I had my lawyer draw it up this afternoon,' he said as she skimmed the first page. 'If you'd like your lawyer to check it over—'

'I don't *have* a lawyer,' she stated, then tapped the paper—savvy business girl now. 'I want that first payment in my account *before* I sign.'

He shook his head. 'That's a substantial sum of money. You're not the only one being cautious here.' He spooned salad onto her plate beside the Brie tartlet. 'What would set your mind at ease?'

'I'm not sure anything will. And I'll tell you why.' She cut off a mouthful of the tempting tart in front of her. 'I trusted a man,' she began. 'He was a lot like you.'

'In what way?'

'The kind of guy women can't resist.'

One eyebrow lifted as he pulled his dinner roll apart. 'You've resisted *me*. Quite admirably, I'd say.'

She felt a smile touch her lips. 'You don't want to know what I was thinking when I opened my front door earlier.'

His gaze clashed with hers and heat met heat across the table. 'If it was anything like what I was thinking, we're going to get along very well.'

An image of them plastered together against her front door, bodies slick with sweat, sent heat rippling like teasing fingers through her lower regions. She almost moaned aloud and her cheeks flushed and she reached for her water. They had more to discuss here than the business arrangements. 'Umm…where was I?'

His eyes flirted, *Wherever it is, I'd like to be there with you*, but, 'Mr Irresistible…' was what he said.

'Ah, yeah. Markos. Call him Mr Despicable.' She cast her mind back to a time not so long ago. A time she'd rather forget but one she needed to remember, particularly given tonight's circumstances and the mission in front of her if she chose to accept. 'A friend's family died in tragic circumstances while she was overseas and it made me think about how long I've been gone… I had some money saved up but I wanted to be able to have enough to show them I'd been successful…'

He watched her without speaking, and neither did she as the mains arrived and the waiter refilled their glasses.

'Why?' he asked when they were alone again.

'My family judges success by how many letters you have after your name and your well-paid *professional* career. I judge success by happiness and how you live your life. It's never been about money for me.'

'And they just didn't get you.'

But he did, she thought, relieved. 'No. Maybe I was home-sick after what happened with Ellen's family and I just wanted to be the person they want me to be for once.'

He drank some champagne, then said, 'Back to Mr Despicable…'

She forked up some of the flaked salmon. 'You heard my story yesterday.' She'd been so stupid, so naive. '"Prince" Markos turned out to be an evil sorcerer. The princess needed money and he was an acquaintance.

'He offered her an investment that promised a quick return. He tricked the princess into parting with what little cash she had, then disappeared. I had barely enough to get me home, let alone a job or accommodation…' *Trust me, Chloe.*

'And you haven't told your family you're back yet.'

She shook her head. *This* man, however—rather, his *offer*—would change her life. Her boss trusted him so she was prepared to take the risk. The only way from here was up, right?

Chloe pushed her half-finished plate to one side, reached for the documents and slid them in front of her. The terms were mostly straightforward. She looked up, met his eyes. 'This clause here…'

'…is saying I won't force myself on you. And the consequences if I did.'

He leaned in so that all she could see were his eyes. No bedroom heat in those brilliant blues right now but they were clear and honest and reassuring.

'What we have is a business arrangement,' he reiterated quietly. 'We'll need to share a room and act like newlyweds up to a point, bearing in mind that in Dubai public displays of affection are unacceptable. But trust me, Chloe Montgomery, winning this contract is worth more to me than—'

Sex. 'You don't need to spell it out, Mr Blackstone. I understand clearly.' *And a golden fortune in compensation if he breaks it.*

So why did his matter-of-fact reassurance that she wasn't at the top of his 'to-do' list somehow disappoint her? 'For the record, if we were to…' She trailed off, flustered as heat bled into her cheeks.

His eyes darkened. 'Take things further?' The way he said it, all smooth and chocolaty. After-dinner delights…

'Forget it.' Chloe pushed the words out before he could respond, digging into her bag and pulling out a pen. Did she sound desperate and dateless or what? She scribbled her signature on both copies, pushed them back to him without looking at him.

Of course abstinence would be the wisest decision, she told herself, studying her hands on the tablecloth. She wasn't a woman who shied away from a man she found attractive, but getting involved on an intimate level with a man she was entering into a business partnership with was fraught with all kinds of danger. Even if that partnership was a faked marriage.

Especially if it was a faked marriage…

Jordan signed too, then tapped into his smartphone. 'Do you have your bank details handy?'

CHAPTER FIVE

WHILE HE STIRRED the froth on his coffee, Jordan watched the girl who'd agreed to help for any sign of how she was feeling. No visible emotion. She was scrolling through her phone options as if he didn't exist. Checking her account balance? International flight schedules to Ibiza or Acapulco? She hadn't so much as glanced at him since she'd signed the documents.

A fleeting self-doubt wrapped around his gut. What was stopping her from doing a moonlight flit with his money tonight? He'd learned not to trust so easily a long time ago, especially where women were concerned; they could literally take off at a moment's notice. And the enormity of this gamble was taking on the proportions of the Hindenburg, with the same potential for disaster.

For God's sake, stop second-guessing yourself. He might have just met her but he knew Chloe was no Lynette.

All that aside, he needed to get them both to Dubai ASAP. He also wanted to keep her with him 24/7 until the deal was done, but he knew that wasn't likely. And he didn't want to spook her by being too full-on and risk the deal going wrong.

On the other hand, she'd told him money wasn't a motivator, and, from the expression in her eyes when she'd said it, he believed her. He'd seen firsthand that she was the sort who was willing to step in and help out in a pinch—for her employer and her family…and Jordan too.

Trust issues aside, it was blatantly obvious she was as attracted to him as he was her and he was hoping they might mix a little pleasure with their business. There was nothing in the agreement to prevent that, provided both parties were willing. He reached for his own mobile. 'We should get some details out of the way tonight.'

'Hmm…'

'Do you have any commitments over the next few weeks?'

She finally looked up from her phone. 'Dana's just given me full-time work, so, yes, I do.'

'Apart from that.' He sent Roma, his PA in Perth, an email confirming his schedule. 'Can you be ready to leave tomorrow?'

It didn't sound like a question and she blinked. 'You're kidding, right? I just told you, I've got a new job. I'm trying to be responsible.'

'That's very commendable, but I'm paying you to be responsible with *me*. Our business has priority over everything else. That includes your social life, by the way.'

She raised a brow. 'It's fortunate then that I have no upcoming social events on my personal calendar, isn't it?'

He frowned. He didn't know why he'd made that brusque demand. Except that he didn't want anything or anyone interfering with his plans, which included having Chloe exclusively to himself for the next week or two. He was confident it wasn't going to be all work and no play. 'I'll make sure Dana holds your position,' he said more reasonably. 'That's if you still want it when we come back.'

'Of course I'll want it.'

Her quick and definite response surprised him. It wasn't exactly a highly paid sought-after career move they were talking about.

'I don't have any paper qualifications so I'm limited in choices,' she said, as if reading his thoughts. 'I never studied.'

He caught a wistfulness in her tone. 'You'd have liked to?'

'Yeah. Maybe counselling.' A wry smile tipped one corner of her mouth. 'Even if it's just to understand myself better. And you need to be settled in one place and I don't know if I can after all this time. Staying power, perseverance and tenacity are not my strengths.'

'But in a couple of weeks you'll have the money to make it happen.'

'Yes,' she said, almost as if startled by the revelation. 'I suppose I will. I've never had my own money—not *money* money. And this is like...wow...'

Her dreamy expression lingered as if she was already wishing herself far far away. *Staying power wasn't one of her strengths.* 'Very well, you've got tomorrow to get organised.' While he finalised travel arrangements and his business plan with Qasim. He signalled the waiter for the bill.

'Hang on...' She cleared her phone's screen. 'We're not going home already, surely? We don't know nearly enough about each other yet. Or how to do this...thing...'

Exactly.

He nodded. 'It could take a while.' *This thing* needed careful consideration and exploration. 'It could take all night.' His voice suddenly sounded lower than his belt buckle—which was no surprise given where his thoughts were leading—and Chloe noticed too because she looked at him sharply, those whisky eyes splashed with awareness.

'To make plans,' he clarified, not taking his gaze off hers.

'And get better acquainted,' she agreed, staring back and shifting forward in her chair. A hint of inviting cleavage caught his attention as she rested her forearms on the table ready to begin.

He liked the prospect of getting better acquainted. A lot. He leaned closer so he could smell that scent of cinnamon, citrus and jasmine that was fast becoming one of his favourites. 'We'll be more comfortable at home. We could go to my apartment, but yours is closer. Is it okay if we go there?'

'I only have a single bed...' She gave a little hiccup and shook her head, looking dismayed. 'Omigod. Did I say that aloud? That's not what I meant.' Pause while she blinked at him. 'Is that what *you* meant? Not that I was thinking about bed—not in that way. Because this is a *business* arrangement. I get that. We need to talk. I need to pack. I probably won't have time to sleep at all—'

'Chloe.' He kept his smile on the inside. 'Take a deep breath.'

She stared at him another beat, then closed those panicked eyes and sucked in air deeply. Exhaled in one long slow stream.

He took the opportunity for a leisurely all-out perusal of her face and he couldn't decide which he wanted to kiss more—her pulse doing star jumps at the base of her throat, or the scattering of freckles across her nose. After reacquainting himself with those plump, pouty lips, that was.

When she opened her eyes again, she seemed to have regained some composure, but she wasn't looking at him, she was staring at the tablecloth. 'I tend to go on when I'm stressed or excited or...plotting fake marriages.' She blew out a strangled-sounding breath, dropped her phone into her purse. 'Let's just get out of here.'

What had she done?

Chloe chewed her lower lip as Jordan pulled up outside her place. Suggesting getting better acquainted in that smoky, siren's voice she'd never heard coming out of her mouth before?

Then the bit about her single bed had literally popped out. She stifled a groan. *Because* he'd been talking about how it might take all night and being more comfortable and...and looking at her as if he wanted to devour her at the earliest opportunity, and her focus on the trip had got muddled up with a sexual fantasy and *how was she going to keep things strictly business?*

She'd never had a problem compartmentalising the men in her life. With one past regrettable exception, it was either business or pleasure—simple and uncomplicated. Her male acquaintances either fitted in one or the other.

Until Jordan.

He switched off the engine. Silence and anticipation thickened the air. Not hanging around to see if he'd try a squeeze or a kiss; she was already out and halfway up the path when she heard Jordan's car door shut and the alarm's *meep.* Her shoes tapped a staccato on the pavement, oddly loud and a tad desperate in the quiet suburban evening.

The scent of damp leaves and smoky log fires gave way to old wood and last night's reheated tandoori chicken as she pushed open the front door—the front door she'd imagined them naked against. Her fingers clenched around her keys and, instead, she imagined telling him she'd changed her mind and shutting it in his face.

She tried telling herself good looks and sex appeal were nothing. *Nothing.* They didn't influence Chloe Montgomery. Except Jordan was already on her doorstep, towering over her and making her swallow those lying, superficial and *treacherous* thoughts.

She realised she'd already partially closed the door on him. 'Sorry,' she murmured, motioning him in. 'My mind's everywhere tonight.'

'I imagine it is,' he said, stepping inside.

Up close, his sheer size in the cramped, dim foyer, lit only from the street lamp slanting through the glass door panels, accentuated their height difference. All her life she'd hated her lack of stature and accompanying feelings of insignificance. Yet somehow Jordan made her feel small and feminine and *not* insignificant in any way.

Not good if she was going to maintain her distance and keep things on a business level. She should have insisted on the safer option of conducting their conversation in its entirety at the restaurant. She'd been too quick to allow him to take control. 'Another coffee?' she asked, flicking on the passage light as she turned away and headed to the kitchen.

'Yes, please. Chloe, wait up.' A firm hand closed over her shoulder and he turned her to face him. 'You're not afraid of me, are you?' Both hands were on her shoulders now, his thumbs drawing tight little circles.

'Me? Afraid? Of you?' She choked out a half-laugh.

'Nervous as a kitten in a tiger's cage since we signed the paperwork.'

There was a lot more truth to that image than she wanted to think about. Jordan radiated that big-cat power and dominance—she could feel it tingling through his fingers and deep along her collarbones, turning them and every other extremity to rubber.

And so help her, Chloe Montgomery, who refused to allow others to dictate her life, who strenuously avoided the type of testosterone-fuelled, take-charge man that was Jordan, wanted to surrender to all that male dominance. Craved more of his lips on hers—and wherever else he wanted to put them—again.

She stiffened her spine and took a deliberate step away, only to end up with her back against the wall. Had she learned nothing in the past couple of years? 'It's myself I'm nervous of—if that makes sense.'

'Yeah. It does.' The massage stopped and he trailed his hands lightly over her shoulders, down her arms and up again, his eyes staring into hers with a smile that matched his mouth.

'You can't keep your thoughts off us getting naked together either.'

A distressed sound bubbled up her throat and fiery heat exploded into her cheeks. Was it that obvious?

'And how it's going to be when I come deep inside you,' he went on in a kind of murmur that swept up Chloe's spine like a big tabby cat's hot, wet tongue, making her shiver—in a dangerously delicious way. 'But that's not what we're about, not what we've agreed on, and it bothers you.'

'No, I… Yes…' This whole one-sided, erotic conversation *bothered* her.

And the fact that somehow, without her noticing, he'd moved closer so that the front of his shirt was brushing against her bodice while her useless arms hung limp. Only her fingers curled and uncurled at her sides.

He toyed with the tips of her hair as if he'd never seen fair hair before. 'Rest easy, Blondie, it'll be *you* inviting *me*,' he assured her, his deep voice resonating against her breasts and making her nipples tight and achy.

'*Me* inviting *you*.'

A slow confident smile spread across his features. 'You're worried about how that's going to work. Trust me, it'll work just fine.'

Trust me, Chloe.

'I am *not* worried because I intend to stay away from you as much as possible. And don't call me Blondie.'

'What will I call you, then? We should have pet names for each other, don't you think?'

'No. And there's that clause in the agreement that states—'

'We're not talking coercion here, *Blondie*,' he said smoothly. 'And we both know it.'

Drawing herself up taller, she dared to meet his blue-eyed intensity, but only succeeded in bumping up against another bit that she was sure hadn't been there a moment ago…and she froze, which was odd since she felt so, so hot. 'It's strictly business—you said so yourself.' Her words were crisp, cool and PA efficient to counteract the heat emanating between their bodies. 'You laid out the terms very clearly.'

'That's true.' Leaning down, he traced the neckline of her dress with a finger. 'Just because we have a business arrangement, doesn't mean it has to be all work. We can still keep it professional—' he removed his finger from the top of her dress and placed his palm flat on the wall beside her head '—but there's no reason we can't make it a bit of a holiday as well.'

She stared up at him, hair burnished teak by the suspended old-gold light in the foyer, not trusting herself to argue with his thought process. But a holiday fling? With one's business partner? *And* keep it professional? Wasn't going to happen.

She lifted her chin. 'You said our arrangement had nothing to do with the fact that you were attracted to me.'

'It doesn't.' He grinned, revealing even white teeth. 'We'll keep business and personal separate.'

'So what's this evening about, then? The *now* part of this evening.'

'Getting better acquainted.' His gaze slid to her lips. 'Isn't that what you said earlier?'

'I… Yes.' Didn't have to mean anything sexual, right? Of course they needed to get to know each other better. She could feel her legs giving way, her back sliding down the wall. 'But I don't think kissing's a good idea…'

'Why not? We really need to practise if we're to pull off the newlyweds charade.'

'No PDA's in Dubai, remember, so it's *really* not necessary. Since we won't be kissing in public. Or anywhere else…'

'But it'll give us that aura of implied intimacy. You know that look you see between two people that signals to the rest of the world that they're lovers?'

Her head bobbed once. 'Uh-huh…' Just as she recognised the look he was giving her now signalled *Danger: Intimacy Ahead.*

'Whisky eyes.' His breath feathered over her lips as he looked at her, his cobalt eyes dark with desire. 'I could get intoxicated just looking at them.'

'Seductive words.' And she refused to be seduced so easily. 'So were you intoxicated the last time you kissed me?'

'Stone-cold sober, as a matter of fact. And it was hardly a kiss.'

And she'd have agreed with him no matter how devastatingly intimate the kiss had seemed at the time, but before she could get a word out his mouth pounced on hers. Bold, predatory and without warning.

Reacting on instinct, her hands rushed up to push at his chest—to push him away—but her fingers had a mind of their own; they clutched at his jacket lapels and held on tight. Forget keeping her distance—how could she push him away when right now she wanted his mouth on hers more than air? Her eyes slid shut.

He deepened the kiss and she answered, her lips parting willingly beneath his demanding tongue. His taste was dark and rich, smooth and velvety—a moan rose up her throat—those *after-dinner delights* she'd been thinking of earlier and then some.

He dragged his hands down her sides, over her waist, the flare of her hips. Lower. Big hands spreading across her buttocks, tucking her in close, so that she could feel the hot, hard length of him.

Heat and sizzle and danger. It was like being swept up in a forest fire and her entire body was turning to flame. She might have tried again to stop him and to make some sense of…whatever this was, but her brain was frazzled from all the heat and the message wasn't getting through to her limbs.

He lifted his lips a fraction. 'Now *that's* a kiss,' he murmured. She felt his hands lift away from her body, coolness drifting in to take their place. She pried her heavy-lidded eyes open to see him staring down at her, a gleam in his gaze that had nothing to do with the hall light's reflection.

Ah... 'Mmm-hmm.' She cleared the sigh from her throat and admitted, 'That's a kiss all right...' Pressing her tingling lips together, she kept her back propped against the wall, still captive beneath his gaze. 'I just need to...' *breathe*. 'I need time. To think.' If she still had any brain cells left intact, that was.

'Think fast, then. We're booked on the evening flight out tomorrow night. It's non-stop, which gives us roughly forty hours before we arrive in Dubai.'

'What?' She felt some of her precious independence trickle away. 'You booked before I agreed,' she shot at him.

'I was—'

'Confident,' she snapped. 'Yes, I get that.'

He nodded, his eyes smiling. 'It pays to think positive.'

She glared. 'You even asked if I had prior commitments. You had no intention of letting me honour them, did you?'

No response. Conversation over. His body heat mingled with musky male scent and suddenly he was too close, the space between them too confining, and she shuffled to one side.

He remained still, allowing her to step away. But she knew tigers were motionless just before they moved in for the kill. She tore her eyes free and moved as swiftly as her rubber legs allowed towards the kitchen.

She heard Jordan's heavy footsteps on the floorboards. His dark flavour lingered on her lips, her tongue. 'Coffee,' she muttered, then over her shoulder, 'We don't have a coffee machine. It's instant or nothing.'

'Instant's fine,' he said, all easy-to-please, but she could feel his eyes on her back and something potent and irresistible shivered down her spine. That big tabby cat tongue again.

She slowed at the doorway to the lounge room and gestured inside without looking at him. 'Why don't you make yourself comfortable in there? Put the heater on if you want. I won't be long.'

Jordan sank onto the couch but he was hardly comfortable. With the way his body reacted to this woman, he wondered if he'd ever be comfortable again. A way too full-on, over-the-top response for a girl who wasn't supposed to be his type.

The last thing he needed was a gas wall furnace; what he needed was a cold shower. He tried focusing on his surroundings. A couple of mismatched armchairs, coffee table covered in a Christmas print cloth and topped with an untidy pile of magazines. Travellers' photos on the walls; presumably her house-mates', the flight attendants. Nothing in the room said Chloe. Maybe she'd not had time to put her mark on the place or maybe she never stopped long enough to make a place home.

Despite her insistence that she loved her solo lifestyle, he found the thought of her alone and itinerant for so long a little sad. Her words and actions proved she also believed family was important despite how they'd treated her. He found that sad as well.

'Couldn't remember if you take sugar.'

He turned at the sound of her voice. 'I gave it up.'

'Good for you.' She handed him a cup, then moved to the gas heater mounted on the wall. 'You're not cold?'

'No, but go ahead if you are. Or you could come over here.' He patted the empty space beside him.

'I think we both know that's not a good idea.' Her eyes swirled with more of that heated awareness but beneath it he saw a reserve, a barrier, that hadn't been there before he'd kissed her against that wall. She stood in front of the grille, hugging her mug to her lips while the heater powered up. 'When I mentioned "getting acquainted", I meant everyday things we should know about each other like…'

'Family,' he said for her. 'You can start.'

'Okay,' she said slowly. 'I have a brother and a sister, both much older than me. Donna's married to Jason, an accountant, and they have a teenage son. She has a degree in arts and another in classical studies but she's been a stay-at-home mum for the past fifteen years. Caleb's a physio with a degree in architecture on the side and married to Jenny, his receptionist, who's studying natural medicine.'

Wow. Academic over-achievers, all of them. No wonder Chloe felt she didn't fit in. He frowned as something occurred to him. 'Donna's the one expecting your financial rescue package?'

Chloe sipped her coffee, then nodded. 'She's the one who kept in contact, as infrequent as that is.'

'So tell me something,' he said, slowly. 'With two older siblings, why is the onus on you to bail the parents out?'

'Caleb's mother-in-law's a widow, she's terminally ill and he's footing the medical bills. Brother-in-law, Jason, the accountant who should know better, lost his money in a failed business venture last year. Donna's "looking for suitable work".' She shrugged. 'Donna's been "looking for suitable work" for the past ten of those fifteen years.' She raised her mug towards him. 'Your turn.'

'You know about Dad. My mother's not in my life and I'm an only child.'

She studied him over the rim of her mug. 'You're going to need to do better than that.'

The old bad lodged in his gut, the familiar lead ball he'd carried around since childhood. He didn't want to talk about the woman who'd given birth to him. Ina was nothing to him.

She didn't exist. But he couldn't ignore the fact that she was married to the man who wanted this deal as much as Jordan.

His emotions must have showed because her eyes turned soft and compassionate. 'I'm sorry, Jordan, if it's a painful topic for you, but I need to know more if we're going to do this thing. Is she...?'

She trailed off awkwardly and Jordan helped her out. 'Ina's alive and doing very nicely for herself.' Jaw tight, he filled Chloe in on his mother's second marriage with the owner of his business rival. He did *not* delve further into their relationship and was relieved when Chloe didn't push it.

'I'm understanding more about why this is all so important to you,' she said, still watching him with those liquid sympathy eyes. 'I'm sorry you and your mum can't get on.'

He'd never seen that look directed at him before. Or maybe he'd never looked for it. He wasn't looking for it now; it was just...there. Was he seeing more in Chloe's eyes than he saw in other women's? Which begged the question, why? He wasn't sure he wanted to know.

He did know that he didn't want sympathy, didn't want what it stirred up inside him, or the associated feelings that came with it. 'I like to win.'

It wasn't revenge or even satisfaction he was seeking. This deal with Dubai was about honouring his father and closure. Chloe nodded. 'And I like to finish what I start.'

As long as it doesn't take too long, he finished for her. Frankly, the fact that she liked to finish things surprised him.

So, this little adventure wouldn't take long and the reward was huge, for both of them. He pushed up from the couch and raised his mug in salute. 'We *will* win this, Chloe.'

She raised her mug too, and smiled, her eyes alive with enthusiasm. 'Dubai, here we come.'

CHAPTER SIX

'HOW NEWLYWED ARE we talking?' Chloe asked when they got down to business ten minutes later. She'd unearthed a notepad from the kitchen and was committing their ideas to paper for future reference. She'd drawn up two columns: one for plans—flights, accommodation, sightseeing she intended to get in while she was there; the other for 'getting acquainted'. Such as background and personal details, real and invented. It kept her hands busy, her eyes down and also helped her to keep everything on a professional level.

'We're combining business with our honeymoon.'

A small smile hooked the corner of her mouth. 'That doesn't make you a very good husband.'

'But you're a very supportive wife and you understand my commitment to business. Besides, once you'd manipulated me into popping the question, you didn't want to wait another day.'

Manipulated? She did look up at him then and noticed a tightening around his mouth, which transformed into a lopsided grin when he caught her staring at him.

'But I'm happy you did, Blondie,' he assured her quickly.

'Yeah? For how long?' She couldn't imagine anyone manipulating Jordan but the stormy depths of his gaze told her someone had tried.

'Eternity. Right?'

She narrowed her eyes. 'Have you been married before?'
'No.'

Do I look stupid? She received his message loud and clear. His blatant cynicism annoyed her. 'You'd better change that attitude before we get there or it'll be game over before we start,' she said, frowning back at her notes. 'Seriously.'

'I am serious. How can you doubt it after the time and effort and expense I'm putting in to make it happen?'

'Right.' She wrote COMMITMENT PHOBIC in her 'getting acquainted' column. She believed in marriage when two people loved and trusted each other and were committed to making it work. But after Stewart, she didn't believe that she personally could do the trust or even the long-term bit. Or maybe she was afraid to believe.

Did that make her as commitment phobic as him? she wondered momentarily. Not at all, she told herself. She wasn't phobic, just…careful. Right?

'I'm also serious about sharing a little pleasure around the business aspect,' he said.

'Well, maybe I'm not.' She added APPROACH AT OWN PERIL to the list and slapped her notepad shut.

'You were enjoying it fine a few moments ago.' His eyes dared her to take issue with the inconvenient truth.

'You didn't give me time to…to change my mind,' she said, dismissing their kiss. 'I wasn't ready.'

'You've been ready since the last time we bumped lips.' Bracing his forearms on his knees, he gave her that sexy grin that made her want to throw herself onto the couch next to him and beg him to do it again.

'No.'

'Come on, you were curious. And it was good, right?'

She exhaled through her nostrils. 'Okay. Fine. It was good.'

'As good as you expected?'

He just had to keep pushing, didn't he? 'It was right up

there with white-water rafting, New Year's Eve sky shows and soft-centre chocolates. Satisfied?'

'Not nearly.'

'But it's not going to happen again,' she went on, tapping her notebook with her pen. 'It muddies our business relationship.'

His grin widened. 'I disagree. Our business relationship is about making our "recent marriage" look legitimate to our target audience.'

'We can still do that. *I* can still do that. It's what you're paying me for.' Which reminded her—the purpose of tonight's meeting. 'Think of me as a conservative, no-nonsense, PA...'

'Hard to imagine when none of those labels suit you.'

'Then *don't* think or imagine, just listen and discuss.' Flipping open her notepad again, she clicked her pen. 'Accommodation—'

'Already taken care of.' He grinned, the lines around his eyes crinkling. He shrugged when she glared. 'Can't help it—I do like an enthusiastic partner.'

An image played behind her eyes. A very active, very inappropriate image. *He means business partner, Chloe.* Didn't he? 'I... You're making this difficult.'

'Tell you what, we can go over this tomorrow evening at the airport or onboard our flight,' he said, setting his mug on the coffee table in front of him. 'It's late. We'll call it a night.'

She let out a sigh. 'You don't know how relieved I am to hear that. I have so much to organise. To pack.'

But her entire wardrobe fitted into one large suitcase and her relief was short-lived. The Jordan Blackstone she'd seen online dated stunning, statuesque women who knew how to dress to impress. He'd have been better off choosing someone with a sense of fashion who already knew the role to play the part. 'I'm not a fashionista—I'm more of a jeans and T-shirt kind of girl. What am I expected to wear?'

'We'll have a day to shop when we get there.' He rose, pulling a bunch of keys from his trouser pocket and drawing her attention to where it shouldn't be drawn. 'I'll call you in the morning.'

She followed his broad shape down the hall, trying not to admire the back of his tanned neck below the neat trim of dark hair. That earlier anticipation was sparking again, like two live wires touching.

Was he going to try to kiss her good night?

Was she going to let him?

But he opened the door then leaned close, kissed her chastely on the cheek. ''Night, Blondie.' He stepped out into the evening.

''Night…' She felt like a teenager, giddy with first-date fever, hanging on to the doorframe and wishing he'd come back and kiss her again, properly this time. 'And thanks for the wonderful dinner.'

His playful gaze didn't waver but a hint of something more intimate infused the cerulean with shades of midnight, making her heart leap beneath her breastbone.

'The first of many wonderful things,' he said, jingling his keys in his hand. 'Now get some sleep.'

She intended to. She had a feeling she was going to need it. *The first of many wonderful things*. His words—a promise?— danced in her head like sugar plum fairies. It was going to be next to impossible to keep her mind focused where it needed to be.

It was going to be next to impossible to keep his mind focused where it needed to be. Jordan lowered his window and let the winter's damp chill wrap around his neck as he drove back to his apartment. Perhaps it would help cool his blood and redirect it to his brain instead of his groin.

For God's sake.

He barely noticed that the view of Melbourne's CBD through his windscreen was blurred with rain—he was too preoccupied with thinking about the way Chloe's hair had felt against his fingers. Its cool, delicate fragrance and how it would feel brushing low over his belly as she—

Damn. He blew out a disgusted breath, shifting in his seat and tightening his grip on the wheel. He'd never had trouble focusing and he wasn't starting now. Chloe Montgomery might be his current red-hot fantasy but she was a means to an end and he was forgetting what was important here. She was being paid to play a role, and with her help he was finally going to settle an old debt.

But he recalled her stunned surprise when he'd planted that first proper kiss on her soft lips and couldn't help the smile that touched his mouth. The delightful way she'd tried to push away only to change her mind. The feel of her firm breasts against his chest. Her taste—sweet and spice and everything nice.

He turned into his apartment complex's underground parking. The security door rose with a hum. Not the only thing humming, he thought, still smiling, as he drove through then manoeuvred into his parking spot. He couldn't wait for tomorrow evening. To see her again. To be on his way. To move forward with the next stage of his life.

Yeah, everything about this trip was going to be sweet.

Dawn was grey with a dusky pink glow, the city's twinkling blanket of lights spread out below when Jordan embarked on a rigorous morning workout a few sleepless hours later.

In the interim, he'd spoken at length with Qasim and everything was arranged with their meeting in two days' time.

He'd confirmed the accommodation, the best that money could buy, and organised a driver to be on call while they were there.

He was cycling hard and going nowhere to the beat of his favourite rock band when a lemon sun, partially obscured by high-rises, lifted into the sky at seven-thirty. Through his gym's floor-to-ceiling glass, Jordan watched the caterpillars of traffic below crawl along and figured Chloe should be up by now.

Still pedalling, he disconnected his music, scrolled to her number and turned his phone on loudspeaker.

She answered on the second ring—''Lo'—filling the room with her husky, sleepy, too-close-for-comfort murmur.

'You're not still in bed, are you?'

A pause, followed by a shushing, shifting, tantalisingly erotic sound that seemed to reach through the speaker to stroke his crotch. 'Why?'

Why? Because he didn't want her to be still in bed *because* he didn't want to imagine her still warm and soft with sleep, firm flat tummy exposed beneath rumpled flannelette pyjamas. He stepped up his pace on the bike and said, 'I took you for an early riser.'

'Did you? Why?'

Hell if he knew. 'So you're not?'

'Not what?' Breathless pause. 'In bed?'

'No—an early riser.' He blew out a harried breath. 'Are you still in bed or not?'

'No. Actually I've just stepped out of the shower.'

Naked. Worse, much worse. She was naked, and the shifting sound was more like a rubbing sound now that he knew it had to be a towel. Against heat-pinkened flesh. He let out a long, low groan.

'Are you okay?' she said sharply. 'What are you doing?'

'You shouldn't ask a man that question first thing in the

morning when you're naked and rubbing yourself with a towel.'

He heard a slight catch of breath then, 'Oh… *Oh*.'

'I'm riding a bike, Chloe.' And damn uncomfortable it was, too.

'Where?'

'Home gym. I'd invite you over for breakfast,' he said, dismounting and heading to his en-suite, 'but the traffic's chaos.'

'I've eaten already.'

So she was a step ahead of him. 'Flannelette pyjamas,' he murmured, toeing off his trainers along the way.

'What?'

'Never mind.' He turned his attention to more immediate matters as he stripped down and flung his jocks in the laundry basket. 'We need to shop this morning. I'll drop by around twelve. Be packed, we won't be going home after.'

'I thought we were going shopping in Dubai?'

'There's something we need to get before we leave.'

'Twelve's okay…but—'

'I'll see you then,' he told her before she could quiz him further, and disconnected.

He padded back to his bedroom for a change of clothes. He had two more calls to make. 'Hey,' he replied when Sadiq answered. 'Hope I'm not catching you at an inconvenient time?'

'On my way out but I was going to call you later this morning anyway since I hadn't heard from you. What's happening with Dubai?'

'Yeah. I've talked with Qasim again. The meeting's all set and I'll be flying out later this evening.'

'Sounds promising.'

Jordan pulled a caramel toffee-coloured jumper from a drawer. 'I'm taking Chloe with me.'

'Chloe.' Jordan could almost hear Sadiq's ears prick up.

'I took your advice.'

'So you're stealing her away from Dana?' Sadiq chuckled. 'Dana won't be pleased—Chloe's her new favourite worker.'

'I'll write dear Dana a cheque to cover a fill-in temp's wages for a couple of weeks—she'll be pleased enough.'

'How did you manage it?' Sadiq queried. 'Chloe didn't look too happy to see you at Sunday brunch. Did you work the Blackstone charm again?'

Jordan rifled through his sock drawer for his favourites, tossing a couple of orphans on the floor in the process. 'I simply made her an offer she couldn't refuse.'

'And...'

'Let's just say we have an arrangement.'

'Sounds...cosy.'

'A business arrangement. And not for public knowledge.' Not even Sadiq need know the details, except Jordan had the feeling the man had it figured out already. 'Not a word to anyone, my trusted friend,' he cautioned as he headed for the shower. 'I want the press kept well out of it.' He paused. 'And if Qasim and you talk at any stage and I happen to come up in conversation...just play along with whatever he says, okay?'

'Aah.'

Perceptive man, Sadiq. 'Thanks. Gotta go.'

'Good luck.'

Chloe was out on the veranda with her travel-battered bag by eleven forty-five. She'd left a note for her absent house-mates on the kitchen table along with the next rent payment in cash. With her new-look bank balance that she was still getting used to, it had been easy peasy.

She'd also deposited a five-figure amount in her parents' account and it had only made a small dent in the overall balance. The knowledge blew her away. And there was still the other half of the payment expected at the end.

An icy wind snuck in under the roof and around the veranda posts, chilling her face, but she rubbed sweaty palms down her jeans. This trip was a whole new experience, like a scary fun park ride in a new dimension.

Dana had rung a couple of hours ago to wish her a successful trip. Chloe had detected a knowing smile in her boss's voice when she'd told her to 'take care and enjoy yourself'.

What had Jordan said to the woman? Or had Dana just assumed Chloe would be bowled over by his charm and ready to run off with him at the drop of a hat? She told herself as long as her job was still available when she came back, she didn't care what Dana assumed.

She was checking her watch for the zillionth time when a luxury car pulled up. Jordan unfolded his long body from the front passenger seat and stepped out to open the rear door. Dark glasses shielded his eyes. His caramel V-neck jumper over an open brown shirt and well-worn jeans that clung to his butt like a denim glove elicited a soft sigh of feminine appreciation from Chloe as she walked down the short path to the gate.

'Morning.' He smiled—a tempting smile that reminded her all over again of last night's kiss—and raised a hand in greeting. The wind tossed his hair so that it stood up in short tufts on top of his head.

'Morning.' She'd not seen him in casual clothes before. He almost looked like a different man—more accessible, more fun perhaps, than the corporate suited guy she was still getting acquainted with—but no less impressive. Or gorgeous, or sexy. Or beddable.

Bad thought, very bad thought. She mentally berated herself and whisked her trolley bag to the kerb. There was going to be none of that. She exchanged greetings with the uniformed driver as he loaded her bag into the boot.

'Right on time.' Jordan gestured her into the car.

'You sound surprised,' she said, climbing in.

'More like pleased.' He shut the door, rounded the boot, and climbed in beside her on the other side. Even though the car was more like a limo, his long legs took up most of the floor space, leaving her to cram up alongside. Or maybe he'd just engineered it that way.

'You make it sound as if men are the only ones capable of time management.'

'I've yet to meet a date who hasn't kept me waiting.'

With the high-maintenance, salon-treatment-three-times-a-week siliconed and Botoxed beauties she'd seen hanging on his arm in the glossy magazines, she didn't doubt it.

Or was she being unkind? Worse, jealous?

No, of course she wasn't. And because she was a big believer in punctuality being all about respect, she couldn't resist saying, 'You've been dating the wrong women, then.'

He was checking inside the pocket of his jacket that lay on the seat between them but his gaze shifted and focused on her. Not smiling. Prickles of heat rose up her neck, into her cheeks. He seemed to take an eternity before he said slowly, 'Maybe I have.'

Oh, no, she *had* sounded jealous. She wished she knew how he felt about that but she couldn't read his eyes behind his dark glasses. And she so wished she'd never spoken those petty little words just because those glossy glams got to her. Who was Chloe to tell Jordan Blackstone, millionaire, what kind of woman he needed?

Rather than try to explain her way out, she crossed her arms over her chest and glared out of the window as they neared the city. A tram rattled past as they drove along Collins Street, congested with lunch-time office workers. 'In case you've forgotten, this is not a date.'

'I haven't forgotten. It's much more important than that. Chloe, look at me.'

She continued to stare at the street-scape but his powerful

gaze on the back of her head drew her against her will—how did he continually manage that?

'Are you still okay with everything?' he asked. 'Because being defensive and prickly around me isn't going to help us.'

'I'm not being prickly…am I?' She deliberately breathed out, smoothed and relaxed taut muscles. 'I don't mean to be.'

'Just be aware of it when we're with other people,' he said as the car pulled into the kerb in front of a shiny black granite office building. 'Here we are.'

'Where, exactly?'

'We have an appointment.' Jordan withdrew his wallet from his jacket, slipped it into the back pocket of his jeans. 'You might want to put on your sunglasses,' he said, opening his door. 'I promised to protect you from the press but they're always where you least expect.'

She fished around in her bag while he came around the car to her side, then slid them on her face.

He hustled her towards the revolving glass door. 'What about our driver?' she asked as they approached the bank of elevators. 'I assume you know him?'

They stepped into an empty lift and he pressed the button for the tenth floor. 'He's a member of my staff here. I pay him to be discreet.'

She took off the glasses, put them in her bag. 'What do you mean by "here"?'

'Rivergold's head office is in Perth. I divide my time between the two cities.'

The doors slid open and they stepped out into a foyer with deep violet walls and concealed lighting. The word *Gilded* hovered above the reception desk in flowing gold script.

Jewellery, Chloe realised. Expensive, exclusive jewellery. She discovered first up that Jordan and the receptionist—Trudi—were on a first-name basis.

Trudi was all smiles for Jordan—naturally—and led them

down a wide corridor, keyed a code into a heavy door and showed them into a comfortable room overlooking the city. She offered them refreshments, Jordan ordered water for the both of them, then another staff member called Trudi away, which left the two of them alone.

Chloe had always insisted jewellery didn't match her lifestyle. She'd choose an airline ticket to an exotic destination over pretty but essentially useless baubles any day. 'I...um. I'm not much of a jewellery person.'

He glanced at her hands. 'I've noticed. But we need wedding rings.'

'Wedding rings...' she echoed. *Of course, wedding rings.*

'You're okay with that, I hope.'

'I just hadn't given it a thought. But this place is...' *ridiculously expensive and overpriced.* She waved her hand to encompass the leather armchairs, the glass-topped table for private showings with its neatly rolled up little black velvet mat on one end. 'We could've gone somewhere cheaper, is all I'm saying. After all, it's not as if it's for real.'

But for a brief heartbeat in time, she wondered how it would feel if it were and something inside her yearned before she shoved it away, deep in that place where she'd never find it again. Never wanted to find it again. Not with a man like Jordan—rich, powerful, gorgeous. Like Stewart.

A heartbreak waiting to happen.

She realised he was staring her down, his eyes a shade of cool logic. 'I own a *gold* mine, we're meeting a *gold* manufacturer in the hope that he and I will do business. With *gold.* What if he or his wife asks to look at your shiny new ring? And even if they don't ask, do you think he's not going to notice?'

'Oh...of course.' She closed her eyes briefly, embarrassed at her own stupidity. 'I hadn't thought about it.' And she needed to start—thinking about it. All of it. Like how *not* in his class she was and how impossible anything long-term or meaningful between them could ever be.

A smartly dressed middle-aged man entered the room with half a dozen jewellery trays. 'Jordan. So good to see you.' He beamed as he set the trays on the glass table and shook hands with Jordan, then extended his hand to Chloe. 'And Miss Montgomery, welcome.'

'Chloe, this is Kieron,' Jordan said as she shook the man's hand.

'Thank you, and call me Chloe.'

'This must be an exciting time for you.' He smiled, clearly expecting an answer.

'Yeah…um…' How much did he know? She glanced at Jordan for help but he was checking out the goodie trays. Damn him. 'We're…um…looking forward to it…' Whatever *it* was.

'What's your colour preference in gold?' Jordan asked without turning around.

She shifted, vaguely awkward in Kieron's presence and cursing Jordan some more for not paying attention. 'I'm not particular.'

'In that case we'll go with yellow,' he said. 'Sit down and let's get started.'

Kieron spread out the mat and placed a tray on the table, exquisite rings, all embedded with diamonds and other precious stones and sparkling in the down lights.

Jordan selected a couple of highly visual and elaborate rings and set them on the mat. 'Which do you prefer?'

'Do you have a plain gold band?' she almost pleaded with him. 'Thin. Plain.'

Jordan met her eyes. 'Kieron, can you give us a few moments, please?'

'Of course. I'll see what I can find in plain gold—'

'No need,' Jordan said, his gaze not leaving hers. 'I'm

sure we'll find something here. I'll give you a call when we're done.'

'What do you mean?' she demanded in a tight, low voice almost before the man had closed the door behind him. 'I don't want—'

'It's not about what you want. You—rather, *we*—need something ostentatious.'

'What about you? Your ring? Is this marriage going to be one based on inequality?'

He opened his palm, revealing a thick gold ring. 'Men's wedding band channel-set with black diamonds.' He set it in front of her. 'I can't have mine outshining yours.'

'Why can't *you* choose something simpler?'

'Because the ring has to make a statement. It has to shout, "We're married and exclusive and we want the world to know". It also says only Rivergold's gold is good enough for the love of my life.'

'So Gilded is your business?'

'One of them. What about this?' He picked up a smaller ring from the tray, a band of gold filigree, its dainty vine-leaf pattern studded with tiny diamonds. Kind of classic yet modern and delicate.

She told herself it wasn't the most gorgeous ring she'd ever seen. It wouldn't fit. It wasn't practical. But this time perhaps she could have the exotic destination *and* the pretty bauble. And oh... She sighed at the misty-eyed romance of it.

And just for once, she *wanted* misty-eyed romantic and impractical. It wasn't forever, she reassured herself. It didn't mean she was going to fall into bed with him—or worse, into love. No way. No how. No—

'I think it'll suit you. Try it.' Jordan reached across the table and took her hand.

As if from a distance, she watched him slide the ring onto her finger. The abrading sensation of his fingertips against hers, every nerve ending he touched tingling like tiny pin-pricks of fire. Her hand looked so small in his. His fingers were long and tanned, his wrist thick and dusted with dark hair.

She couldn't seem to move, couldn't seem to drag her eyes away from their linked hands. It was like being in someone else's dream—someone else's because Chloe no longer allowed herself to dream such fantasies.

He eased the ring over her knuckle. Perfect fit. Perfect design. Perfect.

'Chloe...' he said, deep and dreamy and masculine. *Will you be my wife?*

CHAPTER SEVEN

HEART SONG FOR the romantic soul.

Chloe might have sighed or murmured, but the touch of Jordan's finger beneath her chin as he tilted her face up to him shattered her dreamy illusions as loudly and irrevocably as fine glass smashing on marble.

'The ring,' she heard him say over the echoes still reverberating in her mind. The *only* thing he'd said.

She stared up at him, caught in the blue depths of his gaze. 'Yes?'

'What do you think?'

I think I'm starting to imagine stuff. 'About the ring?'

A perplexed expression crossed his face. 'Yes, the ring—what else?'

'Right. The ring…' *Of course, what else?* She breathed in deep, ordering herself to focus, adjusting to the sight of it glittering on her hand. 'It's lovely.' Oh, she could so spin a softly romantic story out of this—

'Good. Let's go, then.'

His emotionless tone brought her back to reality with a thud. She rubbed the fingers of her right hand over her left knuckles, then flexed them. 'Shall I leave it on?'

He nodded once. 'Wouldn't do to lose it now, would it?'

She noticed he was already wearing his when he pressed a buzzer on the table and she felt a flutter around her heart.

Even though it was for show purposes only, that no words had been exchanged—not even a meaningful glance—the symbolism gave her the odd feeling that they were connected somehow. That they belonged together.

Of course, that was dumb and stupid and very, very dangerous. She'd return the ring when they were done and that would be the end of it.

Still, she needed a moment to get over herself, so when Kieron met them at the door Chloe did a quick trip to the restrooms while the two men continued to Reception.

As she washed her hands she checked that the precious band wasn't too loose on her finger. Where had his ring appeared from? she wondered. She'd seen no men's rings on the tray. But everything was happening so fast, she could forgive herself for getting confused.

When she returned, they were deep in conversation. 'If it wasn't for you, I don't know where we'd be,' she heard Kieron say.

'Okay, all set,' she said, to announce her presence in case she heard something she wasn't supposed to.

Jordan clasped the other man's shoulder. 'Look after that special lady of yours.'

Kieron clasped him back and Chloe wondered what Jordan had done for his employee and his special lady that inspired such awe and gratitude.

She decided to ask him about it as his driver chauffeured them to a restaurant for lunch.

'Kieron worked for us in Perth. His wife's chronically ill and the specialised treatment she needs is only available in Melbourne, so we transferred him.'

His manner was casual, almost dismissive, but Chloe had seen the admiration on the man's face and sensed there was more to it than a simple location transfer. 'And...?' she prompted.

'And what?'

'Tell me more. What else does Jordan Blackstone do for his staff?'

He looked away, out of the window. 'The man had no private health insurance; they were renting basic accommodation. I'm his employer—I do what I can.'

A warm feeling spread across her chest. 'Good for you. You're a compassionate boss. More than that, you're a generous one.'

'I can afford to be.' He sounded curt and irritated. 'Don't make a big deal of it.'

'Okay.' She smiled at him and reached out to touch his arm. 'I won't mention that you're a generous boss again.'

She could have sworn he flinched at her touch. 'Just so we're clear,' he said, still watching the traffic. 'I'm not *your* boss—we're equals. Partners.'

'*Business* partners,' she finished, in case he had the wrong idea. It was nothing more. Right?

In a private dining room with a view of the Docklands and Westgate Bridge, they discussed the finer details of the trip, covering etiquette, customs and dress code. They were keeping their story simple and as close to the truth as possible. They'd met in Melbourne a couple of months ago and it had been love at first sight.

Jordan explained that after the formal introductions, Chloe wouldn't be expected to participate in any business discussions. Any strong feminist ideals she might have were to be left at Tullamarine Airport. She would be entertained by the sheikh's wife and the women in his family. There would be an evening dinner or two but during the day she'd be free to do as she chose. A driver had already been arranged to take her wherever she wanted to go.

By mutual agreement, they filled in some of their time at

the airport separately so as not to attract any unwanted media attention. Chloe wandered the duty-free shops for a couple of hours then returned to the relative privacy of the business lounge and read a couple of women's magazines while Jordan studied some heavy-looking manual he'd brought with him and surfed the net on his laptop.

And every so often she'd feel the ring's unfamiliar weight on her finger or catch its prettiness winking in the light. Then her eyes would flick to Jordan's hand and she'd see his wide band and a strange feeling like silken ribbons would flutter through her, twining around her heart, making her restless and cheated somehow. Dissatisfied.

Over a late light meal served on board the flight, they relaxed and enjoyed a movie together, although at times Chloe sensed Jordan's tension. Whether it was business related, she didn't know, but he didn't seem inclined to pursue anything romantic and that was a huge relief. Really. She was *not* disappointed.

This trip wasn't the travel experience she was accustomed to. The aircraft's business-class luxury gave them privacy in their individual wraparound fully reclining seats, and at midnight Chloe donned her eyeshades to try to get at least a couple of hours' sleep.

It didn't help. Excitement buzzed through her limbs so that in the end she tossed away the eyeshades and let her flickering personal TV screen lull her rioting thoughts. She couldn't wait till morning when she'd step into a different world and a different life.

She just needed to remember that the life part and the *wife* part weren't for real. It was short and it was temporary.

The glint of gold caught his eye as Jordan turned the page of the document on the aircraft's table in front of him. He stared at the sight of the familiar ring on his finger. How long had it been since that day he and Lynette Dixon had decided they were getting married?

Six years.

And in the madness of that moment they'd walked into a local jewellery shop along the coast and bought their wedding rings—a man who owned his own gold-mining company, for God's sake. He still didn't know how she'd managed it. How she'd manipulated him into it. The way his mother had manipulated and deceived his father his entire life.

He turned to the night-dark window where the aircraft's flashing red light swept rhythmically over the engine, but it was Lynette's picture-perfect face he saw reflected there.

He'd met the blonde bombshell at uni and fallen for her with the speed—and devastation—of an avalanche down a ski-slope. Jordan Blackstone, who could charm any girl he set his sights on with a virtual crook of his little finger, had become the charmed. At twenty-six, when he'd been old enough and wise enough to know better, he'd lost his brains, his willpower, his self-respect. And his heart.

Because on the morning they'd arranged to elope to Las Vegas, he'd learned he'd been played for the fool he was.

He twisted the ring that suddenly felt thick and heavy and confining. Yes, he should have known better. Hadn't he lived through a prime example of what not to do? He'd seen the power his mother had wielded over his father, and all because Fraser Blackstone had loved Ina without reservation. All his life Fraser had been a slave to that love. Blind to his wife's treachery—or he'd chosen to ignore it. Either way, it just went to prove that love made you weak.

Which was why he'd kept the ring. A reminder of his foolishness. A reminder that, without due care, women could be a costly distraction. A reminder of his vow never to allow it to happen again.

He would be no woman's slave. His will would prevail.

When he wanted a woman to share his bed, *he* would do the choosing, not the other way round. And that woman might touch his body—in any way she pleased—but no woman would touch his heart.

At sunrise the aircraft touched down in Dubai. The desert air was dry and cool after the plane's stale air conditioning as they walked out of the terminal.

Chloe breathed deeply. Aside from the odour of aviation fuel, everything smelled foreign and exciting.

'Ready to go, Mrs Blackstone?' Jordan said beside her.

'Ready, Mr Blackstone.'

A uniformed driver was waiting to take them to the city and opened the limo door. *'Ahlan wa Sahlan.'* Welcome.

'Ahlan bik.' Jordan waited while Chloe settled herself, then slid in beside her. 'Get ready to be amazed,' he said.

'Okay.' He sounded little-boy excited and she glanced at him, saw the enthusiasm reflected in his eyes. 'Are we talking about something in particular?'

He smiled but didn't enlighten her. 'Wait and see.'

So she immersed herself in the scenery, from the low sand dunes that came up to the edge of the road in some places to the sky's palette of pink and tangerine against unique silver-glinting architecture spiralling into the stratosphere. They travelled over the Dubai Creek, and everywhere she looked construction was frenetic. Cranes, roadworks and traffic hazards, dust.

Dubai's famous seven-star hotel suddenly reared up in front of them, its proud billowing shape catching the sun. 'Now that's something amazing. Is this what you meant…?' She trailed off as the vehicle turned onto the dedicated road that led to the grand entrance. 'Are we staying here? *Here? Really?'*

Bubbles of excitement fizzed through her veins. She

shifted to fling her arms around him, reining herself back just in time. She needed to maintain a respectful distance while she was here. Not only because this was the United Arab Emirates but because right now she wasn't sure she'd be able to stop if she started.

But he didn't seem bothered about the etiquette they'd discussed the other night. They were in a private car with tinted windows, after all. Leaning close so that his lips touched her hair, he murmured against her ear. 'A honeymoon to remember, Blondie.'

She told herself flirting was okay. Harmless. 'I'm sure it will be. *Pookie.*'

His brows shot up, his lips forming the word, but no sound came out. She meant the whole Arabian experience, not what he was obviously thinking she meant with that name—sex on tap—but she smiled and patted his arm, feeling safe in the knowledge he'd not touch her unless she allowed it.

Moments later as they entered through the massive revolving door her breath eased out in awe. The outside view of golden sand curving around the ultramarine to turquoise sea was echoed in the atrium that seemed to rise forever.

A row of staff greeted them as if they were royalty, offering miniature steaming towels, dishes of dates, coffee poured from exotic-shaped carafes.

It was all about the bling—in the mirrored walls, the ceilings, the rich crimson drapes, the waterfall over blocks of green and gold tumbling down beside an escalator. They were still sipping from tiny coffee cups as they shot skywards in a glass-walled elevator.

Their split-level suite had breathtaking views of the beach framed by the building's white bars and steel rope. While staff delivered their luggage and immediately unpacked their belongings, Jordan took charge of a master remote that controlled everything from curtains to TV and music to opening the door and calling up room service.

Chloe explored. A swimming-pool-sized spa set in polished granite, gold fittings, a gallery of mirrors and a view of the skyline. An opulent office with every amenity at one's fingertips. Bowls of tropical flowers on polished tables.

By the time she found the bedroom, their luggage had been unpacked, their cases removed out of sight. The vast purple-hued Arabian nights fantasy bed with its gold trimmed canopy dominated the room, reminding her of a flying carpet.

But there was only one.

And there were two of *them*... Images of soaring into the night sky filled her head...and those images didn't involve aircraft. She turned away. *Remember why you can't. Remember why you're here.*

She didn't want to jeopardise this important deal that meant so much to Jordan because of something she'd done or not done. She was being paid a sheikh's ransom to support him. Her feelings for him weren't professional, never had been, so it was already a struggle to stick to the business relationship she herself had insisted on.

She found him sitting in a bright alcove overlooking the sea and slicing a mango onto a gold-rimmed plate. She sat down opposite him and looked at the opulence about her. 'I could get seriously used to this.'

'Enjoy, but don't get used to it,' he suggested. 'It's a one-off.'

'Ah, yes, the honeymoon. And you're writing it off as a business expense, right?' She smiled. 'As your bride, I'm still annoyed about that.'

He offered her the plate. 'But you couldn't wait to be married, remember?' He raised a brow. 'Which reminds me— *Pookie?*'

'It was your idea to have pet names.' She took a slice of

the fruit, slipped it between her lips and savoured its cool, pungent taste on her tongue.

'There's a certain eroticism attached to that particular endearment, however, and it *does* conjure images.' Hot cerulean eyes lapped at her.

'It does?' It did. She felt the mango sliding down the wrong way and cleared her throat, which suddenly felt tight and scratchy.

'Maybe you've been subconsciously considering my suggestion?'

Nothing subconscious about where her mind had been. 'What suggestion? Sorry, haven't given it a thought.' Heat was spreading over her neck and even in the air conditioning she felt her T-shirt sticking to her skin. 'Pookie's just a little white rabbit with wings…'

'Is he?' He smiled and sliced off another piece of mango but she could tell he thought she was making up one of her fairy stories.

'Yes. He is. Was. It was my favourite storybook when I was young and… I'm going to take one of the hotel's famous rain showers before we head out.' In that luxury shower room big enough for an entire football team. Or one blue-eyed golden man. She caught his hopeful look as she stood up, and shook her head. 'Don't even think about it.'

'Can't stop a man thinking,' she heard him say as she walked away.

A couple of hours later, they were wandering the narrow alleyways of the textile souq with its shuttered shops and rainbows of colourful silks and exotic fabrics. Everything from jewelled Arabian slippers to belly-dancing costumes to the latest fashion in business suits.

Desert heat and unfamiliar scents and a lone Arabic voice chanting prayerfully assaulted Chloe's senses. Tourists and locals in Western dress rubbed shoulder to shoulder with those in more traditional clothing.

She chose a couple of skeins of silken fabric for the simple reason that she couldn't imagine leaving Dubai without them, so Jordan insisted she visit one of the resident tailors and have something made up while they were there. He offered extra cash for the garments to be constructed and delivered to the hotel by the end of the day.

'But you paid me already,' she told him, feeling awkward about the expense. 'I'd not have bought it if I'd known. I pay my own way.'

'Not this time. I want you to play the role you've accepted, and play it well. My wife's wish is my command.'

Jordan was a proud man and she knew his tone well enough not to argue about it for now.

So Chloe made it her Pretty Woman adventure. But it didn't end with the textile souq; it was on to the Burjuman Centre with its high-end fashion labels where she purchased off-the-rack garments. Business attire for their meetings and attractive, modest casual-wear.

And one of the best surprises she discovered was that shopping with a man could actually be fun. Well, shopping with Jordan was fun. He had a good eye for women's fashion; little wonder with the gorgeous types she'd seen draped on his arm in the media pictures. He was protective of her when he saw other men, even women, staring at her blonde hair as if she were some sort of curiosity. And the way he looked at her every time she modelled something for his advice or approval…well, it was…flattering.

More than flattering. It was hot. And she hadn't felt the kind of hot Jordan made her feel in a long time. The kind that spread like nettle rash over sensitised skin. The kind that made you itch and burn and yearn for something to ease and soothe.

And he knew it.

He was playing the role of adoring, indulgent husband to the hilt. His not-so-subtle, underhanded way to lure her with the promised pleasures of afternoon delights didn't faze her, oh, no.

It only cemented her decision to maintain that professional distance. Men like him were far too sure of themselves, and she was getting in over her head with this one. That yearning ache was a reminder of her vulnerability where relationships were concerned. Any relationship.

I don't fit in.

After this charade was over and done they'd go their separate ways because what would a millionaire gold-mining magnate want with a short-stack wandering adventurer like her? *Walk away first.*

So after lunch in one of the mall's shaded courtyards, when Jordan suggested—with a twinkle in his blue eyes— that they return to the hotel because he had business to catch up on, Chloe stayed in town to do some exploring on her own.

Jordan closed down his laptop and scowled at the magnificent ocean view from the suite's magnificent gold-and-mahogany desk. He hadn't expected to end up spending the rest of the afternoon on his own. His suggestion to return to the hotel had been business motivated—he *had* left Australia sooner than he'd anticipated, sending his PA into a spin—but not entirely. He'd hoped Chloe would have accompanied him back here, given the looks they'd exchanged while she'd modelled some of the world's great fashion labels for him.

Contrary Chloe. He couldn't remember a time when a woman had held out for so long, given the obvious attraction. There was something about anticipation that heightened the senses, but it came with an impatience that staccato-tapped up and down his spine.

His phone buzzed on the desk and he reached for it with a grin—not so long after all. 'Miss me already, Blondie?'

'Mr Blackstone?' The unfamiliar Arabic-accented male voice brought Jordan crashing down.

Hell and damn. 'Yes—*na'an*. I apologise, sir, I was expecting Chl—my wife to call.' Jordan reined in his sudden tension and tried to remember the Arabic he'd learned for the trip. '*Marhaba.* How can I help you?'

'*Marhabtayn.* I am calling on behalf of Sheikh Qasim bin Omar Al-Zeid.'

Jordan straightened, his fingers tightening on the phone. 'Yes?' His voice came out clipped and terse.

'Sheikh Qasim will not be able to meet with you tomorrow as planned. A family emergency has occurred. He will be in contact soon. Meanwhile he sends his apologies and would have you accept a special gift instead. You are on your honeymoon, *na'an*?'

'*Na'an.*'

'Please be ready to depart on the helipad of your hotel with your wife at noon tomorrow. It will be an overnight stay, so you may want to bring any essential items with you.'

'*Shukran.* That's very generous. Please convey my thoughts regarding his family and my gratitude to Sheikh Qasim on behalf of myself and my wife.'

The words 'my wife' felt strange and foreign on his lips but Jordan shook off the odd discomfort and disconnected with a smile. His would-be business partner had not changed his mind as Jordan had briefly feared. He'd given a show of faith and arranged something special for their honeymoon.

Pushing up from the desk, he punched the air and thanked whatever good luck demon had been riding on his shoulder when he'd decided an accompanying 'wife' would be a clever tactical move.

Meanwhile, he had a surprise evening of his own to plan,

which included sand, sea and celestial sights. He walked to the bathroom to shower and change before Chloe returned. Sex might also be on the agenda if he played his cards right.

But his anticipation in sharing the evening with his woman of the moment was marred somewhat when he recalled his sheer stupidity in answering a call without checking caller ID. He *never* answered without checking caller ID. Thoughtful, he narrowed his gaze as he stripped off and stepped under the spray. Was his fascination with Chloe interfering with his work?

No. Fascination equated to captivation, which implied a weakness on his part. That he wasn't in full control, that Chloe wielded some sort of power over him. Switching the spray to cold—and full power—he let it pummel his back and assured himself what he felt was lust. Honest to goodness lust.

And women did *not* interfere with his work. This small blip was nothing to worry about. It was just his pent-up libido demanding action. He set the lather to his hair and worked his fingers hard. Soon everything would return to normal. It would all settle down once they'd had sex. Then he could focus on what he'd come to Dubai to do.

CHAPTER EIGHT

'I'M GOING TO knock your socks off tonight, husband of mine,' Chloe announced when she returned late in the afternoon with purchases trailing behind her, carried by staff who discreetly disappeared as soon as they'd set the bags down. 'At least I hope I am.'

He was rather hoping she'd be knocking—or, rather, *taking*—more than his socks off. When she plonked herself on the nearest brocade chair, kicked off her shoes and massaged a foot, he couldn't help but notice the slender shape of her ankle. His groin tightened. He wanted to put his hands there. His mouth. He wanted to kiss his way over that sexy arched instep and up her calf. Her thigh. All the way to paradise... 'Let me do that for you.'

He half rose but she shook her head and waved him away, hugging one knee to her chest, whisky eyes flashing a warning. 'Uh-uh. You do *not* want to smell my feet after a day in the desert.'

He grinned. There was that. 'Okay. Later maybe.'

She didn't look at him, chin resting on her knee as she squeezed and flexed her foot. 'I'm going to need an hour to get ready for this romantic dinner package you arranged for your devoted wife, and you need to be somewhere else while I do.'

'Ah, a little mystery, I like that in a relationship. Keeps it alive, wouldn't you agree?'

'No.' She yanked the band from her hair and shook it out like a cloud of curly sunshine but thunder darkened her expression. A moment later she shrugged and lost some of that vehemence as she met his eyes and acknowledged, 'It depends on the mystery.'

'And the man. Don't let one bad experience with a Mr Despicable spoil everything for you, Chloe,' he told her softly.

'Jordan…' She stopped, then said slowly, 'Mr Despicable hasn't spoiled everything.'

'Glad to hear it.' As she turned away to fiddle with her hair he got the distinct feeling Despicable wasn't the only man who'd hurt her.

Grabbing his suit jacket and a tie, he went downstairs to wander the plethora of fountains and gardens in the hotel complex before heading back to the lobby to wait.

Chloe appeared punctually at the top of the escalator as arranged. And taking his breath away in a long, loose sheath that flowed like an emerald river to her feet where shimmering amethyst sandals peeked beneath the hem. An embroidered purse no bigger than a CD and suspended on black silk rope hung on her shoulder. Everything about her was casually elegant and perfect for intimate dining on the water's edge.

Even as she descended he could smell her skin, as if she'd soaked in a bath of jasmine, then been dusted with golden cinnamon. Her hair was scrunched in a tortoiseshell clip on top of her head, and as she reached him he had to restrain himself from burying his nose against her neck and filling his hands with her sweet flesh. *No PDAs, Blackstone, remember?*

He stuck his hands in his trouser pockets instead and said, 'Consider me sockless.'

Her smile danced across her features, topaz eyes reflecting the setting sun's brilliance a thousandfold. 'Thank you. And you look pretty snappy too, as usual.'

He held out his arm. 'Shall we?'

'We shall.' She tucked her hand around his elbow, her wedding ring glinting. 'Such a glorious evening.'

'And it's only just begun.'

She flicked him a glance from beneath her lashes but didn't reply. At least she hadn't shattered his vision and hopes yet.

They walked the short distance to their reserved table. The romantic package lived up to its name with crisp white-covered chairs protected from the sand by a Persian carpet, Moroccan brass lanterns, the scent of incense on the marine air mingling with the delicate tropical blooms on the cloth-topped table. Gleaming gold cutlery, sparkling crystal.

And Chloe.

'Does your friend Sadiq know about this arrangement between us?' she asked when they'd ordered their meal and toasted the evening with one of his favourite Australian whites, chilled and fizzing to perfection.

'He knows you accompanied me. What about you? Have you told your family yet?'

She shook her head, then sipped again, thoughtful. 'Maybe I should. Then when we go home we could…'

We. The word speared through him—not a word he wanted to hear in the context of home and family—and his muscles tensed.

Then she sighed, her gaze focused inward. 'No. That wouldn't work.'

He dared ask, 'What were you thinking?'

She barely flicked a hand and he glimpsed something in her eyes—defeat or resignation? 'Nothing sensible, that's for sure.' Straightening, she set her glass on the table with a decisive *plunk*. 'I've deposited ample funds in their account, so now I'm thinking maybe I'll stay on in Melbourne for a bit, work for Dana. Who knows? They don't need to know I'm back in Australia just yet.'

'You wouldn't go see them?'

'Why? I'm their mistake. I *am* a mistake.' She spoke matter-of-factly, no malice, no anger. 'The "clever" genes had run out by the time I was conceived.'

Jordan frowned, angry on her behalf that her parents and even her siblings had made her feel she was worthless in their eyes. At the same time he understood where she was coming from because Ina had also blamed him for being born and punished him for it every day of his young life.

In Jordan's eyes, Chloe owed her family nothing. 'Why would you want to bail them out?'

'Because whoever they are, whatever they've done or not done, they're family.' She looked at him, honest eyes reflecting the vermilion hues of sunset. 'I know you understand. This trip, your goal here in Dubai, is about family.'

He couldn't respond to that because what she said was true. And it wasn't as if his dad had been perfect. Far from it. The man could've done much more for Jordan as a child. He could've been a stronger father and banished Ina from their lives years ago instead of turning a blind eye for love. Because Dad had loved his cheating wife more than he'd loved his only son.

Love makes you weak.

He shook it away. With the lavender sky tossing up flames of scarlet and purple, the air thick with barbecued meats and spices, the sound of water lapping lazily on the sand, not to mention the company of an attractive and interesting woman, he refused to let the past crowd in on the present.

He tilted his glass towards her. 'Tonight's not about family, Blondie. It's about us.'

They sampled each other's dishes. Moroccan chicken with orange and cinnamon tagine, and Syrian flame-grilled kafta kebabs with sour cherry sauce on pitta bread and topped with pine nuts.

Jordan found Chloe an intelligent and stimulating conversationalist who wasn't afraid to challenge or even disagree with his views, unlike so many of his dates who went along with whatever he said, testing the limits of his boredom.

They shared a double chocolate ice-cream fantasy as the blaze of sunset surrendered to the deep purple of evening and the stars blinked on and the air cooled. A waxing moon hung like a misshapen pearl in the sky.

Chloe rested her elbows on the cleared table and stared up at its cold ethereal beauty. No matter where she went in a sometimes unfamiliar world, the moon was a constant. 'I could watch that pretty ball for hours,' she said. 'First an amazing sunset, now this.'

'I did promise you celestial sights.'

'Oh?' Her brow lifted. 'I think I missed that memo.'

'Maybe I forgot to mention it.' He rose, shrugged off his suit jacket, slung it over his shoulder and took her hand loosely in his. 'Let's walk. I want to show you something.' She slipped off her shoes and he led her onto the sand, away from the glare. He stood behind her and pointed to two bright celestial objects in the west and close together. 'That's Venus and Jupiter.'

'Uh-huh.' She knew her way around the night sky too, loved the changing panorama the different hemispheres brought, but she'd never found it quite as exciting with Jordan standing behind, their bodies not quite touching, his deep voice rumbling by her ear.

The wine in her system had blurred the line she'd promised herself she wouldn't cross and she turned her head and stared up at his face. Moonlight carved hills and valleys into his strong features and for a moment their gazes meshed in silence while the marine breeze blew gently across her skin and the water slapped on the beach.

'So…where's the Big Dipper?' she asked, all innocence—buying into his game.

'Over here. See that star just above that palm…?' With light hands, he shifted her position—as she knew he would—so that she was facing a more northerly direction, and his right arm lifted in front of her. She smelled soap and fresh cotton and tempting man, and her body started to quiver.

He traced the shape in the air for her. 'You can't see it from Australia.'

'But we can see the three brightest stars in the sky, and the Southern Cross is by far my favourite constellation.' She turned so that she faced him fully, taking a step away to see him better. 'And Saturn is visible in the morning this month. Near the Pleiades.'

His grin was slow and wide. 'You had me fooled for a moment.'

She grinned back. 'I did.'

His eyes took on a molten silver glint. 'And this is payback time where I haul you into my arms and kiss you senseless.' Except he didn't.

'And I let you,' she murmured, melting fast beneath his gaze. 'But that's not going to happen. We're not on Bondi Beach now.'

'I wouldn't do what I want to do to you on a public beach, Blondie.' His gaze flicked to her feet, then strolled all the way up her body to her eyes. 'I'd take you to a very private place where, short of a tsunami, no one and nothing would interrupt us for a very long time.'

Her nipples tightened viciously in the wake of his leisurely perusal. She knew she shouldn't poke a tiger but she returned the favour, giving her gaze permission to slow when it reached the suspicious outline of a bulge in his dark trousers. She was safe here with people not far away—not only from him, but from herself. 'And what would you do in this private place? Theoretically.'

His jaw firmed, his eyes sparking like a welder's blow-torch. 'Come here.'

'Come? Here?' She glanced around them and stifled a naughty giggle. '*Here's* going to get you in a lot of trouble—'

'Us,' he said, his voice tight. 'It's going to get *us* in trouble. Follow me.' He set a fast pace across the sand towards a row of luxury recliner chairs on a deck a short distance from the tables where diners were still enjoying their meals.

Jordan had coupled them in a sexual context, sending a thrill zipping down her spine. Shoes dangling from one hand and her feet tripping over themselves in the sand, she followed.

On the decking, he stopped and turned around. Smouldering desire in the eyes that captured hers. For a guy who worked out, his breathing was on the fast and shallow side, drawing Chloe's attention to his chest as he dragged in air. Her fingers itched to touch, to get to work between those buttons—

He tossed his jacket down, unbuttoned the top button of his shirt and loosened his tie with swift sharp movements. 'You want to know what I'd do and I'm going to tell you. Right here. Right now.'

He sat on the side of a recliner with his shiny black shoes on the ground, and gestured for her to sit facing him on the recliner next to his as if they reflected one another in a mirror. His knees were a hand-span from hers, their torsos within touching distance, but he didn't reach for her, nor did she for him. To anyone passing by they looked like a respectable couple discussing the weather.

'Place your hands on the chair either side of your thighs,'

Jordan said. 'Move them back a bit, so you're leaning back slightly and I can see the shape of your breasts.'

Her nipples responded instantly to his request, tight buds pressing against her bra as she followed his instruction.

'Spread your legs a bit—not too much—just enough room for my hand to fit between.' He must have glimpsed her alarm because he said, 'Don't worry, this is sex without touching.'

'Like phone sex?' She did as he asked, her loose ankle-length dress hiding any hint of impropriety. To any passer-by she looked as if she was perfectly relaxed and admiring the moon. And she told herself she was—relaxed and totally in control.

'Better than phone sex because I can see you.' His voice rolled over her like honey. 'I can smell you. I can watch your responses and know I'm turning you on.'

For all she knew, he might have been complimenting her perfume, but the earthiness of the image that spun through her mind's eye was as intimate as it was shocking and a surge of liquid heat pooled low in her belly.

'I'm turning you on already.' He cocked his head to one side, studying her. 'Your breath caught and your eyes have gone wide and dark. What were you thinking about?'

No, he most definitely hadn't been talking about her choice in perfume. 'If I tell you, where's the mystery?' She squirmed on the seat and cleared the lust frog from her throat. 'Is this going to be all about me or do I get to return the favour?'

'All about you, Blondie.' He waved away her attempt to turn the tables. 'Your hair's gorgeous, even at night, but you need to let it down. So I'm removing that torture clip.' He gestured with a hand. 'You could do that for me.'

'I could, but...' Blue eyes mesmerised and entranced and the rest of her sentence trailed away forgotten. She freed her hair and finger-combed it so that it drifted down around her shoulders.

He nodded. 'That's a relief, right? All that tension in the scalp draining away.'

How did he know? she wondered. Of course the answer was obvious—he knew women. He knew what they liked, what they wanted. And he knew how to give it to them.

'I'm massaging my fingertips against your scalp,' he continued. 'You used the hotel's shampoo—I can smell peaches.'

Yes. She closed her eyes. To concentrate on his voice or to shut out that piercing gaze that suddenly seemed to know her too well? Maybe she wasn't as in control as she'd thought.

'Under the stars your hair looks like milk and feels like satin. I'm caressing your throat with light fingers. Smooth, like china. My lips are there now, where your pulse is galloping with anticipation. I'm lapping your sweetness while my hands slip around and lower your zip, my knuckles grazing every vertebra until I reach the base of your spine. Bra hooks next. I draw the dress and bra from your shoulders. Down your arms in one slow stroke. The heat from your skin rises to my nostrils, bringing your scent. Oriental spices. Jasmine. Arousal. Open your eyes, Chloe. Look into my eyes and see what you do to me.'

What she saw in those sparkling blues made her whole body limp. What she heard in his voice stroked her insides with a silken glove. Desire, heat, arousal, anticipation. And she felt like a kitten, arching her head against that touch.

He nodded. 'And I do the same to you.'

'Yes…' Her voice trailed away on a wisp of night breeze, to hang around the stars that seemed to be slowly spinning overhead like a kaleidoscope.

'Don't look away again.' His command was low and firm. 'I've been imagining your breasts since that first night you had them stuffed into that too-tight costume.' Greedy eyes stroked her bodice. 'Washed with moonshine, they're firm and luscious with nipples the colour of...a watermelon smoothie,' he decided. 'And they taste like pink champagne.'

Her blood fizzed, the sound almost shattering her eardrums. 'Jordan...stop...' She tried to look beyond him and focus on the inky splashed silver beach, the moonlit curve of the Arabian tower against a black velvet sky, and get herself in order, but the powerful lure of his voice dragged her back.

'You don't mean that,' he murmured, low and sure and seductive. 'Can you feel the pull of my tongue as I draw one nipple inside my mouth and tease it with my teeth while I tweak the other between my fingers?'

Her nipples cramped; pleasure in the pain as she arched her back, craving more. 'Jordan...please...'

'Since you asked so nicely...' Humour and playfulness in his voice.

So powerful, so intense, Chloe swore she felt him swap breasts. Moist heat fanned her skin as if he were breathing against her décolletage and she couldn't tell if the slippery abrading sensation was her clothing or her vivid imagination.

'I'm taking their weight in my hands now and blowing on the wetness.'

His voice was dreamlike in the stillness of the evening, emptying her mind while he filled her with image upon image, sensation upon sensation. 'I...I think that's enough...'

He shook his head once, his eyes like blue lasers in the dimness. 'I'm just getting started.' He stroked her knees with those eyes and she wondered if he could see them tremble. 'Relax and let me touch you. My hand's gliding up over your thighs, an inch at a time, spinning out the anticipation. They're a little flushed and feel incredible, like you bathed in rose petals and cherry liqueur. My fingers reach the edge of your panties. Can you feel the heat?' His eyes drew her inside him. 'I can.'

'Jordan...I need... We need—'

'Yes. I know.' He smiled. 'That control you had earlier has melted away like an ice-cream sundae under an Arabian sun, hasn't it?' It wasn't a question.

No. Yes... She rolled her lips together as moisture pooled between her legs, ready for him. So ready...

'You sigh and shift your legs farther apart and my thumb finds you slick and wet and hot. Do you feel hot, Blondie?'

Her eyelids fluttered down as she shifted on the recliner. 'Yes...'

'Here? Where I'm letting the tips of my fingers glide? Or here, where my mouth is lapping at your neck. Or maybe—'

'Hot,' she moaned. 'Everywhere.'

'That ripping sound is me tearing that scrap of silk from your hips, dragging it out of the way so I can slide one finger inside you. One's not enough for you, is it? You want more. Spread your legs wider—I want to see all of you.'

Her eyes snapped open and met his and just like that she complied, her long skirt dipping into the V between her thighs. 'See all of me,' she murmured. 'Touch me.' Her voice lowered to a husky whisper and she tossed caution to the wind. 'Taste me.'

His eyes turned black, a muscle jumped in his cheek and his knuckles turned white on the edge of the recliner. 'Y—'

His mobile ringtone shattered the fantasy. Chloe jumped like a guilty thirteen-year-old caught behind the bike shed with the school's bad boy. For a moment neither moved, nor spoke, staring at each other while the beat of some rap tune jiggled and vibrated in his trouser pocket.

She bit her lips together. *Don't answer it.*

He pulled the offending object out, glanced at the screen then back to Chloe, the spark in his eyes doused but not extinguished. 'I have to answer this.' He rose, explaining, 'It's my PA,' and already walking away into the nearby shadows. 'Roma. What's the problem?'

He halted at some potted tropical plants. Chloe couldn't hear the words but he spoke in short, sharp sentences, his movements jerky and impatient, indicating a problem, possibly urgent.

Her whole body wailed in protest as she threw a glance up at the night sky. As if she didn't have an urgent problem herself—one that needed his immediate and undivided attention.

A breeze blew off the water, cooling her flushed skin, and she counted to ten. It was enough to clear the sensual fog that had enshrouded her, and she rubbed her upper arms with brisk movements. She needed to think, which wasn't easy when her brain cells were melting from an overload of X-rated images.

She turned away from the sight of the man responsible and watched the water lap against the sand. *Pull yourself together, Chloe Montgomery. Take back that control you were so proud of and walk away. Now.*

Because obviously the social part of the evening was over and it was just as well because another moment and she'd have been begging him to take her to their room and finish what he'd started. Worse, he knew it.

She'd been about to allow a man to override her decisions. Again. It was still a raw gash; how easily Markos had persuaded her into bed that night and to part with what little money she'd had. How he'd played her body like a piano while convincing her that he knew the financial markets and could triple her money in a week. *Trust me, Chloe.*

'Chloe.'

She swivelled on one heel, her arms across her chest. She didn't dare look directly at the gorgeous man in front of her who was her *business* partner. 'I'm heading up to the room now,' she clipped. 'Don't try anything because I've already made it clear I will not compromise our business relationship. *You* may be able to switch—'

'That was a call from Perth.' The tension in his voice drew her attention as he walked towards her. 'There's a problem at one of the mines.'

CHAPTER NINE

'OH, NO.' THEIR fantasy vanished like moon dust down a black hole. A mine emergency could change everything they'd come here to do. 'Is it serious?'

'No one seems to know yet.'

'Is there anything I can do? Would you like me to wait with you till you find out?'

He was too busy on his mobile to look at her, the screen casting a pale glow across the grim slash of his mouth. 'Not your problem, Chloe. Go on up to the room.'

'But I… You might…' She trailed off. The man was in no need of her assistance. The tone, the body language clearly told her he didn't want her here. 'If you change your mind…'

He glanced her way as if suddenly remembering he had a dinner companion. A wife. 'I'll escort you up, then I have to make some calls, find out what the hell's going on. I'll do that down here or in the lobby.'

'Please…' Chloe gave a half-laugh '…I can find my own way.'

'I said I'll see you up.'

'*No.* I'd prefer you didn't.' She touched his arm lightly. 'Stay and make your calls. I'm perfectly safe and you're busy.' She stepped away. 'Just remember I'm here if you need someone.'

'Right…'

She didn't exist to him and she turned away, pointed herself in the direction of the hotel and didn't look back. She didn't know why he'd opted not to avail himself of the luxurious office in their suite to make his calls. After what had just happened between them, perhaps he needed space and privacy to get on with the job. No distractions. Perhaps he thought *she* did.

Or perhaps he was more like her than she'd imagined— used to doing everything on his own. Except that he did so by choice whereas she'd learned through necessity.

Some instinct whispered that maybe it hadn't always been his choice either, and as soon as she reached their suite she opened her laptop and logged on to the internet. She'd seen something so sad, so haunted in his eyes when they'd spoken of family. Up till now, she'd refrained from learning more about the man than was necessary for the job requirement, but his expression earlier this evening had aroused her curiosity.

She found an article on his charity. Rapper One was a fund he'd set up that took troubled teenage boys from broken homes and situations of neglect into the bush for some team-building and adventure every six months. He didn't stop at fund-raising. He hired the services of counsellors and psychologists and mentored these kids personally, teaching them how to pan for gold while building trust and self-esteem amongst the group.

There was so much more she wanted to know, but tonight was about being here for him if there was bad news and he needed someone to talk to. She closed the computer and prepared to wait up.

Jordan dragged off his tie and swiped a hand over his hair, willing his phone to ring, waiting for word and feeling so helpless. What the hell was happening on the other side of the world? If he didn't hear something soon, he—*they*—would be on tomorrow's first flight to Australia. He needed to be there; his mine, his responsibility. Was it some safety issue he'd not addressed? Some management concern he'd overlooked?

At the first flicker of life, Jordan stabbed the answer button, barked, 'What's going on?' then listened as relief poured through him. Seemed there wasn't a problem after all. It had been a misunderstanding. A couple of miners they'd thought missing underground had turned up safe and well. Very sorry to have troubled him, to have worried him. *Enjoy the rest of your trip.*

He swore long and hard as he disconnected—even though it was the best outcome possible—and headed to one of the empty tables, ordered a double Scotch, no ice, from the waiter who appeared at his side.

He glared at the recliner chairs where he'd last seen Chloe and his jaw tightened. He'd almost chosen not to answer his phone because he'd been too focused on the red-hot blonde all but coming apart in front of him. He'd been tempted to put a woman before his work. The repercussions of that choice echoed with eerie familiarity.

Eight years ago he'd allowed a woman he barely knew to persuade him to 'stay a little longer'. He'd missed his flight and his father had died that day. He'd put personal desires before what was important in his life.

And then there'd been Lynette. He'd been willing to put her first without question until he'd learned she'd been using his feelings for her all along.

The waiter placed his crystal tumbler on the table. Jordan thanked him and raised it to eye-level. *The colour of Chloe's eyes*—ah, yes, she'd made damn sure he'd never forget her, with that whisky gaze of hers, hadn't she? He downed the contents in one go, needing its full-bodied burn as it slid down his throat.

Women manipulated.

But tonight, he had to admit that generalisation wasn't fair. This evening with Chloe, he'd been the one doing the manipulating. He'd known precisely what he was doing and where it was leading.

Then when his phone had rung with such incredibly bad timing, had she told him to ignore it like some women he knew would? No, *he'd* been the one telling himself to ignore it. When he'd told her the problem, he'd seen genuine concern and caring in her eyes. She'd put his problems before her own needs or any promise of mutually satisfying pleasure.

And he'd almost been tempted to share the uncertainty, to ask her to wait with him for news, good or bad. The way a husband would with his wife. But he never involved the women he dated in his business concerns. His father was a not-so-shining example of what could happen if you did.

She wasn't a date.

Half an hour later he let himself into their suite and walked straight to the bedroom. Chloe wasn't there but she'd put every available cushion down the centre of the bed. A half-grin hooked the corner of his mouth. If he wanted, he could have her lush little body arching wantonly—and willingly—beneath him in a matter of moments, cushions or no. But it was a symbolic action and he'd respect her decision. He wouldn't even try to change her mind.

Not tonight anyway.

From the corner of his eye he saw movement in the semi-dimness of the adjacent room. Chloe was standing at the window and staring out at the moonlit sea, framed by the structure's white lattice and looking little-girl lost in a too-big sweatshirt that might have been red once but was now a sad pink flecked with grey. 'Chloe.'

She whirled around, anxiety etched on her face, fatigue smudges beneath her eyes. 'What happened? Have you heard?

Is everything okay?' She rapid-fired questions at him as she crossed the gold-brocade-edged carpet towards him.

'Everything's fine. There was no emergency after all.'

She huffed out a breath. 'Well, why the heck didn't they get their facts straight before calling you and worrying you like that when you're so far away? I hope you gave them a piece of your mind.'

Her indignation on his behalf made him smile. 'I expect them to keep me informed with up-to-date info. Maybe they just didn't like the idea of me over here enjoying myself.' The lines bracketing her mouth didn't relax and his smile faded almost before it began. 'I thought you'd be asleep by now.'

Her eyes flashed, concern shifting to annoyance. 'You thought wrong. Did you assume I'd just go to sleep and think nothing of your emergency?' She shoved her hands into her hair, making it stand up like a wild halo. 'Of course I waited up. You wouldn't let me wait with you but that didn't stop me from worrying right along with you anyway.'

He frowned. His assumptions had been way off, and something vaguely disquieting skittered down his spine. He fiddled with his shirt cuffs, slid the buttons free. 'I didn't expect you to do that. I *don't* expect you to do that.'

'Isn't that what a good wife would do?' she demanded, a fire in her eyes that twisted something inside him. 'Wouldn't she be there to support her husband anyway she can?'

'I didn't pay you to be involved in my business problems, Chloe.'

Rather than soothe that fire, it inflamed. '*Pay* me,' she repeated, tersely. 'You *paid* me to be your wife. I don't know why but you make it sound cheap. You make this whole arrangement sound cheap.' She flicked her hand and her ten-thousand-dollar wedding ring glinted in the half-light.

He raised a brow but not his voice. 'That's not my intention since this *whole arrangement's* costing me a great deal of money.' *Keep emotion out of it; stick to the facts.* 'You're tired, Chloe. Go to bed.'

'I intend to.' She walked past him then stopped and met his gaze full on. 'For the record, I wasn't worried because you were paying me to be worried. I happen to care.'

Her words struck him like a velvet fist mid-chest. He started unbuttoning his shirt. 'That's not necessary,' he bit out. *Care* was not a part of their deal.

'So sue me for breach of contract,' she tossed back, and climbed into bed.

Hell. He didn't answer because for once in his life he didn't know how to respond. He suspected that any further conversation at this point wouldn't end well, and he could allow nothing to jeopardise their agreement.

He told himself her disposition would perk up with tomorrow's getaway, which he'd surprise her with over breakfast. And he'd do what he knew how to do best. She'd return to Dubai refreshed and satisfied, her cheeks bright with a lover's glow, her eyes sparkling.

And the deal with the Dubai gold buyer would be in the bag.

Chloe dragged the heaven-soft quilt over her shoulders and lay stiff and tense and facing away from Jordan's side of the bed. Clearly, he didn't want her involved in his personal life. She'd been *paid* to be his wife. But not a wife who mattered in the great scheme of things. Not a wife who could be a support if he'd let her.

Not even a friend or someone to confide in.

She closed her eyes. But her ears were working fine. Too fine. She heard the shoosh of fabric shifting over all that golden skin as he removed his shirt, the clink of his belt buckle, the *zzzz* of a zip as he shucked off his trousers...

Was he still wearing underwear or was he going to get into

bed naked? She'd lay bets on the latter because that was the type of man he was—arrogant and cocky where women were concerned. Especially the women sharing his bed.

If she wanted, she could roll over and see if the reality lived up to her vivid imagination, and—no doubt in her mind—he was counting on her to do just that. She squeezed her eyes tighter and wished she'd thought to bring earplugs because he sounded as if he was scratching…somewhere. She did *not* want to know.

There was a slight disturbance in the air as he slid beneath the quilt but the mattress remained as still as a lake at sunset, and almost as wide. With the Great Dividing Range between.

She'd half expected him to sweet-talk her into finishing what they'd started but she didn't hear so much as a murmur. Was he waiting for her to make the move? *It'll be you inviting me.* His words echoed in her head.

Her body was still wide awake and tingling and he hadn't laid a hand on her. Imagine what the real deal would be like… The residual heat between her thighs intensified once more and spread to every yearning and unfulfilled place he'd awoken with nothing more than his voice and eyes.

She pressed her lips together to stifle a moan and forced her restless legs to remain still. She only had to slide across the silky lake, climb over the mountain range and she could live the fantasy for real.

She feared it was only a matter of time before Jordan's charisma and smooth talking overcame her resistance. And worse, much worse, it wasn't only his charm that she was falling for, it was the man. He'd been fun today, a great sightseeing companion, good-humoured and patient while she'd trawled the fashion boutiques. He was also a man who took responsibility seriously, cared for his staff and troubled teens.

But it would be a dangerous mistake to let him close. So she would fight him and his charms with every ounce of will power she had.

When Jordan surfaced from a disturbed sleep interrupted by erotic dreams, Chloe's side of the bed was empty. Which was just as well, he decided, all things considered. He could smell her fresh-from-the-shower scent overlaid with the equally enticing aroma of a full English breakfast.

Pulling his jeans on over his boxers—not an easy task in his state—he followed his nose in search of the coffee pot. He found Chloe sitting at the breakfast table flicking through sightseeing brochures. She'd tied her hair back and he approved the conservative elbow-sleeved navy dress that met Dubai's fashion etiquette. 'Good morning.'

She looked up, her eyes instantly drawn to his chest, then quickly looked back to her reading material. 'Good morning.' She waved a hand at the table and said, 'I didn't know what you liked so I ordered everything.'

'Everything.' His eyes roamed over the sea of silver domes on the table and he had to grin. It appeared she was serious.

'The staff were waiting to serve you but I sent them away… I didn't know what time you'd be getting up.'

He stepped up to the table. 'And you wanted to make sure you wouldn't still be in bed when I did.'

Bingo. Chloe felt the blush explode into her cheeks. She lowered her head farther and reached for another pamphlet. 'I…I'm an early riser.'

'So am I,' he murmured, all lazy innuendo. The tips of her ears burned like a furnace, and she felt him lean in so that his lips grazed one to whisper, 'Why didn't you wake me?'

Honey over sand. Her breath caught, her pulse blipped. That sleep-husky voice was a reminder of last night and how she'd come so close to losing control, and in the glaring light of day she felt the flames of embarrassment all the way to her toes.

She gritted her teeth and decided a women's-only spa session was on this morning's agenda. Maybe she could make it last all day. 'We both know the reason for that.'

'I wonder if it'll still hold true for tomorrow?' Thankfully, he moved away, lifting domes and piling a plate with bacon and eggs. 'You've eaten, then.'

'Yes.' She replayed his words in her head then turned, studying him with narrowed eyes. 'Tomorrow morning won't be any different.'

He looked far too smug as he poured himself a coffee. 'Ah, yes, it will. Because tonight, Mrs Blackstone, we're to be treated to an Arabian honeymoon special, courtesy of Sheikh Qasim.'

Her heart thumped once, hard. 'What?'

'The sheikh's had some family emergency. It's an apology for postponing our meeting.'

'Postponing?' Chloe stared at him, a spurt of panic trickling through her bloodstream. 'How long for?'

'I don't know yet. I'm sure we'll hear very soon.' He smiled—a hint of wicked fun—over the gold rim of his cup. 'Don't look so worried.'

That devil's smile was supposed to reassure? 'So what's this honeymoon special we're being treated to?' More importantly, what did it involve and how did it impact on her decision to keep that space between them?

'It's a magical mystery tour for me too. We have to be ready with an overnight bag by noon.'

All night. Just the two of them in some romantic getaway spot? This wasn't good. She shook her head. 'You go. I… have a salon appointment this afternoon.'

His eyes cooled, as rapidly as molten steel turned black

when dropped in water, and a muscle tensed in his jaw. 'Then cancel it.'

His reaction and demand stunned her. She'd never heard him speak that way to her and shock curdled with something akin to fear beneath her breastbone. That loss of control feeling reminded her of Markos and the subtle but dangerous power he'd had over her. It was her worst nightmare and she struggled against it. 'I…don't want to cancel.'

His expression hardened further, the lines around his mouth deep, drawn. He set his cup down with a snap. 'Have you forgotten why you're here?'

'No.' She lifted her chin, determined not to let him forget either. 'And it's not to please you in bed.'

Something in his eyes warned her she'd overstepped some boundary. 'You're here as my wife.' He wasn't the smooth charmer now; he was all sharp spikes and business. 'This is our honeymoon and we're going to smile and act like honeymooners.' His jaw was tight. 'For our host at least.'

'But our host won't—'

'His *staff*, Chloe.' His eyes pinned her in place, his warning as clear as thunder over water. 'The status of your bank balance is testament to our *new and happy marriage*.'

'Yes…fine. Okay.' She gulped, embarrassed and humiliated that he'd had to point it out, then nodded. He was right, of course. All the way right. And Jordan had every one of those rights to point out his expectations and her responsibilities. She was glad this incident had happened because for a time there she'd lost focus on the real reason she was in Dubai with Mr Blackstone, gold-mining magnate.

And relieved because now there was no way he'd want anything to do with her beyond their written agreement. He thought she'd tried to weasel her way out of it because she had a nice deposit in her bank account. His opinion of her would be rock-bottom.

He wouldn't know why she'd said what she had—that she was afraid of her developing feelings and her increasing vulnerability. That the more time they spent together was increasingly dangerous. Let him think she was someone who couldn't keep her promises. As agreed, she'd play the part of happy honeymooner for an audience, but anything more wasn't going to happen.

CHAPTER TEN

IT WAS A quiet, awkward morning, both keeping out of the other's way as they packed for their overnight stay. Jordan informed her he had to leave the hotel for a while and asked if she needed anything while he was out. She politely told him she was fine and continued to pack, relieved she had some breathing space on her own.

The helicopter arrived right on time. The pilot soon had their bags stowed and explained their journey would take thirty minutes, travelling along the coast. Chloe had never flown in a helicopter and she compared it to a magic carpet ride as they lifted off the helipad, the Arabian tower growing rapidly smaller as they gained altitude and speed.

Jordan slung an arm around her shoulders, drawing her close and pointing to a ragged group of animals moving across the sand dunes below.

Chloe put aside their differences as his hand pressed against her shoulder, his unique scent filling her nostrils as she leaned over to peer out of his side. 'Camels?'

He nodded. 'A bride's dowry amongst Bedouin tribes.'

She laughed but she wasn't feeling the humour. 'My father would never have had enough camels to get rid of me.'

'I'd have taken you, Blondie,' he assured her, his voice mischievous. 'Even without a camel.' He squeezed her shoulder and she forgot they were acting a part and leaned into him, absorbing the view and simply enjoying his company.

Low grey vegetation dotted the dull red sand dunes as the helicopter began its descent. Trees and date palms came into view followed by a magnificent home that reminded her of a kid's sandcastle. Then they were touching down on a helipad in the middle of a courtyard, surrounded by wide arches leading to cool dark verandas.

A driver on staff met them in a Jeep and introduced himself as Kadar. They were quickly through the huge security gates and bumping over red sand towards nearby dunes.

Two minutes later they topped a rise, a virtual Garden of Eden appeared, the vista spread out before them like a scene from an exotic movie set. A blinding white tent like those used for outdoor weddings had been erected, gauzy curtains at the entrance swirling lazily in the drift of hot desert air. Nearby, water spilled over a rocky outcrop and into a white grotto. A shimmering sapphire and emerald pool reflected lush palms and other vibrant vegetation.

'Oh, wow. It's beautiful,' she breathed.

'And near enough to the coast to take advantage of the sea breeze in the afternoon,' Kadar said, his teeth white against his swarthy complexion as he swung down their bags and carried them towards the tent.

'Come on then, Blondie,' Jordan said, taking her hand. His eyes met hers in shared subterfuge as she climbed out of the vehicle. 'Let's explore our home for the next twenty hours or so.'

The inside of the tent was surprisingly cooler than she'd expected as she removed her sunglasses and stepped past the gauze curtain. Sheer decadence greeted her when her eyes adjusted to the relative dimness. It was more like stepping into a palatial home, or maybe the magical interior of a genie bottle. Low swathes of crimson and purple and gold silks. Plush black sofas arranged around the edge of an intricately designed Persian carpet. Scattered cushions, Moroccan lamps, a bowl of fresh fruit and a bottle of wine chilling in an ice-bucket on a low table.

At the far end a massive four-poster bed covered in black silk with gold and vermilion drapes. Pillows plumped and inviting. Beside her, Jordan reached out and turned her towards him with a smile and a playful eyebrow jiggle. 'A great way to spend a lazy…or not-so-lazy, afternoon.'

Kadar cleared his throat. 'If there is anything you require at any time, a staff member will be at your service. You will use this.' He handed Jordan a communication device. 'Buzz when you are ready for meals.' He gestured to his right. 'The cooler is stocked, there is extra linen. Communication with the outside world is not possible in the tent. If you need to contact anyone I can collect you and take you to the house. The amenities block, when you wish to bathe, is outside to your left.' He glanced at both of them in turn. 'No one will interrupt you here. It is private.'

Jordan squeezed her hand. 'The perfect honeymoon retreat, right, Blondie?' His conspiratorial twinkle had a rippling effect all down her body.

'Couldn't be more perfect. *Pookie.*' She knew Jordan expected her to play along but the word didn't sound as if it was spoken by a loving wife sharing an intimate relationship. It sounded forced. It *was* forced.

If Jordan thought so, he didn't show it. He shook hands with their driver. '*Shukran,* Kadar.'

'Yes,' Chloe agreed. 'This is very kind. Very comfortable. I'm sure we'll enjoy ourselves.'

They stood in the tent's shaded entrance and watched the Jeep disappear over the rise. Remained standing until the sound faded, leaving them with only the splash and trickle of water in the pool, the intermittent sound of an insect in a nearby salt-bush. So quiet she could hear her heart beating. Loudly.

And it was like paradise, the jewelled colours of sky, sand and foliage reflected in the water and dappled sunlight glinting like gold through the palms. If only—

'I've got some business to attend to,' he told her, still watching the sand dunes, that twinkle in his eyes she'd seen earlier gone. He walked to the table where he'd put his briefcase and pulled out a pile of document folders. 'I'm sure a girl like you can entertain herself for a while.' She felt the sudden distance between them like a physical ache.

Arms crossed, she tapped her fingers against her upper arms. 'Too right, I can. I've been doing it all my life.' She was relieved he was going to be too busy to bother with her. His remoteness and lack of interest in sharing this amazing place did *not* disappoint her. It was what she wanted, right? It was totally unnecessary, but she couldn't resist the clipped, 'Don't let me distract you from your work.'

She crossed the room and unzipped her bag, pulled out her swimsuit, a floppy hat and sunscreen. She'd seen an outdoor garden setting beneath the shade of the palms. She'd sit there and read awhile, then cool off in the water. 'Is that little pool safe?'

'Kadar told me it's an underwater spring,' he said, shuffling papers. 'The water's clean if you want to take a dip.' On the table, the intercom buzzed and Jordan reached for it. 'Yes, Kadar…'

Jordan disconnected a moment later, adrenaline zipping around his body. Qasim had left a message at the house to say he was looking forward to meeting Jordan the day after tomorrow. Finally.

He fingered a report he'd requested into mine expansion that he'd been meaning to read since they'd left Australia, then shoved it away. Dammit. He'd told Chloe he had work to do—a lie. What he'd needed was some distance to think about where he'd gone wrong this morning.

His reaction to her plea that he come alone had been swift and vehement and over the top. If he wasn't mistaken, he'd seen fear in her eyes, and despised himself. There was no way he'd have given her a choice, but he'd gone about it all wrong. This tension was his fault.

Pushing up, he paced to the cooler, pulled out a couple of frosty bottles of cola. When did a happy-go-lucky adventurer refuse a free and easy side-trip into the desert?

When it came with conditions—him, for example. But he might never know her reasons because he'd shot first and asked questions later. Actually, he hadn't asked anything at all, he'd simply demanded. And it had spoilt the rapport they'd been building.

He wandered to the tent flap and saw Chloe stretched out on a bench on her stomach, reading a book. Her hat and sunglasses shielded her face so he couldn't tell her mood. Her slim body was poured into a sunny-yellow one-piece, her legs glistening with suntan lotion.

His fingers itched to stroke the backs of those legs, starting at her well-turned ankles and working his way up to those incredibly toned thighs... Blowing out a breath, he wrenched off the top of one of the bottles, drank deeply. Still watching her. Still *imagining*, for God's sake.

She'd had every right to point out that he hadn't paid her to give him pleasure in the bedroom, that it had never been part of their deal. He'd just assumed he could change her mind... His track record with women had made him over-confident.

In two days' time he'd need his focus razor sharp for what was probably the most important deal he'd ever made. The only sure way to clear his mind and give him that focus was to get Chloe out of his system. And he *knew* the attraction wasn't one-sided, that she'd not stop him.

He stepped into the sun and began walking towards her.

He was done watching.

He was done fantasising.

Chloe knew Jordan was approaching. It was as if she'd developed a sixth sense where he was concerned. Her skin got that hot shivery sensation and her heart bopped like a teen at a rock concert. Too late to feign sleep.

And didn't they both want the same thing after all? Wasn't that what all this snapping and tension and tiptoeing around each other was about? Acknowledgement was like fuel adding to the fire singing through her body.

She didn't *want* to acknowledge it. This had to stop—

At the first moist contact, she gasped, then let her breath out slowly as he drew a line of suncream down her spine. 'Stop it.' At least she *thought* it was suncream. Yes, it smelled like suncream. She refused to react. Closing her book, she stood. Her legs felt hot, like melting cheese. The pool looked safe and inviting and she really needed to cool off.

'Hey, Blondie, that needs rubbing in first,' he said behind her.

'You put it there,' she accused, taking off her hat and tossing it on the sand. *Not* turning around. 'You *knew* I'd have to ask you. You did it on *purpose*. That's…*cheating*.'

'I know.' His voice was dark silk with an edge. 'The nice thing about a one-piece is it comes with plenty of bare back.' He punctuated his opinion with a glide of his fingertips along one edge of her swimsuit to the base of her spine.

And so help her, her feet were stuck in the sand. His body heat was a furnace. She could feel it pulling around her like a cloak, drawing them together. 'Rub me, then.' She pressed her lips together before she said any more and cleared that annoying husk from her throat. 'I can hardly go in the pool and leave a trail of white goo…'

'Definitely not.' He sounded amused as he set to work. 'Whatever would our host say?'

'I can't imagine...' She trailed off on a moan. His fingers were firm and skilled and sensuous as they worked from her nape and all the way down. Warm breath tickled the back of her neck and there was a trace of his familiar aftershave in the still air.

'That's enough.' She whirled around to face him, clutching at her elbows to keep from reaching for him and begging him to rub other more sensitive parts that were now throbbing with excruciating intensity. 'I...think that's quite enough. I should be right now.'

He smiled, that big cat gleam in his eyes mesmerising her, holding her captive yet at the same time calling to her to come of her own accord and play the game—a choice, but still his game.

She glanced at the pool—her refuge since he was still fully dressed—and edged towards it. 'You um...have work to do. I won't keep you.'

'Work's over for the day. It's playtime.' He toed off his shoes, began unbuttoning his shirt. He glanced at the table where she saw two bottles of cola. 'Care for a drink before we start?'

Start? 'No, thank you.' She ran the last few steps to the palm-shaded water and slid in feet first, breath catching with the initial shock of hot to cold. When she surfaced, Jordan was gloriously shirtless and pulling off his socks.

She slashed the water from her face and drank in the incredible definition of muscle over bone like a woman too long in the desert. He was a bronzed god, broad shoulders gleaming in the sun, his chest dusted with a smattering of dark hair. Her pulse stuttered and her lungs seemed to be fast running out of oxygen. 'What are you doing?' *Duh*... Not only her lungs, her brain was obviously low on oxygen too.

He unbuckled the belt around his jeans. 'What does it look like?' With a flick of his wrist he unsnapped the stud, revealing a neat little navel and an arrow of hair that pointed to—

'Jordan...' She sank onto a ledge at the edge of the pool, grateful for the water's buoyancy. Her eyes refused to look away from the front of his jeans—it was like being drawn to a car wreck. Which she desperately feared *she'd* be if she didn't slam on the brakes before all control was lost. 'Jordan, don't. I'm serious.'

'So am I.' He grinned. A boy's own, kiss-the-girls-and-make-them-smile kind of grin that would have had schoolgirls running towards him rather than away. His long fingers toyed with the zip. 'Turn around if you don't want to see.'

Turn your back on a predator? She bit her lip. 'You wouldn't...'

Red flag to a bull. As soon as the words were out she realised she'd made a big mistake. The repercussions were already clamouring in her head. 'No. I didn't mean...' She trailed off as he shoved his jeans off, kicked them away.

Temporary relief coursed along her veins. He still wore boxers. Red silk with rearing black stallions...and an impressive tent in front. Oh, good gracious...

Somewhere far overhead she heard the faint sound of a jet on its way somewhere. Progress and technology. Yet here she was in the middle of a desert that probably hadn't changed in thousands of years.

Nor had the attraction between man and woman.

Simple, she thought, *this* man was attracted to *this* woman. And vice versa.

'You're confused, Blondie.'

His richly amused voice reminded her she was still staring at his crotch. 'No, I'm not.'

And she wasn't. Not any more. Her mind was as clear as the ochre horizon. She wanted him. Around her, over her, inside her. All of him. Why pretend otherwise? This attraction wasn't going away and she was through fighting it. Next week she'd deal with the fallout, but next week was a million years away.

'I'm coming in.' Eyes the same colour as the desert sky met hers leaving her in no doubt that he wasn't talking about the pool.

'Thank God,' she murmured.

He didn't look away from her eyes as he walked to the pool and slid into the water so they were both waist-deep…and close. Her heart beat strangely, as if it recognised him and was welcoming him home. But he made no move to touch her. He was waiting for her to make the first move.

'I want you.' She reached out to caress the hard square jaw, then watched her hand travel down the column of his throat, the hard planes of his chest, then over and around tight male nipples. Leaning closer, she pressed a kiss to one, then the other, and heard him groan, felt the strong thump of his heart. She explored his abs, watched his muscles contract beneath her fingers.

Lower, beneath the water's surface until her fingers twisted in the waistband of his boxers. The hard ridge of his erection nudged her hand through the silk and his breath hissed out.

She looked up at him, the tension in his jaw, an unholy fire in his eyes. And murmured, 'Oh, yeah.'

'Chloe.' No teasing pet-name games now, just urgent need and barely leashed control. 'Invite me in.'

'Yes.' She smiled, touched her lips to his briefly and curled herself around him, the heat of his sun-warmed skin a stunning contrast against her water-cooled body.

'Chloe.' His fingers raced over her shoulders and beneath her straps to drag them down her arms so she could shrug out of them. And then he was holding her bare breasts in his palms and whisking his thumbs over her taut nipples and her skin was turning goose-bumpy all over and it was like last night's adventure game in the hotel garden only much, much better.

'Jordan. Ooh-aah,' she managed, her breath hitching.

He was in total agreement and she knew there was no way he was going to allow anything or anyone to interrupt them this time. 'Swimsuit all-the-way off.'

He pushed his boxers down, but not before he produced a foil packet from somewhere and ripped it open with his teeth and sheathed himself beneath the water line while she peeled the Lycra down her thighs, then used her toes to push it the rest of the way. She tugged the band from her hair and ran her fingers through it, feeling like a goddess to his god.

They slid deeper into the cool blue depths together, eye to eye, skin to skin, foreheads touching, legs entwining, his erection hot and hard and heavy against her belly.

Not close enough. Not yet.

Water lapped at their shoulders, the palm fronds above them lazily limp in the heat that shimmered off the sand surrounding them. Nothing moved, nothing changed in this timeless spot, and for a moment it was as if the world were holding its breath, waiting.

Chloe knew *their* world wasn't waiting, the world of high finance and corporate luncheons to cater was far away, though in days this magical time would be over.

'This place is ours,' she said fiercely. 'This memory is ours.' And nothing could take that away from her. Gripping his jaw in her hands, she fused her mouth to his as if she could draw him into herself.

But he was the one who took control, took her under. Dark, dangerous delight as his tongue swept in to tangle with hers. Demand in his hands that seemed to be everywhere at once; her shoulders, her breasts, down her spine to cup her bottom and yank her closer.

Last night's starlit fantasy melted in the white-hot glare
of a desert afternoon. There were no seductive word pictures
this time, no whispered images and moonlight imaginings.
Only moans and groans, need and greed.

Strong, relentless fingers found her centre. Fast slippery
strokes, the glimpse of glory to come, and she gasped, her
head falling back as the world spun out of control. Faster. Her
entire body trembling now until the sky seemed to shimmer
to white and explode into a million suns.

Before she could collapse, he caught her in the steel cradle
of his arms and plunged inside her with a groan—one deep
thrust to the hilt—driving her up again.

All she could see was him. In his eyes she saw blazing desire, demand and desperation. The words he muttered were
hot and harsh and shockingly explicit against her mouth. She
licked them from his tongue, then matched them with equal
intensity, while her fingers kneaded and plucked and scraped
whatever flesh they came in contact with.

Chloe raked unmerciful fingernails down his back, and
Jordan gritted his teeth, pleasure balanced on a fine needle-
point of pain. Her amber eyes shone—she knew exactly what
she was doing.

The need for speed hammered through him, his blood
echoing the same frantic rhythm, but he pulled out slowly,
slowly, watching her eyes widen, her pupils dilate, a little
panic filter through the haze. He smiled. *Payback*. Then
plunged deep, back into that hot, tight paradise.

He'd known Chloe wasn't the submissive sort but he hadn't
been sure if her adventurous spirit extended to her sexual
preferences until now. Greed matched greed, heat matched
heat, passion matched passion. Never had he found a woman
so compatible with his own sexual desires. When he groaned,
she sighed. When he bowed, she arched. When he asked, she

gave. She was a sensual whirlwind of perfume and water-slick skin. Peaches and cream and wild abandon.

She convulsed around him, her hands fisted against his chest, eyes glazed while she cried her triumphant release. His own vision blurred as he leapt over the sweet abyss with her.

CHAPTER ELEVEN

IT WAS A while before he could clear the haze from his mind and find his way back to something approaching rational. Somehow he'd managed to manoeuvre them both near enough to the edge of the pool to stretch out on the sand without drowning, and they lay wet and entwined like a couple of pieces of ragged river weed.

'We're going to burn,' she said lazily. 'All over. It won't be pretty. And it's guaranteed to be painful.'

He turned to look at her. Her arms were crossed over her eyes and her skin glistened with water but a satisfied smile curved her lips. In fact, she looked like the kitty cat who'd happily wallowed in a pond of cream.

His own smile was quick to follow. He rubbed the flat of his palm over the nearest breast and felt the hard little bead beneath. 'You'd be pretty whatever colour your skin was.'

She swiped at his arm. 'Charmer,' she said, not looking at him. 'Everyone knows lobster's *so* last century.' Shading her eyes, she sat up. 'I seem to have lost a swimsuit.'

'You don't need one. Skinny dipping's much more fun.' He caught the glint of his ring on her finger and something strange stole through him. Something almost possessive. He firmed his jaw. Whatever it was, it was dangerous. 'Time to move, then, if you don't want to burn.'

He gripped her wrists and pulled her up. Their naked bod-

ies bumped, those deep amber eyes met his. And again he
was flooded with a wave of unfamiliar emotion.

They'd had sex, that was all, he told himself. Good, fast,
honest, mind-blowing, mutually satisfying, all-the-way-to-
heaven-and-back sex. So what was this tender afterglow of
feelings? Why did he feel this...deep rush? Did she feel it
too? He remained still, cuffing her wrists, and staring into
her eyes searching for an answer. 'You okay?'

A fleeting shadow crossed her gaze but maybe he'd mis-
read it because it vanished with her smile. 'Besides needing
a shower and missing out on my spa session?' She planted a
kiss beneath his jaw. 'But I'm feeling entirely too ravished
to be annoyed. You?'

'We both know there was never a spa session and my back
will need some TLC later.'

'Ah...sorry about that...I'll make it up to you.'

She watched her finger tracing his left bicep and the in-
ferno he'd thought they'd doused for now sparked anew with
a speed and brightness that shocked him. More shocking; it
wasn't just spark that he wanted—he wanted *Chloe's* spark.
'I intend making sure you do. Chloe...'

'Yes?' Her finger remained where it was but her eyes
flicked to his again, alive and alluring.

*I want that feeling with you again. I want it so badly it
scares the hell out of me.* Her hand shifted slightly and the
ring drew his attention for a second time. Frowning, he
stepped back and brushed sand off his shoulders rather than
haul her closer and test how soon and how bright that spark
could catch again. 'Why don't you go have the first shower?'

'What, no showering with a friend?' Her voice was light
and teasing. 'This is the desert—we should all do our bit for
the planet.'

He walked to the table, picked up the bottles of cola now
wet with condensation and held one out to her. 'If we get into

that shower together, we're going to end up using a hell of a lot more water than our quota.'

She blushed, which was odd, he thought, considering she was unashamedly stark naked, and after what they'd just done to each other in broad daylight. She took the bottle from his fingers. 'Thanks.'

'I'll check out what's on the menu for dinner,' he said, deliberately turning away first.

Mindful of water conservation, Chloe showered fast with the fragrant gel provided. Her whole body sang—everywhere she touched she remembered how it had felt when Jordan had touched her. His magic fingers had wrought the most exquisite responses from her. No man had ever made her feel so alive. So feminine and desired.

She spent a longer time choosing from the scented massage creams on display and decided on a blend of frankincense, sandalwood, neroli and ylang ylang. The jar promised 'To instil peacefulness'. She figured she needed it. Because eventually somehow she'd have to pay the price for what she'd done.

She'd succumbed and made love with her business partner. Jordan Blackstone, millionaire bachelor and playboy. And she wasn't even sorry.

Yet.

She pushed negative thoughts away. Her reflection smiled back at her as she ran her fingers through her damp hair. Her shimmery off-one-shoulder kaftan with swirling colours of raspberry and tangerine highlighted the honey-blonde streaks. Her eyes looked bigger, brighter. I've-got-a-new-lover eyes. And with that warm glow to her skin, she actually looked pretty for once in her life.

You'd be pretty whatever colour your skin was.

Warmth closed around her heart like a gentle hand. Of course it was a line, and he'd been fondling her breast at the time, but it had made Chloe feel special. Sexy. Sensuous. Desired. And his eyes…she sighed…she was almost tempted to believe it hadn't been just about sex because for an instant she'd seen something deeper before he'd blinked it away. He'd asked her if she was okay then gallantly insisted she take her shower while he organised dinner.

He wasn't going to hang around when they got back to Australia—she wasn't his tall, glamorous brunette type with PhD and whatever else tacked on the end of her name. Their lives were worlds apart. But she'd discovered Jordan wasn't the shallow man she'd first thought. He was involved in charity work and genuinely cared about his staff and friends unlike so many men she'd met over the last few years. During this trip he'd been protective, considerate and generous.

She trusted him in a way she'd never trusted a man before. And against all the defences she'd put up, she was falling for him in a big way. It was so much more than just the business aspect of their relationship. He'd made her feel as if some dreams could come true. If nothing else, she was learning he was someone she could count on no matter what. He made her feel special.

She had a horrible fear there'd be tears when they parted. But hurts and disappointments and moving on were her life. She wouldn't change anything just because she was falling for a guy who wouldn't be there in the long term. She'd do what she always did—live for today and think about the future when it arrived.

While Chloe spent the next hour reading and relaxing in their luxury accommodation, Jordan showered then went over his plans for his meeting with the sheikh. She couldn't resist looking up every now and again to ensure it wasn't a dream. That the bare-chested man in the loose khaki shorts who'd done the wild thing with her was still there, and still as gorgeous and sexy as ever.

As the golden afternoon sky turned to crimson and purple and the air lost its sting, the Jeep arrived. The pair greeted their hosts and waited while Kadar and his wife unloaded fresh scented towels and trays of aromatic food.

Kadar raised flaps at intervals around the tent to let in the cooling breeze and bring the desert atmosphere inside while his wife spread the feast on a low table and lit fragrant sandalwood and beeswax candles inside the Moroccan lamps. The flickering light cast an intimate glow. They wished them a pleasant evening, then left discreetly.

'Hungry yet?' Jordan set his paperwork aside.

'Famished.' Chloe stretched luxuriously, then strolled to the table where Jordan was sitting and massaged his shoulders a moment. She loved that her new status as his lover gave her permission to touch him whenever she pleased. 'How about you?'

He grasped her hands over his shoulders, pulling her close and catching her ear between his teeth. 'So ravenous I could start on that delectable bare shoulder.'

'Later,' she promised. 'What have you ordered?'

'Come and find out.' He stood, and, fingers still linked, they walked to where the food was set.

He poured the chilled wine into what were probably genuine gold goblets, handed her one. 'To success.'

'To success.' Setting her goblet down, Chloe stabbed at a falafel with her fork, lifted it to her mouth and chewed. 'These are yummy.' She reached for another.

'Slowly. You'll give yourself indigestion.' He chuckled at her fast-food habit. 'This isn't Burger Supreme Central. Food is meant to be savoured and enjoyed. Try this.' He ladled something from a bowl, held the spoon out to her. 'Close your eyes and tell me what you can taste.'

'Turmeric, coriander, ginger and chilli. What is it?'

'Goat curry. One of my favourite dishes.'

The faint trickle of water and rustlings of tiny desert creatures beyond the tent could be heard between conversation that concentrated mainly on Jordan tutoring Chloe in the arts of leisurely fine wining and dining.

Eventually, Chloe excused herself to go to the bathroom. She almost laughed as she swished her hands beneath the tepid water. She'd served at fine dining functions rather than dined. But unlike Stewart, Jordan didn't seem to care about class distinctions; he treated people as equals.

She was drying her hands when she saw Jordan's wedding ring beside his toiletry bag and picked it up. Heavy. Must be worth a fortune. Why would he want to spend so much on a wedding ring for a fake marriage? As she held it in her palm she caught sight of some text inscribed inside. *Jordan and Lynette forever.* It was dated six years ago.

That lighter-than-air, on-top-of-the-world feeling deflated under the weight of doubts and questions.

Okay. Calm down, she told herself, her fingers curling around the ring. He wasn't married now.

Or was he?

Spots danced before her eyes. Had he been lying to her all along? Making a cheap and sordid mockery of what they'd done this afternoon?

No! She refused to believe it, but nevertheless a band clamped around her stomach, so tight she thought she might throw up.

Some things were none of her business but he hadn't simply left this information out of their conversation; he'd specifically told her he'd never been married.

By the time she went back inside, she had her nerves under control and joined him on the sofa where he'd poured Turkish coffee for both of them.

She took her cup and sipped. 'You're not wearing your ring.'

He glanced down at his bare finger. 'Noticed like a true wife.'

She fixed him with a stare. 'And you'd know this how? The wife bit,' she clarified, when his brows drew down in confusion. Or was it guilt?

'The suncream got under it when I rubbed you down. I took if off when I had a shower and forgot about it. It's in the bathroom…' His hesitation and his eyes told her what she wanted to know. 'You found it,' he said unnecessarily. Along with the information he'd neglected to mention.

'I did.' She held it up between finger and thumb, looked at the inscription again. 'Want to explain?'

'Not particularly.'

She wished her own expression were as skilled in keeping secrets as his was. 'I imagined you'd say that.' She set the ring on the table in front of him with a clink of metal on wood. 'Jordan and Lynette forever, huh?'

He tensed and a muscle in his jaw tightened. 'I'm not married, Chloe.' When she didn't answer—which in itself *was* her answer—he said, 'Don't you think the media would have had a field day with that information by now if Lynette and I had been married?'

She hadn't thought that far. 'You owe me some explanation at least.'

He raised his brows as if to say he owed her nothing of the kind. 'Do business partners need to know the intimate details of each other's love lives?'

He was coolly twisting this around to suit the circumstances. To suit himself. She reined in her resentment and the hurt. 'We went way past business partners this afternoon and you've made me feel like an idiot. You know about my family and why I agreed to this arrangement with you. I told you about Markos and how he made a fool of me.

'But you?' She pointed an accusing finger at his chest.

'You've kept yourself to yourself. And no one makes a fool of Jordan Blackstone, right? Because unlike some, you can afford to cover up a scandal.'

In the flickering light his expression changed, changed again. Acceptance to defensiveness to…understanding? 'Chloe. No scandal, I promise. And I'm sorry you feel that way. It wasn't my intention.'

'Not your intention to make a fool of me or not your intention to tell me about Lynette?'

Jordan saw a suspicious chin wobble and despised himself. His pride and his need for control—his *evasiveness*—had hurt the one person he least wanted to hurt. He reached out and cupped her jaw between his hands and looked into her eyes. 'Listen to me. You are *not* a fool, Chloe Montgomery. You're clever and honest and witty. You're generous and compassionate. And one of a kind.'

'High praise coming from my employer.' Her smile was tinged with sadness—as if those qualities he valued in her didn't count in her mind. As if she wanted more.

'Partner.' He hesitated. 'Friend.'

'Does the term *lover* scare you, Jordan?' She pushed his hands away from her face. 'But you're changing the subject. Again. If you don't want to talk about Lynette, that's *fine*.' She shrugged. 'It's not as if we're going to see each other after this week anyway.'

The words were unexpected and something flashed through his system and was gone, like lightning, leaving a strange burnt-out, hollow sensation. 'There's nothing in our agreement that says we can't continue to see each other if we want.'

Doubt and something like resignation clouded her eyes. '*If* we're in the same city. Or even in the same country.'

'Come here, Blondie.' He pulled her to him, tucked her against his side and kissed her sweet-smelling hair. Their relationship might be temporary but it wasn't over yet and he wanted to give her at least something of what she wanted to hear. 'Lynette was someone I met at uni.'

'Just *someone*? You had a wedding ring. Presumably she had one too. Oh…Jordan.' She turned her face up to his, a groove between her brows, her eyes worried. 'Please, don't tell me she…'

'No. We were going to get married. It just didn't happen.'

'Why not?'

'We wanted different things.'

'But you kept the ring,' she said softly. 'You wanted a reminder.'

Hell, yes. 'Not for any foolish sentimental reason. I keep it to remind me that I'm not, and never will be, a marrying man.'

Her eyes welled up with sympathy. 'What did she do to destroy that for you?'

Frustrated that she'd assume a woman could wield that kind of power over him, he grabbed the damn thing, jammed it on his finger. 'What makes you think it was her? What makes you so sure I didn't break *her* heart?'

'I'm *not* sure. Because you haven't told me. But your words and actions since we agreed to this arrangement would indicate she's the one who did a number on you and not the other way round.'

The woman's insight and gentle compassion weren't something Jordan knew how to deal with. She was scraping dangerously close to a raw spot he'd almost forgotten he had. 'It's in the past—leave it there.'

As a distraction, he touched her bare shoulder with a finger—smooth ivory—and felt a little shiver run through her. 'We're never going to have another night like this, Blondie. Let's not waste it.'

Whisky eyes turned black in the amber candlelight and a

slow smile drifted over her lips. 'Let's not.' She rose and stood before him, gaze locked on his, confident in her femininity.

Sensing she wanted his attention for the moment but not his touch, he remained where he was. A messy flaxen halo around that elfin face with her too-big eyes that drew you in until you lost a part of yourself. Confident, yes, but also small and delicate and easily damaged. He wanted to tuck her inside the pocket of his jacket and keep her safe, next to his heart. *Just keep her...*

She pushed the garment off her shoulder and the silk slithered to the floor in a vibrant kaleidoscope of colour, leaving a vision of alabaster skin and lush curves and violet lace.

His heart pounded, his groin tightened and he curled his hands into fists on his thighs to stop himself reaching for her. Maybe it was the mystical romance of the silken tent or their exotic location or the drift of beeswax and sandalwood from the candles, but no woman had ever enchanted him so.

Was he ready for another woman in his life? he wondered. Then stopped wondering anything at all because all his blood drained from his brain as she unclasped her bra and dropped it at her feet. Her breasts were perfection, like succulent ripe fruit waiting to be relished.

She pushed the lace panties down over her hips and stepped out of them. A symphony of shadows and light played over her body. He might have groaned but he was no longer certain of his own responses, so absorbed was he with the vision in front of him.

Deep, intimate silence shimmered in the air between them, broken by the intermittent sputtering of a candle, a night creature fossicking in the palms outside, the sound of their own heightened breathing.

She held out her hands, candlelight gilding her eyes. 'Take me to bed, Jordan.'

He needed no second bidding. Scooping up her slender

form, he held her against his chest, and as he watched the emotion flicker over her face he lost himself for a moment in a fantasy.

She was as light as the desert breeze wafting through the hanging silks as he carried her to their bed. Because he just wanted to watch her a moment, he made a place for her amongst the mountain of pillows and laid her down. Stripping off his shorts, he climbed onto the bed, his thighs straddling hers.

To please himself, he fanned her hair out on either side of her head. To please her, he stroked her body from neck to thighs with feather-light touches that roused goose bumps along her flesh. To please them both, he lowered his mouth to one breast and closed his lips over the puckered tip while he brushed his fingers slowly over the curve of its twin.

They had all night so he lingered where he might have rushed. Took the time to enjoy the nuances of flavour and texture and fragrance—of her skin and hair, mouth and tongue. And she responded like a dream. Low intimate murmurs, the slow, sensuous glide of flesh on flesh, her hands and mouth unerringly seeking out places where he liked to be touched.

Rumpled silk sheets and air warm with the scent of passion. Candles sputtered and died. The velvet night seduced and soothed as the moon drifted across the sky, its cool light shafting through the tent's open flaps, painting skin an ethereal silver.

And when at last he lost himself inside her and the sounds of shared passion filled the air, it wasn't with a rush of speed, but with an abiding tenderness he'd never known he possessed.

CHAPTER TWELVE

CHLOE WOKE WITH the dawn—a rim of gold against the sand dunes and a chill in the dry air. She wanted to sigh and smile at the same time and hold the last few precious hours in her heart forever. Their magical Arabian night was over.

She didn't move lest she wake the man beside her. She wanted to look her fill of him first. Long black lashes swept down over his cheeks but that was where the innocent appearance stopped. A disreputable-looking night's growth dotted his square jaw; those lips, almost curving into a smile, were made for sin.

And she was tempted to sin some more. To taste, and touch and tease again. Tempted beyond all sane, logical reason.

Instead, she slid carefully out of bed, and, drawing a light shawl around her bare shoulders, she crept to the tent's flap and watched the harsh landscape welcome the day.

She needed to think where this thing with Jordan was going. Its speed and intensity scared her. *There's nothing that says we can't continue to see each other.* She remembered the expression in his eyes when he'd said those words. As if he meant it. The same look she'd seen when he'd made love to her in the moonlight.

I'm not a marrying man.

He confused her. She felt as if she were on a seesaw. He didn't want commitment—had made no secret of it. He wanted no-strings for as long as whatever it was they had lasted. Wasn't that what she wanted too? Free to walk away. No complications, no regrets, no tears.

I want to belong.

'What are you doing out of bed?' a sleep-husky voice said behind her.

And maybe it was his tone or something in the air between them because she imagined him saying that to her a year from now. Two. Twenty.

But she must keep it simple because he wouldn't be around; even a month was stretching it. Just sex, just for now. She dashed a suspicious moisture from her eye before she turned, her smile in place. 'Waiting for my lover to come find me.'

Warm hands drifted over her shoulders, then slipped beneath the shawl to stroke bare skin, but he'd seen her furtive action.

'He's here,' he murmured. 'And he wants to know who the low-life who hurt you is so he can go run him through with his sword.'

Her breath caught and she shook her head. She couldn't tell him how she really felt—how he would hate that. 'What are you talking about?'

'The scumbag who hurt you.' His voice tightened on the words. 'I asked you in the diner that first night we met. It's not Mr Despicable—he was never in your heart. There's someone else. Who was he, Blondie?'

Jordan's perceptiveness surprised her but the image that rose behind her eyes no longer harmed and humiliated. She was a stronger person than that naive young woman Stewart had used then tossed aside. More experienced. Wiser. It had taken Jordan to show her that.

'He doesn't matter. Not anymore.' Stewart was less than nothing. A faded scar. A lesson learned.

'You've never got him out of your system,' Jordan murmured against her neck. 'Now's a good time.'

He was right—the lying SOB needed to go. 'Rich English aristocrat. Widower. Huge country home. I was his son's nanny. Naive little Chloe fell in love and thought her love was returned. I was in such a hurry to tell my family the good news of my success and too stupid to realise that success didn't mean finding a rich man and falling in love.

'When he...' *threw me out* '...when I left, I didn't mention my failures to my family or that I'd moved on. Because we didn't keep in touch, they still think...' She shrugged.

'You are *not* a failure, Chloe.' He lifted her hair to kiss the back of her neck. 'You're a remarkable woman. You're gutsy and trustworthy. Someone others can count on.'

'Thank you.' He'd never know how much his words meant, more so because she knew they weren't empty platitudes. They lifted her up and made her want to sing. 'You can slay my dragons and demons for me any time.'

'Consider him slain.' His breath tickled the hairs at her temple. 'What would you have your lover do now?'

'I'd have him carry me back to bed and then...' She turned her head and whispered something in his ear that had that gorgeous mouth tilting up at the edges.

'My lady's wish is my command,' he said, and swung her up into his arms.

Twenty-four hours later they were preparing to meet the man Jordan hoped to forge a business deal with. The reason they'd come to Dubai. The reason she was here, Chloe reminded herself, checking her appearance in the mirror.

Satisfied she looked the part of wife with her conservative navy blue business suit and demure cream blouse and her hair swept back into a neat chignon by the hotel's stylist, she exited the bathroom in search of Jordan.

They'd returned to the city late yesterday. Their honeymoon night was a beautiful memory but, if last night was an indication, the rest of their time in Dubai promised to be almost as memorable.

She saw him standing by one of the panoramic windows overlooking the beach scrolling through emails on his phone, brows drawn in concentration. His made-to-measure suit accentuated his broad shoulders and long legs and his shirt looked whiter-than-white against his tanned skin. A navy tie completed the corporate image.

But now she knew the body beneath the clothes. The man behind the image. She knew what he liked, what made him come. Who he was when he wasn't being Jordan Blackstone, gold-mining magnate.

She admired that man. She respected him. He'd given her a new belief in herself and lifted her self-esteem. He'd shown her that not all men were bastards.

Almost reluctant, she stepped farther into the room and announced her presence. 'When do we leave?'

'In a few moments.' He looked up and smiled, checking out her appearance with a nod of approval. 'Perfect. I swear I've never met a more punctual woman. Punctual *and* beautiful.'

'That's why you married me, right, Pookie?'

His smile dipped a moment like the sun skimming behind a solitary cloud in a blue sky. 'Very good, Blondie. Keep it up and it's going to work to both our advantage. Only a few more hours and if everything goes to plan…'

They'd be going home. She crossed the space between them and straightened his tie even though it didn't need straightening—everything about Jordan was precise. Understated and refined. His aftershave was cool and subtle. 'You'll wow him with that fantastic business plan of yours and with your commitment and morals. He'd be an idiot to refuse you over that other Xmining company.'

'X23.' He tipped her chin up and looked into her eyes. 'Thanks for your confidence in me—it means a lot. And thanks for doing this entire thing on such short notice.'

'You paid me to do a job.' Hardly aware she was doing it, she twisted the ring on her finger.

He nodded. 'So it's the beauty session at last, then. Or is it a spa?'

'Spa and massage. I can't wait. You see, I have these tight muscles…'

Jordan chuckled, and she smiled back at him, sharing the humour and fun. She'd been expecting to spend the day with Qasim's wife and other female members of his family but the elderly woman was still by her sister's bedside since she'd suffered a severe heart attack. It had been decided that Chloe would meet the sheikh, then be free to choose her own activities for the day.

'One more thing before we leave.' Jordan pulled a slim box from his jacket pocket and opened it. 'This is for you.'

She stared at the slim gold chain and a pair of gold filigree hoop earrings nestled in royal blue velvet. Was this a thank-you gift or a lover's gift? Or investment pieces to wear for the day? She didn't ask. Not now.

'I bought it from one of Qasim's shops the other day,' Jordan explained and lifted the chain from its box. 'He'd expect the owner of a successful gold mine to shower his new wife with gold. Chosen specifically for her, even if she's not into jewellery. Turn around.' He fastened it around her neck. 'I'll let you do the earrings.'

'I need a mirror.' Distracted, she withdrew her compact and removed the tiny sleepers she'd worn for years then slid the golden hoops in. Maybe it was the residual passion from the past couple of days but she looked different wearing Jordan's jewellery. And he'd chosen it for her.

'Sophisticated and classy,' he said.

'They're not words I associate with myself,' she replied, still studying herself critically.

'Well, you should start associating them, because they suit you—the words and the jewellery.'

Sophisticated? Chloe Montgomery? He meant it but with every second that ticked by she felt less like herself and more like a woman she'd never met and didn't know.

Or maybe he'd brought out the real Chloe, the one she could be if given a chance. She spun away towards the elevator, tossing her compact in her purse. 'You do *not* want to be late. I'm making sure you're not.'

'Aren't you going to give me a kiss for luck?'

'You don't need luck—you already have enough of everything else to make this work.'

Their meeting was scheduled in one of the hotel's private meeting rooms. They were received by one of Sheikh Qasim's advisers and ushered into a luxurious blue room large enough to hold fifty people. The man promptly disappeared, leaving them in a kind of limbo. Which Jordan seemed to expect.

Not to worry—smiling waiters served them spiced tea and a variety of delicacies while they waited. And waited. And waited. If Jordan was nervous, he didn't show it. He assured Chloe waiting was the norm here.

A long, fraught hour or more later, the door opened and the elderly man walked in, his robes swirling about him.

Jordan and Chloe both stood. Jordan stepped forward, extending his hand. 'Sheikh Qasim bin Omar Al-Zeid. *Salam alaykum.*' Peace be upon you.

The sheikh met Jordan and clasped his hand firmly. *'Wa alaykum as-salam.'*

'Sheikh Qasim bin Omar Al-Zeid, I'd like to introduce my wife.' He placed a light hand on her back and smiled into her eyes. 'This is Chloe Montgomery.'

The sheikh turned to Chloe, nodded respectfully. *'Salam alaykum.'*

'Wa alaykum as-salam.' Smiling, Chloe inclined her head.

A short time later, the introductions over, pleasantries exchanged and sincere thanks given for the 'honeymoon special', Chloe was finally able to escape to her massage appointment. Gratefully. *Very* gratefully. Tricky etiquette in this part of the world. For Jordan's sake, she hoped she'd got it right. He'd paid for her services and she'd smiled and acted the docile, adoring wife and just prayed it had worked. If it was successful, they were booked on tomorrow's flight. Which meant tonight was their last night.

Her heart was already bleeding. So she did what any woman would do under the circumstances—she distracted herself. If she didn't do *something*, she'd end up pacing a bald track in their suite's very expensive carpet. And she needed, desperately, to maintain some control over her circumstances.

Hours later Chloe received a call. 'Break out the champagne,' Jordan told her with a grin a mile wide in his voice. 'I'm on my way up to the room.'

And she could visualise that familiar spark in his eyes, the way his cheeks creased when he smiled, and wished she could be there right now to plant one on him. 'Jordan, that's wonderful news, congratulations. I'm so happy for you, but I'm not there.'

Jordan frowned as he stepped into the elevator, his effervescent mood losing some of its fizz. What did she mean, she wasn't there? Surely a massage didn't last that long? 'It's gone three—where are you?'

'I'm in the Burjuman Centre making the most of what's left of my time here.'

'Shopping.' A ridiculous feeling of disappointment rolled through him. He stared unseeing at the world falling away as the elevator soared skywards. She was shopping while he'd been making one of the most important deals of his life.

'I'm sorry,' he heard her say. 'I lost track of time. I'm leaving right this minute. Don't start without me, okay?'

'Okay.' He disconnected, stepped out into their suite muttering to himself. Her stories must be having an effect on him because for some insane reason he'd expected her to be waiting with bated breath for his triumphant return, the way a lady waited in the castle for her battle-weary hero.

Blimey, what an idiot.

When it came right down to it, why would it matter to Chloe how his meeting went? She'd done her bit. For her this whole business was over. She could walk away now, well recompensed for her time and trouble, and never have to see him again.

The question was, would she?

The more disturbing question was would he let her?

He ordered the most expensive bubbly on the menu then strode to the windows and watched the afternoon sun shimmering on the gulf. Forty-eight hours ago they'd been making love in a desert oasis under that afternoon sun. Now... He dismissed the wet and wild images. *Priorities, man.* He'd secured a buyer for his gold as he'd promised his father; that was what was important here.

But when she rushed across the room towards him thirty minutes later, pink-cheeked and pretty in a new fuchsia sundress with a matching bolero, her eyes sparkling with excitement—for *his* success—he wondered for a few mad seconds whether his long-held, sharply focused priorities had blurred.

'Congratulations!' She didn't give him time to clear that haze, dropping her bag and launching herself at him with an enthusiastic 'You did it!' and smacking her lips to his.

When she might have pulled away he clamped his hands to her head—he wasn't settling for anything that brief. Prying her lips apart with his tongue, he swirled inside and turned a simple kiss into something deeper and a lot more complicated. She yielded without surrendering, her familiar taste spinning through his senses like a favourite whisky.

'Not without your help,' he murmured when they finally broke apart, gasping and staring at each other as if they were looking at strangers. As if something had changed.

Everything had changed. It was time to go home. And they both knew it.

'We made a good team today,' she said, quickly busying herself kneading his shoulders with her thumbs and nipping at his jaw with her teeth.

He walked his fingers all the way down her spine and tucked her close so she fitted against him, snug as moss on a log. 'We're good together.'

'Yes…'

Rucking up her skirt then winding her arms around his neck, she practically climbed up him and hooked her legs around his waist. Her feminine heat pressed against his pelvis, her intoxicating eyes…he could drown in those eyes… If he wasn't careful. If he was honest…

'There's something I want to tell you first,' he said, holding her close. 'I came clean with Qasim. I told him we weren't married.'

She leaned back to look at him, her hands still around his neck. 'After all the trouble and expense you went to? Why?'

'It just seemed wrong. It *was* wrong. I've wanted this for so long. Winning this meant so much to me that I lost sight of everything else. But I realised today when I walked into that room that I wanted to win it without resorting to deception.'

She nodded. 'I'm glad. It's much better this way.'

He saw the questions in her eyes and he suddenly wanted to share his story with her. 'I want to I tell you why this is so important to me.'

'Okay,' she said quietly, and slid down his torso until her feet touched the ground.

Without letting her go, he led her to a window seat and sat her down and looked into those liquid amber eyes. 'You already know my father died before he could close an important deal he'd set up in the UAE. But what I didn't tell you was that I was a selfish, self-centred undergraduate who was flunking his course and should have been there for him when he needed me...'

When he was done telling her, she squeezed his hand, her eyes filled with understanding and respect. 'You'd have made him so proud today.'

'I promised him I'd fix it if it was the last thing I did and I think I managed that.' He felt lighter, as if a huge weight had been lifted. Finally, after all the years of hard work, he'd found some sort of closure. And sharing the moment with Chloe was something he'd always remember.

'So, what did Qasim say when you told him about us?' Chloe asked.

'That he appreciated my honesty. He told me I was the best man for the job whether I was married or not.'

She nodded. 'You didn't need me after all.'

He shook away a sudden melancholy her words invoked and dragged her onto his lap, spreading her thighs on either side of his. 'It was much more fun with you along.'

'It has been fun.' She seemed as keen as him to change the mood. 'And I've made plans. Tonight's on me. And you too, if you like.' She grinned and he caught her meaning.

'I like.' Grinning back, he spread his hands beneath her buttocks, fingers skimming the edge of her panties. 'Very much. But I thought you liked being on top?'

'I like being any which way with you. But about dinner— why don't we go back to our little beach-side place? This is our Last Supper—I'd like to end where we began. Closure and all that.'

'We don't have to leave tomorrow,' he decided. He'd change their flights. 'We could take a couple more days…' He wasn't ready to go home to his all-work no-play world yet. They weren't done. In fact, they'd only just started.

Her agile body stilled. 'And then what?'

'Try skiing Dubai style and sleeping in till noon with not much sleeping going on…' He trailed off because the eyes staring into his weren't the let's-have-fun ones he'd just been looking at.

'It's not going to change anything, Jordan.'

What wasn't? 'Not sure what you mean.'

'It's only delaying the inevitable. We agreed to do this. And now it's done. Over.'

Jordan stared at her, a not-so-good feeling in his gut. 'What are you saying?'

'I don't want us to linger on and die a slow, painful death. And that's what's going to happen with us. We might have a fantastic meal tonight and follow it up with equally fantastic sex—*Pookie*—but if we let it continue eventually it's going to fade because that's all we have in common. And that's not taking into consideration your busy schedule and my propensity for not sticking around.'

'Yeah, but until then—'

'So when we get home—'

'That's it.'

She nodded, her eyes not quite meeting his. 'I told you, I finish what I start. No loose ends before I move on.'

Or did she leave before someone else finished whatever it was for her?

'Chloe…' He trailed off because what could he say? She had it right. No loose ends. They'd had fun and they'd always known it was only about the business deal with a little diversionary side-trip along the way. She didn't want to live in his world, nor had he asked her to. Sometimes he didn't want to live in it either. There were days he wished he could chuck the whole thing in and be like Chloe—free as the wind, no employees depending on him for an income. An unknown face in the crowd.

If she wanted to leave tomorrow, so be it. 'We'd better make the most of the rest of the time we have left, then.'

She leaned in so that every luscious part of her touched every wire-taut part of him, then reached for his belt buckle. 'That's what I was hoping you'd say…'

Chloe was determined to make the evening special—a time to remember. She'd arranged the table with the best view over the beach, best French champagne to toast their success. She recounted her adventures and challenged Jordan to pick the fake—the near disastrous white-water rafting expedition, her night in a haunted castle with a team of paranormal investigators, the evening she and a girlfriend had ended up in a well-known movie star's suite sipping bubbly with the cast of her latest blockbuster.

He listened to her as if what she had to say was worth something. Not only listened, but actually conversed with her on topics they'd never covered. He seemed to understand her on so many levels and, for the first time in what seemed like forever, she felt uplifted, valued, appreciated.

After dinner they strolled along the beach talking of anything and everything, then sat on the sand, stared up at the northern constellations and shared the evening's silence. Their fingers were barely touching yet it was as if he'd become an integral part of who she was. Warming her body, unlocking her heart and breathing life into her soul.

She couldn't allow herself to fall further and yet she feared it was already too late.

* * *

Later, in their suite with the moonlight casting bars across the floor, he took his time removing her clothes, lingering over every centimetre of skin he bared as if each were a rare jewel. When she was naked, he knelt before her and worshipped her body with a skill and expertise she could only shiver and sigh and moan over.

And when she could no longer stand, he laid her on the bed and continued his homage to her womanhood with hands and mouth, teeth and tongue. Time drifted like the gentle lap and wash of the tide and she clung to him to keep from floating away. Who knew a man's touch could be so slow and easy? Or his body so finely crafted that he was masculine perfection?

He slid his perfect body on top of her then—hard muscle and warm skin a spine-tingling friction. She drew a luxurious breath, inhaling his personal scent and the faint fragrance of Eastern spices. Then forgot to breathe at all as she looked into his midnight-blue eyes and flew with him over the edge of their magic carpet fantasy.

I love you.

Simple.

Impossible.

Finally, energy spent and desire sated, tangled together on the silken sheets, they slept.

CHAPTER THIRTEEN

THEY LANDED IN Melbourne late at night during a rainstorm. The heavy sky was still spitting its vengeance on the windscreen as Jordan's chauffeured car neared the CBD. Which was only fitting, Chloe thought. She'd wear the weather as an accessory. That way no one would notice her mood or her tears. Except she was determined not to cry until she reached the privacy of her bedroom.

She'd planned to get her own cab but there was no press around and cabs were thin on the ground, so Jordan's car it was. They'd barely spoken during the flight, made easier by their individual wraparound seats. Thank God for wealthy businessmen. Both of them had been tired after almost no sleep the previous night, so, apart from when Jordan had been working furiously on his laptop or on the phone, most of the time one or the other had been asleep.

Or in Chloe's case, pretending to be. It had been hard, but necessary, and it had left her almost dead on her feet, a blessing, she hoped, that would help her crash out for the next twelve hours.

The car turned into her street. 'It's late,' he said. 'Stay at my apartment tonight.'

Her heart leapt at his invitation, but she pressed her lips together and looked out of the window. It was only delaying the inevitable and she didn't want to see his apartment. To know where he lived and imagine him there. Worse, imagine him there with another woman. 'No, Jordan.'

'Then let me stay here. With you.'

Something in his tone had her turning to him. She'd never seen that look in Jordan's eyes. Clearly, he wasn't used to being turned down. 'I told you my bed's too small.'

He looked as if he might argue, then glanced at the driver up front, and Chloe realised it was costing Jordan to sweet-talk her into something he must know she'd refuse in front of his staff.

'I have a headache,' she improvised for the sake of his pride as they pulled into the kerb. 'Jet lag. I need an uninter-rupted night's sleep.'

The driver climbed out to retrieve her luggage from the boot, leaving them alone in the back seat. She dug through her bag ostensibly looking for her keys.

'So this is it, then.' His voice was hard and remote-sounding.

'Yes.' She heard the tremor in her voice and tightened her fingers around her keys, then hoisted her bag onto her shoulder, desperate to get away. 'Thanks for—'

'Save it.' He wrenched his door open. 'Like it or not, I'm walking you to your damn door. You can *thank* me then.'

Rain spat on her face, chilling her as she hurried up the path, Jordan following with her bag. Somehow she got the key in the lock, then turned to him. Thankfully the security light didn't seem to be working and it was dark under the veranda. But not dark enough to miss the granite set of his jaw, the flash of—was that temper?—in his eyes.

Why? Because he hadn't got his own way? Something inside her responded in kind. And far better for her self-preservation to turn her misery into irritation or annoyance. Just because she'd gone and fallen in love with him didn't mean she was going to let him change her mind and go against what she knew was the right decision. For both of them.

So toughen up, Chloe. She wasn't going to apologise for her choice. He had a masters degree in seduction and another in persuasion and she wasn't going to allow a man to make her decisions for her ever again.

'Chloe. Listen up.' Stepping close, he tilted her face up to his with a finger so she had no choice but to look into his eyes, shuttered now, betraying little of what he was feeling. His temper seemed to have dissipated and he spoke with a measured calm. 'I don't want to stop seeing you but I made a promise when we signed our agreement. I'm not going to force you into something you don't want.'

'Tha—'

'Or should I say, what you *do* want but you're too afraid to admit.' His hand fell away and he stepped back, leaving her feeling chilled to the bone and totally exposed because he read her like a book.

She firmed her chin. 'With regards to our *business* arrangement, if anything changes with Qasim or the deal, and you need my assistance, please let me know.' She knew she sounded PA prim.

His eyes held hers captive. 'If you change your mind about *us*, or decide to come clean with me, you have my contact details.'

He didn't kiss her goodbye, just spun on his Italian leather shoe's heel and walked down her path, his black cashmere coat flapping behind him. Taking her heart with him.

But not her independence, not her identity. She still had those, at least. *And will they keep you warm on a cold winter's night?* a little voice whispered.

At the gate he turned back, spine rigid, his eyes darker than midnight. 'You say you like to finish what you start. We started something and it's not finished, so I'm wondering, how do those loose ends sit with you, Chloe?'

Then he was gone.

Three days later, from his expansive view in one of Perth's newest office buildings, Jordan rolled his executive chair back and watched the western sky grow pink behind a bank of mushroom-coloured clouds. It was the first time he'd taken a break since he'd started work at five a.m.

He'd sent his PA away and told her he wasn't to be disturbed under any circumstances. Roma had asked did that include coffee? before his frown had answered for him and he hadn't seen a glimpse or heard a peep from her since.

A knock sounded at his door and an unsmiling Roma poked her head in. She was an attractive forty-something brunette and Jordan valued her highly. 'I'm leaving now,' she said, and held a small packet out for him. 'This came this afternoon, registered express post. Thought it might be important and I didn't want to just leave it...'

Hell. Her tone and body language made him feel as if he'd kicked a puppy. 'Thanks, Roma.' When she didn't come any closer, he crossed the room and took it from her. 'Bad day.' He forced a smile. 'Guess I won't win employer of the year.'

'Maybe not this year.' A tentative smile crossed her face. 'I know this trip's been stressful...' She hesitated, as if waiting for an explanation. When none was forthcoming, she went on, 'I'll be going, then, if there's nothing further you need. Or if you want to talk...' She shook her head once. 'Guess not.'

'I'm fine, Roma. Thanks. See you tomorrow.' If she hadn't tendered her resignation, that was. Ah... 'Roma?'

She turned, warily. 'Yes?'

'How's Bernie?' Roma's husband was also an employee, a geologist up north in one of his mines.

Her brows lifted, puzzled. 'Fine, last we spoke. He's due home in a fortnight.'

Jordan nodded. 'I find myself in the rather desperate position of being dateless for the Rapper One ball and—'

'You want me to find you a *date*?' Her eyes widened and her voice rose a notch.

'No, no. Not that. I know you and Bernie attended last year so I was wondering—rather, *hoping*, since Bernie can't be here with you this year—that you'd accompany me instead.'

'Oh.' A long awkward pause. 'Well. That sounds…nice.'

'I'll ring Bernie myself and check with him first to make sure he's okay with it. I promise to work on my social skills in the meantime.'

Her smile warmed a few degrees and the Roma he knew shone through. 'You do that and I'll talk Bernie into letting me buy a new outfit.'

'Great. Have a good evening. And I'll put the word on Bernie about that new dress.'

He watched her leave, then turned the mystery packet over in his hands and read the sender's address. *Chloe Montgomery*. His gut cramped and he traced her scrawled handwriting as if he could bring her to him by touch. Images of her shot back. Hair that reminded him of sunlight. Her smile that could light up his day—and his night. The last time he'd seen her, on her veranda and telling him it was over.

She hadn't been smiling then.

He ripped through the packaging and withdrew a familiar box. 'Dammit, Blondie,' he muttered, already knowing what he'd find—the gold jewellery and the wedding ring.

And what the hell was he supposed to do with them? He ran his fingers along the slim gold chain, remembering how she'd looked that morning he'd clasped it around her neck. Understated elegance. The kind of woman who'd make any man proud to have her by his side, be it business or pleasure.

He'd never forget the way she'd supported him that day, her enthusiasm when he'd told her he'd won the old sheikh over.

And now she'd tossed his gift back in his face. By remote. Did she care so little about him that she wanted no reminders at all? Had what they'd shared meant nothing? Had she just been waiting for that second payment to go into her account—which he'd attended to first thing this morning—and now further contact was unnecessary? Unwanted?

His fingers tightened on the chain momentarily before he slipped it back in its box, flipped the lid shut and shoved it back in its post pack.

No loose ends.

Her words echoed in his head and he refused to acknowledge the way his whole body tensed and constricted as his control over his emotions slipped a notch. He'd all but begged her to let him stay the night. He stalked grimly across the room. He never allowed emotion to gain the upper hand. Why waste time thinking about a woman who was probably already on her way out of the country?

On an oath, he shoved the packet in his wall safe, slammed the door shut, effectively putting a full stop at the end their relationship. *Done.* She had her clean break as she wanted.

And wasn't that what he wanted too?

'So you're serious about leaving Melbourne?'

Dana's voice penetrated Chloe's thoughts and she realised she wasn't in a silken tent in Dubai, she was in a commercial kitchen prepping for tomorrow morning's breakfast function and had no idea what her boss had just said. She blinked away the daydream. 'Pardon?'

'Are you sure about moving on? You just started here and you said you like it.'

'I'm sorry, circumstances have made it necessary for me

to move on.' The possibility of running into Jordan was just too likely here working with Dana.

'By "circumstances", you mean Jordan.'

Chloe was slicing glacé cherries and her knife slipped. *'Ouch.'*

'You okay?'

Chloe checked that no skin was broken and continued. 'Yep.'

'Can you check the inventory on my PC for me?' Dana slid the last tray of cheese platters into the fridge and indicated her PC tablet on the nearby desk with her chin. 'I want to make sure we didn't forget to add those canapés tomorrow night's client ordered at the last minute. And watch your fingers. I don't want blood in my fruit compotes.'

'Watching,' Chloe murmured, and set her knife down, wiped her hands and crossed the room. At her touch the screen lit up and she found herself staring at a society news page.

Jordan.

For an instant her heart soared like a bird, then dived to her feet as if she'd been shot. Jordan, looking sexy as sin in his tux and escorting an attractive brunette to some charity event in Perth two nights ago. *His* charity. He'd never mentioned the function to Chloe.

Ridiculous to be jealous. She refused to think about the fact that it had been nearly two weeks since she'd told him it was over—obviously he'd wasted no time moving on to the next available woman.

No thanks to Dana for interfering.

She slapped the cover over the screen, and met her boss's eyes. 'Not fair, Dana.' Her lips felt numb, her legs felt like water. Untying her apron, she headed for the door.

'Chloe, it's his PA. Roma West. And she's very married.'

'So?' She stopped, told her trembling self it didn't matter. 'What's your point?'

'You're in love with him. I wanted to be sure. And I do know what you were doing in Dubai.'

Not everything, Chloe hoped. She crushed the corners of her apron between her fingers and forced herself to walk back to her station. Calm, steady. 'You're way over the line. And you're wrong. Why would I want to fall in love with an arrogant, domineering man like your friend Jordan Blackstone?'

'Wanting has nothing to do with it. And do *not* pick up that knife.' Swooping in, Dana finished slicing the last few cherries, popped them on the top of the little glass bowls then carried the tray to the fridge. 'If he meant nothing to you, you wouldn't have reacted that way.'

That jealous, vulnerable way. Chloe swiped up a cloth and began wiping down surfaces. 'So what if I am?' Then she sucked in a breath because suddenly her secret was out and she hadn't ever meant for it to be.

'It's okay,' Dana said quietly. 'I won't say anything.'

'Is it that obvious?' God, no, please not.

'The look on your face just then? And you came back to work even though Jordan had paid me enough to cover your wages for the next week. Believe me, *that's* not normal behaviour.'

'I like to work,' Chloe told her. 'It's therapeutic.'

No matter how healthy her bank balance was— 'Does *he* know? Did he say something?'

'Not to me he hasn't. And if he knows, would that be so bad?'

'Absolutely.' Oh, she'd be mortified. Her one-sided love was tragedy enough without letting the hapless victim in on it. A man who saw women as manipulative and money-hungry.

'Why?'

She feigned indifference and rinsed out her cloth. 'A man's too complicated. I'm not in one place long enough…'

'Sometimes you need to stop a while and listen to your heart.'

'I… Maybe.' And suddenly something inside her yearned for a piece of that slow-down time. Time to make a home of her own where she could paint the walls whatever colour she wanted. Where she could plant bulbs and watch them flower for more than one springtime.

Not some palatial English manor she'd never belong in, but her own place.

A place to put down roots like those spring bulbs.

And she could do that now, she realised. Ironic that it was Jordan who'd made it possible when he wasn't going to be a part of it. Her heart plunged down the sinkhole with the water. She knew enough about him to know she loved him, but not enough, perhaps, to fully understand him. 'That function he was at…his charity, isn't it? It obviously means a great deal to him.'

'Yes.'

'Why is he so devoted to helping troubled teens?'

'It stems from his past. He had a tough childhood that no kid should have to grow up with.'

'I know he loved his dad, so was it his mother? He refused to speak about her.'

'He won't speak about her to anyone, but, according to Sadiq, she was a witch and his father was too weak to stand up to her.'

'Poor kid.' She understood rejection, and her heart twisted for what Jordan the child must have endured that he refused to acknowledge his own mother and counselled troubled youth.

'Whatever you do, don't let him hear your sympathy.' Dana cleaned the knife and put it away. 'Let's call it a night here.'

'But I haven't fin—'

'The morning's soon enough.' Dana glanced at her watch, answered an incoming text before slipping her phone in her bag and marching Chloe to the door by her elbow. 'Come on, we're going to unwind with a cappuccino at my favourite Chapel Street café. My treat, and I'm not taking no for an answer.'

Chloe frowned down at her flat shoes, work trousers and 'Dana's Events' monogrammed uniform top. Unlike Dana, who hadn't been wearing a uniform and had managed to grab her high-fashion fur coat on the way out.

'I'm hardly dressed for going out. Are you sure you don't need to be somewhere?'

'Only somewhere warm and cosy and familiar where the coffee's hot and the lights are low.'

'So you and Chloe enjoyed your *honeymoon*.' Sadiq leaned back in the dimly lit, high-backed booth specifically chosen for its privacy in the back of a classy out-of-the-way upstairs café on Chapel Street and studied Jordan over the rim of his glass. 'Qasim mentioned it.'

'Of course he did.' Jordan tipped back his glass, swallowed long and deep. 'Did he tell you the rest?'

'He admired your honesty and courage and thought Chloe would be a good partner for you when you decide to make it legitimate. He's not as unyielding as we thought.'

Jordan didn't answer. *In a magic kingdom far, far away lived a princess with flaxen hair and amber eyes.* Storybook stuff.

'Is she the reason you're back in Melbourne again so soon?'

Sadiq's question interrupted Jordan's thoughts and he blinked away the image. 'Had some work on the Tilson mine.'

'Right.'

'Yeah.' *Have you seen her?*

'No. But I reckon you need to.'

Crikeys, had he spoken aloud? 'You're starting to sound like your wife.'

'Just saying. No reason to get defensive. Or is there?' he murmured. 'You never said how you two got on.'

Jordan took a while to answer. This was Sadiq, his best mate. The one who'd been there when Lynette had disappeared. 'She was different. She wasn't like any woman I've ever met—she saw me…differently.'

'And it scares the hell out of you. Is that why you've relegated her to the past tense?'

'Fact is, she didn't want to continue what we had—how did she put it? No loose ends. So it's a moot point.'

'And you didn't try to convince her otherwise?'

'Why would I? One thing I'll say for Chloe, she's got a sensible head on her shoulders.' Those beautiful creamy elegant shoulders…

'What if she walked in here now?'

'What if she did?' He shrugged, unwilling to contemplate that scenario because there were too many unresolved questions.

'What if she told you she'd changed her mind?'

'Maybe I'd tell her I'd changed mine now.' His fists tightened on the tabletop. 'I won't be manipulated by a woman's passing whims.'

'No one's manipulating you, mate. Chloe's not Lynette.'

'There you are.' At the sound of Dana's voice, Jordan looked up and was confronted by not one manipulative woman, but two.

And then I saw her face… As he stared at the woman he hadn't seen in twelve days, give or take a couple of hours, the words from a familiar pop song danced through his head, carving up a path straight to his heart where they continued to stomp and stamp like a wild rock concert.

He heard Chloe's stifled gasp and even though the lights

were dim her eyes looked like saucers, her complexion as pale and fragile as eggshell. She looked a hell of a lot like he felt. She was also wearing one of those unflattering Dana's Events uniforms so maybe she was as innocent in this set-up as he.

Sadiq slid out of the high-backed bench seat and rose. 'Dana and I are off to check out the latest sci-fi movie. Catch you two later.'

'Hang on—'

'No—'

Both he and Chloe protested at the same time.

Jordan stood, their partners in crime left and the two of them stared at each other.

'I know you think I had something to do with this,' Chloe said before he could speak, her eyes willing him to believe her. 'But I didn't.'

'Seems fate threw us together one more time.'

'Not fate, just two meddling friends of yours.'

'They'll keep. Might as well have a seat now you're here.'

She hesitated before sliding into the seat opposite. 'I won't stay long, I've got an early start tomorrow.'

'Don't we all? Coffee?'

'Thank you.'

He summoned the waiter hovering nearby and ordered two cappuccinos. 'You caught up with your parents yet?'

'Only by email but they're very grateful for the money. So thanks. I told them about…the breakup with Stewart and leaving—thanks to you for that too because I needed a kick up the backside to make it happen.'

'That's good to hear.'

'Mum actually asked when I'm coming home. She's finally emailing me herself now.'

'She misses you. They all miss you.'

'Maybe. I never thought they did.'

'Maybe you never gave them a chance.'

'Maybe I was afraid to.'

'You're going to tell them everything then?'

'Not everything.' He heard the hint of humour in her voice.

'I've missed you too, Chloe.' The words slipped from his mouth before he could call them back.

'Oh.' Her whole being seemed to light up like the sun appearing after morning mist and her eyes splashed with warmth and for a crazy second he thought maybe she'd missed him too, but then that grey mist rolled back and her smile wasn't the smile he wanted to see. It was brittle and way too bright when she said, 'Bet you say that to all the girls.'

Dammit, Chloe. He'd thought he'd conquered vulnerability years ago but the iron fist squeezing his chest disabused him of that notion. That old feeling of craving even a scrap of his mother's affection slid back like a dark tide. A kid's lack of understanding. The hurt of being ignored. Resented.

'Knowing my reputation with women, wouldn't those sentiments be counter-productive?' He pasted some kind of a grin on his lips that felt as if it didn't belong. 'After all, I wouldn't want them getting the wrong idea, would I?'

Chloe's expression froze and she didn't answer, sliding the sugar bowl around on the table between them in quick little circles and changing the topic. 'I read your charity ball was a success. Not that I was checking up on you,' she added quickly. 'Dana *happened* to arrange for me to see a picture of you and your PA posing for the cameras.'

'Did she?' he clipped.

'You're big news in W.A. Australia-wide, in fact.' She waved a hand about them, reminding him again of the way she moved—with elegance and a charming carelessness that had fascinated him from day one. 'No wonder this place is so hard to get into and dimly lit and private for the right people. You really are a celebrity.' Her eyes were dark honey tonight and everywhere but on his.

'I'm as ordinary as you.' Reaching over the table, he wrapped a hand around her busy one, waiting until he had her full attention to say, 'I know a place not far from here that's much more private.'

CHAPTER FOURTEEN

'MY CAR'S PARKED not far up the street. Are you game?' he asked when she didn't say anything.

Chloe was too stunned to answer. His voice was like velvet and addictive. She'd missed hearing that voice. The only time she heard it lately was in her sleep; when she managed to get to sleep, that was. She knew it was a bad decision, but always-up-for-a-challenge Chloe allowed her hand to be swallowed up in Jordan's, and her head nodded almost without her consent.

She saw his eyes darken to midnight-blue as they slid out of the booth together. She followed him through the dimly lit café, down the narrow stairs and outside where the air was fresh and the bump of nearby music throbbed up through the pavement.

He didn't ask what transport she'd used, escorting her protectively past a throng of party-goers. She breathed in his scent, the warmth of his hand at her back familiar and as comforting as it was arousing.

They passed a trendy clothing store, its light spilling over them, neon and bright. Every second stretched, every step seemed to take forever. Her breaths became shorter, shallower as urgency twisted like a live wire inside her and she realised they were almost running.

That might have been the reason they almost crashed into

a middle-aged couple coming from the opposite direction, but the instant they greeted Jordan by name Chloe knew they recognised him and had stepped into their path deliberately.

'Well, if it isn't Jordan Blackstone.'

'Evening, Jordan.' The couple spoke at the same time. The woman dripped with jewellery of the genuine kind, the man's voice vibrated with the sound of money.

'Good evening,' Jordan replied amiably enough, still, Chloe felt his frustration hum through his fingertips as his hand tightened on hers. Courtesy demanded they stop. 'Chloe, I'd like you to meet Wes and Sybil Hampton.'

She waited for more from Jordan; something that might indicate who she was and what she meant to him. Some kind of acknowledgement at least.

Nothing. Not a word. Pain cramped her whole body. She withdrew her hand from his—or maybe he let her go—and nodded at the couple with a murmured, 'It's nice to meet you.'

Wes said something about being pleased to meet her too and Sybil gave her a brief condescending smile and maybe she even spoke, but Chloe barely heard over the rushing noise in her ears. Because Jordan couldn't have made it clearer that he didn't want to be seen here with her.

The way Stewart had reacted when they'd bumped into friends on that last day.

'Fancy running into you again so soon after the ball,' Sybil gushed, touching Jordan's arm, her rings flashing in the street light, Chloe forgotten. 'We're just on our way to meet the Brodericks for a light supper, if you'd like to join us…' She trailed off, looking at Chloe, who was clearly *not* invited.

'Not tonight, Sybil.'

'Tomorrow, then. We're touring a few wineries—it's not too late to add an extra. The limo's booked for nine a.m. Wanda's coming and she's been dying to catch up with you. I was only saying the other day th—'

'Thanks, but I'm going to be busy,' he said, edging away.

Her face creased with disappointment and she cast a telling glance at Chloe. 'Well. Another time, then.'

'Come on, Sybil,' Wes muttered, nodding at Jordan as he prodded his wife forward. 'Let the man and his lady friend go.'

Lady friend in her uniform and work shoes. Way out of Jordan's league and the Hamptons knew it. She could only be with him for one reason. Sex.

The interaction was enough time for Chloe to shake off the momentary insanity that had taken hold for a few unguarded moments. Insanity that would truly be her undoing if she succumbed to it.

As the couple walked off, Jordan reached for Chloe's hand again, but she moved out of his way and stopped. 'I'm not coming home with you, Jordan.'

His expression remained passive but there was a flash of… something…in his eyes. 'Why not?'

'I need to go.'

'We'll go to yours, then.'

'No. I mean I need to move on. With my life. I've been in Melbourne too long.'

He studied her a moment, then shook his head. 'That's not what you're really saying, is it.' Not a question.

She lifted her chin anyway. 'Who are you to tell me what I'm saying?'

'I'm someone who cares,' he said quietly. 'Someone who knows you better than you think.'

Care wasn't love, and it wasn't enough—not from Jordan. She shook her head. 'I'm going to Sydney. Catch up with my family.'

'Great—I hope you enjoy the family reunion but I'm not buying your story this time, Chloe.'

'It's not a story,' she said desperately.

His gaze narrowed. 'You're afraid to be with me.'

'Those friends of yours—'

'They're not my friends, they're business acquaintances. However they do donate huge sums of money to my charity.'

'You didn't introduce me to them as anyone who meant something to you.'

He paused, looking nonplussed. 'I assumed you wanted to keep your anonymity. Sybil's a busybody with connections in high—'

'*No.*' She jabbed a finger in the air. 'You didn't know how to introduce me because I don't fit into your life like your other women. I'm a problem for you outside the bedroom. I'm not educated and wealthy like the people you associate with. I don't belong here. With you. In your world.'

'What the *hell* are you talking about?' His body radiated an impatient energy and he shoved his hands in his pockets and shifted to the balls of his feet so he appeared to loom over her. 'You'll never belong anywhere because you never stay long enough. For once in your life, stop running. You might find what you're looking for right here.'

The way he said it, the expression in his eyes, almost tempted her to believe. To hope. To take a chance…

'What are you saying, Jordan? That you're offering something permanent?'

She swore he paled beneath his tan, his eyes flashed *PANIC* in big blue letters and she had her answer. Any foolish dreams she might have had died right then and there on the footpath. 'I didn't think so.'

'Permanent's a big leap… I didn't m—'

'Enough.' She shot out a staying hand. 'Don't worry, Jordan, South America's next on my travel itinerary and *Carnaval* in Rio is only a few months away.' Lies, all lies. 'Thanks to your generosity. This time it'll be first class all the way.'

Was it possible to smile when your soul was dying? But she managed it as she backed away, committing his face to memory, etching his image on her heart. 'I'll send you a postcard.'

'Chloe—'

'*Don't* follow me.' She turned around and began to walk. She knew he'd respect her wishes because she remembered the first night they'd met when she'd asked the same of him.

This time it was different. This time she was leaving her heart with him.

The next few days went by in a blur. She was truly sorry to tell Dana she was leaving with almost no notice—Chloe had never left a boss in the lurch that way. But not nearly as sorry as she was to be leaving Jordan without the right and final words being said between them. Dana said she understood Chloe's decision but made her promise to keep in touch and leave her contact details.

It didn't take much time for Chloe to pack her stuff and organise to relocate it to Sydney. She rode her scooter interstate, keeping at a leisurely pace and stopping twice overnight in little country towns.

When she arrived in Sydney, she found a clean, comfortable motel only forty minutes' drive from her childhood home and adjacent to a park. It gave her time to think.

Jordan had said something that last time that she could not get out of her head: *You'll never belong anywhere because you never stay long enough. For once in your life, stop running. You might find what you're looking for...*

True words, she realised, now. Every one.

With him, no matter how short their time had been, she'd learned how it felt to belong with someone. She'd realised he'd been protecting her, not embarrassed by her. That when their fling was over, he was assuring her privacy by not revealing their past to the rest of the world. No one would ever call her Jordan's ex-lover. He'd always accepted her as she was and never tried to change her.

It had taken Jordan to show her that running away wasn't an answer. The big *P* word had scared him, no denying it, yet she'd run before giving him a chance to respond.

Left him before he could leave her.

And who could say how things might have ended? How it might have gone if she'd stayed and had a conversation about it?

So instead of renting, she put down roots for the first time in her life and bought a little Victorian terrace home in Paddington that was unoccupied and available immediately. *A renovator's dream,* according to the ad. She spent the next couple of weeks keeping busy and focused on choosing furniture and fabrics, cushions and crockery.

Signing up for a three-year counselling course online that was starting in three months was thrilling and scary but that was a challenge she was confident she'd meet.

Meanwhile, exchanging regular emails with her family who still didn't know she was back in Australia gave her time to plan how to re-establish those ties without letting them walk all over her.

But every night when she lay alone beneath her feather quilt, other thoughts and images tumbled through her head like a noisy street parade. Then she'd climb from her bed and sit for hours by the quaint glass doors that opened onto her narrow balcony with its panoramic view of old tin roofs and iron lace. By fate or coincidence, it faced south-west, so whichever city Jordan was in Chloe imagined him there. She also imagined having the guts to walk into his office and finally tell him what was in her heart and why she could never be with him.

* * *

In his Melbourne apartment, Jordan lay on his bed staring at the darkened ceiling. Nearly midnight. He supposed he should fix something to eat or even rouse himself enough to go out and grab some takeaway but his appetite was non-existent.

Who knew a month could pass so slowly? Or that he'd be such disgustingly bad company? Finally tonight Dana had told him not to turn up at her place until he'd made a decision. Yep, Jordan Blackstone, who prided himself on his decision-making skills.

The man who also prided himself on his ability to control his circumstances and never allowed emotions to interfere with his life.

That man was history. He barked out a harsh laugh that seemed to echo back at him in the stillness. Yeah, a joke.

A woman had brought him to this. A tiny woman with mussed blonde hair and a smile that could tempt any man to lean in for just one taste.

Which was exactly how he'd got himself into this situation.

But unlike other women he'd known, Chloe had never tried to manipulate him. She might have fallen into his lap but she hadn't fallen at his feet. A willing listener and friend, even when he'd pushed her away.

She wasn't after fame or fortune. He'd discovered earlier today that an anonymous donation had been made to Rapper One. The exact same amount he'd deposited into Chloe's account the night they'd returned to Australia. She'd donated her second instalment to his charity.

Money truly wasn't important to her. She was proudly independent with a sense of humour and adventure. She'd accepted him for who he was, not what he could do for her.

She also had a vulnerable side she worked damn hard to hide by feigning carelessness and not sticking around—for fear of being left. A front, a mask. She'd never told him why the man she'd loved had left her—and he was certain he'd left her and not the other way around—but clearly the scum was the reason she was always moving on.

Switching on his bedside light, he studied the paper Dana had given him again. Chloe's address. An inner Sydney suburb. For how long? he wondered. How long would it be before the adventurer in her beckoned and she took off for places unknown?

And the next time he might never find her.

The thought struck out of nowhere with the speed and devastation of a lightning bolt. He sat up so fast he knocked the lamp to the floor with a crash of broken glass, plunging him into darkness.

He barely noticed. Urgency was pounding through his system, stabbing through his brain until all focus narrowed to a single pinpoint, one thought.

He couldn't lose her.

He *wouldn't* lose her.

He would *not* lose the woman he loved.

Hang on... *Love?* Every muscle in his body tightened. Every fibre, every sinew, vibrated as if he'd been tuned in to some great musical humming through the universe. His skin prickled, he heard his pulse drumming in his ears, the blood pumping through his heart. He didn't know what to do with the energy so he sprang up off the bed and paced to the living room. Yes, he realised on a burst of something that felt like relief mingled with surprise—he loved Chloe, and he'd never felt so intense, so energised, so alive.

He'd always thought love made a man weak and yet he'd never felt so strong.

Strong enough to toss away his flawed and outdated ideas and reach out for something he'd never known he'd wanted until now.

He snatched up his phone. It was only a little after ten in

Perth and he paid Roma an exorbitant income to be available at odd hours.

He had much to consider and decisions to make. Urgently. Then he needed to put those decisions into action....

CHAPTER FIFTEEN

Two days later

'HERE GOES…' CHLOE said, smoothing her paintbrush on the wall and watching the happy yellow colour slowly hide the drab beige beneath, transforming her kitchen into a sunny room where she could teach herself to cook and grow herbs. *Her* kitchen. She smiled and jiggled her hips to the rock'n'roll party happening on her tinny radio on the window sill alongside her first pot of parsley.

She dipped her brush again, working rhythmically while she sang along and considered new possibilities. She could raise hens. Or ducks. Or get a cat. Now she'd committed to staying in one place for a while, a whole new world had opened up to her.

There was just one vital part missing in that world…

No—there he was again. In her head. In her heart. And she must let him go because she knew now she'd never fit in his world. This time she slapped her brush against the wall and felt its resulting cool, thick splash on her brow. She swiped it away with her forearm. She needed to get this place in shape so that she could invite her family over and show them she could be the person they wanted her to be. *Correction, Chloe.* The person *she* wanted to be.

Because being the person she wanted to be would surely

impact on others she came into contact with in a positive way. Confident in herself and her abilities, wholly focused, steady and reliable. Constant. Jordan had taught her how to bring out those qualities she'd not realised she had.

The call she'd made this morning had been the hardest she'd ever made, but worth it. The familiar sound of Mum's voice had brought so many emotions to the surface, she'd been tempted to tell her she could be there in forty minutes, but she needed to stick to her plan, no matter how hard, and take things slow for the next couple of weeks.

They'd talked for an hour. About the man who'd made it possible for Chloe to help out financially. About the prejudiced SOB who'd humiliated her. About the one who'd ripped her off. Both women had voiced regrets but Chloe spoke firmly about how she wanted things to be from now on.

Filled with new hope, she smiled, tempted to paint a rainbow arc across the wall with her little pots of trial colours. And why not?

The sound of a car pulling up outside had her glancing across the living space to the sitting-room window. Through the faded lacy scrim she could see a hulking black four-wheel drive with dull and dented bodywork that indicated it had endured its fair share of off-road adventures.

The driver climbed out, staring at her place behind mirrored sunglasses, and everything inside her stilled. The kind of tall, dark, broad-shouldered male who could send shivers down her spine just by being alive. Her heart bounded into her chest. Only one man could do that…

The paintbrush slid from her grasp and landed on the tarp she'd spread over the scarred timber floor. *Dana, I'm going to kill you.* She watched, frozen, as he trotted up her worn stone steps, then reared back when he disappeared from view and rang the little antique iron bell she'd painted blue and hung beside the door.

'Chloe,' she heard him say and he rang the bell again. When she still couldn't move, he tapped on the door and said, 'I know you're there, Chloe, and I know you can hear me. I've come a long way and I'm not leaving until you see me, so answer the door. I just want to talk, so...'

So she pulled the door open and there he was and her heart raced and turned and tumbled over in her chest. Because he looked as if he'd done the ten-hour drive from Melbourne in seven and without a break. His face was shadow-stubbled, his shirt rumpled. And his eyes...they were bleary and bloodshot but there was also a clarity and resolution and maybe even a glimpse of something like fear that she'd never seen before and it had her heart tumbling some more.

'Hello, Blondie.'

'*How* did you know I could hear you?' she demanded without a greeting and hanging on to the door for support.

He shrugged. 'Took a chance. Can I come in?'

Oh, she missed that voice...but right now it sounded raspy and raw. 'I think you'd better.' She pulled the door wider. 'You look...awful.'

One eyebrow lifted. 'And you look gorgeous.' His grin was lazy. Tired. The grin that always made her heart race.

Her mind awhirl, she gestured him inside. 'Um...excuse the mess. I'm renovating.'

'*Renovating?*' His eyes widened in surprise, then he nodded. 'So that's what the splotch is.' He raised a hand toward her brow, then let it drop and moved back as if he'd overstepped some boundary.

'I wasn't expecting...visitors.' She glanced down at the paint-stained man's flannel shirt she'd thrown on over her leggings and wanted to groan. 'I'll just go and—'

'Don't go.' His gaze captured hers. 'I just want to look at you a moment. You're a balm for tired eyes.'

She tore her gaze away. 'At least let me take off this paint shirt.' Peeling it off her arms, she let it fall to the floor. 'Better,' she murmured, then frowned down at herself. 'Or maybe not.'

Jordan's fatigue-blurred vision still delighted in the sight of Chloe in leggings and an oversized shirt that reminded him of that faded T-shirt—the one she'd worn in Dubai the night she'd waited up for him when things hadn't looked good for the mine. 'You look beautiful whatever you're wearing—oversize paint shirt or too-small rhinestone-covered costume.'

She paused at mention of that but didn't look at him, heading towards a tiny kitchen cluttered with paint pots and rags and smelling of turpentine. 'You should get some sleep—obviously your sight's impaired,' she said as she walked. 'I'll make you a warm drink—what do you want?'

You. Only you. 'Whatever's handy.'

'Herbal tea, then.'

'Fine.'

She cleared a space at a little round table, told him to have a seat, then fussed with the makings of the tea. The beat of an Aussie band on the radio masked the lack of conversation.

He waited until she set two cups of camomile tea on the table but she remained standing, twisting her fingers together and smelling of paint and perfume. 'Sit down, Chloe.' He leaned across and pulled out the chair next to him. 'We need to talk.'

She took the chair opposite instead. 'Yes.'

He sipped his tea thirstily to wet his dust-dry mouth before resting his arms on the table and looking into her eyes. 'First off, I've been giving a lot of thought to why you ran away that last night. And when I say a lot of thought, I've thought of nothing else. Nothing. My work's suffered and my PA's probably going to quit unless I start being human again.'

'I'm sorry,' she said, her gaze darting away. 'I didn't mean for that to happen.'

'You accused me of something I didn't understand. Still don't understand.'

'I know. And I'm sorry for that too.'

'Amongst other things—which I'll get to directly—you said you couldn't live in my world because you didn't belong.' He saw the pain in her eyes and wanted to reach out but didn't know whether she'd welcome it. 'Help me understand that, Chloe.'

She sighed, spread her hands on the table and studied them rather than look at him. 'Remember the dragon you slayed for me in our desert honeymoon? Well, seems he's not quite dead after all.'

Jordan's eyes narrowed. 'What the hell...?'

'No, no, nothing like that. I've never seen him again.' She blew out a breath and fixed her eyes on Jordan's. 'Okay, it was like this. We spent our time together in his home with his son. And that was fine—I was happy with that because I loved Brad too. But he never took me out unless it was to a private booth in an out-of-the-way restaurant. I never met his friends. Until one night when we bumped into a couple accidentally.'

A picture was forming in Jordan's mind and making a lot of sense. 'Like when we bumped into Wes and Sybil.'

'Exactly like that. When we got home he told me it was over. I was devastated, and tried to discuss it. Long story short, he accused me of sexual harassment, made sure I couldn't get a job with any nanny service in the UK. They wouldn't take my word over his. He *used* me. Which is why I was so angry and upset with you that first night when you accused me of coming on to you.'

The blood simmered hot and dark through Jordan's veins. 'You should've told me. I would've understood, but you ran away.'

Chloe realised that now. Her pulse sped up. Was it too

late? 'You told me to stop running and I asked if you were talking about something permanent and I've never seen a guy so panicked.'

'You caught me by surprise. You didn't give me time.'

'Well, I took your advice about running and bought this place. It's mine. All mine. And I'm not going anywhere.' She lifted her chin. 'I'm going to raise chickens.'

He smiled slowly. 'Can I tell you a story?'

She didn't answer straight away. 'Depends. Does it have a happy ending?'

'I hope so.' He leaned closer, so that she could smell the road and travel dust on his skin.

She nodded. 'All good stories start with "once upon a time".'

He smiled, the light in his eyes reminding her of springtime and new beginnings. 'Okay. *Once upon a time*, there was a guy called Jordan who was locked in a tower. A prison of his own making, because he couldn't see beyond his work and his meaningless relationships, and he thought he was content. He had no desire to escape until a girl called Blondie, who lived for adventure, fell into his lap. She was beautiful and kind and clever and he realised he'd be missing out on something amazing if he didn't make this girl his.'

Make her his? Her heart stopped beating. Literally stopped. And swelled. And sang.

'But now he's not sure she'll have him because it took him so long to realise he loves her and he's not even sure whether she loves him back.'

Tears welled up into her eyes. 'Oh, J—'

When she would have touched him, when she would have wept with joy and flung herself at him, he held up a hand. 'Let me finish.'

He paused, then said, 'So he wants adventurous Blondie to come on an adventure with him to explore what they have.

He's packed enough gear into his well-used off-road vehicle for the two of them for a few weeks. Or months. However long and however far she wants to go. He wants to take her into gold-mining country because he knows a thing or two about it. He wants to teach her a new skill—how to pan for gold during the day and…well, he has other things he'd like to teach her at night, under the stars.'

She drew a few stunned breaths while she processed everything. 'What about his work? They can't roam the gold-fields forever. Where will they live? Blondie just bought a house.'

'He's organised to have time off. He's not taken leave since he took over the company so he figures he's entitled. As for living arrangements, Jordan has responsibilities in Perth and Melbourne but he's been thinking of opening up a branch in Sydney. There's no reason why they can't spend time in each place. As long as they're together. As long as she loves him back. He thinks—'

'Blondie's pretty sure she agrees. She does know she's definite about loving him back. Enough talk.' Chloe scraped back her chair, plonked her butt on his lap and pressed her mouth to his to shut him up.

And he tasted so good—dark and rich and *hers*.

Then he hauled her against his chest and carried her to bed and they spent the next little while making warm slow love and not talking at all.

Hours later, when they woke and the evening sky was turning yellow, he reached for his discarded jeans and pulled a small square box out of the pocket. '*Now* will you wear this?' He flipped it open and the familiar little gold ring glinted on a bed of blue velvet.

'It's a wedding ring,' Chloe said, staring at it, remembering all the adventures they'd had while she was Mrs Jordan Blackstone. 'We're not married.'

'Do you want to be?'

'I always thought I couldn't do marriage but I know now that it was because I was afraid. But with you—you give me the courage to give it a try.'

She looked up to see the sun shining in his eyes. 'What about you? You told me you're not a marrying man.'

'I didn't think I was. Until I found you.'

'But you nearly married Lynette.'

The sun slid behind a cloud and his eyes sombred. 'A manipulator. A liar. A gold-digger. And I was a fool.'

'No. You were never a fool.' Chloe rested her chin on his chest but didn't take the ring. Not yet. 'Will you tell me what happened now, since I've come clean with you?'

The corners of his mouth turned down as if he didn't want to talk but needed to. 'She was attractive, outgoing and intelligent and soon after we met I asked her to be my date at my annual charity ball. She showed a keen interest in the kids I was working with and it wasn't long before she was talking about how if she had a house she'd do it up and provide a place-slash-time out for troubled kids blah, blah, blah.

'Meanwhile, we were falling in love—at least I was. Or thought I was. So when she hinted several times that if we were married, we could foster kids in our own home, I fell for it. I understood those neglected kids because I'd been one of them. Not quite the same but even a rich kid knows how it feels to be unwanted.'

'Your childhood wasn't good…'

'Ina never wanted kids. When I was born she refused to have any more, then as soon as she could she shipped me off to boarding school. On school holidays Dad used to take me out into the bush gold-panning. I loved those times.'

He shook his head as if he wanted to rid himself of the memories. Remembering Dana's advice about him loathing sympathy, Chloe remained still and waited for him to continue.

'Anyway, I owned a place in the city I'd been thinking of selling but I gifted it to Lynette as a wedding surprise the week before. I stupidly put it in her name.

'We were due to get married in Las Vegas. She told me she had a last-minute errand to run before we flew out but she never turned up at the airport. She'd sold the house already and disappeared. I never saw her again.'

'You didn't try to find her? Get something back?'

'I suppose I could have, but why would I expose myself for the idiot that I was? Even Foolish Freddy wouldn't try to find her. That's an end to it, Chloe. I don't ever want to talk about her again.'

'Thank you for telling me. Let's make a deal to not talk about our past again.'

'Done.' His stomach grumbled at that moment, and, glad for the opportunity to change topics, she smoothed her palm over his lean, hard torso. 'Hungry?'

He covered her hand and brought it to his lips for a nibble. 'Since I haven't eaten since I left Melbourne, yes.'

'Gosh, when was that?'

'It was dark, that's all I remember. Chloe.' He slid the gold band onto the finger on her right hand and eased it over the knuckle. A tight fit but manageable. 'Wear your ring on this hand until we get married. Whenever that might be—a month from now or a year—up to you. But I want to see my gold there and know we're partners. That we've made a promise. A commitment. That you're prepared to take on the biggest challenge of your life.'

She smiled at that man she loved through misty eyes. 'It's a deal. And now we've made that promise…how does Christmas sound?'

Jordan felt a grin break out on his face, a relief after the tension he'd endured since he'd made his decision. 'It sounds amazing. Like you.' He breathed in the scent of her hair and let it out on a sigh of contentment. Home. He was finally home. 'Do you want the big event or the register office?'

'I don't care, but do know I want my family there when we do it.'

That knowledge pleased him immensely. For all her adventures, he knew she missed them, that she needed that bond of family. 'So have you seen them yet?'

'I was waiting till I got this place fixed up...' She shook her head. 'I know I said I was up for any challenge, but, even though I've talked to Mum and we understand each other better now, I'm still a bit scared of actually facing up to them.'

He reached for her hand, his fingers sliding over the ring of golden promise. 'We'll go face them together.'

'We will?'

'Of course we will. We're partners, a team. And they're my future in-laws. I'm looking forward to being part of a family again.'

Chloe rested her chin on his chest, looked into the cerulean-blue depths of his eyes and saw forever. 'Partners. Pookie and Blondie.'

He nodded, those eyes crinkling up at the edges. 'And they lived happily ever after.'

* * * * *

THE HONEYMOON
THAT WASN'T

DEBBI RAWLINS

This is for Logan, the newest edition to our extended family. The cutest baby in the world.

Prologue

To: The Gang at Eve's Apple
From: LegallyNuts@EvesApple.com
Subject: Insanity

I'm not sure why I'm writing to you guys. Besides the fact that it's three in the morning and I can't sleep. I know the reason for the insomnia, which doesn't help one bit. Tomorrow night, no, <sigh> I guess technically tonight, is my sister's wedding rehearsal dinner. That part's great. She's met this terrific guy and I'm really happy for her.

The problem is that I'll see Tony again. A friend of my sister's. He's part of the wedding party. I met him only once, almost a year ago at the job site where they worked. He was wearing a tight white T-shirt and, my, oh, my, what a chest.

He's tall, too, at least six feet, broad shoulders, dark wavy hair, chocolate-brown eyes and a kind of square jaw. You get the picture. The guy is hot.

So why am I dreading tonight like I would a trip to the dentist? But I'm also looking forward to it. Does that make sense? If so, explain it to me, would you?

Oh, by the way, I'm not new to the group but I've been lurking for a while. To be honest, I never thought I'd post anything. Too busy. And besides, it's not my style. Or so I thought. This guy has my brain going in circles.

Frankly, if I were by myself and met him at a bar, it would be a no-brainer. I'm not into one-night stands though for him I'd make an exception. But that he knows my sister, and will be meeting my parents and brother tonight, complicates every-thing. I'm definitely not interested in anything long-term. Anyway, he's not someone who's in the game plan. No one is, really. I've been lucky. My career is taking off. A social life? What's that?

I'm a lawyer and due in court in six hours. I'm so tired. I truly wish I could sleep. But that's not going to happen. And now I'm rambling. Enough. If anyone is out there with some advice or even to confirm that I'm totally out of my mind, I'd appreciate it.

Thanks for reading this.

D

DAKOTA STARED at her laptop's screen for a moment. She was tempted to erase the e-mail. Writing it had been therapeutic—she didn't need to send it. Nor did she really need a reply. Nothing anyone could write would make her act on her impulse to spend a carte blanche night with Tony. She was too chicken to do anything like that. Not to mention that her family knew him. Or they would by tonight.

Her fingers hovered over the keyboard. What did she have to lose? If she were to get a response, at least it would be something to do since she couldn't sleep anyway. Besides, what would it hurt to get some feedback? She pressed the send button before she could change her mind again.

After setting the laptop on her nightstand, she got rid of one of the pillows she'd stacked behind her back and plumped the remaining one before sliding down, cradling her head in it and staring at the shadowy ceiling.

How totally bizarre was it to e-mail a bunch of women she didn't know—well, in a way she knew them. After hours and hours of reading their uncensored, heartfelt outpourings, she knew them, all right. Maybe even better than their friends and family.

Sheer genius had inspired the concept for the Eve's Apple Web site. Membership was simple. If there's a guy you're hot after you qualify. Not the right guy, in fact, more likely the one you absolutely wouldn't take home to Daddy. But he's also the guy you can't stop thinking about. You know you have to have him just so that life can get back on track. So that you could eventually settle down with Mr. Right and not have to wonder. Posting was like going to a twelve-step meeting. Anonymous so you could really vent, and everyone there really got it. They shared experiences, and gave advice when asked. Kind of like free therapy.

Odd how she could put it all out there for these strangers, but not talk to Dallas about Tony. Not that her sister would disapprove. On the contrary, she'd likely urge Dakota to go for it. But that was the difference between them. Dallas did whatever she wanted. Family expectations meant little to her. Not Dakota. Always the good girl, she'd even followed in her father's and brother's footsteps.

But it wasn't a sacrifice. She loved the law. In fact, she adored everything about her job. Dakota Shea for the defense, Your Honor—was her favorite expression. She wouldn't change any of it. Her social life, on the other hand, was a joke. If she could even call having a drink once every other week at the local lawyers' hangout a social life. Oh, and dinner at her parents' Tarrytown house one Saturday a month.

She closed her eyes, praying for sleep. When it wouldn't come, she tried thinking about work, mentally preparing herself for her court appearance in a few hours. But the distraction only lasted a few minutes before her thoughts drifted back to tonight. Back to Tony.

Groaning, she rolled over onto her side and grabbed the pillow she'd discarded. Comfortably sitting up again, she placed her laptop in front of her. She turned it on and saw she had a new e-mail. Good God, someone from Eve's Apple had already replied.

To: LegallyNuts@EvesApple.com
From: BabyBlu@EvesApple.com
Subject: Losing it

Hey, D, just read your post. Yeah, I'm an insomniac, too. And we share another similar problem.

A guy. Go figure. While it's not too late for you though, I've already blown my chance.

You see, I was once exactly where you are. Worried about my career, worried about what my parents thought (I'm Jewish, he isn't), worried about having all the right accoutrements to my upwardly mobile life.

Dakota stopped reading. Similar problem? Where had this woman—Dakota glanced down at the name—Carson, gotten all this crap? Rather large assumption. Dakota hadn't mentioned anything of this nature. None of it applied. Not really. Okay, so maybe her parents were an issue, to the extent that they'd had a vision for her early on, encouraging her to study law and now strongly hoped that she'd eventually become a judge. Just a minor issue. It wasn't as if she allowed them to govern her life. Sure, she relished their approval but what child didn't?

As far as her career went, well, she was sufficiently secure. No worries there. Not that she wanted to test the waters… But that didn't mean she was anything like Carson.

Her gaze was drawn back to the e-mail. She couldn't help herself and resumed reading.

And to my parents' delight, I became wildly successful. Mainly thanks to the real estate boom, doncha know? Yep, I'm a realtor, commercial sales mostly—high end. And that's how I met Larry. He was a finish carpenter working on one of the buildings I was showing to a client.

Dakota abruptly stopped reading. A carpenter? That was creepy. Tony wasn't a carpenter but a construction worker. Close enough. Professional woman meets blue-collar guy. Sounded like one of those awful talk shows on television with everyone screaming at each other.

She shuddered. Fatigue was really doing a number on her imagination. She left the rest of the e-mail unread and then skimmed a couple more that had popped up, both encouraging her to go for it. Then she signed off. She needed sleep. Not just for her court appearance, but to get through this evening. Without making an ass out of herself.

1

"SHE'S GOING TO BE LATE."

Tony San Angelo looked at his friend Dallas. "Who?"

She smiled and sipped her martini. "Dakota's always late on Friday nights. Too much happening at the office."

"Hey, you're getting married. It's a big thing. She can't make it to her only sister's rehearsal dinner on time?"

"As long as she's not late to the church tomorrow, I don't care." She elbowed him. "Relax. She'll be here."

"Like I care."

"Uh-huh." Dallas took another sip, trying to hide her smile.

"Nice place," he said, pretending interest in the private dining room of the swank Manhattan restaurant. Hadn't Dallas already told him he had zero chance with her sister? Not that he believed that. "I hope you and Eric didn't have to spring for this little soiree."

"Eric insisted on it because my parents are paying for the wedding. My father did try to argue because

Eric's parents are gone. Yada, yada. You know how all that male posturing goes."

"What are you looking at me like that for?"

She grinned.

"Hey, I'm wounded."

"Kidding," she quipped. "You're the least macho guy I know."

"Ah, man. Now I'm irreparably wounded."

"Okay, I'll try this again. You're macho without the macho mind-set. Better?"

"Hey, hey, break it up. People are talking." Eric joined them and clapped Tony on the arm. "Good to see you."

"I wouldn't miss this. Our little Dallas getting married. Hope you plan on keeping her barefoot and pregnant."

She socked him in the arm.

Eric chuckled. "Now, now, children."

Tony liked him. Great guy for Dallas, even if he was a suit who worked off Madison Avenue.

A waiter came in, and said something to Dallas's father. He nodded and then called for everyone's attention, giving them a two-minute warning before dinner would be served.

The rest of the bridal party was already there, nibbling on shrimp and imported cheeses, and guzzling drinks, all the really premium stuff. Even Dallas's snobby brother had made it on time, and he was one of the head honchos at the law firm where Dakota worked.

Tony drained his beer, the trusty domestic kind,

and sat at the far end of the long, elegantly set table. The seat gave him an excellent view of the door, not that he was that anxious to see Dakota again. Okay, maybe he was. The woman was totally beautiful. Light brown hair, gray-blue eyes, incredible legs. But his strategy had more to do with keeping his distance from the senior Sheas.

Dallas's parents had been cordial enough, but that didn't mean he'd like to make small talk with them. They were different, too serious in his opinion; both scholars, he a judge, she a professor. Tony was strictly blue-collar. A college dropout. No regrets. He liked his no-headache job, liked living life on his own terms, not getting calls in the middle of the night like his pop did.

Nancy sat next to him. She was the only other person here he knew besides Dallas because they'd all worked on the same construction crew at one time.

At first he thought Nancy had bumped his knee by mistake when she scooted her chair closer to the table, but then she did it again. He looked over at her.

"Why do we have so many forks?" she murmured, her lips barely moving.

"Beats me. But I know you're supposed to work from the outside in."

"Okay." She dubiously glanced around at everyone else and, mimicking them, placed her white linen napkin on her lap.

"The hell with it, I'm eating with my fingers."

Her stricken gaze flew to him.

"That was a joke."

She gave him a reproachful look, and then smiled at the white-gloved waiter as he set her Caesar salad in front of her.

Tony sighed. That was the trouble with these high-class places. You couldn't relax. Have fun. Of course he'd keep his opinion to himself. He'd never hurt Dallas. This wasn't just her wedding—these were her people.

His attention strayed to the door. Still no Dakota. No one seemed concerned. Not even Mr. and Mrs. Shea. In fact, from what Dallas had told him, they probably approved that she put work ahead of everything else.

Man, he didn't understand these people. His parents would've given him or any of his three siblings a lecture right then and there. In front of everyone. The deal had always been, if the kids were willing to screw up in public, then they got reprimanded likewise. Even though none of them were kids anymore.

While being on time for a party in the San Angelo family was never a problem. When his older sister had gotten married the party had started two days before the wedding and didn't end until three the morning after the reception.

The salad plates were cleared and the rack of lamb was just being served when Dakota showed up. Still dressed in her navy-blue power suit, she had her hair pulled back in an awful, matronly style. Nancy and the other bridesmaid were all gussied up, Dallas more causally elegant in a simple cream-colored silk dress.

Dakota looked directly at him, and he smiled. Her gaze fluttered away and his smile broadened.

"I've never had lamb before," Nancy whispered. "Have you?"

"Yeah." He briefly glanced over to see her skeptically staring at her plate, and then his attention went right back to Dakota.

She took the vacant seat Dallas had saved next to her, and damned if Dakota didn't slide him another look.

"Tony?"

"What?"

Nancy made a face. "Are you listening to me?"

"What did you say?"

"I want to know what this green stuff is. It looks like jelly."

"It is. Mint jelly. It goes with the lamb."

"Right." Nancy snorted. "Come on. If you don't know just—what are you looking at?" Until Nancy followed his gaze, he hadn't realized he'd been staring. "Oh, Dakota's here." She waved excitedly, and Dakota waved back.

Only at Nancy. Not at him. Good sign.

He smiled, thinking about the first day they'd met. The *only* day they'd met. She'd appeared at the job site to see Dallas. It was love at first sight for him. Okay, more like lust. Dallas had noticed his interest. Told him to forget it. But the eye contact he'd made with Dakota told him otherwise. If it had lasted one second less, it would have been a different story. And when she got to the end of the block and turned around, he knew.

"How do you know her?" he asked Nancy.

"Well, duh. She's the one who helped us with all

our legal stuff to scare Capshaw into taking our harassment complaints seriously. For free, too."

Tony's gaze returned to Dakota. A woman full of surprises. He thought she'd be too busy to help a group of women fight discrimination against the state's second largest construction company.

"You haven't met her." Nancy leaned closer, eyeballing him with far too much interest. "Have you?"

"Why?"

"Have you?" She darted a look at Dakota, probably wondering why she hadn't acknowledged Tony. Nancy seemed to arrive at her own conclusion, judging by the smirk on her face as she settled back in her chair. "She shot you down."

"What?"

"There's actually a woman in this city who isn't gaga over you."

"Get out." He grabbed his beer and took a deep pull.

"Tell me you don't know that all the women at work are in heat over you."

"Yeah, right. Especially Jan."

Nancy rolled her eyes. "I meant the straight ones. So what happened?"

"I met her once for about forty seconds."

"You must be slipping." She grinned. "It usually takes only ten for women to start getting stupid over you."

"That how long it took you?"

Her grin disappeared and her cheeks got pink. He knew that would shut her up. What he didn't know was that he'd been the subject of gossip.

Shit.

Hadn't he been the only guy on the work crew who'd been willing to speak up on the women's behalf? Although most of the other guys were guilty of the harassment management chose to ignore. Still, he could've kept his mouth shut. But he hadn't. And now he wasn't working for Capshaw Construction anymore.

Fine by him. Being discussed by a bunch of chatty women wasn't.

Through the rest of dinner, he and Nancy didn't speak much.

She was busy choosing forks and eating, and he was busy trying not to stare at Dakota. The woman really needed to smile more. She looked too damn serious. The way she wore her hair pulled back didn't help.

All of a sudden, her gaze swept toward him, meeting his eyes dead-on. She locked into him for one long hypnotic moment, and then blinked and looked away.

Excitement thrummed through him. The awareness in her gray-blue eyes was like a vice around his neck, restricting air, making it hard to breathe. To say nothing of the effect she was having on him south of the border. The woman definitely had him by the balls. What did she intend to do with them?…was the question.

"DID MOTHER TALK to you about the photographer?" Dakota foolishly asked her sister, in a vain effort to keep her mind and eyes off Tony.

"No." Dallas frowned, immediately setting down her wineglass. "What about him?"

"Oh, nothing. I mean she wants to make sure the wedding party knows they don't have to stop at his studio before the reception."

"Right," Dallas said slowly, her frown deepening. "I knew that."

"Good. Just checking." Dakota gave her a weak smile and then finished off the rest of her chardonnay.

The corners of Dallas's mouth twitched and she glanced toward the far corner of the table. At Tony.

Damn.

Dakota clenched her teeth. Was she really that absurdly obvious? Probably. Her sister knew her better than anyone. Which also meant Dallas should understand that Tony was unquestionably the wrong kind of guy for her.

The thought struck like a bolt of lightning, coming from some dark void and stunning her. Shaming her. She glanced around worried that someone could read her ugly thoughts.

Her parents were chatting with Eric's friend Tom and his wife Serena, both of whom were in the wedding party. Nancy, a woman who'd worked with Dallas, and Dallas's roommate, Wendy, both sat on the other side of Eric.

And then there was Tony. Looking directly at her, his dark eyes sparkling in the mellow glow of the crystal chandelier. His lips curved slightly, and then he winked.

She lowered her gaze, removed the white linen napkin from her lap and brought it to her lips. Even though she'd yet to take a bite of her entree. The others were already being served dessert and coffee, and she could have easily skipped eating altogether except she didn't want to upset her mother.

Sighing, she picked up her fork and knife. At least while she ate she could politely ignore Tony. Dallas and Eric were tête-à-tête and Cody had vacated the seat to Dakota's left five minutes ago to make a phone call. Not that she had much to say to him. Being with her brother at the office for twelve hours a day was quite enough.

She slid a glance toward Tony. The chair next to Nancy was empty. Dakota jumped at the hand on her shoulder and swung her gaze around.

Tony grinned, his teeth brilliantly white against his tanned face. "Dakota, right? Dallas's sister?"

"Yes, we've met once before, haven't we?"

The corners of his mouth quirked up slightly and he gestured to Cody's vacant chair. "You mind?"

"Suit yourself." She cringed at the defensive lilt to her voice.

He didn't seem to notice, just lowered himself into the chair, mindless of the way his thigh brushed hers. How when he angled toward her, his knee touched her knee. When he stretched his arm along the back of her chair and leaned close, her heart nearly exploded through her chest.

"I have a question."

"Yes?" She inched back to look at him without coming nose to nose. Bad enough his warm sweet breath managed to caress her chin. God, he had such thick dark lashes. So not fair. And his smile as he got closer...

"It's kind of personal."

She swallowed. What could he possibly—

"Ah, Tony." Dallas leaned over. "Glad you decided to slum it."

"Right." They exchanged the look of longtime friends.

"You remember Dakota," Dallas said, the impish gleam in her eyes all too familiar.

"Yeah, we were just getting reacquainted until you butted in."

Dallas laughed. "So charming, isn't he?" She glanced briefly at Dakota and then turned a more serious expression toward Tony. "I need to talk to you before you disappear tonight."

"Disappear?" He grinned at Dakota. "My motor is just getting revved."

She tried to keep a straight face. Tried not to look around to see if anyone heard. Especially not her mother. She picked the napkin off her lap again and pushed back her chair. "Excuse me, please. I have to make a phone call."

"Something I said?" Tony asked, his amused dark eyes watching her rise, lingering briefly on her breasts. Not long enough to be rude, but long enough to make her feel as if she were twelve again, awkward, nervous and wanting to suddenly disappear rather than face her parents' reaction, her mother's accusing eyes because Dakota had put herself on display.

She dropped the napkin over her plate and pushed in her chair.

"Aren't you going to finish your dinner?" Tony couldn't quite keep his amusement in check. "No dessert unless you clean your plate."

She ignored him and addressed Dallas. "You two go ahead and have your talk."

"Come on, Dakota. You just got here. Besides, I need to talk to you, too." Dallas gave her a pleading look that almost had her caving. After all, tomorrow was Dallas's big day....

As hard as it was to say no to her sister, Dakota shook her head and picked up her briefcase. Tony was headed someplace she didn't want to go. At least not here. Certainly not with an audience. "I'm leaving."

"I'll have them bring your bananas Foster."

"Think I'll pass." In spite of herself, Dakota glanced at Tony.

"Hmm, that's what you call that stuff. Some guy named Foster must have come up with it, huh?"

Dallas laughed.

Dakota couldn't tell if he was kidding or not.

"They're supposed to offer cognac and then we're done here," Dallas said, looking over her shoulder at the headwaiter, who'd already brought out the bottles of brandy. "So if you can't stay—"

"What?" Tony spread his hands. "No dancing?"

"Down, boy. That's tomorrow night," Dallas quipped. "As if you can dance."

"You talkin' to me?" Tony scoffed. "Do you have any idea who taught Travolta his moves for *Saturday Night Fever*?"

"What were you, about three?"

He shrugged, a grin curving his mouth. "I'm just saying…"

Dakota shook her head, a little envious of their easy camaraderie. "As I said, I'm leaving."

Tony stuck out his chin in acknowledgment. "See ya tomorrow."

"Right." Everyone at the table seemed preoccupied so she skipped a farewell and headed for the door.

"Don't be late," he added.

Dallas half groaned, half laughed.

Annoyed, Dakota stopped, but then thought better of turning around and calling attention to them. She kept walking, wondering how in the hell she'd ever found this man attractive.

WATCHING HER SISTER walk out in that ramrod straight   I'd-better-get-out-of-here-before-I-kill-somebody posture Dallas knew too well, she sighed. "Why do you have to antagonize her?"

Tony dragged his gaze away from the empty doorway. "I think she likes me."

"You're impossible."

He smiled. "A little wine, a little tango tomorrow night…" He flattened a hand to his belly and made a swaying dance move. "She'll be ripe for the picking."

"Excuse me? We're talking about my sister here."

"Hey, I'm just talking about asking her out. Where's your mind at?"

She gave him a mock glare. Tony was a great guy. Perfect for Dakota if she'd give him a chance. But she wouldn't. Too many expectations blocked the way. Father wanted her to be a judge, and Cody, a senior partner at the law firm where Dakota worked, not only expected her to rake in the dough but attract high-end clients. Mother, well, she always expected too much of everyone.

"Seriously, Tony, I need a favor."

"Shoot."

She glanced over at Eric's friend to be sure he wasn't listening, and then leaned closer to Tony. "Remember how I met Eric. Through a prank his friend Tom pulled?"

"Yeah."

"We think he's up to something again. Like sabotaging our honeymoon."

"No way." Tony gave Tom a harsh look. "Not your honeymoon."

"You don't know Tom. He lives to create the perfect practical joke."

"Want me to talk to him?"

"No, no. I don't even want him to know we suspect anything. What I would like you to do is act as a decoy." Dallas felt Eric stirring behind her. Obviously he'd heard, or at least knew what she was doing. They'd discussed the ploy. He didn't agree with her interference. But of course he didn't understand the complexities of growing up a Shea.

"Decoy? How?"

"You can take a long weekend, right?"

"Uh, yeah," he said slowly.

"Ever been to Bermuda?"

Tony frowned in disbelief. "You're not saying—you're kidding."

"The plane leaves right after the reception. The hotel is already booked and paid for."

"Do you know how crazy this is?"

Eric's cheek touched hers as he leaned close enough for them to hear. "That's what I told her."

She elbowed him. "Be quiet."

"Just tell him you're going to Hawaii." Tony chuckled.

"He heard Eric making the arrangements but he doesn't know that we decided to go on a cruise instead. I want to keep it that way."

"This still sounds crazy. It's not like he's gonna follow you to Bermuda."

"Have I ever asked you for anything?"

"Wow, Dallas, go ahead and turn the screws, why don't you?"

"It's a free vacation, for goodness' sake."

"You realize there's one huge hole in this plan," Tony said, giving Eric that smug condescending male look she hated. "Don't *two* people normally go on a honeymoon?"

It was her turn to look smug. "Of course. That's why Dakota will be going with you."

Hell, why didn't she say that in the first place?

2

"I NOW PRONOUNCE YOU man and wife."

Tony watched Dallas and Eric embrace, and then looked at Dakota. Her eyes were glassy, blinking rapidly, and her smile quivered slightly as she gazed at her sister.

Today was the first time he'd seen her with her hair down, longer than he'd expected, hanging just below her shoulders, light brown and full of honey-colored highlights. And really shiny. Outside he'd caught a glimpse of her entering the chapel, her hair a brilliant silky mass floating around her shoulders.

He was one of those suckers for women with long hair and Dakota was way up there on the perfect scale. His groin tightened, thinking about tomorrow, Dakota, a sunny beach, a skimpy bikini and all that hair.

Assuming she'd agreed to the plan. Dallas was supposed to have talked to her this morning. Him, he already had a small bag packed, waiting in his car to be transferred to the limo. Dallas didn't think there'd be a problem with Dakota, only that she might not want to stay the whole weekend. Just turn around and come back to Manhattan tonight. That's where he'd have some convincing to do.

She looked over at him just then and he smiled. Her lips curved ever so slightly. Ah, progress. But she gave up eye contact, her gaze going back to her sister as the cello music started, signaling them to leave the altar and start down the aisle. Dallas and Eric went first and then everyone else in the wedding party followed in no particular order. The men wore tuxedos and the women long dresses. The way Dakota filled out the dark red dress made it hard to keep his eyes on Dallas and Eric. The neckline wasn't too low but it showed off a tempting amount of pale satiny skin and a hint of cleavage. He was lucky enough to walk behind her, or maybe unlucky, because the gentle sway of her hips and the way the dress cupped her curvy backside got a reaction from him that he had trouble hiding.

They got outside and pews of friends and family followed, hugging, kissing cheeks, shaking hands, but not a single grain of rice was thrown. Probably not a custom at high-class weddings. When his sister had gotten married, his pop distributed a whole twenty-pound bag of rice. Made a special trip to Chinatown to get it.

"Okay, everyone." After the initial commotion, the photographer motioned the wedding party to stand in front of one of the large stained-glass windows.

The Union Church of Pocantico Hills was really something. Even tourists stopped to see the stained-glass windows created by two modern artists, Matisse and Chagall. Not that Tony knew squat about either of them, but he'd read the literature put out for tourists. Today the place was off-limits on account of the wedding. The Sheas obviously had some major clout in Tarrytown.

Impressive circle of friends, too, who stood off to the side in their expensive suits and silk dresses and pearls. Tony recognized several faces from the legal community. Couldn't place their names. He'd seen them on the news or in the newspaper.

"Excuse me, sir. Stand here, please." The tall, thin hawkish-looking photographer gestured for Tony to stand beside Dakota.

The guy didn't have to ask him twice. Tony sidled up beside her, their arms and hips touching, and inhaled her mysterious scent. Maybe he'd sniffed a little too enthusiastically because she gave him an annoyed look. Or maybe it was the touching part she didn't like.

"Dallas looks beautiful," he whispered while the photographer got everyone else into place.

Dakota immediately softened. "And happy."

"Is it gonna seem weird that she's married?"

"Not really." She shrugged, her arm rubbing his. "Nothing will change."

Tempted to ask about tonight's plan, he kept his mouth shut while the photographer finished positioning everyone. Tom stood too close to risk him hearing of the counterattack.

"Everyone ready?" The photographer clicked off two shots.

For the next twenty minutes, they were separated, pushed back together, coupled, shuffled from one stained-glass window to the next, the entire time the photographer muttering how difficult this was with everyone chatting and laughing.

Mrs. Shea stood back, commiserating, shaking her head and sliding her husband long-suffering looks. The honorable Judge Shea didn't seem to give a crap. Good for him.

Once the photographer was satisfied, or maybe because Dallas had whispered something to him, they disbanded and got into the waiting limos. The guests followed in their separate cars and everyone headed for the reception at the Shea's country club.

Tony was lucky enough to share a limo with Dakota. Too bad Nancy, Trudie and Wendy climbed in behind them. Could've been worse. He could've gotten stuck with Mr. and Mrs. Shea, and Cody and his snotty society date.

"Hey, how do you like being surrounded by all these women?" Wendy asked, while trying to get her long legs into a suitable position. She was a dancer, an extra on Broadway if he remembered correctly.

He stretched an arm out along the back of the seat and got comfortable, then gave her a cocky grin. "I can handle it."

"I bet you can." She gave him an inviting smile he wished Dakota had given him.

But she sat across from him with her face turned toward the window and didn't even react to what was going on.

Until Wendy said, "Hey, Dakota, I guess you're next."

"Next?"

"To bite the dust." Wendy grinned at Dakota's wide-eyed expression. "Tie the knot. Whatever they say these days."

"Why me? You're older."

"Ouch."

Dakota grinned. "Shouldn't you be the one getting antsy? Watching that biological clock."

"Ruthless, aren't you?"

Trudie laughed. "That's what makes her a good lawyer."

Dakota's grin tapered off.

No one seemed to notice but Tony. They all kept teasing each other back and forth while Dakota shrank back against the seat. Good to know she was touchy about the lawyer thing. Not that he was stupid enough to repeat the jokes he'd heard. Okay, so maybe he would've let a couple slip, but now he knew.

"So is like everybody gonna stay dressed like this, or can we change?" Wendy asked as they turned off the street and onto the lush country club grounds.

"I don't know, but I was hoping somebody would ask." Nancy looked to the others, and then focused on Dakota.

"I doubt Dallas cares one way or the other," she said, "but we'd better wait until after dinner so the photographer can get the rest of the pictures."

"Yeah, we don't want your mom freaking out."

Wendy tugged at her dress. "The same moron who invented high heels must have come up with this gem."

"Fair is fair." Tony couldn't resist. Not that he was particularly fond of ties. In fact, he hardly ever wore them—only when he absolutely had to.

Wendy smiled at him. "You are so damn cute. I can't believe Dallas kept you from us all these years."

Heat crawled up Tony's neck. Thankfully he knew he wouldn't turn red. He didn't embarrass easily but Wendy was something else.

"Now that Dallas has ditched me, I'm looking for a roommate if you're interested." Wendy gave him an impish grin, shifting so that their legs touched.

"Hey, he's already taken," Nancy said, rubbing a familiar shoulder against his.

He gave her a sharp look. So did Dakota.

Nancy laughed. "My six-year-old thinks he's it. She lights up like the Fourth of July every time she sees him."

Tony reared his head back. "Megan's six already?"

"Yep, she had a birthday two months ago."

"Man, then I haven't seen her in almost a year."

"You should come by sometime." Nancy smiled. "It would make her day."

"Yeah, maybe next weekend. I owe her a teddy bear for her birthday."

Wendy spoke up. "Nanc, I didn't know you were married. I thought you were one of us." When she frowned, Wendy added, "You know, single."

"I'm divorced," Nancy replied. "Does that count?"

"Oh, yeah. Definitely." Wendy peered out the

window at the impeccably manicured greens and small man-made lakes, stretching on for acres. "Wow, this place is awesome." She looked at Dakota. "Do you know if any Broadway people were invited?"

Dakota shrugged. "I don't think so."

"Just the boring legal types, huh?"

Trudie groaned and darted a look at Dakota. "Wendy, would you shut up?"

Dakota just laughed. "I know what you mean." She faked a yawn. "Bunch of long-winded, pontificating blowhards."

Everyone got quiet and stared at her.

Tilting her head to the side and smiling, Dakota added, "With a few exceptions, of course."

God, she was gorgeous. Tony just stared. He couldn't look away. With that soft smile on her peach-tinted lips, the way the late-afternoon sun filtered into the windows and lit her hair, she should have been spread out across a billboard. Wouldn't matter what product she peddled. Hell, even nail clippers. Any red-blooded guy would buy it.

Obviously he wasn't the only one with that opinion because Wendy said, "Jeez, Dakota, why aren't you modeling like Dallas?"

"I like what I do."

"You can practice law later. Make the easy bucks now while you still have the looks."

Trudie shook her head with disgust. Apparently she also noticed Dakota's defensive posture. "What part of keep quiet don't you understand?"

"Come on, Trudie, I'm just saying—"

"Hey, we're here. There's Dallas and Eric." Tony's timely interruption was met by a quick smile from Dakota. He winked back and she abruptly turned away, and he could've sworn her cheeks had started to pinken.

But she hid it while stepping out of the limo and leading them to the foyer to stand in the reception line where people were already waiting to congratulate the bride and groom.

Why the rest of the wedding party had to stand there was beyond him. Nobody cared if they were there or not. But now wasn't the time to question the tradition so he obediently positioned himself between Nancy and Trudie as Mrs. Shea instructed.

After more pictures were taken and everyone had had a crack at Dallas and Eric, the wedding party was finally allowed to enter the private dining room. More like a ballroom with tables and chairs for at least a hundred and fifty guests. Fresh flower arrangements, mostly orchids, were everywhere. Two bars were set up on either side of the room, manned by bartenders wearing tuxedos. He couldn't imagine how much this had set the Sheas back. Of course that kind of money was no sweat to them.

"Hey, where are the balloons?" he asked Dakota.

She gave him a weird look as if she hoped he was kidding but wasn't sure. And then surprised him by asking, "Do you want a drink?"

"Sure."

"Come on."

He followed as she led him around the guests who had already lined up in front of the bars. Several white-gloved waiters stood to the side and she whispered something to the short husky one who nodded and smiled ecstatically as if she'd just agreed to have his children.

Tony watched the guy abruptly turn around and then disappear through a side door that blended with the wall and had been invisible to Tony. "Where's he going?"

"To get our drinks."

"Ah." He nodded. "Come here often, do you?"

She arched a brow at him. "You want to wait in that line?"

"No, ma'am."

"All right then."

"Do we stay right here and wait or is there a rendezvous point?"

A smile tugged at her lips. "Don't worry. You won't get mobbed. This is a very civil bunch. They'll only complain to management."

"That I can handle. By the way, tell me you didn't order me champagne."

"I didn't order you champagne."

"Not to sound ungrateful."

"Uh-huh."

The waiter reappeared holding a small tray in one hand, and used the other to hand Dakota a glass of white wine and Tony a bottle of beer, his usual. Without a glass, too. Obviously she'd noticed what he was drinking last night.

The weekend was starting to look up.

Maybe she planned on taking Dallas up on her offer of a free minivacation with him. Before bringing it up, he glanced over his shoulder to make sure Tom wasn't around. No, but Wendy was headed their way.

Damn.

The only consolation was that Dakota looked just as disappointed.

Her red hair windblown, Wendy smelled faintly of tobacco as she approached. She looked from the glasses in their hands to the increasingly long line at the bar. "Where did you get the drinks?"

Dakota gestured vaguely over her shoulder. "A waiter was walking around with a tray."

"Cool." Wendy wandered off in the direction Dakota had sent her.

Tony chuckled.

"I didn't lie."

He didn't care. She'd gotten rid of Wendy. That's what counted. Not that he didn't like Wendy, but he wanted Dakota to himself. He wanted to lose himself in those sexy gray-blue eyes, and bask in the anticipation of tonight. Miles away from here. Alone. Nothing to do but get to know one another. Spend long leisurely hours of exploring each other's bodies.

That line of thinking had to stop. He shifted his weight from one foot to the other, trying to stop the blood from rushing south. He took a healthy gulp of icy cold beer and then met Dakota's amused eyes.

Dakota smiled and took another sip, her lashes long and thick resting on her cheeks. She barely wore any makeup, didn't have to. Her features were almost perfect. High cheekbones, a pert nose, full lips, her skin so flawless it was almost translucent. Her eyes were smaller than Dallas's, more gray than blue and deeper set, but she was every bit as gorgeous.

Man, he'd like to see the faces of everyone the first time she walked into a courtroom. Not the typical lawyer, that's for sure. Unless she always dressed for work the way she had last night, conservative and drab.

A trio of violinists in the corner started playing elevator music, but at least they kept it low-key. Up front there were two stages, one slightly elevated with band equipment and the other a parquet dance floor.

"Uh-oh." Tony saw Mrs. Shea heading toward them with obvious purpose. "I think we're about to be summoned."

Dakota looked over her shoulder, immediately tensing. "I have a feeling she wants me."

Interesting how tense she got at the mention of her mother. He knew a little bit from Dallas about the formidable Mrs. Shea, prominent college professor and demanding mother. The woman had done one really good thing for her girls. She'd encouraged them to go for an education instead of trade on their extraordinary looks. Had to give her credit for that.

Dakota sighed. "I'd better go see what she wants."

"I have a better idea. Let's take a walk."

She looked at him, the disbelief in her eyes slowly fading to uncertainty. "We just got here."

"So. Do you want to ditch her or not?"

Her lips parted in indignation, but a flicker of excitement sparked in her eyes. She briefly glanced over her shoulder again, caught her mother gaining on them and said, "Let's go."

3

DAKOTA LED Tony out of the banquet room to a side patio, knowing she'd pay hell for the disappearing act. In fact, she wouldn't put it past her mother to hunt them down. Except it was getting cold outside, with nothing on the fairway to block the biting wind, enough that it might insure them some privacy.

She swallowed. Was that what she wanted? To be out here alone with him? This was foolish. She knew how it would turn out. They wouldn't just talk. Facing him, she smiled. "Bad idea. It's a little too cool."

"Here." He shrugged out of his jacket, the white dress shirt straining against his broad chest. "Put this on."

"No, really, that's okay. Then you'll be cold. Let's go back—"

He slipped the jacket over her shoulders, and then turned her to face him. Unfortunately, she couldn't see his expression. The patio was very dimly lit by a pale blue glow, courtesy of the parade of solar lights staked along the perimeter. The thought infused her with a dangerous excitement that made her nipples tighten and her resolve weaken.

"This should keep you warm." He pulled the lapels together and she stumbled toward him, steadying herself with her palms against his chest.

"Sorry," she whispered and straightened, reluctantly letting her hands fall away.

He released the lapels and cupped her shoulders, then ran his palms down her arms. "You smell good."

She shivered when his warm breath fanned her cheek, and he took her cold hands, sandwiching them between his slightly callused ones. She'd never been with a man with work-roughened hands. How would they feel touching the tenderest part of her body? Stroking the area around her nipples? The soft skin between her thighs?

He lowered his head and her breath caught when his lips brushed hers. But only briefly before he whispered, "I can't wait for later."

"Later?"

The sound of the French doors opening had them guiltily jumping apart. Thankfully it was Dallas, the long white gown obvious even in the dim light.

"Hey, you guys, dinner is going to be served in twenty minutes."

Dakota sighed. "You came out here to tell us that?"

"Better me than Mother. Anyway, Dakota, I need to talk to you."

"Now?"

"Yep. Sorry, Tony. I need her for five minutes."

He gestured with his hand. "I'll see you inside."

"Here's your jacket," Dakota said, pushing it off her shoulders and then handing it to him.

"Keep it while you're outside."

"I'm not staying out here. It's cold."

"Trust me," Dallas said, "it would be better if we talked out here."

Dakota didn't like the sound of that. Even Tony frowned as he tried to give her back his jacket. She shook her head. "I'm okay."

After shooting Dallas a curious look, he left them alone. Dakota was pretty curious herself. "What's going on?"

"I have a favor to ask of you."

"Okay."

"It's kind of big, but I really, really need you to do this for me," Dallas said. "Okay?"

"Well, what is it?"

"Promise me you'll do it first."

Dakota snorted. "Right."

"Come on, Dakota, have I ever asked you for anything? You're my sister. It's my wedding, and I need this favor badly."

"What already?" She waited, but Dallas's chin stubbornly went up, and the truth was Dakota would never refuse her sister anything. "All right. I promise."

"I need you to play decoy for me tonight after the reception."

"Why?"

"You know how Eric's friend Tom likes to play practical jokes. We're pretty sure he's going to try and sabotage our honeymoon."

Dakota shook her head at her sister's paranoia. "He wouldn't do something so juvenile."

"He'd think it was hilarious. I know him, and you need to help me out." Dallas rubbed her bare arms. "It is cold out here."

"So you want me to do what exactly?" Dakota asked as her sister linked an arm through hers and steered her toward the entry into the banquet room.

Dallas opened the door and the light inside illuminated her smile. "Go on my honeymoon for me. With Tony."

DAMN THAT Dallas. As soon as they got inside someone called to her sister and she was off with no further explanation other than she'd already packed a bag for Dakota. As if the matter were settled.

Dakota headed straight for the bathroom, her thoughts spinning so quickly she literally felt dizzy. Or maybe it was the excitement of what lay ahead? The whole idea was crazy. And perfect. A weekend with Tony? She couldn't have come up with a better plan herself. Except she had a lot going on at work, and it wasn't as if she could just *not* show up on Monday.

Two older women, colleagues of her mother whom she vaguely knew, stood at the mirror talking and applying lipstick. Dakota smiled at them and then hurried into a stall, put the seat down and sat on the john. She hadn't even asked her sister if Tony knew about the plan and if he'd agreed to go. Is that what he'd meant by "later"? She straightened. If he'd known about this before she had that would really tick her off.

She took a deep breath. Dallas had purposely

waited to tell her. Just so she wouldn't have time to come up with an excuse not to go. She was a coward. She admitted it.

Dallas was the independent one. She did as she pleased. Dakota, however, was the good little lamb. Always doing what she was told.

She still didn't like it that Dallas had conspired with Tony. For that reason alone she ought to tell her sister to find some other flunky. Yeah, right. Like she wasn't ready to leave the reception right now, get him alone and rip off his clothes.

Feeling a little flushed, she bent over, crossing her arms over her knees and breathing deeply. She was crazy for even considering doing this. But she'd be even crazier for refusing the opportunity. The ladies' room door opened and she heard someone murmur about dinner starting. She had to go or someone would surely come looking for her.

Straightening, she smoothed back her hair, and then checked the front of her dress. Smiling, she stood, ready for the games to begin. She'd go but that didn't mean she'd go easily.

"Guess what Mother wants." Dallas met her partway.

Tony followed Dallas, who gave him an exasperated look.

Dakota sensed an undercurrent but they didn't seem angry with each other. "What?"

"To change the seating."

"I would've guessed that."

Dallas snorted. "I'm having the big formal wedding like she wanted, and I kept my mouth shut when she invited half the legal and academic communities, most of whom I don't know. But that's it."

"Calm down." Tony slipped an arm around her shoulders and squeezed lightly. "That's one of the first rules of weddings. Mothers get to show off their kids and put their husbands in the poorhouse. Just ask my pop."

Dallas rolled her eyes. "Gee, if I'd known that was a rule I wouldn't have gotten upset."

"Now you know."

Sighing, she smiled and kissed Tony on the cheek. "Entertain my sister, okay?"

"I don't need entertaining," Dakota said, but Dallas had already flitted over to another couple Dakota didn't recognize. She turned toward Tony. "I don't—"

"I know." His mouth curved in a sexy grin that made her heart skip a beat. "So entertain me instead."

"BETTER TAKE IT EASY with that stuff." Tony eyed the brandy snifter in Dakota's hand, her second cognac as far as he could tell. And that was after several glasses of wine with dinner. A different variety was served with each course. Him, he stuck to his beer. Two glasses of wine and he'd be kissing the floor. For some reason, the stuff really got to him.

"One mother is all I can handle, thank you very much." She took a deliberate sip, smiled and said, "I'm fine. Really."

"Okay," he said without conviction. The fact that

she'd said that a little too loudly was proof enough she better give the booze a rest.

Although he had to admit she wasn't sloppy. If he hadn't been sitting next to her at dinner he wouldn't have known she'd had that much wine. Plus each course had been spaced out so that dinner had ended up being the longest, most quiet meal in history. At least for his family. When the San Angelos got together for a party, talking, eating and dancing were not mutually exclusive.

They'd finally finished dessert a half hour ago, and people had started dancing the moment the band struck the first note. He wanted to ask Dakota to dance but the song had to be just the right one. Despite his mouthing off, he wasn't all that swift on the dance floor. The beat had to be slow and easy so he didn't have to think too much about what his feet were doing.

He'd skip the idea altogether, but the way Mrs. Shea had been giving him the eye, he figured dancing with Dakota would be the only way he'd get close to her. Dallas and Eric were already out there and so were Trudie and Wendy who'd pulled Tom along with them. At the end of the table, Serena and Nancy seemed deep in conversation.

The song ended and the band eased into another, slower, moodier one he could handle. He turned to Dakota but her father beat him to it.

Mr. Shea was taking her by the hand. "Hope you saved a dance for your old man," he said, smiling fondly at his daughter.

"*Save* a dance? No one's asked me yet," she said, with a teasing smile at Tony as she set down her brandy.

"My mistake." He met her eyes. "I claim the next one."

Laughing, she got to her feet and allowed her father to lead her to the dance floor. The way that dress hugged her curves bordered on illegal. Her hips moved with a little extra enthusiasm almost as if for his benefit. Hard not to stare, but he sensed someone over his shoulder and looked up.

"Mind if I sit with you for a moment?" Mrs. Shea didn't wait for an answer. She lowered herself gracefully into Dakota's chair.

"Gee, here I thought you were going to ask me to dance."

She smiled and gazed out toward the dance floor. "Everyone seems to be having a good time."

"Yes, ma'am. Free liquor does it every time."

Annoyance flickered in her eyes. One blink and it was gone.

He tried not to smile and sipped his beer.

"Didn't you like the wine we selected?"

"I'm sure it was just fine. I prefer beer."

"Ah." She turned again to watch the dancers.

The woman hardly looked as if she could have three adult children. Tall, blond and trim, she didn't look much over forty. In fact, she could've passed for Dallas and Dakota's sister.

She caught him staring.

Tony coughed. "I was just thinking how you look more like your daughters' sister. They'll be lucky to look like you in twenty years," he said and meant it. She was a very attractive woman.

She looked annoyed again, her pinched expression adding a decade to her face. "Looks hardly make the person."

"Couldn't agree more." Tony took another sip of beer to avoid saying something sarcastic. Like her being a perfect example.

"Take Dakota." Mrs. Shea's gaze went to her daughter. "She could have had a successful modeling career. But she was smart enough to realize the foolhardiness of such a move. Wisely she chose to further her education, secure her future." She looked at him then, steadily meeting his gaze. "Did you know she's got a good shot at a judgeship?"

"Yeah, I heard something about it from Dallas. The thing I don't understand is that she's only been out of law school for what—three, four years? I'm sure she's really bright and I don't know how the system works but isn't that kind of fast?" He smiled and brought his beer to his lips. "But then again your husband probably has connections if that's what you two want for Dakota," he said before taking a long pull.

He had to give the woman credit for keeping a straight face. Maybe she should've been the attorney. The only sign that he'd dented her composure was that it took her a few moments to come back with, "Where did you attend college, Mr. San Angelo?"

"NYU. And call me Tony." He enjoyed the surprise on her face. Probably figured he hadn't made it through high school. Yet she wouldn't be disappointed for long.

"What was your degree in?"

Ah, well, the fun lasted all of thirty seconds. "I dropped out the middle of my sophomore year."

Her eyebrows went up. "Really?" He didn't think he imagined an inkling of satisfaction on her face. "May I ask why?"

He shook his head. "School just wasn't for me. I like working with my hands."

"Yes, but—"

He held up a hand. "No offense, Professor Shea, I understand where you're coming from but that's the way it is. I like what I do. I'm not going to change my mind."

"Forgive me. I didn't mean to sound as if I'm interfering. We all make our own choices."

The song ended and Dakota and her father headed back toward them. Even from this distance he could see the alarm on Dakota's face, and surprisingly what looked like disapproval in her father's.

Mrs. Shea pushed back her chair. "I suppose we were lucky all of our children valued their education." She smiled at him as she rose to her feet. "Nice chatting with you, Tony."

Tempted to remind her of Dallas's detour he decided to keep his mouth shut. It didn't matter. He got the message. He lived on the wrong side of the fence.

She slipped away a second before Dakota returned to her seat. Her father nodded at Tony and then followed his wife back to their table.

Frowning, Dakota watched until they both sat down. "What was that about?"

"What?"

She fixed him with a pretty intimidating glare. One she'd probably perfected in court. "What did my mother want?"

He grinned and got up, pulling her with him. "She wanted me to dance with you."

"Right."

He was lucky. The song was slow. He shouldn't have too much trouble keeping up. They got to the center of the floor and he guided them to the middle for some privacy. Not much, but better than having her mother's gaze boring into his back as he slid both his arms around Dakota, his hands resting just above the curve of her sweet little backside. No holding one hand out in the air crap. He wanted to feel her chest pressed against him. Feel her thighs move with his.

She sighed softly, and then tilted her head back to look at him. "Come on. What did she want?"

No way was he getting into this conversation with her. He couldn't without bad-mouthing her mother, and he wasn't doing that. "Why isn't your brother being groomed to be a judge?"

Her lips parted slightly as she hesitated, and if they were anywhere else, he would've accepted the invitation. And if she didn't quit soon…

"Cody is far too mercenary, hardly civil servant material." She laughed softly and swept a quick glance around. "Oops, did I say that?"

Civil servant? That stopped Tony. He hadn't thought of it that way. "Defense attorneys make more money, huh?"

"Oh, please." She chuckled and then squinted at him. "Are you kidding?"

He shrugged. "How would I know?"

"Defense attorneys can make oodles of money. Especially defending white-collar clients." She whispered. "My brother's favorite kind of criminal."

"What happened to innocent until proven guilty?"

"I wasn't referring to the innocent ones." She paused thoughtfully. "Although they usually end up racking up a lot more legal fees."

"You're so cute when you're being materialistic."

"Hey." She lightly pinched his shoulder. "I was being analytical."

"Oh." He smiled and brought her closer so that she pressed her cheek against the base of his throat. His lips were touching her forehead. This is where he wanted her. Not leaning away from him analyzing the legal profession.

Besides, the dance floor had gotten more crowded. Good for him. It gave him an excuse to draw her closer. Bad for her in that she could be overheard and, since half the people there were either lawyers, judges or somehow related, she'd be better off zipping it.

Her arms tightened around his neck and she rubbed her cheek against his jaw. His body immediately reacted. If the song suddenly ended and he had to walk back to the table, he'd be screwed.

"Hello, Dakota."

She lifted her head and smiled at the distinguished-looking older man dancing beside them with a much younger blond woman. "Hi, Judge Hawkins."

He nodded to Tony and then said to Dakota, "We're not in the courtroom. I think it would be okay to call me David."

"That would feel a little too strange."

He smiled, nodded and they moved apart, but not before the man gave Tony a sizing up.

Tony ignored him. "Is that his wife?"

"Nope. He's divorced. Three times now."

"He looks old enough to be her father."

"Probably is. He likes them young."

He obviously liked Dakota, but Tony didn't point that out. The song wound down and he hoped like hell the band would stick to a slow beat. They did and everyone on the dance floor stayed. Several other couples crowded in and damned if they didn't all seem to know Dakota. Their once-private area was getting to be as bad as Grand Central Station.

When it was announced that it was time to cut the cake, he didn't even mind. Maybe after that they could get out of here. Even if he and Dakota just rode to the airport together, alone, no parents, no coworkers, and the evening ended there, he'd be okay with that. Not happy, but okay.

Glasses of champagne were passed out while Dallas and Eric got ready to cut the cake. Dallas got a little impatient when the photographer kept trying to reposition them and she dug into the cake with her fingers and offered the piece to Eric. Everyone laughed. Except Mrs. Shea, but that was no surprise.

In Tony's experience, shortly after the cake was cut the bride and groom usually left the reception.

That meant he and Dakota would be leaving, too. He glanced at his watch. No matter, they'd have to leave within half an hour to get to LaGuardia in time for their flight.

An older, distinguished-looking man had intercepted Dakota right before the cake cutting, and Tony scanned the room locating her in time to see her drain a flute of champagne and exchange it for another. She caught his eye and smiled, then raised the glass to him before gulping down half the contents.

What the hell? Was she on some kind of mission to get plastered? Maybe she didn't like flying? A lot of people didn't. Better that be the reason than anything personal. He wanted to be with her this weekend, but not if she had to get loaded to be with him.

"We're going to have to leave soon." Dallas dabbed at the white frosting clinging to the corner of her mouth. "Where's Dakota?"

"Over there."

"Ah, she's talking to Judge Mayfield and his wife. She shouldn't be long. We'll meet at the door in fifteen minutes. Eric is having the limo brought around front."

"Is she okay?" he asked.

Dallas smiled "Yes. Trust me."

That's about all he could do. "I'll be ready." His gaze went to Dakota.

She was laughing at something the judge said, her face slightly flushed. She tossed her hair back over her shoulder, the honey-colored strands catching the light from the chandelier. The red dress shimmered as she moved, emphasizing the tempting curve of her backside. Yeah, he was ready all right. He had been from the first time he saw her.

"WHO EVER HEARD of a limo without champagne?" Dakota sighed, hiked her dress up to her thighs and then swung her legs up on the seat where she sat opposite Tony. Predictably his gaze went straight to the hem of her dress, and then ran down the length of her legs. "We'll simply have to have the driver stop for some." She lifted her fist to knock on the dividing glass, but Tony lunged from his seat and captured her wrist.

"Don't you think you've had enough to drink?" He got up and joined her on her seat, using his hip to nudge her legs aside.

"Excuse me?" She indignantly lifted her chin, and slightly slurred her words then asked, "Do you think I'm drunk?"

He hesitated, exhaling in exasperation, and she had to really struggle to keep a straight face. "Look, we can't stop. We'll miss our plane."

"Plane? What plane?"

He stared at her. "You're kidding, right?"

"Of course I'm kidding." She pulled her hem up a little higher and used her pointed toes to trace a path across his back. "Remind me."

"Oh, God," he muttered, passing a hand over his face, and then covering his mouth and exhaling loudly.

"What's the matter?"

"Nothing."

"Why are you still holding my wrist?"

"What? Oh, sorry."

As soon as he let go, she knocked on the dividing glass.

"Yes, ma'am?" The driver's voice immediately came over the intercom.

Tony pressed the response button. "Sorry, my mistake. We're fine."

"Hey, I wanted—"

Tony cut her off with a brief kiss, and then whispered, "When we get on the plane you can have all the champagne you want."

She slipped her arms around his neck and pulled him closer. "What if I want something else?"

His breath warm and uneven against her cheek, he said, "Such as?"

She shifted so that her hip rubbed him right where it counted, and he tensed. She made him wait a few seconds and then whispered, "Chocolate."

"Ah…" He chuckled softly. "When we get to the airport you can have that, too."

"For now I'll settle for a kiss."

"You will, huh?"

She nodded, and then waited, surprised by the uncertainty in his eyes. Maybe it was a trick of the shadows, or maybe he didn't want to take advantage of her because he thought she was drunk. The idea softened her and she tightened her arms around his neck, bringing him close enough that their noses touched. She slanted her head and met his lips.

His reluctance lasted all of a second before he kissed her back, going down with her when she laid back against the cushioned seat. The tinted dividing window prevented the driver from seeing anything and it would be easy to get carried away. Especially with Tony's broad chest pressed to her breasts, his arousal growing against her lower belly. But they were too close to the airport and if she really wanted to torment him, now was the time.

He'd conspired with Dallas and deserved a helping of torture. Just a little before they got down to the good stuff, she reminded herself, when he parted her lips with his tongue and her determination started to evaporate. She moved her left thigh to rub his hard-on and he groaned against her mouth.

She hadn't planned on torturing herself, too, but every pore in her body had come alive, her nipples so ripe they ached, and it was a good thing she'd opened her eyes in time to see the first sign for LaGuardia. Knowing they were about to be interrupted, she reached for his zipper. And then secretly smiled when he groaned, and stilled her hand.

"THE CAPTAIN HAS turned off the seat belt sign and you're free to move around the cabin. However, if you remain in your seat, we ask that you keep your seat belt fastened. Thank you."

The flight attendant had barely finished her spiel and Dakota reached for her seat belt.

Tony stopped her. "Where are you going?"

She gave him a sleepy smile and twisted around in her seat to face him. "Nowhere."

Neither of them had a coat so he'd given her his

jacket to wear over the dress but this particular position gave him a sneak preview that he didn't need right now. She'd gotten him so damn worked up in the limo that he didn't trust his cock anymore.

Getting checked in had cooled him off. Replaying the scene in his head helped do it again. The ticket agent looked as if she thought he was kidnapping Dakota. Fortunately she pulled it together long enough to provide her identification and tell everyone who'd listen that they were on their honeymoon.

"Where are we going?" she asked, and promptly covered a yawn.

"Dakota. You know where we're going. Dallas talked to you, remember?"

She blinked at him. "Sort of."

God, he didn't like this. He cleared his throat. "What exactly do you remember?"

"She packed a bag for me, right?"

He nodded.

"Did she remember my toothbrush?" She yawned again. "My electric one."

"I'm sure she did."

"I think I'll take a nap now."

"Good idea."

She shifted so that she could lay her head on his shoulder, and with one hand he shook out a blanket the flight attendant had given them earlier. He draped it over her, and she snuggled closer.

Man, he sure hoped Dallas knew what she was doing. She swore Dakota wasn't drunk. Just a little tipsy. That she understood exactly where she was going. And who she was with. Because if she didn't, this weekend or any chance they might have had was going to be so messed up.

4

"THANKS, OTIS. I'll take it from here."

"May I get you some ice, sir?"

Tony shook his head. "Nah, we're okay." He tipped the bellman three times what he normally would, hoping the guy didn't call security. Or worse, the police. All the way up on the elevator ride, he'd eyed Tony as if he were Jack the Ripper. Not that he blamed the older man. The way Dakota was acting, everyone from the flight attendant to the cab driver had to be wondering if Tony had drugged her.

He'd practically had to hold her up just to get her off the plane. And then she was so disoriented she kept asking where she was up until three minutes ago when they'd arrived at the suite.

"Do I have any clothes?" Dakota asked, yawned and then stretched, before sinking onto the couch.

Otis stopped on his way to the door and slowly turned around. "May I assist you in any way, miss?" he asked solemnly, his gaze steadily on her and deliberately away from Tony.

She'd taken off his jacket in the taxi and the way she sat, her dress slightly askew, exposed a lot of cleavage. Her lips curved in a teasing smile. "I don't think so. We're on our honeymoon."

The relief on the man's face was almost laughable. "Ah, I see. Very good." Backing toward the door, he looked approvingly at Tony. "Very good, sir. I'll bid you good-night then."

"See ya, Otis." Tony hurried to double lock the door as soon as the man was gone. When he turned back to Dakota, she had her eyes closed.

She looked pale against the navy-blue-and-cream floral cushions. But a couple of days on a sunny beach would fix that. The problem now was whether he should leave her here in the living room.

"Dakota," he said low enough not to wake her if she was sleeping.

She sighed and snuggled down deeper into the cushions, letting one of her high heels slide off her foot. Her feet were long, narrow but dainty, and shining through the sheer black hose her toenails were a bright red.

Her tousled hair looked more sexy than messy, and thinking of how soft and warm and willing she'd been in the limo had him itching to get down to business. But not when she was like this. Coffee. Strong and black. He wondered if that really worked.

He looked away and studied the living room. The tropic-styled suite had to have cost a small fortune. Tony was no expert on decorating or art but he knew about wood and carpentry and the hardwood floors alone had set the owner back a year's rent for a Queens apartment. Anyone could tell that the rattan furniture was of the highest quality and the artwork on the walls and interesting native pieces casually set on corner pedestals weren't cheap knockoffs. Expensive knockoffs maybe.

Even the bar area was no afterthought. At least ten feet across against a mirrored wall, the back shelf was stocked with full-size bottles of premium brands and not the miniature version. The refrigerator was full size, too, and loaded with different varieties of beer, according to Otis. Four bar stools with blue-and-cream-colored seats that matched the couch were arranged around the tall, curved rattan bar.

No fake plants either. Eight-foot palms stood on either side of the sliding glass door to the balcony. It was dark but he knew they faced the ocean. Not just because the front desk clerk had told him. Tony could hear the waves lapping the shore.

Man, it sucked that Dallas and Eric had spent all this money and Tom was screwing up their plans. No doubt they had something equally nice someplace else but that wasn't the point. It wasn't even about the money. Tony had already decided he'd pay for the suite and everything else this weekend. He didn't care what Dallas said. But it was all the hassle she'd gone through to counter Tom's prank that irritated Tony.

He couldn't think about that right now. It pissed him off too much and he had another problem to consider…sobering up Dakota. His gaze went back to Dakota. For a second he thought he saw her eyes open, but as he moved closer he realized it had to have been a trick of the light.

He'd already lost the bow tie and shrugged out of the jacket. He draped it over the rattan chair that matched the couch and bar stools, and then grabbed their bags and carried them to the bedroom.

The friggin' bedroom was almost as big as the living room, with a canopied king-size bed and one of those white nettings you only see in movies draped over it and tied back to the bedposts. There was another couch and another sliding glass door that led to a separate balcony. More palms, more paintings.

He found the large walk-in closet and placed their bags on the built-in luggage racks. Kicking off his shoes, he unfastened his belt at the same time and then hung it on a gold-plated hook behind the door. He pulled his shirt from the waistband of his pants and started unbuttoning it as he walked out into the bedroom.

Dakota stood in the doorway, leaning against the frame. Frowning slightly, she tried to smooth her hair. A few curls sprang back to rest on her cheek. "Tony?"

"Yeah?"

"Where are we?"

He cleared his throat. "You don't remember anything."

"Well, yes, of course I do." Her gaze slid down to his exposed chest, lingered for a long satisfying moment.

"What exactly do you remember?"

"The wedding."

"I hope so." He chuckled. "And?"

She put two fingers to her temple. "Wow, do I have a headache."

"Yeah, a vat of wine will do that."

She gave him a glare that was immensely reassuring. Yup, she was definitely coming around.

He grinned. "Let's see if Dallas packed any aspirin for you."

He brought the bag from closet and set it on the bed, then left her to root through it while he went to get some water from the bar.

The refrigerator was stocked with Evian and Perrier. He grabbed two Evians, one for each of them, and then returned to the room.

She shook her head. "No aspirin."

"Wait a minute. Let me check in here." The place had everything else and he wouldn't be surprised if the bathroom was stocked with personal items.

He slowed as he entered and let out a low whistle. He'd seen some fancy bathrooms before but this was totally awesome. A huge bathtub with three marble steps leading up to it. The entire floor was cream-and-tan marble. Not the cheesy fake kind either. The tub and dual vanity fixtures were gold and in the corner was a glass shower large enough for three people.

If you were into that kind of thing. Tony was a simple man. He just wanted Dakota. Naked. In that tub. Or shower. It didn't matter. As long as it was with him.

"Tony?"

The sound of her voice made him jerk. "What?"

"What's taking you so—oh, my." She walked past

him, her fascinated gaze sweeping the room. "I definitely could get used to this."

"You mean you don't have one at home?"

"I wish." She swayed a little but other than that she seemed steady and coherent.

"I haven't checked to see if there's any aspirin."

"A shower," she said. "That's what I need."

"Good idea." He backed toward the door. "I'll call room service. Order some coffee."

"Wait. I need help with this zipper." She gave him her back.

He moved in and found the small tab and slowly drew it down, his heart thumping at each inch of pale silky skin he exposed. She wasn't wearing a bra, which surprised him; she was so firm and high he'd had no idea. As he pulled the zipper down past the curve of her backside, he saw that she was wearing a red thong.

Drawing in a sharp breath, he stepped back. "Anything else?"

She slid her arms from the sleeves, and then holding the dress over her breasts, she turned around. "Thank you."

"You're welcome." He looked into her eyes, found them focused and aware, and leaned toward her.

She met his lips, tentatively at first, brushing lightly, using the tip of her tongue gently along his lower lip. His groin tightened. But then she slipped her tongue into his mouth and pursued him with an eagerness that brought him to his senses.

This wasn't Dakota. This was the booze talking.

The last thing he wanted or needed was her mortification tomorrow morning.

With every shred of willpower he possessed, he pulled away.

"What's wrong?" She clutched the dress tighter.

"Want me to start the water for you?"

She lifted a shoulder, the move casual and sexy as hell. "Sure."

He rolled back his sleeve and stuck his hand in the shower to turn it on. The heat of her stare seared his back and he took his time getting the right water temperature while he tried to figure out just how noble he wanted to be.

"There you go." He dried his arm on a white fluffy towel and pulled his sleeve back down, carefully avoiding looking at her.

"I'm not drunk," she said, "if that's what you're worried about."

He looked at her, his cock twitching at the exposed curve of her bare hip the limp dress didn't cover. "You had a lot to drink."

"Not as much as you think."

He smiled, but then she moistened her lips, the tip of her pink tongue leaving a tempting sheen across her lower lip and he totally lost track of rational thought.

"Want to join me?" she whispered.

He cleared his throat and ran a hand through his hair, and then caught sight of the reflection of her naked backside in the mirror. She had on the thong but that meant nothing. His cock sure as hell couldn't tell.

"Tony."

He looked into her confused eyes. He should say something, but nothing came to mind.

She sighed, and then covered a yawn. "If you're not going to join me, would you get out?"

He smiled, and then forced himself toward the door. The yawn and droopy eyelids had done it. Three more hours and the sun would be coming up. It wouldn't hurt either of them to grab a couple of hours of sleep. He'd take the couch for now. Tomorrow, when she'd be totally clearheaded, was another story.

WHAT THE HELL was Dallas thinking? Dakota started emptying the small bag her sister had packed for her. Two bikinis, one yellow, one red, both so itty-bitty she wasn't even sure how you put them on. The yellow gauzy strip was probably supposed to be a cover-up, although it sure wasn't going to cover up a damn thing.

Even the two pairs of khaki shorts were totally unacceptable. So brief you practically needed a Brazilian wax to wear them. And the halter tops and skimpy sundresses? Dakota shook her head. She'd have to find a hotel boutique first thing. She checked her watch. Nine-ten.

Her gaze was drawn to the bedroom door, the only thing separating her from Tony, and she automatically pulled the lapels of the robe together.

As much water as she'd had to drink last night, she'd apparently had more wine and champagne than she thought. Her head ached and remembering how brazen she'd been made her wince a little. Not that she'd changed her mind about having hot monkey sex with Tony. But she normally wasn't that out there about it. Probably served her right for carrying the tipsy thing so far.

Turned out the joke was on her. She could've been sleeping with Tony instead of alone. He got points for being honorable, but damn... Ironically, the knock came at that moment.

She drew in a deep breath. "Come in."

He opened the door. No shirt. No socks. Just last night's tuxedo pants. A beard-darkened jaw and a gorgeous expanse of muscled chest and pecs so well defined she wanted to run her hands over them. Touch his nubby brown nipples, the crisp swirling hair...

"I heard you so I knew you were up." He gestured toward the closet. "I need my bag."

"Of course."

"And the bathroom. The one out there doesn't have a shower."

She struggled to keep her eyes level with his. Not that he noticed. His gaze had lowered to her chest, and she realized she was clutching the robe so tightly her fingers were starting to ache.

She cleared her throat and released her death grip. "It's all yours. I've had my shower," she said, unnecessarily, considering her damp hair.

"I won't be long." On his way to the closet he stopped, and eyed the pile of clothes she'd left on the bed. "I hope Dallas included something for the beach."

"Um, not really."

"What's that?"

She followed his far-too-interested gaze to the yellow bikini. "My sister's idea of a joke."

He studied her for a moment. "I take it you remember everything now?"

"Of course I do." She started refolding the clothes, too embarrassed to meet his eyes. A shameful flashback to last night made her wish she were in court. She'd even be willing to face Judge Hadley, an attorney's worst nightmare. Anything but standing here, having to lie to Tony. On the other hand, she wasn't lying. She did remember. "I knew what was going on."

"Then you're okay with everything."

She didn't have to look at him to know he was grinning. She heard it in his voice. "I'm here, aren't I?"

"A little testy, aren't we? I heard that a Bloody Mary can take care of that hangover."

"I'm not hungover. I'm absolutely fine."

Hiding a smile, she replaced the clothes in the bag.

"What are you doing?"

Dakota looked at him, startled by his urgent tone. He still wasn't wearing a shirt. Not that she expected one to magically appear, but jeez, how was she supposed to talk to him? "Excuse me?"

"The suite is paid for—we have the rest of the weekend. Don't go."

"I—I'm not." She shrugged, flattered yet embarrassed at his desire for her to stay. "I was just putting away the clothes I won't be using."

A teasing grin curved his mouth. "I'm down with that. We'll stay naked the whole weekend."

"Funny." She tucked in the pseudo cover-up. "I'm going to the hotel boutique and pick up a few more suitable things to wear."

"What could Dallas have packed that's so bad?"

She half laughed, half groaned. "You have no idea. Wait till you see what's in your bag."

"I know what's in my bag." He ducked into the closet and carried out the black leather garment bag. "I packed it myself."

"Really?" She folded her arms across her chest. He'd have to admit the conspiracy now. "When?"

"Yesterday morning."

"Nice that you had that much notice."

He frowned at her. "I didn't know she was gonna ask you at the last minute. That had nothing to do with me."

Dakota sat on the edge of the bed, thinking it over. Now that she wasn't so annoyed or panicked it suddenly made sense. This was all her sister's doing. Dallas had given Tony warning because she figured he wouldn't turn her down. But she'd blindsided Dakota. Because Dallas knew she'd have found another way. Bless her! Dakota tried not to smile.

"Hey, don't get mad at Dallas." Tony set down the garment bag, and then sat next to her. "She had a lot on her mind. Probably thought she'd already asked you."

"You don't have to defend her." It was ridiculous how hard her heart pounded just because he'd sat next to her. Although he really hadn't left much space between them.

"She probably figured you needed a vacation. Working all those long hours like you do…"

"How do you know how much I work?"

"I know more than you think." He gave her one of those teasing winks that she was absurdly susceptible to, and then added, "Have you looked outside yet?"

She shook her head, and then hoped he didn't jump up to open the drapes.

He stayed right where he was, if anything, leaned a little closer. "Wait till you see it, Dakota, sky and water so clear and blue you'll want to pack up your Manhattan apartment and become a beach bum."

"I like the city. Besides, how do you know I live in Manhattan?"

"You look the type."

"Meaning?"

He smiled. "This isn't a courtroom. You can't interrupt. Okay, like I was saying, the sand is as white as fresh snow and the—"

"We live in the city. How would you know what fresh snow looks like?" She didn't know when he'd taken her hand. But he was doing this soothing stroking motion on the inside of her wrist.

"You keep interrupting and I'll have to do something about it."

"Oh, yeah?"

"Yeah." The stroking stopped.

He lowered his head and her heart pounded harder. All he did was brush his lips over hers and she thought her chest would explode. He slid his tongue inside and she hoped that whimper didn't come from her. When he put his hand on her thigh, turned out she didn't care.

She tentatively touched his chest, his skin taut and warm beneath her palm, the swirling hair just as soft and crisp as she'd imagined. His kiss deepened and the robe slid off her shoulder. She shivered, and his warm lips left hers to trail down the side of her neck, slowly making its way to her collarbone. His tongue swept the hollow and she shivered again. So violently that his head came up.

"Cold?"

She shook her head.

He smiled. "Sure? I can warm you up."

She smiled back. "You've already done that," she said and let the other side of the robe slip off her bare shoulder.

5

TONY'S MOUTH WENT DRY. God, she was beautiful. And soft. He'd never been with a woman with skin this amazingly soft. And he'd had his share. Especially in the early college days. But Dakota, she was something.

He used his forefinger to trace the exposed satiny skin at the edge of the robe. She didn't even flinch when his finger dipped lower, following the curve of her breast.

The front door buzzer sounded and he cursed himself. He'd forgotten he ordered room service. Did they have to be so efficient?

Dakota pulled away. "What was that?"

"I ordered coffee and rolls."

"Ah." She gathered the front of her robe together.

He hooked a finger under her chin, lifted it and lightly kissed her. "If we don't answer, they'll just leave it out there in the parlor."

The ringing turned to a persistent knock.

"Or not," he said wryly and pushed a hand through his hair. "I'll be right back," he said, getting to his feet, knowing the mood had taken a nosedive.

"I'll get dressed and come out for coffee."

He made a face. "Do you have to get dressed?"

She laughed, got up and gave him a small shove. "Out. I need caffeine."

"I'll show you what you need," he said, taking her hands and pulling her into his arms.

Her lips parted and a small sigh breached, drifting across his chin. She wove her arms around his neck and tilted her head back.

Another knock at the door.

Damn.

"I know," she said, and moved away. "I'll be out in a minute."

He wasn't happy about it but he went to the door and let in the obnoxiously cheerful waiter. Tony almost forgave him when he caught a whiff of a fresh croissant and the strong Colombian brew. After over-tipping the guy, Tony escorted the waiter to the door, cutting him off when he tried to advise Tony on the best fishing spots. Yeah, as if.

He took the tray to the table and poured them each a cup of coffee, thinking about Dakota and how different she was away from her family. He probably knew more than he should from Dallas. She wasn't a talker normally, but sometimes after the Sheas' monthly Saturday-night dinner, she'd just had to vent while they ate their lunches. Tony had never minded. It was kind of interesting hearing about a family so different from his own.

"I need caffeine, and I need it badly."

Tony looked up and nearly dropped his cup. Through the filmy thing she had tied around her, he could see strips of yellow. A bikini. A very, very tiny bikini. Over the knot where she'd tied the wrap, her breasts swelled. Not too much. Two perfect handfuls. Enough that all the blood rushed south and made his thoughts go crazy.

That was Dallas's doing. Man, he owed her. Big-time.

"This one mine?" Dakota picked up the other cup he'd poured.

"Uh, yeah."

She rooted through the condiments and plucked out a pink packet of sweetener and carefully sprinkled a dash of the white powder. "Cream?"

"Right here."

She splashed in some cream from the small silver pitcher and stirred, not once looking at him. "Do I smell banana bread?"

"I think there's some in that basket." He finally got it. She was actually self-conscious. Why, he didn't understand. She was perfect. "It's nice to see you in something other than a suit," he said calmly, and tried to focus on pouring himself more joe. "These puny cups are ridiculous. Two sips and that's it."

"Would you like me to order you a trough?" She flipped the red linen napkin over to get to the treats and peered inside the basket.

"That would be an improvement." While she was busy avoiding him, he took another heart-stopping look at her long legs. He had no idea what to say next. How to put her at ease, how to calm down his heated body. He deserved a friggin' award for being able to think at all.

She put a slice of the banana bread on a small white plate, then pinched off a piece and brought it to her lips. She took a bite, her eyes closing briefly. "This is awesome."

He watched her walk to the couch, set her coffee on the end table and then sit down with the plate on her lap. His gaze went to the curves of her calves, her slim ankles, the bright red toenails.

"I think I'll go take that shower now," he said abruptly, and this time he avoided her. Headed straight for the bathroom door. Before she got a load of his rising temperature.

DAKOTA WOLFED DOWN the rest of the banana bread and then got another piece. When depressed she didn't eat, but when she was nervous? Look out.

Was she crazy staying here with him? She could've been on a flight home already. She should have been at the office an hour ago. Never had she missed a single Saturday. Everyone knew that. Where would they think she was? There'd be questions. And stares. And…

She looked around for a clock but couldn't find one. Her watch was on the nightstand, but it didn't matter really. She'd call the concierge and find out when the next flight to New York was leaving.

She hesitated, recalled the way Tony's pecs swelled with muscle, the way the black hair got thicker as it neared his waistband. She wanted to explore every inch of him. Discover his muscular thighs. He was a laborer. Used every muscle in his body. Panicked, she searched for the phone. Why had he stopped her last night? It would have been so much easier when she was pretending to be drunk.

God, she was a coward. But she'd hate herself either way. Better not to have to face Cody at work. Would he have questioned her parents and got them concerned?

The phone rang just as she reached for it.

"Hey." It was Dallas.

"Where are you?"

"Still in the city."

"You're kidding."

"Nope. How's it going?" Dallas asked.

"Tony registered us under your names. But as far as I know, Tom hasn't tried to pull anything."

"Good. I think his wife may have reeled him in. Serena's pretty tired of his pranks."

"Oh, well, it's about time." Where had the disappointment come from? She'd already decided to leave. "No need for us to stay then."

"Dakota."

"What?"

"Don't be a chicken."

"What are you talking about?" She couldn't mean Tony. Dallas knew better. The lengthening silence told her otherwise. "Dal-las? What have you done?"

"Nothing."

"Tom wasn't going to sabotage you at all…was he?"

"Look, Dakota—"

"I've never interfered in your life."

"I'm not interfering. I asked you for a favor. You could've said no."

Dakota drew in a breath. She couldn't argue that point.

"I've gotta go," Dallas blurted. "We leave this afternoon for Budapest. We're taking one of those fourteen-day riverboat cruises to Amsterdam."

"Wow! Fourteen days?" Dakota didn't want to fight with her sister. Especially not before she traveled. The old childhood fear that something bad might happen while away had turned into a persistent superstition.

"Yep, after haggling with Mom over the wedding plans, a nice long vacation is exactly what we need."

She couldn't imagine being away from the office that long. It would be horribly nerve-racking. "Well, you guys have fun."

"We will. You, too. Cut loose, okay? No one's looking over your shoulder. And you couldn't find a better guy than Tony." Dallas abruptly hung up.

Dakota smiled wryly as she replaced the receiver. Look who was being chicken now. Sighing, she checked the pareu knot, although it was so short, calling it a pareu was stretching it. She could tie the cover-up around her waist, which was probably how it was meant to be worn, but of course that would cause another problem.

Maybe when they went to the beach, with all that sunshine and clean ocean air, she'd feel better. At least she wouldn't feel so exposed on a beach with other half-dressed people.

She wandered to the sliding glass door, which was still draped, odd considering they had an ocean view. No one's looking over your shoulder, Dallas had said. The weekend, the situation, it was all totally perfect. If she could have e-mailed the gang at Eve's Apple, they would have told her to go for it. Run, don't walk. This is what she wanted. She'd told them so just a couple of nights ago. So why the hell was she vacillating?

She found the cord for the drapes and pulled them open.

"Was that the phone?"

She heard Tony come up behind her but she just stared outside. At a dark sky, a gray turbulent ocean and the balcony wet from a recent rain.

"What are you looking at?" He stood beside her, smelling of soap and the croissant he'd brought with him. To her dismay, he was also wearing a T-shirt. But at least he'd had the courtesy to wear shorts, a little too long for her to get a look at his thighs but he had great calves.

She raised her brows at him. "What happened to the blue skies and sunshine?"

"Oh, that." He took a bite of the croissant. When he finished chewing, he said, "You have to believe, Dakota, have faith that everything will turn out all right."

"What kind of nonsense is that?"

"Nonsense?" He snorted, and then pointed outside. "Look over there."

"What am I looking at?"

"See that patch of blue?"

"Yes." She had no idea where he was going with this. But she loved just hearing his voice. Deep and soothing, sexy yet friendly. Maybe the playful friendliness was what made him sexy. She didn't know but she wasn't going to analyze further.

"You had faith and it's paying off."

"You're nuts."

He smiled, ate the last bite of his croissant and then took her by the hand. "And you're beautiful."

"Stop it."

He tugged her closer. "Like you haven't heard that a thousand times."

She sighed, disappointed. She really didn't want him to be like the other guys. The ones who couldn't see past the package. She'd outscored all of them in law school but it never mattered. "Is that why you're here with me?"

"Partly."

"What's the other part?"

He frowned thoughtfully for a moment while doing those little circles on the inside of her wrist again. "I'm thinking it might be because you play hard to get."

Pretty damn honest of him. "I never played hard to get. Did you ever think I just wasn't interested?"

"Nope."

That startled a laugh out of her. "Are you always this sure of yourself?"

"If I'm not, no one else will be." He ran his hand up her arm. "Want to hear part three?"

"Ah, there's more." She tried to stay cool when he grazed her shoulder and then cupped the side of her neck.

"I know a little about you from Dallas. Now, don't get your knickers in a twist," he said, when her mouth opened in protest. "It wasn't as if she was talking about you specifically. She was talking about herself and you just entered into the conversation."

"How?"

He smiled, massaged the back of her neck. "She didn't tell me you had a temper."

"I don't."

"The eyes don't lie."

She gave him a sugary smile, and said, "Can you guess what they're telling you now?"

"Ouch."

She laughed. She couldn't help herself. Although the fact that he was giving her the best neck rub ever certainly went a long way toward penance.

"As I was saying, part three, even though you're built like a—" At the lift of her eyebrows he paused. "Like a, um—"

"You don't have to stop rubbing my neck while you think."

He nodded and went back to work, his dark brows solemnly drawn together as if he had to decide the fate of the world. He'd missed a tiny spot shaving, right where his skin creased when he smiled. Which he did a lot. She liked that. "Okay, like a goddess," he said looking to her as if for approval.

"Oh, brother." She rolled her eyes.

"You like 'every guy's fantasy' better?"

Heat stung her cheeks and she moved away from him. "Would you stop."

"Hey, wait, there's more." He caught her hand and pulled her against him. She held her breath when his arm slid around her waist, forcing them to melt together. "Despite the fact that you're beautiful and could probably get anything you want, you have a serious career that you've worked hard for. And you took the time to help Nancy and Trudie and the rest of the ladies get Capshaw's attention."

"I really didn't do much."

"The harassment stopped. You did good. Get over it."

She gave him a wry smile. It was the best she could do considering how sensitive her breasts were, how achingly hard her nipples had become crushed against his chest.

His gaze lowered to her lips, and then he dipped his head and touched her mouth with his. Softly. A whisper of a touch, while his hands explored her back, followed the curve of her spine and cupped her bottom. She moved against him, felt his hardness growing, exciting her. Empowering her. Making her bolder.

She ran her tongue across his lips and then drew his lower one into her mouth. He let her take the lead, nibbling, tasting, exploring the inside of his mouth. Tension radiated from his body, fed her own and she fought the urge to back off. Slink to the corner. Run back to her safe, well-ordered life.

What was wrong with her? Had it really been that

long since she'd been with anyone? It wasn't as if Tony was a threat.

He must have sensed her withdrawal because he leaned back far enough to look at her. "Hey."

"Hey."

He touched the side of her cheek with the back of his finger, yet giving her some space. "Did you notice how much blue sky is showing now?"

She gave him a weak smile. "The sun's been out a couple of times, too."

"Is this where I tell you I told you so?"

"A couple of times does not a sunny day make."

He mockingly put a hand to his chest. "She's poetic, too. I think I'm in love."

She gave him a playful shove and felt his hard chest beneath her palms. Getting all heated again, she snuck a look and saw that he was still aroused. Now it was difficult to look away. Difficult to think about anything but dragging him to bed. She doubted he'd mind. And wasn't that why she was here?

"Look at that." He pointed at two couples in swimsuits, carrying snorkels, and walking along the shoreline. "Fellow believers."

Between two fluffy white clouds, the sun peeked out, so bright this time that Dakota had to squint to look up at the sky. It was definitely clearing up. Even the ocean was turning from gray to a pretty bluish-green. Several more people emerged from the bungalows close to the water, all of them in swimsuits and carrying towels.

"Maybe we should take advantage of the beach

while the sun's out," she said, expecting him to balk, to grab her and kiss her and convince her to crawl back into that nice big soft bed with him. Yeah, like she needed her arm twisted.

"Good idea." He took a step back. "I'll go put on my trunks."

She shrugged, trying not to show her disappointment. "After I slip on a pair of sandals I'll be ready."

He took a few more steps backward, his gaze taking her in, devouring her as if she were a hot fudge sundae. "I can't wait for you to baptize that suit."

"You're going to wait a long time. I can't swim."

"Excellent. I'll teach you."

Laughing and shaking her head, she pointed to the bathroom. "Go."

"Can't wait to get me in the water, huh?"

"I'm so embarrassed you guessed."

He winked and disappeared.

She couldn't stop smiling. She'd lied. Of course she could swim. In fact, she'd been ranked number two on her college swim team. But if he wanted to teach her, hey, who was she to argue.

6

WELL, NOW HE KNEW. Tony grinned to himself as he hauled two lounge chairs from the attendant's station near the pool, through the warm sand to a spot close to the water. Ms. Shea was hot for him, after all. Pretending she didn't know how to swim. Right. He knew damn well she'd been on her college swim team. It had somehow come up in conversation with Dallas once.

"Do you want an umbrella?" he asked her after he set his chair next to hers.

"I put on sunscreen."

"Yeah, but sometimes the sun and a hangover don't mix."

She wore sunglasses but he could tell she was glaring. "I don't have a hangover, nor am I as knowledgeable about them as you seem to be."

"Haven't had one myself since my college days. When are you going to take off that thing?"

She ignored the part about getting down to her bikini. "You went to college?"

"I'm wounded that you look so surprised." He kicked off his deck shoes and sand flew everywhere.

"I'm not surprised. Well, yeah, I am, but only because Dallas never said anything."

"So you asked about me?" He grinned at the long-suffering face she always made when he teased her. "I didn't finish. Too boring. I left halfway into my sophomore year."

He pulled off his T-shirt and folded it before stowing it with his towel under his chair. He probably should have put on sunscreen since he didn't work outside much anymore and his tan had faded. Truthfully, he was hoping they wouldn't be out long. He had far more interesting indoor activities planned.

Tony stretched out on the lounge chair and looked over at Dakota, anxious for her to unveil, his pulse racing like when he was a kid on Christmas morning and his parents finally brought out the big wrapped toy they always saved for last. But she was obviously in no hurry. She'd sat down but was still messing with the small bag of stuff she'd brought with her. Maybe she was even stalling.

He still didn't get it. How could she be so self-conscious? Was that why she dressed the way she did for work, or was that just part of the image she had of herself as an attorney? He understood the whole professional look, dress for success bit, but if the two times he saw her in work clothes were typical, then she carried it too far.

"Over there." Tony waited for her to look up and then motioned with his chin at a woman knee-deep in the water. "Now that's what they call itsy-bitsy."

"Oh, God."

"What?"

She just shook her head.

"Yours isn't that—" His heart thudded. "That's not a bad thing."

"I don't see you wearing a Speedo."

"Good point. But I'm just saying—"

He totally forgot what he was about to say when she got up, untied the knot at her breasts and let the wrap fall. Even at the risk of being rude, he couldn't take his eyes off her. He didn't know how she'd even gotten it on. A small yellow triangle took care of the bottom front and two triangles took care of the top. The rest was all her. Soft curves, pale skin and a flat belly she must have had to work hard for.

She quickly sat back down and with a glance over her shoulder said, "At least I don't know anyone here." She got comfortable, stretching out her long legs, her head tilted back so that her face got full sun, her back slightly arched.

He said nothing. With all the blood pooled in his groin, anything coming out of his mouth would probably sound juvenile. Other guys had noticed her, too, even ones with wives or girlfriends. And damned if he didn't get that same adolescent rush as he had when he'd trumped all the school jocks and taken Jackie Ricci, the homecoming queen, to the big dance. But that was seventeen years ago and he wasn't that same cocky kid anymore.

"Here comes a waiter. Do you want a drink?" he asked and she made a face.

She moistened her lips. "Maybe some plain orange juice."

Just watching the tip of her tongue took him to a place he shouldn't go. Not here. "Ah. Come on. Don't you want something with an umbrella in it?"

She sat up and looked in the direction of the approaching waiter. "I'll bet he'll put one in my orange juice."

Tony snorted. The guy would probably do anything she wanted, unless he was gay. Even sitting up her belly was flat. Her breasts weren't large but their size suited her slender body type perfectly. This time when he saw a couple of guys eyeing her it annoyed him.

"You ready for a swim?" His motives weren't entirely pure. A hard-on was starting to make him uncomfortable, and playing in the water invited all kinds of possibilities.

"We just sat down."

"I'll order our drinks, and they'll be waiting for us when we get out."

"You go on ahead and I'll wait for them." The wrap she'd left on the lounge chair, she now gathered to her sides as she settled back again, partially hiding her body.

He sighed and adjusted the towel to conceal the front of his trunks and stretched out again. He kind of liked it that she was modest. In his experience, women who looked as good as her went the other way. But jeez, she was beginning to cramp his style.

The waiter came and took their order and their room

number. Tony asked for juice, too. Didn't want alcohol to hinder his stamina. If he ever got a chance…

"Okay, let's go for a swim." She swung her legs over and her feet hit the sand. "I can't stand to watch a grown man sulk."

"Me?"

"Ouch, this sand is hot."

"Race you."

One second a challenging look, the next she was gone. Headed for the water. Man, she was fast. He didn't catch up until she was thigh deep, the gentle waves lapping against her and turning to foam like white frosting on a bluish green cake.

She laughed as he plodded his way to her, and he resisted the urge to splash her in the face. Dakota, on the other hand, had no such self-control. She got him first. Taking him totally by surprise.

He wiped his face. "Oh, it's like that, is it?"

Giggling like a little girl, she backed up. "Truce. Let's call a truce."

"Before I get even?"

"Come on. I said, truce."

"Tough." He advanced on her.

She turned and dove toward deeper water. Her strokes were clean and she moved at an impressive speed. He followed, and he was a pretty good swimmer himself, but not that good. Finally, he gave up and treaded water, waiting for her to come back.

She took her time, alternating with a backstroke, gracefully cutting through the water. When she finally glided toward him, he was beat just from trying to stay afloat.

"Hey, show-off." He started paddling backward toward the beach. "Thought you couldn't swim."

She grinned. "I may not have told the truth about that," she said and swam past him.

He flipped over and swam the rest of the way, too, staying fairly close on her tail. He'd probably end up having a heart attack but no way was he letting her leave him behind.

They got to the shore and although she wasn't out of breath, she'd obviously exerted herself. Him, he was gonna crawl to his lounge chair and slip into a coma.

"You were right. That felt terrific." She picked up her towel and wiped her face and then drew the towel down her arms and legs, across her chest.

Exhilarated from her swim, she didn't seem self-conscious now or maybe she was just too distracted to notice that a number of people were staring. Both men and women. Probably wondering if she were a model or an actress they should recognize.

She was really that stunning, and he realized that he wasn't that tired, after all. Sighing, he got back into position on the lounge chair, the towel again hiding his stubborn cock.

The waiter had left their glasses of juice on a small tray attached to their armrests. It took Tony two gulps to drain his, the icy coldness welcome as he baked under the hot sun. Dakota sipped hers, her eyes closed, before slipping her sunglasses on and then leaning back on her elbows.

Part of her left breast slipped out of the side of her top, just a small strip but enough to stir his imagination. Damn, he tried not to look. Sucked some ice out of his glass and chewed it instead. Tried to forget that her nipples stuck out, pushing against the wet top.

"Tony?"

"Yeah?"

"Are you okay?"

"Fine. Why?"

"It sounded like you were groaning."

He crunched down on the ice. "Nah, I was just clearing my throat."

"Okay." Then she stretched her arms over her head. "Can you believe this warm breeze? I think it was close to fifty when we left New York."

"Yeah, but look at those dark clouds headed our way."

She looked out at the horizon and then her lips curved in a teasing smile. "What happened to having faith?"

Getting rid of the hard-on he was having trouble with blew faith to the back of the line. "Touché, but I still think we should head inside."

"Let's stay just a little longer."

"You wanna see me sulk again?"

Her smile broadened. "I'll close my eyes."

"Tough broad, aren't you?"

"Hey, I resent that sexist remark."

"It's not sexist. It's just a—it's not sexist."

Turning toward the sun again, she huffed. "I suggest you think about it."

"With that tone, you should've been a school teacher." She already dressed like one, but he didn't mention that.

She started to say something but a red Frisbee landed in Tony's lap, and he grunted, cutting her off. The aim couldn't have been better. Damn good thing his arousal was on the downswing.

She bolted up. "Are you okay?"

"No."

A redheaded kid, early teens, ran up to them. "I'm sorry, mister. The wind caught it."

"No problem. Here you go." He tossed it back. "With that breeze picking up you should probably head further down the beach where it isn't crowded."

"Yeah, I guess. Sorry again." Walking backward in the soft sand, the kid almost stumbled over another couple. "Sorry," he said to them and ran.

"It's getting dangerous out here. I'm telling you, we'd better go in." He shifted and winced. The Frisbee had left its mark.

"You really did get hurt." She took off her sunglasses to regard him with concerned eyes.

"Nah, it's okay." Of course he may never have kids...

"Want me to kiss it and make it better?"

At a loss for words he stared at her. Did she have any idea what she'd just said?

"Oops." Laughing, she covered her mouth. The mischievous sparkle in her eyes said her words hadn't been innocent.

Man, was she hard to figure. "You're making me crazy, you know that?"

"Then my work here is done." She slid her sunglasses back up her nose, and returned to sun worshiping.

"Dakota?"

"Hmm?" She turned to him without raising her head.

"I wanna ask you something. If you don't wanna answer, I'm sure you'll tell me to shove it."

"Count on it."

He smiled. "Why do you dress so conservatively?"

Her lips tightened. "I'm an attorney. You want me to dress like a stripper?"

"Now see, there you go," he said, shaking his head. "Getting all defensive for nothing."

"Well, did I criticize how you dress?"

"I'm not criticizing." It was getting harder to keep the impatience out of his voice. "I'm curious because it's almost like you purposely try to look plain." He wanted to say frumpy but thought better of it.

"I think I look professional."

"Let's say you'd packed your own bag for this trip, what would you have brought?"

"A one-piece swimsuit because it's much more practical for swimming, and some shorts and maybe—" She sighed. "Why is this important?"

"Because you don't seem like a prude but you dress like one, and I'm trying to figure you out."

She sighed again and briefly closed her eyes before rolling over onto her side and supporting her head with her hand. The weight of her right breast at that angle kind of rolled partway out of her top and messed with his concentration.

She pushed her sunglasses up on her head and looked at him with frank eyes. "Mother always made Dallas and I dress demurely. Even as little girls, she wouldn't dress us in anything cutesy. So you can imagine how strict she was with us when we were teenagers. The whole reason being, any attention we received would be for our intellect or accomplishments and not our looks."

"Wow! Good intention, I guess." But he didn't get it. "Your mom's a good-looking woman herself, she must have had—" He stopped at the sudden wariness in her expression that told him the subject of her mother was closed.

Instead, he let silence stretch while he thought about Dallas and how she'd been affected. She talked about family stuff and vented about her demanding mother sometimes, but she never mentioned anything about being told how to dress.

And because she'd worked in construction with him, she'd worn jeans and T-shirts like the rest of them. Even when they'd gone for a drink after work, she changed to clean jeans and another T-shirt, totally in line with the bars they went to. But then, too, she had that short modeling career. Rebellion maybe?

Almost as if she'd read his mind, Dakota finally broke the silence and said, "Like Dallas I rebelled in college, too. I didn't want to model or anything like that. I started wearing short skirts, tight jeans and skimpy tops. Nothing horrible, I dressed just like all the other girls. And I found Mother was right." Dakota paused, visibly swallowed. "That wasn't the kind of attention I wanted."

There was more to it. A whole lot more, judging by the way she'd tensed. "Anything you want to talk about?"

"No."

"Okay. How about them Yankees?"

"They play basketball, right?"

"Do you have any idea how sacrilegious that is?"

"Football?"

"I hope you're kidding."

She laughed. "I bet I've been to more Yankee games than you have."

"No way."

"Care to make a wager?"

Either she had one hell of a poker face, or she'd told the truth. Didn't matter. He could keep staring at her all day. Her cheeks were starting to get a little pink from the sun and her gray eyes picked up the blue of the ocean and sky. Her skin would be salty from their swim and he wanted to lick it. Start from her lips and then head down to those silky-looking thighs.

She smiled. "I really do like baseball."

"No way."

"You need to work on your vocabulary."

"Your dad a fan?"

"Somewhat, but my brother is rabid over the sport."

"Cody?"

"I only have one brother," she said dryly.

"He doesn't seem the type."

"He played Little League and then some in high school, which my mother thought was a complete waste of time. But my father insisted it would be good for him and it turned out he liked it."

"Interesting." He couldn't imagine Cody Shea getting dirty. Not even as a kid.

She gave him a smug smile. "Thought you had us all figured out, didn't you?"

"Yeah, kind of."

She gave him a thoughtful look. "You're racking up points for honesty, by the way."

"Yeah? Like frequent flyer miles? After so many I get a free ride."

She bit her lip, obviously trying to hide a smile, and shook her head in mock disapproval.

"Am I right?" Trying to look affronted, he reared his head back. "You don't think I meant—Ms. Shea you surprise me."

"Tony, I have to say you are unique."

"Damn right I am."

"Okay, enough of that, your turn to tell me something."

"What kind of something?"

"About yourself."

He shrugged. "No skeletons in my closet. I had a boring childhood. My pop runs an auto body shop he inherited from his pop, and my mom stayed at home to raise us kids. Two brothers, one sister, a cousin I consider a sister because she grew up with us."

"Are they older, younger?"

He had no idea why that mattered but he answered, "I have one brother older than me."

"Are they married? Do you have nieces and nephews?"

"Everyone but my baby sister is married and they all have a bushel of kids. I can hardly keep the names straight." He lied. He knew each and every one of those rascals, and he hadn't missed a single silly birthday party.

"Do they all live in New York?"

"My younger brother just moved to Atlanta to help my grandfather with his carpet business. My mom comes from Georgia. All that side of the family is still there."

"That's so interesting. How did they meet?"

"She was a tourist. First day in the city a cab driver scared the hell out of her, so she rented a car."

Dakota winced. "Oops."

"Yep. He towed her to the shop the next day. You know the rest."

"A vacation romance that lasted. How about that?" She picked up her glass of orange juice and took the last sip. "How about you? Any particular reason you haven't gotten married?"

"Got a good pair of running shoes."

"Ah." She smiled and tipped the glass to get the last ice cube.

Mesmerized, he stared at the slender curve of her neck, at her well-defined jaw, at the small point of her chin, at her lips, the kind he liked, slightly turned up at the corners. He didn't know many women who were prettier when you got up close.

She sucked on the ice, and he even liked watching her throat work. How sick was that?

"Tony?"

He met her eyes, sleepy and sexy, and man, he had to reach for the towel again. "Yeah?"

"When are we having lunch?" she asked around a yawn.

Great. He was thinking about sex, and she was thinking about food. "Tell me something first..." He kept his eyes on her as she shifted her position, her cleavage deep, and wondered if she was torturing him on purpose. "You asked why I'm here with you. I told you. Your turn."

She lifted one shoulder. "For the sex."

7

DAKOTA KNEW HOW to keep a straight face. She did it in court all the time. But she almost lost it watching Tony's jaw drop. Though it started working again soon enough.

"Now you tell me. After we get out of the water?"

She laughed, the sound shaky, thinking about what she'd just said. Thinking about the bulge he was trying to hide. "We're on a beach. Lots of people. Kind of a deterrent, don't you think?"

"Now you expect me to think."

"Poor baby." She was glad she had sunglasses to hide behind as she rolled onto her back again. He had an amazing chest. Just the right amount of muscle defining his pecs and abs and shoulders, unlike some of the guys at the gym who pumped up until they practically had no neck.

"Is it getting hot, I mean like scorching out here, or is it me?"

She turned to him again, and said, "Race you." And then jumped up and threw off her sunglass before he could say a word.

He was a lot quicker getting to the water this time,

splashing her warm dry back as he ran up behind her. Before she could dive in, he grabbed her around the waist and they both went down laughing.

When she tried to right herself, she found her leg wedged between his thighs, rubbing him intimately with each kick. Good thing the water retarded the impact.

He grabbed her ankle. "Between you and the Frisbee, I'm gonna be out of commission for a year."

"Sorry."

"You could sound like you mean it."

She'd gotten the giggles, which sometimes happened when she got nervous. She'd actually admitted she was here for the sex. The salt air must have rusted her brain. But so what? That is what she wanted. So did he. That was obvious.

She pressed her lips together, cleared her throat and then got a false start. She tried again, and this time without laughing, she said, "I really am sorry."

He grinned, his teeth really white against his tanned face, and the direct sun bringing out some golden flecks in his brown eyes. "Prove it and you're forgiven."

"You'll have to let go of my ankle first."

"Swear you won't swim away."

"I promise."

"Okay." He loosened his hold. "I'm trusting you now," he said before totally releasing her.

"And to show you that trust wasn't misplaced…" She slid her hands up his chest, feeling his hard nipples beneath her palm, and then wound her arms around his neck.

Just as their lips met a wave hit them and they stumbled apart. Tony caught her and they both swung their gazes out to sea to fend off any more surprises. No large swells in sight but the water had definitely gotten choppy as the clouds headed inland.

Tony pulled her close again. The water hit them at chest level so when his hands ran down her back to cup her bottom she moved against him without fear that someone could see them. The funny thing was, she wasn't all that concerned anyway. This whole thing was so not her but it felt incredibly free and exhilarating to be here with Tony enjoying the freedom of doing whatever she pleased. Without censure. Without worrying that one little mistake could ruin her future.

"Look, the clouds are chasing people away," Tony said with a jut of his chin toward the beach.

She briefly glanced that way. Only a few sunbathers remained and some of them were packing up. "Ah, that just breaks my heart."

With both hands, he gently squeezed her backside. And when he slipped his fingers inside the elastic, her entire body thrummed with anticipation.

"Of course we could always go back to the suite." He nuzzled the side of her neck, and she closed her eyes.

"No, let's stay awhile."

"You're the boss."

"I like the sound of that." She shivered when he nipped an especially sensitive spot.

"Sure you don't want to go in?"

She shook her head. She'd never admit what a high this brief walk on the wild side was. He wouldn't understand. This was nothing for a guy like him.

"Here comes another wave. Not too big, but brace yourself." He ran his hands back up, encircling her with his arms and turning so that he received the brunt of the force.

She hid her face against his chest and tasted the salt on his skin. He jerked as her tongue got close to his nipple. Laughing, she looked up at him. "Ticklish?"

"No. You?"

It happened so fast she didn't know how he got his finger inside the elastic between her thighs. Dakota spread her legs a little farther apart. He found what he wanted and probed deeper, rubbing gently yet firmly, until tingling warmth surged through her blood.

She couldn't quite look at him. So she closed her eyes and tried not to claw his chest, tensing when he found the perfect spot to make her melt like warmed honey. She lowered one hand and explored the front of his trunks. He was hard, considering they were chest high in water that was starting to make her own skin shrivel.

Another wave knocked them off course, not a big one, but enough to dislodge his finger, and force her to cling to him with both hands. He gave a wry chuckle and brought his hand up slowly, as if memorizing her body. Finally, he held her by her upper arms.

His mouth curved in a smile that was different

than normal. Or maybe it was his eyes that were different, black almost and so full of desire it made her tremble with want. "Now are you ready to go inside?"

"I am so ready." Her voice came out a whisper barely intelligible above the crash of waves around them. "I'm ready," she repeated, but by the look in his eyes, he'd already gotten the message.

"WHO GETS THE SHOWER first?"

"You're kidding." Tony barely got the door of their suite closed when he took the beach bag out of her hands and dropped it on the floor. "I hope."

"Um, well…" Dakota wished she knew what she'd said that was so wrong.

"I have every intention of washing this very soft, very delectable back," he said, drawing her close and hungrily kissing the side of her neck.

"I see." She let her head drop back. Showering together seemed so intimate for the first time. She thought about what they'd just done in the ocean with a dozen people still on the beach and a giggle threatened to escape. "That makes your back fair game."

Tony chuckled against her throat. "Baby, any part of me you want, it's yours."

She kicked off her sandals. "That's quite an offer."

He kicked off one deck shoe. "I hope you take me up on it." He had trouble with the other one, and taking a small hop, he muttered a curse.

Dakota laughed and offered her shoulder. "Here, hold on to me."

"That's what got me in trouble in the first place."

He cupped her shoulder with one hand and used his other to loosen the shoe.

Looking down, she caught a glimpse of the front of his trunks, and understood what might have thrown him off balance. She swallowed and clutched his arm. Nothing but lean hard muscle. Not an ounce of spare flesh marred his taut belly. And it was all hers for the taking.

Tony got rid of the shoe and they left everything right there in front of the door, slowing making their way toward the bedroom. He untied her pareu, but held on to both ends drawing her along with him, kissing her as he walked backward, oblivious to the table he nearly tripped over, her laughing and the door frame he bumped into.

He pulled back to look at her. "I'm kissing you and you're laughing. How is this thing supposed to work if you take shots at my ego?"

She smiled. "What thing?"

"This thing." He lightly pinched her behind, and she yelped. "And this—"

She blocked his hand, not sure where he was headed, not sure if she really wanted him to stop. "No, I get it."

"You sure?" He bit her lower lip.

"Um, give me a minute."

"Just one." He reached behind her and pulled free the strings of her top before she knew it. Gasping, she caught the front before it fell, cupping a hand over each breast. He smiled, covering her hands with his. "Only looking for something to occupy myself while I wait."

She hesitated, and then he stroked the backs of her hands, and she loosened her grip and let the bikini top fall to the floor. He moved back, his gaze lowering to her bare breasts, his nostrils flaring slightly and his eyes as black as midnight.

"Dakota." He gave a slight shake of his head, and exhaled.

"What's wrong?" She shrank back a little, wanting to cover herself, wanting to replay the last ten seconds.

"Nothing." His laugh came out shaky. "You're just so damn beautiful."

She let out a breath she hadn't realized she'd been holding, and tentatively reached out a hand and put it flat against his chest. "So are you."

"Hey, think up your own lines." He seemed genuinely embarrassed, which was totally unexpected.

Kind of fun, she thought. "You have a perfect man's body—broad shoulders, muscled but not too much—"

"Would you shut up?" He gave her no choice by kissing her hard and cupping her breasts with his slightly rough palms, kneading gently, grazing her hardened nipples, just enough to make her insane.

Lowering his head, he took one into his mouth, sucking, nibbling lightly, the sensation so sweetly satisfying that she moaned softly. Then he took the other nipple into his mouth, using the pads of his thumb and forefinger to console the one he'd abandoned.

Her nails dug into his shoulders. She flinched at what she'd done. He didn't seem to notice. Tony had gotten down on one knee, his hands bracketing her waist as his mouth moved lower, laving her navel, and then taking the bikini elastic between his teeth.

"Hey." She pushed her fingers through his hair and fisted the thick dark strands. "Shower first, remember?"

"Hmm?" He didn't stop. His tongue kept doing wicked things to her skin, and her resolve.

"Tony?"

He looked up, his lips moist, his eyes glazed.

"Shower?"

"Right." He bowed his head again, gave her a quick nip, and then slowly got to his feet, stopping to swirl his tongue around each nipple.

She wasn't so anxious to jump in the shower as she was to see him naked. His blue bathing suit was covering all the important parts and she'd felt enough of his firm, full ass to make her a little impatient. And that wasn't even the main event.

Thinking about it, her composure slipped and she roughly jerked him up. He looked at her, startled, but she kissed him, and then took him by the hand and headed for the bathroom.

She adjusted the water to the right temperature while he stripped off his trunks. She turned around and held her breath. He wore nothing but a tan and budding hard-on.

"Your turn," he said, his gaze going to her breasts, lingering, and then finally to her bikini bottom.

Boy, she'd screwed that up. She should've made him ready the shower. She'd always hated undressing in front of anyone. Way too awkward, even though there wasn't much to take off.

She hooked her thumbs on either side and slid the tiny yellow bottom to her ankles and sure enough, had some trouble stepping out of it. She grabbed the towel bar for support and swore to herself that if he was laughing, she'd sock him. After untangling the bottom from her left foot, she straightened.

He wasn't laughing. His arousal was at full bloom, thick and ready, and she couldn't help but stare. She tried to think of something clever to say. She couldn't even come up with anything stupid. Her brain totally shut down.

Her only consolation was that he seemed just as powerless. He stared back, his gaze so primal and hungry it sent an electric shock down her spine.

She moistened her parched lips and spoke first. "The water is ready."

He grinned. "Me, too."

Her laugh came out nervous. One of them had to make a move. Her feet didn't seem to be cooperating. "I think there's another bar of soap on the vanity."

He turned around. "Got it."

God, he had a great ass. She raised her gaze just as he looked back at her. He gestured for her to go first, and she smiled to herself. That was one for him. She did, and quickly got into the large glass enclosed shower to stand directly under the spray of warm water. He slipped in right behind her, bringing his arms around her middle and pulling her back against his chest.

Her ass pressed against his arousal and when his hands came up to cup her breasts she was certain he could feel her heart pounding so hard and so fast that she didn't think she'd survive. He toyed with each nipple, rubbing and lightly pinching and then one of his hands moved down her belly. She sucked in a breath and slowly moved her hips, her ass taunting his long hard penis.

He groaned, his hand slackening on her breast, and then she felt him shudder. He took her by the shoulders and turned her around to face him. Cupping her face, he kissed her hard, slanting his mouth over hers, he delved in, leaving no virgin territory.

Horribly in need of air, they pulled apart to take a breath. Dakota laughed softly, her breathing still uneven. Wet strands of hair clung to her cheeks and he gently brushed them back, sinking his fingers in her hair and massaging her scalp.

Dakota let her head loll back briefly and then brought it forward before she got too relaxed, and smiled. "You have a thing for water, don't you?"

He grinned. "Seawater, pool water, showers, baths, it's all good when you're naked." He glanced down and muttered a mild oath.

"What's wrong?" She glanced down, too.

"Look what I've done to you." He gently touched the red area on her breast, and then his hand went to his jaw. "I should have shaved first."

"It's okay." She touched his face. It really wasn't too rough yet. "I have sensitive skin." Especially since it hadn't had any roughness on it for so long, but she didn't tell him that. "But I don't feel anything. Promise."

He gave her a look of mock horror, his eyes sparkling and crinkling at the corners. "You don't feel anything?"

She realized where he was going with this and tried to hide a grin. "Nothing," she said, all innocence.

"We'll have to fix that." He didn't hesitate and went straight for the juncture between her legs.

Evading him just in time, and grabbing the soap she said, "Turn around."

His mouth curved in a cocky smile. "Oh, baby, I like it when you give me orders."

"Well, then, do it." She'd make a lousy dominatrix. The urge to laugh was almost too strong.

"Be still my heart." He turned around and flattened his hands against the beige contoured tile.

For a moment she just stared, letting the water pelt her back. His cheeks indented on the sides as flesh molded muscle. With his arms raised, his pec muscles bunched and mounded. Sinew stretched across his powerful back, making him look impossibly broader.

How she wanted to run her palms over every inch of him. Feel every dip and bulge, even the rather long scar on the side of his thigh. She gingerly traced it with her finger.

He looked over his shoulder. "Happened at work about seven years ago. My own stupidity."

She kissed his back and then started soaping him, starting at his shoulders, and then reaching around to his chest. She felt his sharp intake of breath as she brought his nipples to life, and then traveled to his stomach. She stopped there, smiling to herself, knowing his anxiety was increasing. But so was hers, so who was she tormenting?

"Okay, you." He abruptly turned around, and produced a pink squishy bath sponge.

"Where did you get that?"

"Up here."

She followed his gaze to a small ledge that had been discreetly built into the tile. There were two more, housing a tube of bath gel and something she didn't recognize. She got closer and realized that was what was providing the herbal scent she'd smelled. "Wow, how cool is that? I totally missed it. How did you find them?"

He shrugged. "I did something similar in my shower. Only the nooks are bigger, almost the size of the tile and I put—" He smiled. "I'm not telling you any more. You'll see for yourself."

Dakota stiffened. See for herself? She would never see the inside of his apartment. Didn't he understand? They wouldn't see each other once they got back to the city. This was a one-time thing. A brief escape from reality. When they got back, it was over.

She was so swamped with work that she spent most of her time at the office. A social life wasn't optional. Not at this point in her career. Anyway, they'd have no reason to see each other again. Except for sex maybe. But that was way too close to home. She couldn't take that risk.

Tony frowned. "What's wrong?"

"Nothing." She shook her head. "Actually, I'm feeling a little waterlogged."

He looked at his palms. The skin on the pads of his fingers had shriveled. "Yeah, I'm feeling like a prune myself. Let's hurry up and get out of here. I think horizontal might be nice for a change."

She accepted his kiss without the enthusiasm she had earlier. Fortunately, he didn't notice. They finished washing without playing around. Any move he made she playfully blocked. But she wasn't feeling so playful anymore. Not until they talked. Not until she was certain he understood where she was coming from. Not until she presented the terms of their brief relationship.

8

AFTER SHE'D DRIED OFF, Dakota reached for the white hotel robe. While slipping into it, she caught Tony's confused look. He was still naked, although not as aroused. He looked so good she wanted to throw away caution. Forget the short speech she'd been preparing in her head. But she knew better. That would be incredibly foolish. Better to spell out the ground rules first.

"There's another robe behind the bathroom door," she said. "I'll get it for you."

He got hold of her wrist. "I was thinking naked would be best."

"I'm thirsty. Let's have something to drink first. Otis said the fridge is stocked with beer." Headed toward the parlor, she said over her shoulder, "But feel free to stay naked."

She kept going, trying to ignore the puzzled hurt in his eyes. He thought something was wrong. Of course that wasn't true, and the sooner they discussed the arrangement the sooner everything would be fine again.

She found a diet cola in the fridge and brought

it out along with his brand of domestic beer. By the time she got a glass and some ice for herself, he joined her, dressed in the matching robe. Frowning, he sat on one of the bar stools across from where she stood.

"What's wrong, Dakota?" he asked, taking the beer she offered, but setting it on the bar while he looked her in the eyes.

"Nothing." She popped the top of the can and started pouring the cola into the glass. "Seriously. Nothing. But I do want to talk."

"About?"

"Don't look so worried. It's no big deal." She set down the can and came around the bar to face him. She grabbed his lapels and pulled him toward her for a kiss.

He readily accommodated her, taking hold of her hips and pulling her between his legs. She tried to keep a level head, which wasn't easy knowing he wore nothing under the robe and only inches away was the mother lode. This wasn't at all how she wanted things to go.

Tony was a dangerous man. At least for her he was. He disturbed her mental equilibrium. Tempted her to be imprudent. Not good. Not good at all.

She broke the kiss. "The sooner we talk, the sooner we get back to the fun stuff."

"Uh-oh."

"What?"

"This sounds bad."

She stepped back and put her hands on her hips. His gaze immediately went to her chest and she realized the robe had fallen open, exposing one of her breasts. The longing on his face was almost her undoing.

Quickly turning away, she pulled herself together, and then took a deep cleansing breath.

"Okay, let's talk," he said, uncapping his beer bottle and taking a big gulp.

"Okay." She cleared her throat. "I realize this is a little late but I think we should establish some rules for the weekend."

His dark brows drew together in a frown. His hair was still wet and a thick lock fell across his forehead. He looked so adorable she could just eat him with a spoon.

"That's not quite accurate. We don't need rules now. That's what's great about being here. Away from Manhattan. Here nothing counts."

She smiled, but he didn't.

"That's a good thing, right?" She sighed when she got no reaction. "Here's the reality. When we get back to the city, work is going to be a bitch. I'm losing two days I hadn't anticipated. Even in the best of circumstances I don't have the kind of free time to grab a last-minute dinner or if you find cheap same-night theater tickets."

Realizing she'd begun her practiced pacing, like she did in court when she addressed a jury, she moved behind the bar and leaned over across from him. His face was an unreadable mask. And she was damn good at reading people.

She cleared her throat again. "I'm sure this is a relief for you. No expectations once we leave the island."

He didn't look relieved. He didn't look anything.

"Tony, do you understand what I'm saying?" They stared at each other for a long time, and she was tempted to point out his remark about good running shoes.

"Why do you feel the need to bring this up?" he asked finally, flatly.

"I just wanted to set the record straight. I'd think this talk might put you at ease."

"Oh. So this is for my benefit."

"For both of us." She sensed his anger, yet didn't understand it. "I'm not saying any of that affects us now. Maybe I didn't need to bring it up."

"I'm glad you did." He nodded pensively, his gaze straying out the glass doors before coming back to her. "Finished?"

"You're taking this totally wrong. Remember that I didn't have the benefit of preparing the night before this trip. Plus I wasn't exactly sober last night, if you recall." Panic needled her. "Not that I'm unhappy to be here."

He got up, without a word, leaving his half-full beer on the bar.

"The silent treatment doesn't help," she said when he headed toward the bedroom.

"I'll be right back." He didn't even turn around, or spare her a brief look.

She stared after him, angry, bewildered and a little sad. He just didn't understand. And she wasn't sure how to explain her situation. Her career had become increasingly demanding. So had her parents. She laughed humorlessly. Her brother, too. Everyone seemed to want a little piece of her and she didn't have anything left to give. To top off everything, it meant she was a miserable coward.

Not three minutes later he emerged from the bedroom. The moment she saw him wearing the blue-and-tan tropical shirt and khaki shorts, she knew she'd blown it. He had something in his hand and laid it on the bar in front of her. It was her airline ticket.

"The concierge should be able to help you get the next flight." Emotionless words and a shuttered face, and then he gave her a reluctant smile, full of weariness, disappointment and resignation. "Have a safe trip."

When he kissed her lightly on the cheek, he might as well have slapped her.

NORMALLY TONY APPRECIATED reggae music. Not now. Half the tables were taken, couples mostly, talking and laughing, some of them too loud. He wished the band would disappear and everyone would shut up. Though he was the idiot who had chosen a bar for him to wallow in misery. He could've walked the beach. But it was drizzling and he didn't feel like getting wet again.

Hell.

He probably couldn't splash his face again without thinking of Dakota. Naked. Water streaming down her incredible body. Her perfect pink nipples glistening with moisture. Hell, all he'd have to do was picture her in her office, behind her big important desk, doing whatever important things she did. That would cool him off real quick.

"You want another one of those?" the stocky bartender asked.

"Sure, why not?" Tony pushed the empty bottle toward him, and squinted at his name tag. Edward. He liked calling people by name and normally would have learned the bartender's name right off the bat. But a certain pain-in-the-ass woman had him in a tailspin.

"Thanks." Tony brought the new bottle to his lips.

"Sure you don't want a mug." Edward wiped his hands on the yellow towel he kept thrown over his shoulder. "I keep 'em nice and frosty."

"No, thank you." Tony snorted, and then muttered, "I left something pretty frosty upstairs."

The bartender chuckled, his black eyes sparkling as he leaned his short beefy forearms on the bar. "You have a problem, you talk to Uncle Eddie. He's heard everything."

"Me? Nah. No problem at all." This time he took a long drink of beer and then reached for a handful of pretzels from a wooden bowl sitting on the polished mahogany bar.

"You like nuts?" Eddie asked in a whisper. "I save them for my favorite customers." He brought out another bowl, this one with peanuts and cashews. After setting it in front of Tony, Eddie helped himself to some. "You don't look so good, buddy. You sure you don't wanna talk."

"That customer is trying to get your attention." Tony motioned with his chin toward the balding guy wearing a loud Hawaiian shirt and holding up an empty glass.

"Be right back." Eddie grabbed another handful of nuts and moved to the other end of the bar.

Tony hoped he'd stay there. Eddie seemed like a

nice enough guy, but sometimes—times like these especially—a person just wanted to be left alone. Amen. The guy was slick, bringing out the nuts, giving Tony that favorite customer crap. He didn't blame Eddie, bucking for a good tip. And Tony would give him one, if he left Tony the hell alone.

Chuckling, Tony took another pull of beer and then stared at his wet napkin.

His stomach growled and he went for the nuts. Tilting his head back, he dropped some into his mouth through an opening from his fist. Nice and salty. He dropped in a few more. No use saving room for lunch. Or dinner. After Dakota left, he'd probably fly back, too.

Damn her.

He sighed. Why'd she have to go and ruin the weekend? Everything was going so well, and then pow! He'd felt as if she'd hit him with a two-by-four upside the head.

To be fair, she was right about having been at a disadvantage last night. Dallas shouldn't have waited until Dakota had had so much to drink before she explained about the honeymoon decoy thing. And maybe when he'd seen how out of it she was, he shouldn't have let her get on the plane.

Still, none of that mattered. What she'd brought up in that annoying lawyer tone of hers had nothing to do with today. Or tomorrow. She was worried about what might happen when they got back. Like maybe he wasn't good enough to socialize with. That stung.

"Hi."

At the soft feminine voice he looked up, his heart thudding. He knew it wasn't Dakota's slightly husky timbre, so why the disappointment?

"This seat taken?" This unfamiliar woman was blond, petite and young. Real young. Like someone-should-card-her young.

"It's all yours."

She hiked a hip onto the bar stool beside him and then wriggled her way against the rattan back. Her already short dress rode up alarmingly high, which didn't seem to bother her.

"My name is Celine." She put out her hand. "Like the singer." She had one of those soft limp handshakes that he despised. But she was young. Maybe she'd learn that if you offer your hand you should act as if you mean it.

"My name's Tony. Like the tiger."

She giggled. Not the sexy throaty kind of giggle Dakota made in the surf. But an annoying girlish sound.

"Did you just make that up?" she asked.

"All by myself."

"Celine, your usual?" Eddie called to her from the other end of the bar.

She nodded and cocked her head toward Tony. "Give him one, too."

Tony held up a hand. "Nope. I've had enough, thanks."

"Oh." She sighed, her lips forming a disappointed pout. "Are you on vacation?"

"Sort of." Small talk wasn't his thing but he didn't want to be rude. "You?"

"Sort of." She grinned and then picked up the fruity-looking umbrella drink Eddie set down for her. "Although I practically live here. On the island, not the hotel."

"What is that?"

"A piña colada." She removed the pineapple wedge from the rim. "Want some?"

He glanced at Eddie, but he'd already moved on to another customer. Tony frowned at her. "Are you old enough to be drinking that?"

She giggled again, and he made a mental note not to encourage that sound anymore. Not that he'd said anything funny.

"I'm twenty-two," she said, leaning toward him far enough to show some lethal cleavage. "Totally legal."

"When did you get in, Celine?" Eddie joined them, taking the towel from over his shoulder and wiping down the area around their drinks.

"This morning. Daddy wanted to dock by yesterday afternoon but one of the deck hands got sick, and then we got caught in that rainstorm."

"You ought to show him your yacht," he said to her, and winked at Tony when she wasn't looking.

"Sure." She perked up. "Would you like to come see it?"

"Uh, well—"

Something brushed his right shoulder. He turned to find Dakota sliding into the bar stool on the other side of him.

"Hey." She had on a strappy red sundress, low cut, short and tight.

"Hey," he said back. "You're still here."

She nodded, and in a low voice asked, "Is that okay with you?"

He shrugged. "Not my call."

"Are you staying?"

"I don't know yet."

She sighed. "I know you're angry and I don't blame you." She moistened her lips. "I was wrong."

Eddie showed up. "Good afternoon, pretty lady, what can I get you?"

"I, um, I—" Her eyes filled with uncertainty, she looked at Tony and then darted a look at Celine.

"She'll have a white wine. Chardonnay," he added, by way of telling her she was welcome to stay.

"Thank you."

Tony really didn't want to stick around and talk here, but he didn't want to scare her off either. Better to scare off the other two. He turned back to Celine and smiled. "Excuse us. We're on our honeymoon."

The young woman's brows shot up. "Oh, sorry. I didn't know."

"No problem. You didn't do anything wrong." He couldn't wait to get a look at Dakota's face. Probably sitting there all prickly over his lying about the honeymoon part. Tough.

He slid her a look. Surprisingly, a smile tugged at her lips.

"Did you say you guys are on your honeymoon?" Eddie set down the chardonnay in front of Dakota. "For my favorite customers I have some very special champagne."

Dakota winced. "Um, thanks, but I think I'll have to pass on that. Too much at the wedding last night."

"Yeah, she had way too much. Dancing on the tables, the whole bit. I had to step in when she started to strip."

Everyone laughed, even the couple sitting at a nearby table.

She glared at him. "I did not."

"That's okay, honey." He squeezed her hand. "I know you don't remember and I shouldn't have brought it up."

She glanced around. "He's lying."

"She's right." Tony nodded condescendingly. "Yeah, I made it up."

Eddie gave him a you're-asking-for-it look, and shaking his head, ambled toward the other end of the bar.

Dakota's mouth tightened and then her lips slowly curved in a forced smile. "Okay, I guess I deserved that," she said softly.

Tony scoffed. "First of all, I wasn't taking jabs at you. Going for payback. I wouldn't do something that juvenile. Secondly, you need to lighten up. I was teasing. Couldn't you tell?"

"This was a mistake. You're hurt and angry and I should—"

He caught her hand before she got all the way off the stool. "I'm not hurt! Why would I be hurt? What irritated me was you're acting like a damn lawyer."

"I am a lawyer."

"Not upstairs in that bedroom you aren't."

She blushed and glanced to her left.

He was certain no one heard. He'd been careful to speak softly.

"Well, it was nice meeting you, Tony," Celine said from behind him. He'd forgotten about her sitting there.

"Same here."

"I've gotta go find my father." She smiled at Dakota. "Maybe I'll see you guys around."

After she was out of earshot, Dakota's gaze followed her. "Is she old enough to be in here?"

"Her?" He shrugged casually. "Sure."

"She looks so young."

"The older you get, the younger they start looking."

She turned to him with one brow lifted. "I get it. You're teasing, right? Ha. Ha."

"Don't be so touchy."

"I'm not," she said with a mischievous glint in her eyes. "Now if I were over thirty I might be a little sensitive."

"I wouldn't know." Close to thirty-four, he hadn't grown up yet so it didn't count.

"Right." She sipped her wine, and then picked a cashew out of the bowl.

"Hey, you have to ask me for those. I got them because I'm a special customer. Just ask Eddie."

"May I?"

She gave him such an oddly affectionate smile he got the sinking feeling he was about to get the let's be friends speech. "Knock yourself out."

He waited but she just scooped up a couple more nuts and put them in her mouth one at a time and chewed. Something he totally didn't get. How could anyone eat one nut at a time? "How old are you?"

She looked startled. "Where did that come from?"

"We were talking about age. It's not a stretch."

"I'm twenty-eight."

He let out a low whistle.

"What? Too old for you?" She glanced at Celine's vacated seat. "I notice you like them pretty young."

"Yeah, like twenty-eight is *so* old. I thought you were older."

Her eyes widened.

"Not because you look it. I did the math. College, law school, successful career, looking to be a judge already. All at twenty-eight. Pretty ambitious."

"To become a judge you have to look ahead and map out your career."

"Don't get defensive. I'm not criticizing you. Everyone should be able to live how they want."

She looked at him for a long moment, a sad smile on her lips as she switched her gaze to the napkin under her glass.

He couldn't help himself, he had to ask. "What?"

She sighed. "Some people think my parents have pushed me into a law career, that it's my father's ambition I become a judge and not mine. I think maybe even Dallas believes that. But it's not true. I loved law school. I loved learning so much about our justice system." She laughed. "I don't always appreciate the way it works. But I love it. I can't explain it."

"You don't have to. Not to me. I get it. I love what I do. I love working with my hands." He decided he wanted another beer after all and signaled for Eddie. "I just don't like working as many hours as you do."

"I don't always like it." She shook her head, a wistful expression on her face. "I have to. Having a father that's a prominent judge isn't easy. It doesn't mean I'll get a break. It means I'd better *really* measure up."

Eddie brought Tony's beer and while Dakota asked the bartender about one of the tropical drinks he'd prepared for someone else, Tony stared thoughtfully at her profile. He'd thought he understood, but he hadn't. Until now. Dakota *had* to work twice as hard— Being a Shea took its toll.

9

DAKOTA CHOSE a pretty pink fruity drink, minus the alcohol. Drinking hard liquor after wine was a bad idea. Besides, she had plans for tonight. Big plans that could hopefully last all night. And she needed her strength.

She felt the weight of Tony's stare, and purposely crossed one leg over the other, her red toenails peeking out of the sandals and pointing at him. That got his immediate attention. Thank goodness men were so easy.

"Have you eaten yet?" she asked, swinging her calf a little, watching him reluctantly drag his gaze away.

"Uh, no. Just pretzels and nuts."

"Would you like to have dinner with me?" The lack of a quick response made her stomach tighten. Her confidence vanished. Had she totally blown it? Here was this great guy who'd wanted nothing from her but a consensual weekend of fun.

Earlier, when she'd gotten on her high horse and started dictating terms, he could have gone along, agreed to anything just to get to the sex. But he'd stood up for his principles. He wasn't like so many of those guys in college and law school who couldn't see past her looks.

She cringed just thinking about how she must have sounded. As if he were only good enough for a weekend fling. But not good enough to be in her life. That he could never fit into her world. The sad part was, to her utter shame, the thought had crossed her mind. Not that he wasn't good enough, but that she'd be burdened trying to fit a square peg in a round hole. And that her career might suffer.

Revisiting the thought shamed her all over again. When had she become so damn arrogant? Tony was too full of fun and life and self-confidence. He wouldn't even be interested in her narrow, pathetic world. "I guess I should have asked if you're planning on staying," she said finally.

"I doubt I could get a flight out at this point."

"Oh."

"Not that I would." He smiled and winked. "I'd have to be crazy to give up our honeymoon."

Hope fluttered in her chest. "May I assume I'm forgiven?"

He gave her a heart-melting look and then leaned forward to kiss her briefly. "I'm glad you stayed."

"Me, too."

"No more talk about later. One day at a time. Okay?"

"Agreed."

"Now, about dinner?"

"There are three potential restaurants; casual, fancy and one with Indonesian food. You choose."

"Indonesian?"

She shrugged. "Go figure."

"There is another possibility." He picked up her hand and kissed the back, his eyes dark with meaning. "We could have room service."

"Even better. Good plan." She moved her leg so that her foot touched his calf, and then ran her big toe up as far as she could. "I like it."

His dark brows went up. "Except it's too early for dinner."

"True. Any ideas?"

He smiled. "One."

THE ELEVATOR DOORS OPENED and Tony let out a low growl. "Damn it."

"What?" She looked to see what had gotten him upset. One side of the double doors to their suite was open and parked in front of them was the maid's cart. "Oh. No way."

He held the elevator doors open and then followed her out to the corridor. "Maybe she's almost done. If not we'll kick her out."

"Nice."

"Would you like to invite her to stay for tea?"

She jabbed him with an elbow to the ribs, and he grunted. "Wise guys don't get laid," she whispered.

He laughed loud enough for the maid to hear and stick her head out.

A big smile lit her round brown face. "Come, come. I make ready." She motioned with her plump hand and then pushed the cart to give them room to squeeze by.

Dakota took the lead into the parlor. Something in the dining room caught her eye. On the table was a huge bouquet of red roses, white carnations and baby's breath sitting next to a silver bucket holding a bottle of champagne. Chocolates and petit fours arranged on a white lace doily topped a rattan tray.

"Wow, look."

Tony came up behind her and put a hand at the small of her back left bare by the sundress. She could feel his touch all the way to her thighs. She turned her face toward his and his gaze dropped to her mouth.

"Excuse me." Dressed in a crisp black-and-white uniform, the maid hurried by with folded cream-coloured towels, and headed for the bathroom.

Tony sighed, and then went straight for the chocolates.

"Is there a card?" Dakota asked.

"Screw the card. Check this out. White-chocolate covered macadamia nuts, English toffee, almond clusters... Oh, baby."

"You like chocolate. Just a wild guess." She plucked the small white envelope from the bouquet of flowers.

"Not to would be un-American."

"I thought that was mom and apple pie."

"Whatever." He selected one and bit into it.

She opened the envelope. "It's from Dallas and Eric. They wanted to thank us for doing this."

He chuckled. "Yeah, such a hardship."

The maid appeared, smiling, walking briskly from the bathroom. "Everything okay?"

"Everything is great. Thank you."

"I go now."

Dakota walked her to the door, and after she left, secured the dead bolt. She turned around to find Tony grinning at her. It was obvious what he was thinking. Too bad she didn't have a comeback because it was true. She was anxious to be alone with him.

He was munching on his second chocolate. "Dallas say anything else?"

Dakota shook her head, gazing at the flowers and champagne. "I wish they hadn't done this. This whole weekend is costing them a fortune already. Tom needs a swift kick in his butt."

"I know. But don't worry about it. I'm footing the bill."

"What?"

He shrugged. "No big deal. I haven't had a vacation in a long time."

She hesitated, careful not to hurt his feelings. The hotel was expensive. She knew that much for sure. And a suite? He had no idea. "Actually, I'd already planned on taking care of it. She is my sister."

"Actually," he said with a smug smile. "It's already done."

"What do you mean?"

"I stopped at the front desk before I went to the bar. Gave them my charge card and had them transfer the cost."

"Oh." She wanted to ask if he'd seen the bill. If he knew what he was in for. On a construction worker's pay he thought he could take care of it?

Heck, she'd hate coughing up that much. But at least she could and still pay her rent. Yet how could she bring it up without hurting his feelings?

"And yes, don't worry, I can afford it. You want one of these?"

"I didn't—" She shut up. What more could she say without getting in trouble? "Anything milk chocolate." She went over to him, reminding herself she simply had to let it go. He was a big boy.

"Here." He put a piece of chocolate to her lips.

She bit into it and let the creamy smoothness coat her tongue. "Mmm, heaven."

"Give me a taste."

"Too late."

"I don't think so." With a hooked finger he brought her chin up. He kissed her gently at first, and then so greedily her head went back.

She laid her hands on his forearms, thinking she'd slow him down, but instead ran her palms up to mold his rounded biceps. When he put a hand on each side of her hips, the muscles hardened beneath her palms. Wanting his shirt off she went for the buttons. They slid out easily and his shirt hung open.

Smiling against her mouth, he tackled the straps that crossed over her breasts. They wouldn't be easy to unfasten, in fact she doubted he'd succeed, but she'd let him try while she explored the contours of his chest.

He finally gave up and released her. She wasn't so eager to abandon her exploration but he took hold of her wrists. "What do you say we go try that nice big bed in there?"

"I've already tried it. It's wonderful."

"Yeah, thanks, so was the couch."

"Poor baby."

"Fine. I don't want your sympathy. Just tell me how this damn dress works." He started walking her backward toward the bedroom.

She laughed. "It's like one of those puzzles. If you can figure it out you can have the prize inside."

"Ah. You mean the kind that makes me so nuts I tear and rip until I get what I want."

She stopped. "Don't you dare. This is a great dress."

"I agree. Are you going to wear it again?"

"Yes."

"When? Back home?"

She glared, annoyed with his goading. Although his shirt still hung open, and she knew damn well what that totally yummy chest felt like pressed against her breasts, and here they were wasting the afternoon. "Excuse me, but what happened to one day at a time?"

He put up his hands in surrender. "You're right. I concede."

She grabbed hold of the front of his shirt. "The hell with conceding. I want you to kiss me."

"Yeah?" He got up close, his warm lips brushing hers, and said, "Then take that damn dress off."

She made a ridiculous noise that sounded suspiciously like a giggle. She didn't care. Her concentration was directed at getting undressed. Before she even started she was halfway there. No bra. Only thing under the brief dress were uncomfortable thong panties, something with which she really wasn't happy and Dallas would hear about.

Tony got rid of his shirt and had his shorts off in concert with her throwing off the sundress. All their clothes astoundingly landed on the chair near the window. She pulled the bedspread back while Tony did his best to hinder her progress by trailing kisses down her back.

She'd barely gotten to the sheets when he urged her down onto the bed, stretching over her, kissing her mouth, her eyes, her throat. Shamelessly she ran her hands over his chest and shoulders, down his back, and then cupping his backside, squeezing the solid muscle, drowning in the sensation of his rock-hard penis rubbing her belly and the triangle of hair that absurdly felt as if it were on fire.

"Tony?" His name fell off her lips before she really knew what she wanted to say. When he pulled back to look at her, realization took hold. "I'm glad I'm here with you."

He smiled. "Me, too." He brushed the hair back from her face and then drew the pad of his thumb across her lower lip. "Me, too," he repeated, before lowering his mouth to her breast.

He caught her budded nipple lightly between his teeth and touched the tip with his tongue while he kneaded her other breast. She closed her eyes, amazed at the shivery sensation that controlled her body. She wanted to touch him, too, but she couldn't seem to get her arms to move.

When she finally overcame her lethargy and

summoned the strength to raise her right arm, he gently pushed it back down into the mattress. He kept her wrist captive, not in a scary way, but in a way that turned her on more than she could've imagined.

Selfishly she was glad. She wanted to just lie there and soak up all the delicious sensations that her body had been deprived of for too long. As well as she knew her own body, honed her own pleasures, taking care of herself didn't come close to the way Tony seemed to know exactly where and how to touch her. Knew how to push her to the brink, and then bring her back wanting more.

He took his time, laving her, discovering every curve, every crevice. This leisurely pace couldn't be easy for him. Not as incredibly hard as he was, his penis prodding her thighs, rubbing her belly as he moved over her.

Her impatience grew with the desire to touch him, and she broke free to run her palms up the side of his hips, and then down his taut backside. He moved against her, his arms shaking with restraint. Moisture formed at the tip of his penis and she could feel it on her belly, feel her own wetness between her thighs.

"Tony?"

He kissed her, the taste of rich chocolate still on his lips. He started slow, a soft brushing, a light nip, but the urgency increased and he parted her lips with his tongue, taking all she gave, taking what he wanted.

When he finally pulled back, his breathing was ragged, his voice hoarse. "Yeah?"

She stared blankly. "I forgot."

He chuckled and rolled to his side. After touching the tip of each nipple with his tongue, he settled back on his side, his head braced by his hand. His gaze swept her body and then rested on her face.

"Need a breather?" she asked sweetly.

"No, but I figure if I don't take a time-out, you'll need more than that."

"Aren't we cocky?" She reached down and ran two fingers along the underside of his penis, getting to the head and using her thumb to spread the moisture.

He briefly closed his eyes, muttered a mild curse and then maneuvered her hand away.

"Sorry, I forgot you needed a breather." She lay back, moving her hand to a spot right above her breasts.

His gaze followed her hand, watched as her fingers idly grazed a nipple. He took a deep shuddering breath, his chest rising and falling and begging her to touch him.

"You're beautiful," she whispered.

He met her eyes, his both surprised and amused.

"I mean it." She moved her hand to his chest, running her palm ever so lightly over his pecs, tracing the muscled slopes.

He chuckled, shaking his head, and by his self-conscious expression she realized she'd embarrassed him.

"The guys at my gym would kill to look like this." She ran her hand down his flat belly. Touched his arousal, watching her finger circle the head, watching his stomach clench.

He moaned, a throaty guttural sound that turned

her on as much as his hand sliding up her thigh. He got to the juncture and pushed her legs apart. Not that it required much effort. She wanted him inside so badly she shook with the need.

When he put his finger inside her, she arched off the bed and clutched at his shoulder. He moved so that he could watch what he was doing; spreading her nether lips and finding that one tiny nub had her ready to explode. It took seconds for her to cry out as the spasms blinded her, rocked her to the edge of oblivion. She wanted him to stop. She wanted it to last forever.

She squeezed her thighs together and he finally withdrew, slowly, reluctantly, his breaths coming raggedly on her breasts. Her eyes seemed as if they were glued shut. Her mouth wouldn't work. But she wanted more. She wanted him inside.

His muttered oath brought her around and she opened her eyes. He'd sat back and was looking around the room.

"One minute," he said, got off the bed and went to the chair with their clothes. He found his shorts, and when he fished something out of the pocket, she finally got it.

He started tearing the foil packet open on his way back to bed. She lay perfectly still, waiting, staring at the size of his erection, and gritting her teeth with anticipation. As soon as he sat at the edge of the bed, she was on the move, crawling to him, surprising him with a nip on his rear end.

"Oh." He turned around, grinning. "You wanna play rough, huh?"

She smiled coyly, and then took another nip.

"Okay." He finished sheathing himself and then lunged for her.

Laughing, she tried halfheartedly to get away. He caught her ankle and held her until he crawled on top of her, imprisoning her hip between his muscled thighs and planting his hands on either side of her head while he gazed down at her.

He smiled. "You surprise me."

"Not more surprised than me, I bet."

The corners of his eyes crinkled and he came down for a kiss, a surprisingly sweet one. He replayed the kiss on her chin, and then on her collarbone. Without warning, he slid inside of her.

Gasping, Dakota tensed at the initial impact. She relaxed, fisted the sheets and arched her back to take him in deeper. He readily accommodated her plunging so far she thought she couldn't take any more. He didn't stop, and she wouldn't have let him. Again and again he pulled out then thrust in until she was trembling from head to toe.

"Dakota," he whispered. "Now, Dakota." He threw back his head and the anguished look on his face with his final thrust gave way to a primal cry.

Anyone in the next suite could have heard it. She didn't care. An exhilarating feeling completely consumed her mind and body. Fueled her greed. She knew she'd want more. Much more. She already did.

Tony lowered himself and covered her body with his. He still suffered aftershocks, making his arms vibrate with a slight tremble. She understood completely.

"Oh, man." He looked at her, his breathing a series of short rasps. "Wow."

"Yeah." She tried to catch her own breath and moistened her parched lips.

He took it as an invitation and kissed her hard and deep before coming up for more air, and then flopping over onto his back. It took little urging on his part for her to crawl up beside him and lay her cheek on his chest.

It took only a minute longer for them to fall asleep.

"HEY." Tony touched Dakota's soft cheek and then pushed back the hair from her face.

She slowly opened her sleepy eyes. "What time is it?"

"You're on vacation. What do you care?"

"True." She smiled slowly, and then covered a yawn. "Just habit, I guess."

Still naked, they hadn't moved. She'd lain peacefully on his chest for hours. He knew the time. He'd been guilty of looking at the nightstand clock as soon as he'd awoken. Mostly out of curiosity because it was already dark outside.

She made a sleepy sound and rolled her shoulder back. "How long have you been awake?"

"A couple of hours."

She brought her head up, looking fully awake suddenly. "No."

"Yep."

"What have you been doing?"

"Watching you sleep."

She smoothed back her hair and ran her tongue over her teeth. "Tell me you're kidding."

"Why?" He urged her chin up. "You look beautiful. You always do."

Her skeptical look turned into a mischievous smile. "You, too."

"Ah, here we go." He knew she was trying to annoy him and he shouldn't react. Hell, he needed to go to the bathroom anyway.

She stopped him when he started to get up. "Okay, my timing might have been ill-intentioned, but I'm serious. Guys at my club seem to spend hours there and they don't look nearly as good as you."

He scoffed, embarrassed. "Too much sitting behind desks. All they need to do is get off their asses and do some manual work once in a while. Present company excluded." Nothing wrong with her ass, round and firm, and her breasts, crowned with those ripe pink nipples… He had to look away.

"You don't use weights?" she asked, cupping a hand over his bicep, almost reverently following the curve of the muscle.

His ego shot up a notch. "I have a couple of dumbbells at home, mostly to help me loosen up. That's it."

She smiled at him. "We're supposed to order room service for dinner."

"Hungry?"

She reached for his cock. "Not for anything on the menu."

10

THE MIX OF WHITE CLOUDS and darker brooding ones created an awesome sunset. Salmons and pinks streamed through the twilight sky and shadowed the grayish blue water below. The moon had already started to rise, tempting Dakota to run downstairs to the gift shop and buy a disposable camera.

But she was too lazy, the view from their balcony too spectacular and Tony was within arm's length of her. She looked over at him stretched out on the lounge chair just inches from her own.

"Can you believe we go home tomorrow morning?" she asked, reaching over to snag his beer.

With amusement, he watched her take a sip and then put the bottle back on his armrest. "Would you like me to get you one?"

"No, thanks. I'll just share yours."

"By all means, be my guest."

She turned and grinned at him. "I wish we could stay longer."

"Why don't we?"

"You know I can't. I have a court date on Friday and hours of preparation. I still can't believe I agreed to change our flight tonight until tomorrow morning."

He caught her hand and kissed her palm. "Aren't you glad we did?"

She nodded and sighed. "This has been the best weekend of my entire life."

"The best weekend, or the best sex?"

"Both." She gave him a mock glare. "You turkey."

He squeezed her hand. "Me, too."

"Really?"

He studied her for a moment and then frowned. "You couldn't tell?"

She withdrew her hand from his. "I don't know what your social life is like. Or how many women you're seeing. And it's certainly none of my business." She sighed. "And frankly I'm not as experienced as I should be." She pinched the bridge of her nose and tapped her head back against the lounge chair a couple of times. "I can't believe I just admitted that to you. But I'm sure you could tell."

"No more beer for you."

She shot him a puzzled look.

"No, I could *not* tell, because you were terrific. And I know because I'm probably too experienced. Not recently. In my youth." He made a face. "I don't date much now."

"Oh."

"One more thing. How experienced is one supposed to be? Is there a rule I missed?"

"I only meant that, in this day and age, a woman, like myself, who's been to college and law school and out in the workforce, well, one might expect that she's dated more than I have."

He hesitated, and she truly hoped he'd drop the subject, but that wasn't likely. He looked too curious. "Why haven't you?"

Her fault. She'd said too much. How could she possibly have become so comfortable and familiar with him? Certainly not because they'd made love at least seven times in two days. Talked about everything from terrorism to housebreaking puppies. That is, when they weren't having long, leisurely sex.

Sighing, she folded her arms across her chest. "Remember how I told you about my short rebellion in college and then finding out my mother had been right?"

He nodded, the curiosity in his eyes replaced with earnest concern.

"Well, it wasn't pretty." Most of the orange and pink in the sky had vanished because of cloud cover. The forecast for the island tomorrow was rain. A reminder that the fairy tale was over. "I'd gone with some friends to a frat party one night during my sophomore year. I knew most of the guys there. I loosely considered them friends. At the end of the night and two kegs later, two of them tried to assault me."

"Ah, Dakota."

Even in the dim light she could see the pain and rage in his face. She touched his arm. "I wasn't raped. I hadn't drunk much but they had, and I messed one of them up pretty badly."

His brows went up. "You did?"

She shrugged. "Dallas and I both had taken a lot of self-defense classes. Plus, I've always liked to kickbox for exercise."

"Damn. Nice of Dallas to have warned me." He took her hand again. "What happened?"

"I reported them. At first. But then, the dean convinced me to drop the charges. One of the jerks was a key player on the football team so they didn't want the publicity. I didn't either because I didn't want my parents to find out."

"Did they?"

"Oh, God, no. That's all I would have needed."

"You were the victim."

"Yeah, I was." She'd thought the bitterness was gone, but it coated her tongue and burned like acid in her stomach. "Remember that I was only nineteen, humiliated and scared to death my parents would find out. The two guys got slaps on the wrists and I just slunk away. That same day, all my new clothes went right into the trash."

"That wasn't that long ago. I didn't think that kind of stuff still happened to women."

"Hey, when it comes to protecting their star athletes, don't underestimate any schools' ethics." She took another sip of his beer, relieved that she was starting to feel better. "But you know what, that day, I knew without a single doubt that I wanted to study law. I wanted to be an attorney. The best one I could possibly be."

"And make sure that kind of thing didn't happen

to other women." He cupped the back of her neck and massaged the knot of tension.

She closed her eyes and let her head drop forward. "You got it."

"I thought the plan had always been for you to follow in your brother's and father's footsteps."

"The assumption was always there. Don't you dare stop," she said, when he started to remove his hand from her nape.

He continued the massage. "No, ma'am, wouldn't think of it."

"Anyway, I was a good girl and went along with what my parents wanted. I thought practicing law would be cool. But after that ordeal, it became my mission."

"I have a question."

"The answer's yes."

"Hey, I'm good but not a superhero. I have to have some time to recoup."

Laughing, she ducked away from his hand. "Okay, I'll admit it. I'm a little out of commission myself. So you're off the hook."

"Hey, let's not get crazy. I didn't mean no sex. I only meant we'll have to wait an hour."

"An hour, huh? I think I may need a couple." That was an understatement. She ached in lots of places. Really, really embarrassing places. But since tonight was their last night…

The thought stabbed at her heart. She'd miss him like crazy. No question there. But it wouldn't be practical to make plans once they returned to the city. She couldn't imagine the mountain of work that awaited her.

Worse, she couldn't imagine not seeing Tony.

Oh, God, she was in trouble.

She promptly chased all such thoughts from her mind. They were totally unacceptable. Impossible. Not wanted.

"Did you hear me?" he asked.

"What?"

"I was just saying, now don't get defensive, but aren't you letting those assholes win by caving in and dressing the way they think a woman should dress?"

"Valid point. But it's not worth the hassle. It's easier to wear a suit all the time."

"What about during off hours? Or like, while we're here. Doesn't that defeat the—"

"I admit it. I'm a coward, okay?"

He exhaled sharply. "I'm sorry. None of my business."

She didn't say anything. Better silence than to point out he was right. It was none of his business. Anyway, he didn't understand the discomfort of being hit on by married men, clients, bosses, older acquaintances of her father, for goodness' sake. Dressing conservatively and professionally made life much easier.

"Okay, next subject." He adjusted his lounge chair so that he sat upright. "Are you telling Dallas about us?"

Her heart sank. "What about us?"

"You know she's gonna ask about what happened this weekend. If you want we can tell her we didn't stay. She's not getting a bill from the hotel so she won't know the difference."

Dakota relaxed when she understood he wasn't talking about any future commitment between them. "What do you think?"

"She's your sister."

Was this a test? With the increasing darkness, she couldn't see his face very well. But she had the feeling this was more than a casual question. "We'll tell her the truth."

He faked a cough. "Like in the real truth?"

She chuckled. "How many kinds are there? We'll tell her we stayed and had a great time. I doubt she'll ask anything more personal than that."

"Okay."

"If she does..." Dakota paused. How much did she want Dallas to know? "I don't care, do you?"

A flash of white teeth and then, "Nope."

She stretched lazily. "How long did you say it would take you to recover?"

"As long as it takes you to get off your pretty butt." Tony got to his feet and pulled her up.

They'd left the air conditioner off and the sliding door open to enjoy the warm balmy breeze. Hadn't had the forethought to put on a light, though. So they stumbled into the parlor, Tony finding a lamp and switching it on.

Dakota took his hand and started to lead him to the bedroom, but he wouldn't budge. When she turned to look at him he smiled, took her face in his hands and kissed her. The kiss was so different from the others, so incredibly tender, she ached from the reminder that this would all be over soon.

Once she'd returned to her office everything would be fine. Work rarely allowed her time to think about anything else. Tonight, she'd enjoy every minute with Tony, enjoy every touch, every kiss. The endearments he used made her feel special inside.

"Shouldn't we close the drapes?" she asked once he'd moved to her ear, nibbling the fleshy lobe.

"This is the top floor. No one can see in." He reached for the hem of her tank top and drew it over her head.

She wore no bra and stood there baring herself to him, feeling not a shred of self-consciousness. How could she? Not with Tony. God, how could she be so comfortable and familiar with him in just three days? How many times had she tried to analyze the phenomenon in her head? It seemed impossible. But it wasn't.

"What are you thinking about that's making you look sad?" he whispered, cupping the weight of her breasts and kissing her lightly on the nose.

"Just wondering why you still have your shirt on." She grabbed hold of the black T-shirt and yanked it off. It ended up on the sofa with her tank top.

His expression told her he didn't believe her, but he didn't challenge her either. Instead he drew her close, her breasts pressed against his strong chest, her cheek flush with the quickening pulse at his neck.

He ran his palms down her back and rested them at the swell of her backside, just as he'd done a hundred times this weekend. Again heartwarming familiarity engulfed her. Scared her, too.

It wouldn't be easy parting tomorrow. The next couple of days would probably be lonely once she was back in her small apartment. Nevertheless, that's the way it had to be.

FIGURES THEY'D RETURN to a dreary gray day. Rain was forecast and there was a crispness to the autumn air that smelled of early snow flurries.

Neither of them had a coat, and when Tony tried to slide an arm around Dakota to warm her, she stiffened. He got the message and backed off.

"Damn, we wasted the entire plane ride," he said, yawning, as he slid in next to her in the backseat of the cab.

"What did you expect? We slept for only two hours last night."

"Was that just last night?"

She chuckled. "I know what you mean. Seems like a blur now, doesn't it?"

"Not exactly." He put an arm around the back of her seat and this time when she stiffened, he didn't give in. No one else was around. It was just the two of them, so tough. He pulled her against him. "I recall some extremely memorable moments."

She shivered, from a memory or the cold, he didn't care because she snuggled closer and that's all that counted. "Don't go there," she whispered, her breath warming his ear.

"Why not?"

"Because."

"I see."

She laughed softly, giving him a nudge with her shoulder before snuggling against him, her hand on his chest. "I hate to say it but I could probably fall asleep again."

"Go ahead." He stroked her hair. So soft. Just like the rest of her. "In this traffic, we have at least an hour before we get to Manhattan."

"What about you? Where do you live?"

"Manhattan."

"Have you always lived there?"

He shook his head. "I moved from Queens about a month ago."

"Oh."

He waited for her to say something more. He could have sworn she'd been about to ask where in Manhattan he lived. Instead she sat up and turned to look out the opposite window, putting some distance between them.

They'd come to a complete stop because of bumper-to-bumper traffic. Morning rush hour had already passed, but around here it didn't matter. She groaned. "I'm going to be so late."

"For what?"

"Work."

"You're going in today?"

She looked at him in surprise. "Sure I am. I'll probably be there until midnight trying to catch up."

"I thought maybe we'd grab a late breakfast."

"Can't."

"Early lunch?"

She smiled.

"You have to eat."

"I have granola bars in my desk drawer."

Tony looked out the other window. He'd known everything would change once they got back to the city. So why was he getting ticked off? One day at a time. His words, and this was a new day. Other choices to be made. He may not like hers, but that was too bad.

Shit.

Silence settled for a while and then she asked, "Aren't you working today?"

"Maybe tomorrow."

"Maybe?" She snorted. "Your boss may have something to say about that."

He smiled. "I doubt it."

Silence lapsed again as they both looked out their respective windows. The truth was, he had a lot of work to do, too. His new house needed some major renovations. The wood floors had been damaged from a major dishwasher leak, and the first floor walls were an ugly mint green. Even the antiquated bathrooms had to be gutted and totally redone. The stairs could wait for now but down the road they'd also need work. Not that he was complaining. Hell, no, not for the price he'd gotten the brownstone. Even though he was his own boss, he couldn't make a living by not turning over the brownstone quickly and then scooping up the next good deal. Especially in the current real estate market.

This time he broke the silence first. "Where does your boss think you've been?"

"My brother's one of the partners. Dallas handled it with him."

"What'd she tell him?"

"Something about me taking a day off to do her a favor. Believe me, Cody won't pry. He's probably too busy having his secretary pile stacks on my desk. All he'll care about is how much I can get done yesterday."

Tony shook his head. He didn't know how she could live like that. How anyone could? Deadlines on top of deadlines and everything a big rush. Allowing life to take a backseat. But it was her choice.

The rest of the ride into the city saw them alternating between yawning and chatting about everything from the Yankees to the local news overheard on the radio station playing inside the taxi.

They passed a limo on Columbus Circle, and Tony said, "Hey, that's right! How come we had to take a cab home. Where was the limo?"

"We'll have to give Dallas a hard time about that." She reared her head back, a teasing smile on her lips. "I didn't figure you for the limo type."

He snorted. "Are you kidding? Free beer, champagne, you name it."

"Yeah, and where's Otis when you need him?" She sighed, reaching for her purse when she noticed they were approaching her street.

"Hey, I have an idea. We can do this again next weekend. Same hotel. Same suite. What do you say?"

She laughed.

"I'm serious." He covered her hand when the cab

stopped. "Say the word and I'll take care of everything."

A small frown puckered her brows and her lips parted but she didn't say anything.

"The meter's ticking," the cab driver said over his shoulder. "Somebody getting out here?"

"Just hold on a moment," she told him sternly, and Tony smiled at her lawyerly tone. She turned back to him with regret in her eyes.

He shrugged. "It was just a thought."

"A nice one. But it won't work. I really am going to be swamped."

"I know. Hey, I should've done this already." He patted his breast pocket. The only thing in there was the napkin he'd saved from the plane. "Do you have a pen?"

She dug one out of her purse.

After scribbling his cell number, he handed it to her. "I don't have a landline, just this."

She studied the napkin for a long time, her other hand already on the door handle. Bad sign. Obviously she didn't know what to say, like, here's my number.

He swallowed his disappointment, forced a smile and kissed her on the cheek. "Don't work too hard."

"Oh, I will." She smiled sadly and opened the door. "Bye, Tony."

He nodded. That probably said it all.

11

"EXCUSE ME," Sara said as she knocked at Dakota's open door. "Would you like me to bring you back something for lunch?"

Dakota glanced at her watch. Already one o'clock. "Where are you going?"

Sara grinned, her big blue eyes sparkling. "I have a hankerin' for some of that greasy corner pizza, but I'll get you anything you like."

"Aren't you tired of that yet?"

"No, ma'am, I'm fixin' on trying the pepperoni this week." The new temp had a wide smile and fresh look about her that suited her cute southern drawl.

Dakota grabbed her purse from the bottom drawer of her desk. "There's a deli next door to the pizza place with ready-made salads. If they still have a Greek salad I'll take that, otherwise the chef salad."

"No pizza, huh?"

Dakota got up to give her some money and Sara walked in to meet her halfway. "I've lived near or in the city all my life and I've had my share, thank you."

"I suppose I'll get tired of it sometime, but I've only been here a month."

"Where from?"

"Georgia."

Cody entered the office and cleared his throat. Sara glanced over her shoulder at him, and then turned back to Dakota and made a wry face. "Be right back with your salad," she said, then as she passed Cody, her drawl exaggerated, she said, "Afternoon, Mr. Shea."

He didn't respond. At least not to Sara. He exhaled loudly and shook his head with that arrogant look Dakota disliked. "What's wrong?"

"You have to ask?" He laid a folder in the middle of her desk, on top of some briefs she'd been reviewing.

"If you're referring to Sara, I'm missing your point." She rounded the desk, sat in her chair, and made a show of moving the folder to her in-box.

He lifted one condescending brow and then, to her dismay, made himself comfortable in her guest chair. "She's not right for this office."

"Sara? You're insane. The clients love her."

"She doesn't dress particularly well, nor does she—"

"Excuse me, but Sara's a temporary employee. The firm doesn't pay them all that well." Dakota leaned back in her chair, took in his two-hundred-dollar Armani tie and the custom-made Egyptian cotton shirt. "When did you get to be such a snob?"

He stared at her for a moment, concern in his eyes. "You've been prickly *all week*. Ever since your little secret errand for Dallas. I hope she hasn't gotten you into some kind of trouble."

"Please." She sighed. "Of course not." He was right about her being prickly. He may even be right about her being in trouble. She couldn't stop thinking about Tony.

Images of him popped into her mind all the time. At work, while riding in a cab, she'd even found herself daydreaming about him in court yesterday, which was totally inexcusable. Especially when her client paid three hundred dollars an hour for her attention.

But mostly she thought about him at night when she was trying to sleep. That's when her mind proved the most susceptible. Occasionally she swore she could even feel his strong arms around her, feel his warm breath on her cheek. The sensation was both wonderful and terrifying.

"Dakota, I don't know what's wrong with you but I sure hope you pull yourself together."

She looked blankly at her brother. "Why would you say that?"

"Fine," he said wearily and stood.

"I haven't been sleeping well," she said, when she realized he genuinely did seem concerned, and then gave him a rueful smile. "Probably hormonal." That wasn't a lie.

He smiled back. "Getting old, kiddo."

"I wouldn't be throwing stones."

"Tell me about it. I found my first gray hair last week."

"Oh, you'll love looking distinguished."

Cody shot her a wary grin. "Janice and I are going to the theatre next Saturday. We have an extra ticket."

"Janice? What happened to what's her name?"

"Don't want to talk about it." He glanced down at his gray suit slacks and brushed at them. She didn't see anything but if there was a single speck of lint, Cody would find it.

"Okay. Thanks for the ticket offer but I'll have to pass."

He nodded and headed for the door where he paused. "That folder I left—there are a couple of police reports in there pertaining to the Draper case."

She swallowed, her mouth suddenly dry. "Thanks."

He left, and she sat there numb and drained. How could she have forgotten about the Draper case? She still had time, even though it meant working later than usual. What troubled her was that she'd been capable of forgetting.

The problem went back to Tony. He consumed her thoughts too often. The six days since she'd seen him had been dull. And she'd become inordinately restless. Her concentration level was probably a step above that of a puppy going from one toy to the next at lightning speed.

Suddenly paranoid, she quickly flipped through her calendar to make sure there were no other surprises coming her way. Fortunately there were none. She leaned her head back against her black leather chair and applied pressure to her temples, hoping to prevent the headache that threatened.

Tony's cell phone number was still in her purse. She should call him. Just see what he was up to. She didn't have to actually see him. But would hearing his voice be enough? Or would it whet her appetite and make her more miserable? She'd only been asking herself the same questions again and again. It was no wonder she couldn't focus. But then of course, if she did call…

God, she couldn't stand being this indecisive.

She took a deep breath and reached into the drawer for her purse. She had no choice. She had to call him. If only in self-defense.

"SON OF A BITCH!" Dropping the hammer on the workbench, Tony vigorously shook out his hand, hoping the thumb he'd just creamed would quit throbbing.

Yesterday it had been the saw he let slip. Twice in two days he'd been distracted and ended up hurting himself. He was always so careful. He'd had a perfect record, both while working for Capshaw Construction and now himself, until this week.

Damn that Dakota. Why hadn't she called? He knew she was busy with work. But would one quick phone call kill her? Probably lost his number by now. Or had thrown it away.

He went to the refrigerator and got some ice from the door dispenser. If he didn't ice down his thumb and curb the swelling, he was gonna have a hell of a time finishing this job.

He could call her if he wanted. Even though she hadn't given him her home number he knew the firm's name where she worked. But he wasn't gonna call. No way. Making the first move was hers. Hadn't she gotten all weirded out about how things would go when they got back to the city? One day at a time, he'd told her. And just for today, no way in hell he was gonna call.

Good. He'd made up his mind. He didn't have to think about it anymore. He looked at the clock. Five-fifteen. He wasn't going to get any more work done today, not with his thumb feeling as if someone had lit a match to it.

Yawning, he stretched out his aching back. He'd been putting in too many long hours. Getting to be as bad as Dakota. Her again. Sneaking her way into his brain. He had a stiff back. Nothing to do with her. Too many long hours tearing apart the bathroom.

Sleep hadn't come easy since they'd gotten back a week ago. Sometimes he lay awake all night thinking about her smile, about the weight of her breasts on his belly and chest as she crawled up his body to kiss him. To taunt him. To make him insane. He'd picture her that last evening they were on the island, lounging on the balcony at sunset, her eyes closed, her lips curved in the barest of smiles, the look of sheer contentment on her face.

That was the problem with working alone every day. Too much time to think. At least when he'd worked for Capshaw there were distractions. Joking with the guys, lunch with Dallas every day until she'd quit last year. He'd left shortly after that when his hobby of buying and refurbishing brownstones not only became more fun and challenging, but lucrative enough that he didn't need company benefits.

The sloppy wrap he'd made for his thumb slipped.

He checked the injury and decided a few more minutes of icing would help. He got to the refrigerator but before he remade the ice pack he looked in the fridge for a beer. None. What did he expect? He hadn't been shopping since he'd gotten back. Yeah, Dakota had been right. Where was Otis when Tony needed him?

Tony muttered a curse.

He backed away from the refrigerator as if it had bitten him. That wasn't the only time she'd mentioned Otis. Tony couldn't recall the time or details, but no way should she have remembered the guy. Not his name, not his spiel about keeping the fridge stocked. Otis had only been in the suite that one time—when Dakota was half-asleep and totally wasted.

So what the hell?

Dumbfounded at the sudden realization, he sat on one of the bar stools he'd had delivered yesterday. He rested his injured hand on the new brown-and-tan granite countertop he'd recently put in.

She hadn't been drunk that night. She'd known what was happening all along.

What a damn fool he was. Baffled, he replayed some of the events the night of the wedding. She'd had a few, he knew that, but why pretend she was drunk?

He stared out the window at his courtyard garden, withered and bare from the first frost they'd had last night. He just didn't get it. He didn't know if he should be angry because she'd used the pretense to shun responsibility if they were found out, or be flattered and glad that she'd gone to the extreme in order to have those few days with him.

Just when he thought he was beginning to understand her, she turned out to be a puzzle. Not that it mattered. She hadn't called. Probably wouldn't. And he wasn't sure he would either…if he could help it.

He got up and went in search of some tomato juice he thought he'd spotted earlier, when his cell phone rang. Normally he kept it clipped to his belt, but he'd put it down somewhere. He frantically looked around, locating the cell by the fourth ring.

As soon as he flipped it open, a second before he answered, he saw the unfamiliar local number and knew it was Dakota.

"Tony?"

"Hey."

"Busy?"

"Not for you." Amazing how any annoyance he'd felt just minutes ago dissolved at the sound of her voice.

She sighed. "I'm looking out of my office window at some really dark clouds. Looks like it might snow."

"I heard it would rain."

"I'm not sure which is worse."

Tony rubbed the back of his neck. "How come we're talking about the weather?"

She hesitated. "I don't know."

He knew, because he felt the awkwardness, too. No reason for it to be there. Not after everything they'd shared. But there it was. "Well, how ya doing? Working hard?"

"My eyes are crossed and I have an in-box stacked to the ceiling, but other than that everything is great."

"Sounds like you need a little R & R." Man, did he have the perfect thing in mind.

"I'll be lucky to have a whole weekend to myself from now until next summer."

"I hope you're exaggerating, Dakota."

"Not by much."

"That sucks."

She laughed. "That's an understatement. But it's not all bad. At least it's interesting work. I'm working as cocounsel on a big high-profile case."

"How big?"

"Really big. Huge."

"Would I recognize the name of your client?"

"Hmm, most likely."

"Can you tell me who?"

"Not really."

"Okay, then who's your cocounsel?"

"My brother. Why?"

No surprise there. "Just curious." Three years out of law school and already being pushed into a high-profile case. Shoved right into the limelight by Cody. At least the Sheas looked out for their own.

"I don't want to talk about work. I just wanted to see how you were doing."

Tony shook his head. It looked like he had to make the next move. "What are you doing tomorrow night? You like Italian food?"

"I've got to work, Tony."

"My grandmother taught me how to make a mean lasagna."

"Wow, a man who can cook."

"Don't get excited. I can make only five things and lasagna's the best of the bunch."

"Anything sounds better than the peanut butter and jelly sandwiches I've been eating."

"So we're on?"

"What time?"

"Your call."

"Eight-thirty too late?"

"Any time that's good for you. The lasagna can keep."

"Wait, let me find my pen. I've got to get your address."

He paced the kitchen and living room, checking out the mess he'd have to tackle before tomorrow night. His housekeeper wouldn't be back until next week. Maybe he could bribe her to come tomorrow for just a couple of hours.

"Okay, I'm ready."

He gave her the address, it turned out they lived only ten blocks apart. They hung up after that. Dakota was anxious to get her work done, and he was anxious to find his grandmother's lasagna recipe. He had no idea what the hell he'd done with it. He hadn't even finished unpacking yet. There was never any rush because he hadn't accumulated too much stuff since he moved every year or so.

Before each place was finished, he bought another one to renovate. They always sold quickly then and for more money than he'd ever pay for one. Rich people sure liked their conveniences. They wanted to be able to move in, not have to do so much as change the carpet.

He started gathering up his tools, cringing at the amount of dust he'd created changing out the dining room floor. That was the only reason he had a woman come in to clean once a week. He liked to make the mess, not clean it. But for tomorrow night he would. The kitchen was already finished and fortunately the living room didn't need that much work. He'd spruce up the downstairs bathroom and the rest of the house would have to be off-limits.

His thumb started to throb again and he went to look for his ice pack. He still couldn't believe she'd called, or that she was coming over tomorrow. Why the sudden change of heart, he wondered. Did she miss him? Or was meeting him in private kind of like being on the island. It didn't count.

DAKOTA SHUDDERED. What had she been thinking calling Tony? She didn't have time to see him. She had more work than she could handle and now she'd probably given him the wrong message and...

"Do you need anything before I leave?"

At the sound of Sara's voice, Dakota started.

"Sorry, I didn't mean to scare you," Sara said, standing in the doorway.

"I didn't know you were still here. You should've gone home already."

"It's okay. I had a few things to finish up and I'm in no hurry." Sara shrugged. "Besides, I've only been in the city a month. I don't have any friends here yet."

"Manhattan's a big change from Georgia. Are you sorry you came?"

"Oh, no. I love it here. So much to see and do."

Dakota smiled. "That's why you're working late?"

Sara laughed, flashing a cute dimple. "When I meet some people, I'll start getting out more."

Dakota nodded, a little sad for Sara. Meeting people in the city, nice people anyway, wasn't so easy.

"May I ask you a question?"

"Sure."

Sara moved in closer and lowered her voice. "Is Cody, um, I mean, Mr. Shea married?"

"Uh, no."

"Dating anyone?"

"No one seriously that I know of." Oh, God, she should lie. Tell the poor girl he's engaged. But she'd find out otherwise.

"Good."

"He's not married for a good reason." She motioned for Sara to come closer. This woman would be crushed if she went after Cody. He liked his women much more sophisticated, and with a note-worthy surname. "He's my brother and I love him, but he's high maintenance, and tends to be a bit arrogant as I'm sure you've noticed."

"Oh, yes." Sara grinned, as if she thought that flaw was cute, her blue eyes sparkling with the thrill of the hunt. "I know."

"Okay." Dakota sat back. The woman was on her own. "Just thought I'd give you a friendly warning."

"Thanks." Sara smiled and took a couple of steps back, then tucked her hair behind her ear. Dakota couldn't help but notice the woman's watch. It looked like a Rolex, but had to be a knockoff. Much too pricey for a temp's salary.

"Need anything before I leave?" Sara asked again.

"No, thank you. Go home. Salvage the evening." Dakota acknowledged her wave with a nod, and then stared at the empty doorway. Sara seemed like a nice woman, but maybe she was the type who chased after rich guys. Cody wasn't rich, but for someone like that he'd be worth the catch.

But that was *his* problem. Dakota had enough of her own. Tomorrow night she'd see Tony again. The thought both excited her and scared her to death. Her gaze was drawn to her laptop sitting on the credenza.

To her shame, she hadn't checked in with the girls at Eve's Apple since she'd been back. They were all great about sharing accounts of their dates. Not that she would be specific, but she'd at least let them know she'd gone for it.

She grabbed the laptop and brought it to her desk, placing it on top of the mess of papers she should've been working on. Instead, she flipped it open, powered up and then briefly checked her personal e-mail account. Nothing important. Nothing that couldn't wait, anyway. She switched to Create Mail and started to type.

To: The Gang at Eve's Apple
From: LegallyNuts@EvesApple.com
Subject: Mission accomplished
Hi, Everyone,
Just checking in to tell you I did it. Bit the bullet. Had a fabulous weekend at a fabulous resort with the most fabulous guy! All of you who told me to go for it, you were absolutely right. Thank you. Thank you. Thank you. It was exactly what I needed. I'm only sorry the weekend's over. It went way too fast. And reality just isn't quite as fun. :)

But I'm back to work, and God knows I have enough to keep me busy. Won't have time to miss him or the great sex, or anything else. That's the good news. Bad news is…okay…I'll admit it. I miss him!!!

But I'm okay. Really. No worries. Hope all is well with the rest of you.
Your sister in arms,
D

12

DAKOTA PAID THE CABBIE and climbed out in front of the address Tony had given her. The number she'd written down belonged to a three-story brownstone. Like her own apartment, the brownstone had probably been converted into three flats and rented out separately. She searched for a directory or sign indicating which flat was Tony's, but there was only one address etched into the eye-level bronze plaque beside the beautiful beveled glass door, circa early nineteen hundreds, if she weren't mistaken.

She pressed the buzzer and Tony answered the door. He wore faded jeans and a long-sleeved navy shirt that was too loose to give her a good view of that great chest she'd missed all week.

"Hey, good. You're early." He stepped aside, letting her in.

"I guess I should have called to warn you."

"Nah, the lasagna's been ready since seven-thirty, and me…" He winked. "I've been ready for a week."

She smiled, amazed at the warmth and contentment she felt simply being in the same room with him. He led her into the foyer, from which she could see the living room where a cozy fire was blazing in the fireplace.

"Here, I'll take your coat."

She shrugged out of her tan cashmere with him helping. His fingers brushed the side of her neck, absurdly making her heart flutter. "I take it you have the first floor?"

"Actually, I have every floor, but this is the only one that's livable." He hung her coat in a nearby closet. "What about your blazer?"

She hesitated, and then got out of her suit jacket, leaving her in the matching gray skirt and a tailored white blouse.

He put the jacket with her coat, and then turned to her with one of those sexy grins that would have had a wiser woman running for the door. When his gaze flickered to her breasts, she realized that, even through her sensible bra and staid white blouse, her nipples were protruding.

His gaze abruptly met hers. "I have both white and red wine. Which would you like?"

"White," she murmured, backing up to give him room to pass.

The delicious smell of lasagna drifted under her nose and her stomach growled loudly. Embarrassed, she flattened a palm against the sound. It didn't help.

The noise didn't seem to faze Tony, he simply said, "I hope that sucker tastes as good as it smells."

She laughed. "You look skeptical. I thought you made a mean lasagna."

"I did. Once."

"Ah." She pressed her lips together. He looked so earnest. She didn't care how it tasted. It would be the best lasagna she ever had.

"Come in." He led her farther inside, and she followed, her gaze staying on his butt.

She hadn't seen him in jeans before. Well, once, the first time she'd met him a year ago at the job site where he and Dallas worked, but he'd been sitting down so it didn't count. But she sure was feasting on him now. She'd seen him naked so of course she knew he'd look good in jeans, but my, oh, my.

He turned and gave her an odd look, and she prayed she hadn't inadvertently said anything out loud. She cleared her throat. "This is nice." The room had high ceilings, a beige marble fireplace trimmed with ornate brass, lots of polished wood and a large Oriental rug in front of the sofa. "Really nice."

"Thanks."

"Do you own or rent?" Silly question, really. A place like this would cost a fortune.

"I bought it a couple of months ago."

"No kidding."

"A foreclosure. I got a deal." He grinned. "I wouldn't say it needs a lot of work but a tetanus shot is required to go upstairs."

She laughed. "I think I'll stay down here with the lasagna."

"You ready to eat? I just have to toss the salad and stick the garlic bread in the oven."

"For just the two of us?"

"I don't do this often, so I'm doing it right. Come in the kitchen and talk to me."

She followed him into the kitchen, again surprised by the size and quality of the granite countertops and hardwood floors. The appliances were not only new, but top-of-the-line stainless steel.

"Who the heck did you know to get a deal on this place?"

He smiled as he went around the counter to the refrigerator and got out a large glass bowl full of torn-up pieces of romaine. Except for a bottle of white wine, a bottle of ketchup and a six-pack of beer, the refrigerator looked empty.

"When I got it, the wood countertops were warped, like the floors, and the appliances were all that old avocado colored stuff from the sixties." He opened a beautiful wooden cabinet and brought out two wineglasses. "Did you say you wanted white wine?"

She nodded. "White. Thank you. Did you change the cabinets, too?"

"Oh, yeah. The old ones were ruined." He turned on the upper one of the double ovens.

The five-burner cooktop was separate, and there was a convenient butcher-block island in the center. This was a kitchen she'd kill for. If she cooked. Which she didn't.

He poured the wine with a frown, and as he passed her the glass, asked, "Are you having garlic bread?"

"I hadn't thought about it." She lied. She had. Garlic? What was he thinking?

"I don't know if I should bother heating it, because either we both eat garlic bread or neither of us do."

She tried not to smile. "Why?"

"Just in case we do a little kissing later."

"You're a little devil."

His eyes widened and his jaw dropped in mock horror. "You've been talking to my mom."

She laughed. "I figured that one out all by myself." She slowly came around the counter, her high heels clicking on the hardwood floor, and drawing his attention to her legs. "Why wait until later?"

His heated gaze slowly came up to her face. "Can't think of a single reason."

She took another step and he pulled her the rest of the way, bringing her up against him and finding her mouth with an urgency that made her dizzy. As if he couldn't get enough of her, he feverishly kissed her mouth, her chin, her neck...

"What about dinner?" she whispered.

"Mmm..." He bit her earlobe. "It tastes pretty good."

She laughed and hiccupped at the same time. "Tony, I've missed you."

"Oh, baby, not like I've missed you." He cupped her bottom and pulled her in tight. He was already hard and a vivid memory of him naked and ready for her made her whimper.

She buried her face against his neck, her palms running up his back. Feeling him through the shirt wasn't enough so she worked her way under the hem until she hit bare skin. She heard his sharp intake of breath, and then he yanked her blouse from the waist-band of her skirt.

"We should eat first," she whispered.

"Really?"

"No."

He chuckled and started unfastening her buttons. She knocked his hand away and he stopped, a startled look on his face, until she gripped his shirt again. He quickly pulled it off then went back to her buttons. She reached around and unzipped her skirt.

She didn't even know this greedy person she'd become. From the moment she'd seen him at the door she knew she wanted him stripped naked, his penis thick and hard in her hand. She wanted to taste him. Every last inch of him.

He slid her skirt down her thighs to her calves, and she stepped out of it, and then kicked off her heels. Tony moved back to unfasten his buckle.

"Nice bra," he said, the corners of his mouth twitching.

"Shut up." She'd thought about wearing one today that Dallas had bought her, but Dakota always wore a white blouse to the office and this style was appropriate.

"Very practical."

"Shut up or it stays on."

He got rid of the belt and unsnapped his jeans. "No, really, it's great. Very sexy. I'll shut up now."

"Good idea." Something caught her eye above the kitchen sink and she froze. "You don't have curtains."

"Not yet. Low on the priority list."

She looked around for her blouse, found it on the counter and pushed an arm through the sleeve.

"Now, just hold on a minute. No one can see in."

"The hell they can't. If I can see movement, then they can see in here." What on earth was wrong with her? She'd come here to have dinner. Not be dinner. She got her arm through the other sleeve but the collar was all screwed up and she turned away while she straightened it out.

"I swear to you no one can see in." He touched her arm. "I've tried myself. Just to make sure."

She got three buttons fastened and realized she'd started with the wrong hole. She muttered a most unladylike curse.

"Dakota?"

"What?" She didn't mean to sound so bitchy. This wasn't his fault. She was exhausted and embarrassed and…

"Dakota, look at me."

Drawing in a shaky breath, she reluctantly met his eyes.

He smiled and helped her button her blouse, correcting the ones she'd messed up. "Let's have some dinner, okay?"

No shirt, his jeans unsnapped, he stood there looking so yummy she wanted to kick herself all the way down Broadway for being a big wuss. He had to think she was a total nutcase. But being on their home turf while carrying on spooked her.

God, she felt like that one time in high school when she'd snuck out of the house to see a boy her parents had forbidden her to see. Guilt had stuck to her like wet paint for the entire two hours she was with him, and all they'd done was hold hands.

"I overreacted. I know." She thought she saw something and her gaze darted back to the window.

"No, you didn't. I'm not into being watched, either." He handed her her skirt. "Let's not allow it to ruin our evening."

She'd been about to beg out, and tell him she needed to get back to work. But he'd know better, and anyway, it wasn't fair. Not to him, and not to her, either. She'd already smiled and laughed more here, tonight, than she had all week.

Dakota stepped into her skirt, holding onto one of Tony's shoulders for support. When she went to zip it up, he silently offered to do it, reaching around her and pulling the zipper into place.

Close enough for a kiss, he seized the opportunity. She didn't refuse, didn't even glance at the window. Simply enjoyed the moment, enjoyed the warmth of his lips on hers, enjoyed the security she felt in his arms.

He kept the kiss gentle even when she tried to take it to the next level. And then he moved his mouth to her cheek for a light peck and held her tightly for a long tender moment.

Tears burned the back of her eyes. She never cried, and she sure as heck wouldn't do so now, but work pressure and exhaustion were really getting to her. And she really needed this. To be held. To not be questioned or prodded. To just be.

She inhaled deeply, composing herself, and then tilted her head back to look at Tony. "Thank you."

"You're welcome." He brushed his lips across hers. "I don't know what for, but you're always welcome."

She smiled. "Now, are you going to feed me?"

He tapped her on the backside, and then took her shoulders and turned her around. "For distracting me, you have to help with dinner. Get the plates out and toss the salad."

"I can do that." She went to the salad bowl and peered inside. He wasn't kidding. All she had to do was toss. The tomatoes and red peppers were already cut up, the black olives already sliced.

She looked up to ask him for the salad dressing, and with deep regret, saw him putting his shirt back on. Tempted as she was to ask him to leave it off, she knew that wouldn't be fair. Besides, if he humored her, she couldn't be trusted. Sighing she busied herself with looking for the dressing and found some blue cheese.

They decided to skip the garlic bread and he dished up the already warmed lasagna, while she filled salad plates. She ate so many salads for lunch at work, all she cared about was the lasagna so she made him give her an extra piece.

He took another one himself and they carried their plates into the dining room. She sat at the small oak table, which seemed completely out of place in the formal dining room, while he returned to the kitchen for their wine. The hardwood floors were in excellent shape, probably because Tony had already redone them, but the gold foil-like wallpaper was hideously gauche and old-fashioned.

"I love the wallpaper you chose," she said when he got back.

"Yeah, I was thinking about using this pattern in the rest of the house," he said with such a straight face that for an instant she thought he was serious. Then he shook his head. "You should see the stuff they had on the bathroom walls. The previous owners had lived here for sixty years. When they passed away last year, their kids mortgaged the place to the hilt for the equity because they couldn't agree on selling it, and then defaulted."

"That's sad. For all our differences, I can't imagine Dallas and Cody and I behaving that way.' She took her first bite of lasagna. "Oh, my, this is…incredible. Did you really make this?"

"Hey." He showed her the underside of his forearm. "I've got the burn marks to prove it."

She gasped playfully. The marks were faint. "Poor baby. You really did burn yourself."

He nodded, going for sympathy with a forlorn look.

"You'll live. I promise. The good news is…this lasagna is truly amazing." She took another big bite. The compliment wasn't meant to simply be nice. The man could cook.

They talked very little while they continued eating, and too late, she realized she'd eaten too much. Walking home instead of taking a cab would help that problem, but damned if her mind didn't go straight for another way to burn off some of her dinner. Surely he had to have curtains in his bedroom.

"Okay," she said, getting up with her plate and reaching for his. "The least I can do is the dishes."

He immediately got to his feet and took the plates from her. "Domestic goddess that you aren't, you probably haven't heard of one of these newfangled inventions. It's called a dishwasher."

"Wow, imagine." She grabbed their glasses and followed him to the kitchen. Her gaze went directly to the window. Nothing there, of course, but she couldn't help it. "Hey, you drank wine tonight."

"It goes with lasagna. Has to be red, though. Just ask my grandmother." He stacked the plates in the sink, and she grabbed a dish towel. "Another thing I should explain about these dishwashing contraptions, you always let the dishes soak in the sink first." He took the towel out of her hand and threw it on the counter.

"I hadn't heard that one before."

"Trust me." He took her hand and led her into the living room.

At his urging, she sat on the overstuffed leather couch and then watched him look through a rack of CDs. His shirt was untucked and to her knowledge he hadn't put his belt back on. She laid her head back, drowsy from her carb-fest, knowing she should go home, knowing she couldn't leave yet.

"You like Norah Jones?" he asked, and then turned around when she didn't answer.

"I'm trying to think. I know I've heard her before."

"She has a distinctive voice." He slid the CD into

the player. "If you've heard her before, you'll recognize her immediately."

He left on one dim lamp, and turned off the rest of the lights. Then he joined her on the couch, angling himself toward her and pulling her back against his chest.

"If you fall asleep, I'll wake you in an hour," he whispered, his chin lightly resting on top of her head, his strong arms encircling her, crossed gently over her breasts, and imprisoning her arms.

She didn't feel trapped, though. Safe and content, yes. The only scary thing was how easy it would be to forget the responsibilities and pressure of work. But she knew better. Tomorrow morning's meetings and deadlines would come and she'd better be ready.

She turned so that her cheek rested against the base of his throat, and snuggled deeper, bending her elbows so that she could curl her hands around his forearms. She wouldn't go to sleep, but it was nice listening to the bluesy voice of Norah Jones and feeling Tony's strong heartbeat, which was the last thought she remembered having.

ADMITTEDLY, Tony had had other plans for the evening. But this was good. He liked holding her and knowing that for just a little while she wasn't thinking about work. She could relax and know she was safe, and that he was right here if she needed him.

Her grip on his forearms slackened and he knew she'd drifted off. Probably not for long, but a power nap always did him a world of good. He inhaled the vanilla scent of her shampoo, laid his head back and closed his eyes. It would be easy for him to fall asleep, too. After working a twelve-hour day himself, one glass of wine and a plate of pasta was enough to do him in. But he couldn't break his promise to wake her.

He quickly stifled a yawn when his chest expanded and she stirred. He tightened his arms around her ever so slightly and she settled down, and he lay back again, enjoying the feel of her soft breasts beneath his arms.

He could hear her gentle breathing.

Or maybe it was his own.

The voice of Norah Jones lulled him into a pleasant twilight. He fought sleep. Blinked several times to keep himself awake. But his lids felt so damn heavy....

TONY WASN'T SURE what startled him. He opened his eyes. It took a second to realize he was still on the couch. Dakota was with him. And she was unzipping his jeans.

"Good morning," she whispered.

"Is it?"

"Two-fifteen."

"I'm sorry."

"Don't be." She pushed his shirt up and found his nipples.

He smiled. "Come here."

She shimmied up to him, causing unbearable friction in her wake. "Yes?" she said, her lips against his mouth.

While he kissed her, he pulled her blouse from the waistband of her skirt and then unzipped her. She helped him with the annoyingly small buttons of her blouse and he helped her pull off his jeans. Her panty hose was the biggest challenge and he wasn't sure but he might owe her a new pair. But in spite of all obstacles, within seconds they were both naked.

Thank God he'd left the old drapes up.

She ran two fingers along his cock. "Tony, do you have any—?"

He shuddered. "Yep, give me a minute." He got up even though he had condoms in his jeans pocket, but he didn't think it would be cool to just whip them out. Might give her the wrong idea.

He disappeared for a few seconds and when he got back he found her looking over his CD collection. In full light, she was perfect. Standing there, naked, in the dim glow of the lamp, she looked like an artist's rendering. From the graceful curve of her neck to the seductive curve of her backside, she was perfection. Even her sexily tousled hair looked as if it had been arranged. But he knew for sure it hadn't. Not Dakota.

She looked up and smiled. And that was perfect, too.

He couldn't wait. Not another minute.

Taking her hand, he brought her back to the couch, urging her to help sheath him. He kissed her hard and deep, and holding her hips, guided her over him. He stretched his legs out as she straddled him, lowering herself until he entered her, so slick and wet that in three thrusts the explosion started.

13

NOBODY HAD GOTTEN to the office yet. Only six-fifteen. Early even for Dakota. But she badly needed to get a jump on the day. Yesterday, after leaving Tony's place at four in the morning, she'd gotten only two hours sleep before going to the office. The whole day had gone downhill with her first cup of spilled coffee.

She'd functioned at half speed, managing to get in only six hours of work after putting in a twelve-hour day. Last night she'd crashed early when she was supposed to have been preparing an opening argument. Fortunately, she'd always been an early starter so she wasn't late with it yet.

The coffeemaker in the room next to her office made that low gurgling sound it always did when the coffee was done brewing and she went to get a cup before she unloaded her briefcase.

On the way back, her laptop caught her eye. It normally took downing half a cup of strong Colombian brew before she could function anyway, so she saw no harm in checking for responses from the Eve's Apple gang.

She got set up and relaxed in her chair as the

messages started popping up. Jeez, she'd never seen so many responses, most of them calling her an idiot judging by the subject lines. Did she really want to read those?

Curiosity got the better of her and she chose a few to read while she sipped her coffee.

To: LegallyNuts@EvesApple.com
From: Cindy@EvesApple.com
Subject: Who are you kidding?
D,
You're not okay. Reread your e-mail. Be honest with yourself. I felt so sad reading it. Are you seeing this guy again? What happened!?!
Cindy, who's on your side but doesn't get it

That one stopped her. How much had changed in just one day! Yeah, she'd seen Tony again, but what had that accomplished? She liked him even more if that were possible. But that solved nothing. In fact, she'd probably have been better off not contacting him again. To think he lived so close was sheer torture. That in a ten-minute cab ride she could be with him. Kissing him. Be in his arms. Feel the stress miraculously melt away just because he was near.

She looked to the next message, this one with a more neutral subject line.

To: LegallyNuts@EvesApple.com
From: HornyInHenderson@EvesApple.com
Subject: Hey!!!

D,
You really are nuts if you don't think we all don't want to hear more about the weekend. Details, please!!!!!!!!!!!!!

BTW listen to Cindy. She's right.
Love and kisses,
Horny

Dakota shook her head. Details they definitely weren't going to get. She was about to get offline when she recognized the moniker of a woman who'd e-mailed her the first time Dakota had posted. She couldn't resist seeing what BabyBlu had to say and promised herself this was the last one she'd waste time reading.

D,
I'm glad to see you've posted again. I've been thinking about you a lot lately. Better than thinking about how miserable I am, eh? <G> I saw Larry the other day. He was with a woman. She had on an engagement ring. Nice emerald cut, maybe three-quarters of a carat, two small baguettes on the side. Nothing like the two-carat solitaire I bought myself last month for closing a big sale. Good thing I could afford it. No one else to buy me a ring. <<sigh>> I'd trade it for a pop top ring if Larry had given it to me. God, I miss him. So, have you broken down and seen your man again? If not, do it. Don't wait until you see him walking around with some other chick.

Let us hear from you again.
Good luck!
Love,
Carson

Dakota signed off, feeling the same sadness she experienced the last time she'd read Carson's e-mail. Worse, this time, she felt the threat of panic. Could she stand seeing Tony with another woman? It would kill her. Not that she had a speck of right to feel anything but indifference. That knowledge didn't lessen the gnawing in her gut.

The irony was that it could easily happen. They lived in adjoining neighborhoods. Not often, but at times she went up to his corner market for produce or this special cheese she couldn't find anywhere else.

Then again, maybe he wouldn't stick around the Upper West Side. He might have gotten a good deal on the house, but excluding the kitchen, it still needed a lot of work and, from the look of it, he'd run out of money. Plus he had his day job. The renovation could take years.

She had to stop speculating. It did no good and she had too much work to do. If Cody asked her for the first draft of the opening argument one more time, she'd scream.

She heard the elevator ding, which meant her peace and quiet was about to end. So was her chance to get a head start on the day. She was so screwed.

TONY HAD KEPT his cell phone close for two days. No calls from Dakota. Bad enough she hadn't woken him up before she left the other night, but she hadn't given any indication if or when they'd see each other again.

He knew she was busy and under a lot of pressure. And he didn't even mind seeing her on her terms until things settled down for her at work. But she could at least call. He was tired of misplacing his tools because his mind had drifted off, wondering about her. Like his level. He looked on his workbench and then on the dining room table. Second time today he'd misplaced that same level. What the hell had he done with it now?

It wasn't on the bathroom counter, but he did find a hammer he'd been looking for an hour ago. His missing tool belt hung over the doorknob. This had to stop. At this rate, he'd still be working on the house five years from now.

Maybe she was waiting for him to call. She'd made the last move. His turn. He'd already programmed her work number into his phone. Unfortunately it wasn't a direct line and he had to go through the company operator. He waited for the woman to connect him, half expecting to get a voice mail. But Dakota answered, by briskly stating her name.

"Prove it," he said in a gravelly voice.

"Pardon me?"

"Prove you're Dakota Shea."

She hesitated and then laughed. "Let's see...I know this guy named Tony, and I could tell you something really juicy about him that only I would know."

"Okay, okay. I believe."

"I was just thinking about you," she said, her voice

lowering, and then through the phone line, he heard a door close.

Smiling, he sat down on the couch and swung his legs up, not caring about his dusty jeans or work boots. "What were you thinking about?"

"About how late you kept me up the other night and how behind I am at work because of you."

"I kept you up?" He snorted. "I remember quite a different scenario. Like waking up to one hell of a surprise."

She issued a short laugh. "Shh."

"Nobody on this end to hear me, darlin'."

"Okay, I give up. Mea culpa."

"So when are you coming over and mea culping me again?"

She made a tsking sound. "You are so bad."

"Isn't that what you like about me?"

"Probably." She sighed. "Hey, I have—"

She stopped at the same time Tony thought he heard a knock at her door. A man's voice mumbled something about a meeting, and then she was back on the line.

"Tony, I've got to go," she said, papers rustling in the background.

"No problem."

"Thanks for calling."

He didn't like that brusque tone. "How about a drink after work?"

She didn't answer. Even the papers quieted. "Just a quick one, Dakota. Wherever you want."

She sighed. "Okay, I can dash out around six but

I'll have to come back to the office later. Do you know Sargenttis?"

"I know it." A hoity-toity place near Wall Street he'd been to a couple of times. Not of his own choosing.

"Okay."

"See you there."

She hung up first. Almost before he'd finished talking. He didn't take offense. He knew she was busy and that's why he hesitated to call her at work. But she still hadn't given up her home number. Maybe tonight when they met for a drink.

Sargenttis, huh?

Yeah, he knew it. And she wanted to meet there? Interesting.

DAKOTA CHECKED HER WATCH and punched the elevator button again. She was already five minutes late and the bar was another five-minute walk away. She was out of her mind for telling Tony to meet her there. Talk about lawyer central. She didn't go for after-work drinks often, but when she did, it was always to Sargenttis because it was basically the only bar she knew, and only because all the other attorneys went there.

Including her brother. Great. Just great.

Luckily, Cody was still in a meeting. But there would be other colleagues there. And there'd be questions and curious looks and Tony would end up feeling uncomfortable.

It was her fault. She'd gotten flustered when Cody had poked his head in to remind her about the meeting. She'd been gathering the necessary paperwork for it when Tony called. And poof, just like that, everything else flew out of her mind. And in that moment of weakness, she'd suggested the popular bar.

She so wished she had Tony's cell number with her. Fine place for it to be, sitting on her nightstand. All because last night she'd been tempted to call him but had consistently talked herself out of it.

She got half a block away from Sargenttis and pulled off the clip that was holding her hair back. She fluffed the flat strands as she walked, moistening her lips and wishing she'd remembered to apply lipstick before she left the office.

A man in front of her opened the door for both of them and welcome warm air hit her face. In that instant she realized she'd forgotten her coat. She'd walked three blocks in only her suit and it had to be forty degrees.

She was losing it.

The bar was crowded, lots of expensive suits and loud talking. She couldn't actually hear anyone specifically, but she recognized two judges, neither of whom was her favorite, and several self-important attorneys who worked in her building. At a corner table, two of her office colleagues were engaged in conversation.

She didn't see Tony, even as she walked past the group of tables that bordered the ornate turn-of-the-century bar. It was hard to see who sat in the booths but more than one person occupied each one.

She finally spotted him at the end of the bar surrounded by three men and a woman, only one of whom she knew. A black leather jacket hung off the back of Tony's bar stool, and he wore a white T-shirt and jeans and laced-up work boots, clean, not as if he'd just gotten off work or anything, but he looked totally out of place in a sea of expensive tailored fabric. Obviously it didn't bother him. He seemed completely at ease and involved in a lively conversation with the others.

If only she felt that comfortable having him here among her peers. The thought shamed her, briefly, but the truth was that her career was important to her and it was more complicated than just being a good lawyer.

She approached quietly and stood off to the side, hoping to eavesdrop, hoping Bruce, the one guy she did know, wasn't being his usual pain in the ass. He was young, brash, successful and full of himself, but insecure enough that he had to make sure everyone else knew of his successes.

"So, Greta, when are you thinking of taking the plunge?" Tony asked the thirtyish blond woman who was part of the group.

"I'm thinking spring. Any thoughts?"

Tony shrugged. "Any time is good if the price is right."

"Amen." Bruce tipped his head back and drained his martini, and then signaled the bartender for another.

"Yes, but you're talking about a place that needs work. I can't manage paying rent and financing renovations and overseeing the work," Greta explained.

"Look, this is what you do—" He saw Dakota

and a warm smile curved his sexy mouth, making every one of his companions turn toward her direction. "Dakota. Hi."

She felt her cheeks flame. Thank goodness the bar was dimly lit. "Hi." She swung her gaze around to include everyone, and then nodded at Bruce.

Tony slid off his bar stool. "Here, I was saving this for you."

"Thank you."

He stood with the guys. She sat beside the blonde.

"I'm Greta." She offered her hand. "That's Derrick and Sam. We're with Simon and Lloyd."

"I work with Bruce at Webster and Sawyer." Dakota caught the amusement in Tony's eyes. It was professional courtesy to let the other person know for whom you worked.

She thought for a second. Not that it really mattered, she supposed. But when you worked for a prestigious firm it was kind of a high to see the trace of envy in people's eyes.

"May I borrow him for just a few more minutes?" Greta asked, and without waiting for a reply, turned back to Tony. "You were saying about doing a renovation?"

"This is yours," Tony said to Dakota. He'd apparently ordered her the white wine that was sitting on the bar.

She'd planned on drinking orange juice since she had to go back to work, but she smiled her thanks and took a small sip.

He winked and turned back to Greta. "This is what

you do. After you buy the place, you choose one room that you have to have right away, like the bedroom or kitchen, wherever you spend the most time. You get that done before you move in, and then do the rest slowly as you can afford it."

The bartender came with Bruce's martini and put a beer in front of Tony. Just the bottle. No glass. "This is from Mr. Wilson," he said, indicating Bruce.

"Thanks, buddy." Tony gave him a nod, and then said to Greta. "You need to find a good contractor you can trust, so that most of the work can be done while you're at the office."

"Makes sense." Greta smiled. "How about you? Would you be interested in the job?"

"No, ma'am." Chuckling, Tony shook his head. "I've got enough on my plate."

"You didn't finish telling me what to do about the bottom of my boat," Sam said, and Tony gave Dakota an apologetic look before launching into an explanation about the quality of marine paint and barnacle removal.

Dakota didn't mind. She liked listening to him. He seemed to have quite an extensive knowledge of a variety of do-it-yourself improvements. Even Bruce, who was never interested in a conversation unless it was about him or his current case, seemed absorbed by Tony.

"I'm thinking about building a summer house on some land I have on Martha's Vineyard," Bruce said. "Any ideas on how I could save a few bucks without cutting corners?"

"Yeah, don't let anyone talk you into a slab foundation. A crawl space is cheaper. And quit drinking seventeen-dollar martinis at Sargenttis."

Everyone laughed, even Bruce, who then saluted Tony with his seventeen-dollar martini.

"My ride is leaving. I have to go." Greta hurriedly laid a couple of twenties on the bar near her wineglass. "Nice talking to you, Tony." She slid off her stool and whispered to Dakota, "He's adorable. Where'd you find him?"

Dakota just smiled, and then watched Greta join an older man waiting at the door.

The men had already started a lengthy discussion about cars. Dakota took another small sip of wine and then asked the bartender for a glass of water. When she turned around again, she found Tony staring at her.

He smiled. "Everything okay?"

"Perfect."

"You want to get out of here?"

"I'm fine." In fact, the more he talked, the more she liked listening to him. His charm mixed with enthusiasm made even the most tedious discussion interesting. Even Sam mentioned that Tony should host one of those do-it-yourself television shows that had become so popular.

Bruce tried to buy Tony another beer, which he declined. "Anything this guy doesn't know?" Bruce asked, shaking his head.

"Well, while you pretty boys were going to college and partying I was actually reading books."

The guys laughed good-naturedly.

"Well, I'm outta here. Almost dinnertime." Sam signaled the bartender for his tab. "My wife is pregnant and expected me home on time."

"Been there, done that." Derrick ordered another drink.

Tony subtly turned so that he gave the other two his back. "You're quiet."

She smiled. "Like I've had a chance to say boo."

"Uh, yeah, sorry."

"I'm teasing."

"You know I'd much rather be talking to you." The way he looked at her, his eyes so intense, it was as if he'd touched her. He hadn't, not once, even though she knew he wanted to.

She appreciated his restraint, his knowing how awkward it would be for her. Glancing around, she saw that several other colleagues from her office had arrived. But not Cody, thank goodness. He generally worked too late to stop at the local bar but there was always that possibility.

But even if he did, so what?

She took another quick look around, wishing she could be that blasé.

Tony took another sip of his beer. "I seriously think we should go someplace else. Maybe get some dinner. I know this place in midtown that—"

Dakota shook her head. "I have to go back to the office."

"Tonight?"

She nodded. "That's why I suggested this place."

"Bummer."

"Yeah." She saw Bruce wander over to a secretary who worked on the floor below them. "How did you end up talking to those guys?"

"This bar," he said, knocking on the polished wood, "was constructed with pieces of wood from an old Italian vessel. I was asking the bartender what he knew about it, and they overheard."

"How did you know about the wood?"

"I don't know. I was trying to remember that myself." He frowned over his shoulder and then leaned closer. "What's with introducing yourselves along with the name of the firm you work for? Is there some kind of hierarchy with you guys that us mere mortals don't know about?"

She made a face at him. "Funny."

"No, seriously, that was kind of a trip the way you and Greta traded employer information. Is it kind of like my dad can beat up your dad?"

She rolled her eyes at him. "It's hard to explain," she said and checked her watch, eager to drop the subject. It was a little embarrassing.

"Okay," he said. "Have you heard from Dallas?"

"No, but I don't expect to until day after tomorrow. That's when she gets back."

"Ah." He took another sip of his beer.

Silence stretched and she realized he was waiting for her to say something. Only she'd been distracted by the guys from the office who'd taken a corner table. They had to have seen them.

"So what time do you think you'll get done tonight?" He leaned close enough to unsettle her, but not enough that anyone could draw a conclusion.

"I don't know. Late. Really late."

"Did I tell you I'm a night owl?" There was that sexy undermining grin again.

"I can't, Tony. I also have an early morning meeting."

"Sure. I understand." He lowered his voice. "This is hard. Not being able to touch you."

"Yeah, I know." She made a quick grab for her wineglass and took a big gulp. She couldn't give in. She really did have an early meeting tomorrow. "In fact, I have to be going."

"Already?"

"Hey, Mr. Goodwill Ambassador, I'm not the one who started a new social club."

"I'm not the one who showed up late."

"Touché." It'd turned out well, actually. Being part of a group with him was so much better for appearances. Sighing, she got off her stool. "Believe me, I'd much rather be here with you than slaving away in my office. But I don't have that choice."

"Hey, I'm glad I got to see you." He reached into his jeans pocket, the T-shirt pulling tightly across his chest, and she swallowed. Not a man in this room could fill out a T-shirt like that. "Hold up. I'll settle the check and walk you back."

"No. Stay," she said quickly. Maybe too quickly judging from his narrowed gaze. "You didn't finish your beer." Meeting him here was one thing, but she couldn't walk out with him. How would it look?

"Really. I'll call," she added, briefly touching his hand, and then resisted the urge to see if anyone had been watching.

"Okay." He smiled. "I'll talk to you later."

God, she wanted to kiss him.

She abruptly turned and walked toward the door, keeping her gaze straight ahead, acknowledging no one as she left the bar. Once she got outside, she felt this weird emptiness in the pit of her stomach and had the sudden urge to hail a taxi, go home and crawl under the covers.

Ironic really. She'd thought Tony would be a problem, but the problem turned out to be her. Right now, she didn't like herself very much.

14

TONY STOOD BACK and admired the new floor he'd just put in the guest bathroom. He'd gotten a good deal on some discontinued tile and was able to use a higher quality than he'd anticipated. His supplier was looking into another possible discontinued batch for the master bath. A few breaks like that would up his selling price.

He heard a knock at the door and pulled off his work gloves. His mother and sister had been the only visitors he'd had other than Dakota. Against all odds, he hoped like hell it was her. But it was the middle of the day and she didn't even know how to knock off work at a decent time, so he wasn't holding his breath.

Besides, two days since he'd seen her at Sargenttis, and she still hadn't called. She was busy—he got that. But one lousy phone call?

Glancing through the peephole, he saw that it was his Realtor wrapped in that mink coat she started wearing the second the temperature dipped below sixty-five, and he reluctantly opened the door.

"Finished yet?" she asked, and walked past him, heading straight for the kitchen.

"Hi, Sylvia, nice to see you, too." He shook his head and closed the door. The woman could sometimes be too pushy for his taste, but she got results and had made him a lot of money.

"Oh, my God, Tony. This granite is to die for. Where did you find it? I know you didn't get it from that skunk on Fourth." She waved a dismissive hand. "He wouldn't know quality if it bit him in the face."

"As a matter of fact, I did get it from Manny. Gave me a good deal, too."

She narrowed her gaze, her eyes so heavily made up it made her look ten years older. "I very nicely asked him to look into some discount floor covering for me to put in one of my rentals and that worm told me…" She pulled herself up straight, lifting her chin. "I'm a lady so I won't repeat what he told me."

Tony grinned. "What can I do for you, Sylvia?"

"You can finish this job. I have a buyer."

"You what?"

"Don't worry. He's not in a rush."

Tony glanced around the room. "I didn't even decide to sell this one yet."

Her dark brows drew together in outraged disbelief. "What else would you do with it?"

"I don't know." He shrugged. "Keep it maybe."

"Tony, don't be foolish."

"Owning a piece of real estate in Manhattan is foolish?"

"You know what I mean. The market is hot right now. You've made an awful lot of money, and there's a lot more to be made."

"Sylvia, the market's always hot in Manhattan. Besides, it's not all about money."

She frowned, studying him closely. "Of course it is."

He scoffed. "Says you."

"Remember when you first came to me and asked for comps on listings and you said—"

"Okay, okay, but my only goal was to eventually quit construction and support myself this way." Hell, he didn't have to explain anything to her. She made her commission. A damn good one.

"And you're doing a great job. By the way, you look tired. Aren't you sleeping?"

He checked his watch. "I really have to get back to work."

"Can you spare some time for lunch? I'm buying."

"Already ate. But thanks." He started toward the door. She got the hint and followed, and he said, "Look, I don't know what I'm going to do yet. I'll probably sell, but if I don't, I'll find another one to turn over."

"All right." She sighed, then her expression suddenly brightened. "My niece is coming to town this weekend, a real pretty girl, and—"

He opened the door. "Goodbye, Sylvia."

She drew the front of her mink coat together at the throat. "Call me," she said, before hurrying out to a waiting cab.

Tony closed the door. He really hadn't eaten and since he was at a stop he went to the kitchen to make himself a peanut butter and jelly sandwich. His cell rang twice before he was done. Both calls were from guys where he used to work wanting to go for a beer at four. He left it open, telling them that he'd probably make it, but not to send a search party out if he didn't.

He still had the old-fashioned claw-foot tub and ancient commode to move out of the master bath. Later, a couple of buddies he'd hired for extra muscle were coming to help. They always showed up when he called, but never at the requested time. Otherwise, it would be nice to see his old coworkers. It had been a while.

Not since before Dallas's wedding. Since before Dakota had started making him nuts. Shaking his head, he carried his sandwich and a bottle of water to the table. When she'd asked him to meet her at Sargenttis, he'd been pretty surprised. He knew it was a lawyer hangout. Twice he'd had lunch there with his own attorney.

Foolishly he'd hoped the ice was finally broken. That she'd acknowledge they had a developing relationship. But she hadn't been comfortable being there with him. Too subdued, and the constant wary looks around the room she tried to disguise had been disappointing. Maybe it had nothing to do with him. Or maybe the way he'd been dressed embarrassed her.

He'd thought about putting on dress slacks and a nice sweater. God knew he had enough of them, mostly Christmas presents from his mom and sister. But he'd resisted. That wasn't him. He liked the comfort of T-shirts and jeans and he wasn't about to change. Not for anyone. This was him. Take it or leave it. No matter what, she got major points for inviting him in the first place.

Half his sandwich was gone and he didn't remember tasting a single bite. He was tired of peanut butter and jelly anyway. Tonight he'd order in Chinese. Maybe Dakota would miraculously call or show up.

Damn, he shouldn't have made that crack about her and Greta bringing up which law firm they worked for. It was weird though. Kind of like their jobs were their identities. He didn't get it. But it was none of his business and he should've kept his mouth shut.

What if Dakota had overheard Sylvia today? Her claim wasn't true. He loved what he did. No way was it about the money. But man, Dakota could've had a lot of questions, a lot of cracks to make herself. Being able to afford whatever he wanted was nice. Damn nice. But that hadn't been his goal. He just wanted to be his own boss and still make a living.

Simple.

He looked at the beautiful new hardwood floor beneath his boots, and experienced a rush of satisfaction for a job well done. One of the things he liked best about his work was the immediate gratification. With his hands, he created something beautiful out of nothing. That's what life was all about. Personal satisfaction.

Money was the gravy. He inhaled deeply. Easy to say, however, because what he liked to do paid well. Would he still love it without the money?

"I'LL NEED THIS by three-thirty." Dakota handed Sara a thick folder of papers she needed copied.

"They'll be ready. I have something for you to sign, too." Sara gave her a bright smile that was quickly transferred to something behind Dakota.

She turned around. Cody was headed toward them.

She quickly signed the request she'd made for an additional temp. "Thanks. I ordered a sandwich to be delivered. This should be enough including tip." She hastily set down some money on Sara's desk, hoping to head Cody off.

He was really bugging her lately, always stopping by her office over the most minute thing, as if he were checking up on her. That really ticked her off.

He was already behind her. "Got a minute, Dakota?" he asked, his gaze straying to Sara.

"Only one."

Cody didn't seem to notice Dakota's abrupt tone. His gaze stayed on Sara. "I didn't get a hold of those tickets." he stated.

Sara sighed and shook her dark head. "Maybe next time."

"If I hear anything, I'll let you know." Cody continued to focus on the secretary.

Although he sounded slightly gruff, Dakota knew her brother better than that. She stared at him for a moment, bewildered by the way he seemed in no hurry to get down to business, instead lingering near Sara's desk. Maybe his constant dropping by had nothing to do with Dakota. Maybe he just wanted to see Sara.

Dakota silently laughed at herself. She seriously

needed more sleep if she thought for one moment… Maybe when hell froze over.

She led the way into her office, but apparently he was in no hurry to follow her. He showed up a minute later.

"What was that about?" Dakota asked.

He sat across the desk from her. "What? Oh, nothing. Your temp—"

"Sara."

"Yeah, Sara. She wanted tickets for a sold-out show. I thought I knew someone who didn't want theirs."

"Ah." Interesting that they'd talked long enough to get on the subject in the first place.

Her amusement must have shown because he was suddenly all business and cranky, at that. "Dakota, frankly, I'm concerned about you," he said lowering his voice, unsettling her.

She leaned back in her chair. "Why?"

His eyebrows rose. "You're distracted. You're barely meeting deadlines."

"Barely being the operative word." Okay, this conversation was going to be bad. Her temper sparked and her defenses shot up as high as they could go.

"It's not like you. Usually you're more focused."

"I am focused."

He smiled. "You know better."

"Don't give me the big-brother you-can't-fool-me look. It'll only make me angry."

"I'm also your boss, and I need to know that you're committed to working the Draper case."

She shook her head in utter disbelief. "You're questioning my commitment."

"This case isn't just important to this firm, it's a major stepping stone in your career."

"I'll worry about my own career, thank you." She fell silent, trying to rein in her anger and battling the acceptance that he was partially right. She wasn't as focused as she should be.

He let her have her quiet for a while and then sighing heavily said, "I hear you've been seeing Tony. Could that be the reason for your distraction?"

"Who told you that?"

"Someone mentioned you met a guy at Sargent-tis. From his description, that guy Tony is the only person like that we know."

Blood surged to Dakota's face.

When she thought she could speak without biting his head off, she said, "Explain what you meant by 'only guy like that we know.'"

He briefly closed his eyes, shaking his head. "You know what I meant."

"I sincerely hope it's not what I think. I'd hate to find out you're truly that big an ignorant snob."

"You're overreacting."

"Funny, I was thinking the same about you."

"Okay, I see this is going nowhere." He got to his feet while straightening his obscenely expensive Prada tie. "We'll talk later."

"Not about this subject. As my boss, my private life is none of your business. As my brother, I love you, but it's still none of your business." She paused to take a deep shuddering breath. "And don't ever question my commitment to this case or this firm again."

He said nothing, just walked to the door. Before he left, he turned around and asked, "Have you heard from Dallas?"

Taken aback by the innocuous question, she could only stare while gathering her thoughts. "Yes, this morning. They got in late last night so we only talked for a minute."

He nodded absently, and then disappeared from her doorway.

Probably went to sweet-talk Sara, the hypocrite. Well, he had at least one redeeming quality. He cared enough to ask about Dallas.

Why was Dakota angry or even surprised? Hadn't she expected fallout from meeting Tony at Sargenttis? Maybe she had some crazy desire to be outed and that's why she'd chosen that bar?

Outed? The unexpected thought sickened her. Tony wasn't a dirty secret. He was her friend. God, she was as bad as Cody. Must be a faulty Shea gene.

She rubbed her throbbing temple. The truly horrible reality was her brother being right about the distraction part. It wasn't as if she hadn't given the case adequate attention. It simply had taken twice as long to do it. Cody was also right about this particular case. Winning could do more for her career than having been in the top five of her graduating class in law school.

The painful truth was, she didn't have time for Tony right now. Even more painful, she didn't know that she ever would.

"DALLAS?"

"Tony!"

"Is this a bad time?"

"No. I'm glad you called."

He hadn't expected to catch her and put down his chopsticks. Dinner could be zapped in the microwave later. "How was the honeymoon?"

"You have to go sometime. It was an amazing experience. No unpacking or cooking or making my bed for two whole weeks."

He chuckled. "Didn't care for the scenery, huh?"

"That was a whole other amazing. I swear at every turn in the Rhine there was another castle. We have tons of pictures. I can't wait to bore you. You and Dakota will have to come over for drinks soon."

That stopped him. Had she talked to Dakota? "Sure, count me in."

"Well, so how was *your* vacation?"

"Have you talked to Dakota?"

"This morning."

"How did she say it went?"

Dallas laughed. "I only talked to her for a few minutes. I was wiped out from traveling and she was at work, sounded busy."

That made him feel better. Dakota really was busy and not just chumping him. Then again maybe Dallas was backpedaling and didn't want to hurt his feelings by having to repeat her conversation with her sister. Not that he'd ask her to.

"So, I take it you stayed the weekend?"

"Yeah, we stayed."

"Good." Obviously Dallas wanted to ask more questions. Which made him think she really hadn't talked to Dakota after all. But to her credit, all she asked was, "Anything else going on?"

He smiled at her subtlety. "Nothing I can think of. Just wanted to make sure you were back safely."

"Safe and happy." She sighed a contented sigh. "Can you believe I'm married?"

"Yep. You guys are a good team."

She paused. "You and Dakota getting along okay?"

"We got along great," he said, deliberately using the past tense. He wasn't going to say any more. Anything more she'd have to get from Dakota.

"Call her, Tony. Trust me on this, okay?"

He didn't want to go there. "I ordered Chinese and it's getting cold." So was his bed.

"All right, you coward. Go eat."

"See ya, Dallas."

She tsk-tsked. "See ya."

He hung up, set aside the phone and stared at his cold chow mein and kung pao chicken. It wouldn't hurt to call her. The worst that could happen is that she'd tell him to go to hell.

The switchboard was probably closed, he realized when the fifth ring went unanswered. She still hadn't given him her private line and he was about to hang up when surprisingly Dakota answered.

"Hey, you playing operator?"

"She goes home at six."

"Smart lady."

"Yeah, except anyone working late ends up having to answer."

"Which is pretty much always you."

"There's still a lot of us here. Even two of the partners are working late."

"Shining examples."

She sighed. "Did you call to harass me?"

"Oh, baby, that is so not what I had in mind to do to you."

She laughed. "Hold on. Let me get back to my office."

He heard a click and then a few seconds later she was on the line again.

"I was passing my assistant's desk when the main line rang so I grabbed it out there," she said. "We kind of take turns but it's usually pretty quiet after six-thirty."

"I would have called your private line but I don't have the number."

"Oh, damn. It's the main line. Hold on again." Another click.

While he waited he wondered about the timing of that maneuver. If she didn't want him to call, all she had to do was say so.

"Still there?"

"Hanging on your every word."

"I'll give you a word."

He smiled. "I see you're in a good mood."

"Yeah, terrific." She yawned into the phone, and then murmured, "Sorry."

"Are you wearing that big ugly white bra?"

"What?"

"You know, the one you wore the other night. I miss it. I think it's my new fetish."

"You're a lunatic, you know that?" Sounded like she stifled another yawn. "So what's your other fetish?"

"Come over tonight and I'll show you."

Her silence gave him his answer.

"I talked to Dallas today," he said to ease the awkwardness.

"Me, too, but only briefly. I had to go to a meeting. Sounded like she's sold on cruising."

"Yeah, she's gonna be the next poster girl."

Another yawn.

"You sound exhausted. Can't you duck out early tonight? I still have some Chinese takeout here. That's it. Dinner and some quiet time. No ulterior motive. I promise."

"Tony, you can't keep tempting me like this."

He hesitated, not wanting to interfere. That hadn't been his intention. "You're right. Hey, I don't even like calling at work but it's the only number I have."

She snorted. "That's the only place you'd ever reach me."

He hadn't thought of that. It did make him feel marginally better. "Go ahead, get back to work. Sorry I interrupted."

"You didn't interrupt. I'm glad you called."

"Yeah, me, too," he said, taking the high road even though he sorely wanted to point out this should've been her call. "I'll talk to you some other time."

"Okay."

He was about to disconnect when he heard her.

"Tony, wait."

He brought the phone back to his ear. "I'm here."

"You're right. I am tired and not very productive. Want to meet at Samuel's Deli? It's after eight. Most of the dinner crowd should be gone."

"Fine." He knew the place, on a corner halfway between him and her flat. "An hour?"

She paused. "You say you still have Chinese?"

Tony smiled. The evening was looking up.

15

GOD, SHE WAS WEAK. Horribly, disgustingly weak. Yes, she was tired and leaving the office would make her more productive tomorrow morning. But only if she were going home. To bed. Alone. Not running to Tony.

They had to have a talk. She had to make him understand that time was her greatest ally and, yet, also her worst enemy. She had so damn little of it these days. In the end it would be worth it, but right now she had to pay her dues.

She'd knocked twice and when he hadn't answered, she'd started to think that maybe she'd gotten confused over where to meet. But then he opened the door, dressed in snug well-worn jeans, his hair damp, and looking as if he'd recently shaved. Looking as if he might be ready for the horizontal Olympics. Damn him.

He smiled, the warmth reaching his eyes, and stealing a piece of her heart. "Come in. It's freezing out there." Stepping aside, he rubbed his hands together and then quickly closed the door.

"Wow, you've really done a lot since I was here last." She looked around while he hung up her coat.

"The living room floor is new and you've done something to the mantle."

He nodded. "The upstairs guest bathroom has new tile and new countertops, too."

"How did you find the time?"

"First things first." He slid his arms around her from behind and pulled her against his chest. He kissed the back and side of her neck, soft leisurely kisses that gave her goose bumps, and then he slowly turned her around so that their lips met.

With his arms around her and her breasts pressed against his chest, the tension seemed to melt out of her. Disappear just like that. A dangerous illusion. Nothing changed. Tony couldn't change it.

She broke the kiss and reluctantly moved back. "I'm very jealous that you just had a shower."

"We can fix that. I'll even scrub your back."

"Oh, no." Laughing, she backed farther away. "We so can't go there."

"Okay, okay." He threw his hands up. "To the kitchen then."

She followed him, her gaze on his very fine backside, her pulse picking up speed. Why did she keep doing this to herself? She forced her gaze away and noticed the windows. "When did you put the blinds up?"

"About five minutes ago." He grinned, and she rolled her eyes at him. Nothing was going to happen tonight, if that's what he was thinking. She hoped. "I had to order custom because of the size. They were delivered this morning and I put them up while I was waiting for the bathroom grout to dry. Better than curtains, huh?"

"Definitely. The kitchen is modern and that plantation-style blind is perfect," she said, envy surprising her. As much as she'd love to have her own place to decorate, she doubted that would happen for a long while. She didn't have time or money. Certainly not for high-priced Manhattan real estate.

He got the cartons of Chinese food out of the fridge, taunting her with that perfect backside again. "I think I'll replace the living room drapes with the same thing."

She went for the plates, opening one wrong cabinet, then finding them on the second try. "I don't understand how you have time to do all this and still work." She turned and caught him checking out her legs. Fair was fair, she supposed.

He smiled. "This is my work."

"No, I was talking about your full-time job."

"This is it."

She didn't understand. "But you work for Capshaw Construction."

"Not anymore."

"When did you leave?"

"Right after Dallas quit."

"I didn't know...."

He chuckled. "Apparently not. You use chopsticks?"

She nodded numbly. No wonder he didn't understand how crunched she was for time. "I assumed you had a regular job."

He deposited the food in the microwave and started it. "I thought attorneys never assumed anything?"

She gave him a wry smile. "I'm curious. How do you sustain yourself?"

"When I'm done renovating, I sell."

"This one?" Disappointment welled up inside her. What did it matter? Probably better that he moved away. Back to Queens. Or Brooklyn. Or even the other side of Manhattan.

He studied her closely, close enough to make her uncomfortable and she turned away, busily gathering utensils and napkins.

"Why?"

She looked up and smiled. "It's really nice. You've done a wonderful job. I would think you'd hate to part with it."

"That's business," he said, shrugging. "I was hoping you were disappointed that I wouldn't be living so close."

The microwave buzzer went off, signaling the food was ready, but he stayed where he was, his gaze searching her face.

"Like we have a lot of time to see each other." She arched her brows in the direction of the microwave. "Are you going to get that?"

He blinked and looked away, but not before she saw the disappointment in his eyes. "Yeah."

She took a deep breath, getting ready for the plunge. "For me it's not going to get better, either. When Cody was trying to make partner he practically lived at the office. My father, too. When I was a kid, there were some weeks when the only time we saw him was at Sunday dinner."

"What about now?" he asked, totally expressionless as he carried the food to the table. "Does Cody have a life outside of the office? Does your dad?"

That stopped her. "Well, yes, of course," she said tentatively.

He didn't say anything, just pulled out their chairs.

"I mean, they attend all kinds of social events." She sat down, scooted her chair closer to the oak table and placed the napkin on her lap. "Dad's on several committees with the bar association—"

"You don't have to try and convince me." He swooped down and briefly kissed her before taking his seat.

"I'm not." Admittedly it sounded as if she were. "It's difficult to explain but when you love your work—"

"Hey, I guarantee you no one loves their work more than I do, but I still have a life."

She sighed, knowing this conversation would go nowhere. "Pass me the chow mein, please."

"Let's change the subject."

"Great idea."

"How about dinner Saturday night? Not here. I know this terrific restaurant in Soho—" He leaned back and frowned. "What?"

"I can't."

"You're working Saturday night?"

"I have a bar association dinner to go to. It's an annual thing that's not exactly mandatory, but absences are usually noticed." She'd had some trouble keeping the noodles on her chopsticks but she finally got them anchored. "Kind of a boring evening, especially since everyone takes their spouse or significant other."

At the expectant look on his face, she nearly dropped the chow mein, chopsticks and all. Did she have the biggest mouth on the planet, or what? She couldn't take him. He'd be bored silly. Most of the talk was legalese. It wouldn't be at all like chatting with the guys at Sargenttis. Prominent judges would be there. Hot-button legal issues discussed.

Chicken that she was, she shoved the noodles in her mouth so she wouldn't have to say anything more. She stared down at her food, hoping he hadn't seen in her eyes the ugliness that had gone through her head. That he might not fit in. That she would be uncomfortable.

"So even when you have a social life, it revolves around work?"

She kept chewing. The thought hadn't occurred to her, but yeah, pretty much. When she did go to a party, a colleague normally threw it. Her two friends from college both had busy careers and it seemed like every time they made dinner plans, one of them ended up canceling at the last minute.

"But that's pretty typical, really," she finally said after she thought about it. "Once we're out of school most of our social contacts evolve from work. If you go for a beer, I bet it's usually with the guys you used to work with."

He gave a small conciliatory nod. "Point taken. But at least it's my choice and I enjoy going."

She sighed. "Point taken."

He chuckled, and then sobered. "Don't go."

"To the association dinner? I have to."

"Why? You said it'll be boring."

"I also said that absences are noted."

"So what? You're a good lawyer. You have to be if you've been handed a high-profile case. Don't be bullied into rubbing elbows if you don't want to."

Sighing, she laid down her chopsticks. "It's not that simple, Tony."

She had to tell him. That's what she'd come here for. It should have been said already. Before too many other issues got in the way. But she'd kept her mouth shut for the same reason she was in trouble. He distracted her. With that sexy smile and those broad shoulders and strong arms of his, she got lost. Forgot that she didn't have the time to give to a relationship. Forgot that she had a goal, and frankly, he didn't fit into the plan.

She hadn't made the rules, but if she wanted to get ahead she had to damn well follow them. That part was very simple. And she'd known the drawbacks going in. She couldn't cry foul now.

And neither could he. All they'd ever shared was sex. No promises had been made. Not even implied. One day at a time. He'd said it himself.

"I forgot to get us something to drink." He got up. "Orange juice, water, wine or beer. Take your pick."

"Water is good." She watched him walk to the kitchen, his long legs taking slow, easy strides, and she thought about how she never walked slowly anymore. At work, she could be going to get a cup of coffee and she'd practically speed-walk to the lounge.

It seemed as if she was always running to a meeting or running to catch a cab or running to catch the elevator even, because God forbid she should wait five seconds for another one.

Only when she was with Tony did she slow down, savor every moment, every touch. Did she not think about work. Therein lay the problem.

"Here you go." He set a bottle of water beside her right hand and then leaned down for a kiss. His hand cupped her nape and he gently massaged her neck while he performed magic on her lips.

Her traitorous body immediately responded. Her nipples tightened and the flutter that started in her chest went down to her stomach and then settled between her thighs.

"You seriously need to relax," he said, continuing the seductive massage. "And I have just the thing."

"I can't have anything to drink. I have to get to the office early."

"What I have in mind won't give you a hangover. That's a promise."

He withdrew his hand from her neck and her entire body protested. She twisted around to look at him just as he reached for her hand. He pulled her to her feet and led her into the living room. She pretty much knew what he intended. What she didn't know was whether she had the willpower to stop him.

Did she want to? Would it be so bad to have this one more time with him? If this was a last time. It wasn't as if she could never see him again. It would just be a while before she had the time. And if all they wanted from each other was sex then...

She couldn't bear to finish the thought. To think their sole connection was based on sex stung. It simply wasn't true. In the beginning, yes, sex was all she wanted from him. But not now. Which made their relationship all the more difficult.

The thought shook her to her very core. When had it happened? When had she started caring? Wanting? Needing? Damn her. Damn Tony.

He sat her on the sofa, and then knelt down in front of her and slipped off one of her high heels.

"What are you doing?"

He slipped off the second heel, his chocolate-brown eyes sparkling when he looked up at her. "Reflexology."

"Right."

"You doubt me?"

She chuckled. "With all my heart."

"Smart woman."

He stared at her knees for a moment, looking confused, and then he inched up her hem.

"May I help you?" she asked, trying to sound indignant, and trying not to laugh.

"No, I think I got it." He found her garters and started to roll down her stocking.

"Hey." She clamped her knees together. "What are you doing?"

"Trust me."

She made a face. He hadn't tried to take her

clothes off, which would have made more sense. "Is this the other fetish you were talking about?"

"No," he said, frowning thoughtfully. "But this is right up there on the happy scale."

"Come on," she said sternly, "what are you doing?"

"This." He reached up her skirt, between her legs and found his target.

She gasped, stiffening, trying to squeeze her legs together. "Tony, we can't."

"*We* aren't doing anything. You just relax." He pushed the hem of her skirt up as far as he could, which ended up at midthigh, and then he smiled wryly, murmuring, "Plan B."

"Tony." She put a restraining hand on his shoulder. "Please."

"What are you going to do?"

"Can you trust me?"

She moistened her dry lips and nodded.

He kissed her while sliding his hands around her waist and finding the zipper to her skirt. She held her breath while he unhooked and unzipped and then pulled down her waistband as far as it would go. He tapped the side of her hip and she raised her bottom a little. Enough that he easily slid her skirt off, and then carefully folded it in two and laid it beside her on the sofa.

She sat there in bikini panties, one stocking, a lone black garter and her conservative white blouse. The panties Dallas had packed for her that fateful day, and only because Dakota hadn't done laundry in nearly two weeks.

Tony noticed and smiled. But didn't say anything, only got rid of her other stocking, again carefully, setting it atop her skirt. That he was going so damn slow did not help her to relax. Tension mounted with each careful movement even though she pretty much knew what he was going to do.

The anticipation, of course, was killing her. So was the fact that she couldn't touch him. Really touch him, not just clutch his shoulder or push her fingers through his hair when he got close enough.

He ran his palms down the outside of her thighs and she shivered in the warm house in front of the crackling fire. "By the way, honey, I know you weren't drunk."

Her sleepy eyes suddenly widened. "What do you mean?"

"The night of Dallas's wedding. When we flew to Bermuda. You weren't drunk. A little tipsy, I grant you." He kissed the inside of her knee. "You were pretending."

"Why would I do that?"

"Because you didn't know how to ask for what you want, or how to just take it."

"That's absurd." She tried to bring her knees together but he stopped her with a kiss higher up her thigh, inside, on the fleshy sensitive side. And she realized she might have made another faulty assumption about his intentions.

"And now?" He looked up into her eyes, his dark and glassy with a desire she knew well. He wasn't trying to humiliate her. Only trying to make a point. "All you have to do is ask."

She swallowed hard. Briefly closed her eyes. Heat tunneling through her, her entire body alive and waiting, down to the last strand of her hair. "Tony," she whispered, pleaded.

That was enough. He pulled off her panties, spread her thighs farther apart and kissed his way to a spot that made her squirm. Reaching his hands behind her, he pulled her hips toward him, and then his mouth was on her, his tongue delving, tasting, exploring. Plundering.

Reflexively, she tried to wriggle away, even though she didn't want him to stop. He used his fingers to spread her farther and with his persistent tongue found the little nub that made her scream. She put a hand over her mouth, her teeth biting into her palm as he brought her to the brink, and then slowly let her slip away.

Before she could protest, the assault resumed, fiercer, more relentless until she came so hard, so completely her entire body trembled violently. Her hand slipped from her mouth to fist his hair and her cry filled the room.

She started to retreat and Tony slowed his pace, finally bringing his head up to look at her, his eyes glazed and his lips damp. From her.

"I made a lot of noise," she said, her breathing so ragged she barely recognized her own voice.

He smiled and nodded.

"I hope your neighbors don't call the police."

"Let them." He kissed one thigh and then the other. "My attorney is present."

She laughed nervously, taking several deep breaths, trying to restore order, and arranging her blouse so she didn't feel so exposed. "Oh, yeah, that would be great."

He got up from his crouched position, and joined her on the couch, sliding an arm around her shoulders. He drew her close and kissed the top of her head. "Wasn't hard, was it? All you had to do was ask."

She moved her hand to his lap, and he stopped her from reaching his bulging fly. "Tony?"

He squeezed her hand. "Not this time."

She yawned. "I thought all I had to do was ask?"

Chuckling, he put his other arm around her so that she leaned against his chest, safe and warm, in the circle of his arms. "Rest," he whispered against her hair.

She couldn't. Not because she needed to go home, which she did, but because she hadn't accomplished what she'd come here to do. And now it would be horribly awkward.

"Would you hand me my skirt, please?" she asked, pulling away and avoiding his gaze.

Her tone came out formal and polite, which she totally hadn't meant. He apparently noticed, judging by the wariness in his eyes. He delivered the carefully folded skirt and stockings, and then kept his hands to himself as she searched the floor for her panties and then pulled them on.

Still sitting, she stepped into her skirt and pulled it up as far as it would go before she stood and finished the job. After she was zipped up, her blouse neatly tucked in and her stockings securely fastened by the garters, she looked over at him.

"Not even gonna stay for a cigarette?" Despite the wry smile and the teasing words, he knew. She saw it in his eyes.

She cleared her throat, and then lowered herself back to the sofa but kept close to the edge. "This is going to be a little awkward."

He sat patiently, waiting, totally expressionless, not giving her a bit of help.

"I didn't plan tonight to go like this." She briefly looked away to maintain her composure. "I wanted to have a nice quiet dinner and to talk."

"About?" His lips curved in a slow smile and she couldn't tell whether it was sad or strained from anger.

"Us. About how often we see each other." She paused, but he didn't react, just sat there. Annoying, but she had only herself to blame. "I'm under a lot of pressure at work, Tony, with this case I'm working on. What's making it more difficult is that I'm distracted."

He said flatly. "You don't want to see me anymore."

"No, it's not that. I do. I just can't. For now."

He nodded slowly. "I see."

"You don't. I can tell." She started to reach for his hand but stopped. "You should be flattered," she said with a small laugh. "I *want* to be with you. Hence, the distraction."

"I don't wanna be flattered." He held her gaze. "I want you."

Abruptly, she stood. "I can't afford a relationship right now."

"With me." His expression tightened.

"With anyone."

She moved away from the sofa, and he got up and went to the closet for her coat and jacket.

"Tony, please try to understand," she said as he helped her on with them.

Gently he fixed her collar. "I do." He smiled. "Don't let the bastards win again, Dakota." He kissed her on the cheek and then opened the door.

16

BRUCE WALKED INTO her office, his coat hooked on his thumb and slung over his shoulder. "A bunch of us are going over to Sargenttis if you want to—"

She briefly looked up. "No, thanks."

"If you change your mind, we'll be—"

"Have fun." She rudely cut him off, this time not looking up from the brief she was working on.

Damn it.

Sargenttis reminded her of Tony. She shoved the image of him from her mind. Two days since she'd seen him and she could still taste the finality of his last kiss. She couldn't think about it.

"See you tomorrow," Bruce muttered irritably and left.

She glanced at her watch. Six-forty-five. She'd be lucky if she made it home by midnight.

SARA KNOCKED and then entered Dakota's office before she was invited. Normally Dakota wouldn't mind. Today she gritted her teeth.

"I brought you a salad from that new—"

"I told you not to bring me any lunch." Dakota put

down her pen and rubbed her right temple. The headache that had started at seven this morning wouldn't quit. Not even after six aspirins.

"I know, but there's this new Italian deli that just opened and it's after two and you haven't eaten. In fact, you haven't been—"

"Sara?"

"Yes." She shrunk back a step, alarm in her blue eyes.

Italian deli. Hell, was everyone purposely trying to torture her? Four days since she'd seen Tony. He was probably making lasagna for someone else by now. The idea burned a hole in her stomach.

"I know you're well-intentioned," she told Sara as calmly as she could. "But don't you have some filing to do?"

Sara nodded and backed out of the office.

Dakota sighed, annoyed with herself. Sara was the last person she should be annoyed with. She was a great assistant, and a nice, caring person.

Damn that Tony.

"DO YOU HAVE A MINUTE?"

Dakota looked up at her brother standing at the door of her office. "No," she said, and went back to reviewing the new motion she'd received an hour ago. One week and counting since she'd seen Tony. Withdrawal was hell.

"Dakota?"

"I'm busy, Cody. Later."

Sara showed up alongside him, her eyes worried.

Probably thinking Dakota would get fired talking to one of her bosses that way. "May I get you anything? Coffee? Lunch?"

"Yes, as a matter of fact." She smiled sweetly, and looked at Cody. "His head on a platter if he doesn't get out of here in two seconds." Dismissively, she looked down at the motion. "And close the door behind you."

He ignored her, waved for Sara to leave and entered the lion's den. "What's going on, Dakota?"

"Nothing." God, she wished he'd leave. If he didn't she feared she'd say something she'd regret. Like quit being a damn coward and using pretend visits to her in order to see Sara. But she was hardly the person to call anyone else a coward.

"This isn't like you. You've been snapping at everyone who crosses your path for the past week. Poor Sara's even afraid to come in here."

Oh, God, but he was tempting her....

"I think maybe the pressure of this case is getting to you. Maybe I was wrong in naming you cocounsel."

She brought her head up. "Don't you dare."

His eyes were full of concern. "I didn't say I was going to pull you off the case." But he'd thought about doing so. It was written all over his face. "I'm thinking you could use more help."

"No." She shook her head. She knew how that went. Another attorney would be assigned to help her. After a couple of weeks, it would be simple to ease her out. But she'd given up too much already. She's sacrificed a chance with Tony. She couldn't let Cody take this opportunity away from her. "I know

I've been irritable. I apologize. Something personal came up. But I've taken care of it."

He stayed where he was, silently assessing her. She wanted him to speak or leave, but now wasn't the time to bite his head off. So she waited.

"Tony?" he finally asked.

"How would that concern you?"

"I know you haven't been seeing him. You're always the first here, and the last to leave."

"This is so not like you to get personal. Don't start now."

He smiled. "You've been putting in too many hours. It's taking its toll. Take a rest, Dakota."

She stared in disbelief. He looked like her brother. Must be an illusion.

He got to the door, paused and hit his palm against the door frame. "For God's sake, go see him," Cody said and then left without a glance.

Dakota sank back in her chair. Was Mercury in retrograde? Was everyone going crazy? She stared at her phone. It wouldn't hurt to at least call him. Would it?

TONY HAD TO GET to the market soon. One more peanut butter and jelly sandwich and he'd croak. Even Chinese food had gotten old. He'd have to start getting to know the neighborhood and pick up a few takeout menus. Better yet, find the places that delivered.

He didn't like going out if he could help it. Commuting to the coffeepot was as far as he'd gone the past week. Maybe this weekend he'd take his mother up on dinner. She always made a ton of food, which meant she'd send him home with a care package that would keep him fed for three days.

She'd called and asked him to come over twice, and both times he'd made an excuse. Then his sister had called and started bugging him. It was as if they had some kind of radar that told them when he was in a rotten mood and wanted to hide. Could they respect that? Of course not. They had to nag. He loved his family but...

His cell rang again and he pulled it off his belt, prepared to turn the thing off and let voice mail pick up the message. But he saw that it was Dallas and hesitated. He wasn't sure he even wanted to talk to her—the subject of Dakota would come up.

It rang the final time before she would be sent to voice mail.

Shit.

He gave in. "Hi."

"Hey, Tony. It's me. Busy?"

"I just finished a peanut butter and jelly sandwich. What does that tell you?"

"That if you keep eating those you're going to end up weighing a ton."

"That'll be the day." He wiped the counter and put the peanut butter away as he talked.

"How's the house coming?"

"Ahead of schedule. Sylvia already has a buyer."

"Oh." Dallas sighed. "I was hoping you'd keep that one. It's nice having you live in Manhattan."

He snorted to himself. He'd thought so once. "Are you back at work?"

"Oh, yeah. In fact, I only have a minute, but I wanted

to see if you and Dakota want to come over for dinner and look at our honeymoon pictures this weekend?"

He sat down. "Have you talked to her?"

"Not for the past week. I left a message yesterday but she hasn't called me back yet."

"She has a bar association dinner on Saturday." He didn't want to get into it with Dallas about her sister. At least he hadn't lied.

"Oh yeah, I forgot that was coming up this weekend. Are you going with her?"

"No. Look I have another call I've been expecting. I've gotta go."

"Me, too. Call me later."

He disconnected, feeling so miserable and confused he wanted to punch a wall. He missed Dakota, but he couldn't abide by her terms. He couldn't see her exhausted, and be stretched every which way.

And truthfully, he didn't know where he stood with her. He didn't have a comparable education and he didn't wear a suit to work every day. Was that a problem for her? Did she feel that he reflected negatively on her and her career? Is that why she hadn't asked him to go to the dinner? He wasn't sure. But if that was true, he sure as hell wouldn't roll over for that kind of thing. She had a lot to figure out.

The phone rang again, and when he checked, he was surprised to see that it was Dakota. Smiling sadly, he turned it off.

DAKOTA SIPPED her first cup of morning coffee, wondering if she should try calling Tony again. He always had his phone on him, and it wasn't like him to not answer. Unless he was avoiding her. The thought stabbed at her but what did she expect? She was the one who'd told him she didn't have time for a relationship. Maybe it was for the best that he hadn't returned either of her calls. What did she really have to say to him that would change things?

Like every other morning this week, she'd arrived at the office first. Not to get a head start, but to catch up from the day before. Yes, admittedly she'd been distracted by Tony, but that wasn't the only thing hindering her productivity. She hated the case she was working on. She despised the client and thought the smug bastard was as guilty as the devil himself.

Cody had warned her about letting her bias show. Reminded her she wasn't a judge yet. That had royally ticked her off. But her brother had a habit of doing that, anyway. To think she'd agreed to go with him to the bar association dinner.

Just thinking about Saturday night knotted her stomach. The dinner itself wasn't the problem. But it reminded her of the look on Tony's face when she'd brought it up. He'd obviously expected her to ask him to go, but she hadn't, and he'd done the math.

But he had part of the equation wrong. He didn't embarrass her. In the beginning she'd feared judgment and talk because he didn't fit in with her circle of friends and colleagues. What a joke. What friends? Her two law school pals were just as busy as she was and their plans to see one another never happened. If anything, she embarrassed herself, for the kind of person she'd become. So like the peers she privately criticized.

And now she was about to blow one of the best things that had ever happened to her. Sadly, she didn't even know what to do about it. Her workload wouldn't change. She didn't have time to spare. How could she ask him to accept crumbs? How could she go back to her drab life?

She needed to talk to someone before she went crazy. Dallas. Dakota owed her a call anyway. She checked her watch. Only seven-ten. If she called this early, Dallas would bite her head off.

There was always the Eve's Apple gang. Someone might be online, or have posted a bit of wisdom for her to hang on to. Like a junkie looking for a fix, she couldn't get her laptop on her desk and operational fast enough. As she signed on she realized how important the group had become to her. Most of the time she dismissed the advice, often laughed at some of their theatrics, but once in a while, just at the right time, she'd read a thought-provoking post that hit so close to home it lingered for days.

She decided to read first and then possibly post, for cathartic reasons if nothing else. The anonymity of the group allowed her to speak freely and she hadn't appreciated the opportunity as much as she did right now.

A lot of new activity had popped up since she'd last checked in and she scanned the older posts first, some chatty, some more serious stuff, the camaraderie already making her feel better. She read a general posting from Color Me Happy about a reunion with a high school boyfriend after being apart for eight years. Then she found one in response to one of her earlier posts.

To: LegallyNuts@EvesApple.com
From: Colorado Jane@EvesApple.com
Subject: Check out his wallet
D,
Hey, girlfriend, take some advice from a single fellow lawyer also looking to get laid. Make sure the guy has some dough of his own. Yeah, I like the more brawn than brains type, too, who isn't afraid of getting down and dirty. But I've had two different but equally bad experiences with the type. Either they think you're their meal ticket. You know, sit at home and drink beer while you bust your ass at the office. Or the other scenario is the damn Neanderthal gets it in his thick head that you've undermined his manhood because you make more money than him. Either way it sucks. The sex stinks after that and there's no going back. So, girlfriend, I urge you, make him show you the money. Wishing you luck in this crazy singles' world.
Jane

Tony wasn't like that. He'd never be so petty or sexist. He was far too secure and comfortable in his own skin. That was one of the qualities she liked best about him. Besides, money seemed to be the least of his interests. Jane from Colorado meant well but she was so off base.

Dakota's ridiculous annoyance stopped her. She felt like a mother lion protecting her cub. What was she doing taking this stranger's words as a personal affront to Tony?

She calmed down, reminding herself that Jane was venting. Her e-mail actually had little to do with Dakota or anything she'd posted. In fact, Dakota hadn't revealed anything too specific.... She hoped.

Uneasiness had her thinking back on her e-mails. How much had she mentioned about Tony? She'd been careful, remaining vague, except, admittedly, a couple of nights ago she'd been so down and miserable she never should have gotten on the computer. Had she said too much?

It didn't matter. No one knew who she was. She hadn't even used her name. Just her first initial. She scrolled down and one of the subject lines caught her eye.

To: The Gang at Eve's Apple
From: JustSara@EvesApple.com
Subject: Lonely and the City
Hi, y'all,
Thought I'd check in. It's Thursday night. Nothing to do, as usual. I'm all alone in my apartment, except for the little lost kitty who showed up at my door. She's so cute and I like the company. Maybe tomorrow night I'll venture out again and try to meet new people. I'd rather be venturing out with you-know-who from the office but I'm starting to lose faith. Sometimes I think he's interested and

other times, I swear, he treats me like something he picked up on his shoe.

Anyway, I refuse to fret over him. If he's not interested enough to get to know me, well then, I guess it's his big fat loss.

Boy, I sounded brave, didn't I? :) I owe it all to y'all. One of these days I'm gonna have Mr. Big Shot Attorney on his knees begging. You wait and see.

I'll check in tomorrow. Hope y'all are having a good night.

Bye for now,

Sara

Dakota stared at the screen. Reread the moniker and then the sign-off, her pulse doing double time. It couldn't be. Oh, God, not her Sara. How awful would that be? Why hadn't Dakota noticed her posts before now? As if she weren't too self-absorbed. Getting upset was ridiculous. Sara was a common name, and she hadn't said anything about living in New York City. But Mr. Big Shot Attorney? The y'alls? Oh, God. It sure sounded like Sara. And if it was, and she'd read any of Dakota's posts and knew it was her, she'd just die.

She quickly got offline and turned off the computer as if someone from Eve's Apple could actually see her. That was it. No more going there. Except to read posts. Maybe figure out if that was *the* Sara.

So much for that. She drummed her fingers on the desk and stared at the clock. Dallas wasn't exactly a morning person, and she normally didn't go to her office until later. But Eric had to be up by now.

Dakota couldn't stand it. She picked up the receiver and pressed the speed dial number, taking deep breaths while the phone rang.

"Is it too early?"

"Dakota?" Dallas sounded as if she might have been asleep. "What's going on?"

"I can call back later," she said reluctantly.

"No, no, I'm awake. I just haven't had my first cup of coffee yet. Are you okay?"

"Oh, yeah, I'm fine." Dakota sighed. "Relatively speaking."

"Uh-oh. Is this about work or Tony?"

Dakota hesitated. What the hell was she thinking? Did she really want to get her sister involved? But if not Dallas, whom else could she talk to? "Tony," she said quietly, the admission feeling like a lead weight on her tongue. "Have you talked to him?"

"Yesterday. What happened?"

"Did he say anything?"

"About you?" Dallas paused, and Dakota could hear her taking a sip of coffee. "Not really. I asked him if you guys wanted to come over for dinner tomorrow night and he reminded me that you had the bar association dinner. That's about it."

"Oh."

"So?"

"What?"

"So you didn't call me at seven-thirty in the morning just to ask if I spoke to Tony."

Dakota cleared her throat. "No, I, um, I'm not sure why I called to be honest." She wasn't lying. If Tony had said something then that would have opened the conversation. But he hadn't said a word, probably because he hadn't given her another thought.

"I figured you wanted my opinion as to whether you should ask him to go to the dinner."

"No," she said a little too quickly. "I mean how boring would that be."

Dallas laughed. "Tony is never bored. In fact, if the dinner gets too boring, he'll liven things up."

Dakota didn't say anything.

"Are you afraid he'd embarrass you?" Dallas asked slowly.

"Of course not. It's just that Cody and Dad and my boss and, well you know, everyone will be there." Meaning those who could influence her career. She briefly closed her eyes. "Oh, God, Dallas, please tell me I'm not getting to be like Cody."

"You've got a ways to go yet." Dallas laughed softly. "But I'd hate to see you head in that direction."

Cody's world revolved around his career. Everything he owned or did somehow enhanced his position in the firm or legal community. Is that how Dakota wanted to end up? Was being a judge so important to her that the journey should be sacrificed?

Don't let the bastards win again.

Tony's words haunted her.

She knew damn well what he'd meant. College. The dean. Her whole life she'd allowed other people to decide what was right for her. Her mother and father and Cody. But Tony was right. She was a damn good attorney. Her merit alone would have to be enough.

"Dakota?"

"What?"

"Don't snap at me. I wasn't the one who called you."

"Sorry." She looked at her watch. A cab was going to be tough to find soon with everyone trying to get to the office. "Look, Dallas, I have to go."

She had to talk to Tony. Before it was too late.

17

TONY POURED his fifth cup of coffee and then re-membered his cell phone was still in the living room where it had been charging since last night. He didn't expect any calls. Most of them he wasn't answering anyway. But on the off chance that the bathroom wallpaper he'd ordered had arrived early, he'd been checking for messages.

And shit, yeah, he wanted to know if Dakota had called again. Ironically she'd finally left her direct line number. But he just wasn't ready to call her. He was still mad and hurt at being rejected. And since that had nothing to do with her precious career, he doubted she gave a rat's ass, so why put himself through it again?

One message. From his mother. She wanted to know about dinner. Nothing from Dakota. Probably got tired of him not returning her calls. Disappoint-ment made his coffee taste bitter so he set his mug on the end table, then sprawled out on the couch. The good thing about leather was that it didn't matter if his jeans and shirt were dusty as hell. He'd gotten up earlier than usual, close to five, and immediately had gone to work in the guest room.

With so much time on his hands, he'd made awesome progress in the past week. Sylvia was going to be happy. His neighbors most likely weren't. In fact, they'd probably throw a party when he left the neighborhood. Even though he tried to keep the pounding and drilling confined to midday.

The thought of leaving still didn't sit well. Not that it should matter where he lived if he weren't seeing Dakota. Besides, Sylvia had found him another town house on the east side for which he was about to sign a contract. It was a sweet deal and Sylvia already had two buyers who were interested.

God bless lazy rich people. Life had been pretty damn good lately. Only Dakota would make it better. He abruptly stood and grabbed his mug. Sneaky unwelcome thoughts like that really pissed him off. The woman had issues to resolve. Nothing to do with him. Nothing he could do about it.

On his way to the kitchen, the doorbell rang. He looked at his watch. Who the hell could that be at eight-forty? He wasn't expecting a delivery. He used the peephole. What the—?

Dakota stood with her arms wrapped around herself, without a coat, and shivering.

He took a deep breath and opened the door.

"Hi." She looked him up and down. "Glad I didn't wake you."

"Come in."

She gave him a tentative smile and walked past him.

"Where's your coat?"

"I forgot it." She moistened her lips. "I was in

a hurry," she said, her voice breaking when her teeth chattered.

"But it's only in the thirties."

"Believe me, I know." She gave a shaky laugh, vigorously rubbing her arms.

"Come here." He didn't have to say another word. She walked into his arms and they stood quietly in the foyer as he warmed her. "Don't you have enough sense to come in out of the cold?" he whispered, enjoying the feel of her, the smell of her more than he should.

"That's why I'm here." She tilted her head back to look at him, her eyes searching his face, her words loaded with meaning. She had a smudge on her nose, probably from his T-shirt.

He moved back, glanced down at his dusty clothes, and then at her beige suit. He didn't want to think about what her words implied. Better not to read too much into them. "Look what I did."

She looked, ignored it, and smiled at him. "Will you come to the bar association dinner with me tomorrow night?"

Taken by surprise he reared his head back. "Tomorrow?"

She nodded.

"I'll have to check my calendar."

She blinked. "Okay."

"That was a joke."

"Oh."

He stared at her for a moment, wanting to pull her against him but knowing they had some talking to do. "Coffee?"

"Definitely." Rubbing her hands together, she followed him into the kitchen.

"About this dinner, your date cancel at the last minute, or something?"

She gave him a dry look. "No, I was going alone. If you don't count my brother and father."

"Ah, they'll be there, huh?"

She nodded, and immediately took a sip from the steaming mug he handed her.

"And it won't be a problem with me going?"

"Why would it?" She conveniently looked away to pull up a bar stool.

He smiled and poured himself more coffee. "Why?"

"Why what?"

"Why did you change your mind?"

She shrugged. "I—it wasn't that—" Her shoulders sagged. "I'm tired of forgetting my coat."

He laughed. "What?"

"I'm tired of not laughing. I'm tired of not having something to look forward to at the end of the day. And I definitely don't want to let the bastards win again."

Tony smiled.

"Most of all, I miss you." Her lips quivered. "With you I live life in color. Without you it's black and white." She shook her head. "I can't do black and white anymore."

He put his mug down. "I've missed you, too."

She tried to fake a pout but a smile tugged at her mouth. "So why didn't you return my calls?"

"Because I wanted you to figure out what you

wanted. If you thought I'd stand in the way of your career then I was willing to back off."

She opened her mouth to protest, but then said nothing and sheepishly looked down at her hands. "You're right. I'm embarrassed to admit that the thought had crossed my mind that you couldn't fit into my life." Her laugh was terse. "Then I realized I didn't even have one."

"It's okay."

"No, it's not. I was an ass."

"Look, I don't know where this is going," he said, tugging her toward him until she went into his arms. "But I'm on the bus. Wherever it takes us."

"Me, too." Sliding her arms around his waist, she sighed. "Do you know how long this past week has felt?"

He rested his chin on top of her head. "Oh, I have some idea." He smiled and inhaled the fresh herbal scent of her shampoo. "What did you mean about being tired of forgetting your coat?"

She moved back to look at him. "I was in such a tizzy all week I kept forgetting my coat, my purse, where I put my keys. I couldn't even concentrate on work. Basically, I was a mess."

"Ah, so you're just using me."

Grinning, she traced a finger down his fly. "Shamelessly."

"Better not start something you can't finish," he said, his jeans immediately starting to get snug.

"We should go away for a weekend again. To another island, or maybe someplace in Vermont where we could get snowed in for a week." She quickly added, "But this time I'm paying."

"I'm the old-fashioned type. That would hurt my feelings." He leaned in for a kiss but she resisted.

She looked seriously at him. "Would it bother you being with a woman who makes more money than you?"

"Nah, I could get used to it."

She obviously couldn't tell if he were joking or not, and it seemed important to her.

He stole a quick kiss, and then said, "While you're here, would you do me a favor?"

She seemed startled, but nodded. "Of course."

"I need some legal advice."

Her eyebrows rose. "Okay."

He went to the corner cabinet where he kept his paperwork and brought out the contract Sylvia had dropped off. "If you could look over this contract before I sign it…"

"You know I'm not a contract lawyer."

"Yeah, but you've got to be able to do a better job of reviewing this than I can."

"What sort of contract is it?"

"Real estate."

"You're selling this wonderful brownstone?"

"Nope. I'm buying another one."

She frowned. "Let's see."

He handed it to her and watched her face as she read over the document. Normally he wouldn't reveal personal information like this. In fact, no one but his attorney and accountant knew his financial status.

But since Dakota seemed hung up on the money issue he figured this was as good a way as any to let her know he could afford a lousy vacation.

She frowned again when she got to the terms of sale part. "Have you read this yet?"

"Pretty much. Great price, huh?"

"This says you're agreeing to pay cash."

"Yeah, I know. My accountant doesn't like it. Says I'm foolish and I should borrow, but I prefer to pay cash and then get a credit line for the renovation material. It's been working out great so far."

Her brows drew together in confusion. "How did you pay for this place?"

"Cash."

Her lips parted in surprise, and he really wanted to kiss her. He would later. "How many houses do you own?"

"Just this one right now. I don't like to juggle more than two at a time. Then I'd have to start hiring people and I like working by myself just fine."

"Wow!"

"So the contract looks okay?" he asked with a straight face.

"Um, yes, fine."

He took the papers from her and set them aside. Then he took each of her hands and put them on either side of his neck. "One more question," he said, while molding his palms to her hips. "It won't bother you going out with a guy who makes more money than you, will it?"

She pressed her lips together, wincing. "Ouch! I guess I deserved that."

"I'll give you something you deserve." He lowered his head and she met him halfway.

Their lips barely touched but his body had already ignited. Deepening the kiss, he pulled her close so she could feel his desire. She clutched his shoulders and moved against him, swaying and rubbing and awakening every primal instinct he possessed.

"Have a feeling you're gonna be late for work?" he whispered against her mouth.

"What work?"

He pushed off her jacket but he only got her out of one sleeve before she unbuckled his belt. Her nipples were hard and pressing through her bra against her white cotton blouse. He touched one, circling it with his forefinger, and she whimpered softly.

"Want to try another room?" he asked. "Lots of blinds and curtains."

"Hmm, how about the bedroom for a change?"

He smiled. "What a novel idea."

Epilogue

One year later

TONY COULD HEAR the San Angelo clan laughing from clear across the large banquet room. Cousins he hadn't seen in years were here. His great aunt Francesca had come all the way from Rome to see him get married. He was glad to see her.

He stared at Dakota, sitting beside him, looking extraordinarily beautiful in her cream-colored silk dress. "Quite a diverse group we have here, huh?"

"Gee, you noticed."

They both laughed. On the right were the San Angelos, talking, laughing, dancing and sampling the hors d'oeuvres with gusto. On the left were the Sheas' friends and colleagues, looking shell-shocked. They probably still hadn't gotten over the amount of rice that had been dumped outside the small Manhattan church where he'd promised to love and cherish Dakota just a short hour ago.

Like he needed a piece of paper or preacher to tell him to do that. He looked at his new wife, emotion swelling in his chest. God, but how he loved this woman. Smart, gorgeous, kind and the best friend he'd ever had.

By mutual agreement, the ceremony had been simple. No attendants in tuxedos or fancy dresses. The exchange of vows had been kept short. The party, however, they'd gone all out for. With an equal amount of diplomacy and firmness they'd managed to maintain control of the event.

Instead of a formal sit-down dinner, they had food stations set up in each corner serving ethnic finger food. Every form of liquor was available from two very busy bars. His sister and Dallas had handled the decorations and flowers, which turned out tasteful enough to even meet his new mother-in-law's approval.

"This doesn't seem real, does it?" Dakota said softly and laid her head on his shoulder.

"Tired?"

"Exhausted."

"Exactly what we were trying to avoid by having a small wedding."

She brought her head up to smile at him. "But then we invited half of New York to the party."

"Yeah, well, we're only doing this once."

"You better believe it." She leaned in for a brief kiss, then her lips curved in a mischievous smile. "If you're a good boy, you might get lucky tonight."

"I'm always good. Ask any of the ladies."

"Why do I put up with you?"

"I can think of one big reason."

She rolled her eyes. "Oh, brother."

"Speaking of whom." Tony motioned with his chin toward the door where Cody had just arrived. "Did you notice my proper use of *whom?*"

"I did."

Someone got in the way and Dakota craned her neck to keep sight of Cody. Her hair was down and she'd done something to make it slightly curly. She looked beautiful. But of course she always did. Especially when she first woke up in the morning.

"Okay, now watch. I'm not wrong about this."

Tony sighed. "You and Dallas should go into business together. Matchmakers, Inc."

She gave him one of her stern lawyerly looks. "Are you complaining?"

"No, ma'am."

"Anyway, I'm not matchmaking. Sara isn't right for him, and she told me yesterday she's going back to Atlanta. I'm simply observing. In fact, I'll bet you that he makes contact within…" She checked her watch. "Five minutes. Are we on?"

"What's the bet?" He checked his watch, too.

"You don't trust me?"

"Why would I? You're a lawyer."

"Say that louder." Dakota gave him a cheeky look and turned back toward Cody. "Aha!"

Curious himself, Tony spied Cody talking to Sara. "Well, whaddya know. He's smiling. First time, huh?"

"Hey, that's my brother you're talking about." She grinned. "But I think you're right."

She also had the best smile. The best eyes. The best hair. The best heart. She was everything any man could possibly hope for.

And she was all his.

And he was hers.

Forever.

LET'S TALK
Romance

For exclusive extracts, competitions
and special offers, find us online:

Or get in touch on 0844 844 1351*

For all the latest titles coming soon, visit
millsandboon.co.uk/nextmonth

*Calls cost 7p per minute plus your phone company's price per minute access charge